Hush Little Fire

Hush Little Fire

♦ *A NOVEL* ♦

JUDITH NEWCOMB STILES

alcove
press

This is a work of fiction. All of the names, characters, organizations, places, and events portrayed in this novel are either products of the author's imagination or are used fictitiously. Any resemblance to real or actual events, locales, or persons, living or dead, is entirely coincidental.

Copyright © 2025 by Judith Newcomb Stiles

All rights reserved.

Published in the United States by Alcove Press, an imprint of The Quick Brown Fox & Company LLC.

Alcove Press and its logo are trademarks of The Quick Brown Fox & Company LLC.

Library of Congress Catalog-in-Publication data available upon request.

ISBN (hardcover): 979-8-89242-030-3
ISBN (paperback): 979-8-89242-243-7
ISBN (ebook): 979-8-89242-031-0

Cover design by Lila Selle

Printed in the United States.

www.alcovepress.com

Alcove Press
34 West 27th St., 10th Floor
New York, NY 10001

First Edition: May 2025

10 9 8 7 6 5 4 3 2 1

*For my great-great-grandfather
Captain Benjamin Oliver Newcomb,
who rescued the entire crew of a foundering ship
when it hit the shoals during a
nor'easter on December 1, 1851.
The state of Massachusetts named
Newcomb Hollow Beach after him for his
"courage and perseverance."*

AUTHOR'S NOTE

THE LINE BETWEEN MEMOIR and fiction is quite blurry at times. As a twelfth-generation Newcomb, I tiptoe on that line—because, when it comes to family stories, it can be a tightrope.

This book is 100 percent fiction peppered with the truth about this and that. For the record, I, Judith Newcomb Stiles, am an *e*-dropper, along with other good-citizen Newcombs, who long ago dropped the *e* at the end of their names to differentiate themselves from Naughty Newcombes who kept the ignominious *e*.

♦ 1 ♦

MARY'S USEFUL FIRE ACTIVITIES

Mary

2015

ALONE IN MY BEDROOM, I played this game. Light a candle and run a finger through the flame without getting burned. I was quick, so it didn't hurt to glide my skin through fire at the perfect tempo. I would have done this all night until the candle burned down to a nub, but my mother caught me and flipped out. She worried I'd stay up late and burn the house down. I begged for one more minute and promised to move away from the curtains. She blamed the girls in my middle school for teaching me the candle game at their stupid slumber parties, but she was wrong. I learned this game from my cousin, Jimmy, who would close his eyes tight and pass his whole hand back and forth through the flame without saying a word.

A grown woman now, I start a lot of fires, and nobody gets suspicious or mad. That's because fire is my tool, a potter's inferno where I burn the things I make. I know how to tame the flames in a kiln to harden pots so they can hold water and be useful. And there are dozens of other useful fire activities, according to Jimmy. For instance, instead of sulking when he was benched in little league, he filled the coach's rowboat with turpentine rags and dared me to toss the match.

To begin a kiln firing, I don't need matches, even though every liquor store on Cape Cod gives them away for free. Instead, I carry a silver monogrammed lighter in my pocket and light up whenever I want. If I open the kiln burners to hissing gas, I flick my lighter, and poof, swirling flames will singe my eyelashes if I'm not careful. My silver lighter is handy too whenever I feel like a cigarette or if it's time to light a candle for my birth mother. After all, for centuries, the churchgoing wives of seamen lit candles for the disappeared to come back, so you never know, my birth mother might get the message. She's out there somewhere. I hope so. I am told she forgot to give me a name, so I was Baby Girl Number Two with the nuns for the first three months of my life. When the stork handed me over to my new mother, they had me baptized Mary Newcombe, and that was that.

Every woman in the Old Ladies Gossip Militia of Wellfleet will tell you my birth mother had three choices back then. 1. Keep the baby. 2. Call the stork. 3. Get a secret procedure to end it. In those days, Dr. William Newcombe, my adoptive father, was in charge of numbers two and three. He was never much of a talker, especially with me, so I don't know how and where my life began. Besides, he's dead now. Tell me, why can't finding the woman who slipped me out between her legs be as simple as striking a match?

Unfortunately, going back to the *Mayflower*, none of the Newcombes were talkers or scribblers in ledgers or diaries, and they wrote almost nothing about their Pilgrim adventures for

HUSH LITTLE FIRE

me to read. They didn't save a single letter about anything important. Too bad for me. But one thing I do know, the Newcombes stayed on the crooked peninsula of Massachusetts, and here, fire is the way people settled disputes.

Burn it down.

♦ 2 ♦

NURSE BARBARA HASKINS SUCKS HER THUMB

Barbara

TONIGHT, I AM SQUIRMING around in hell, a little hell of my own doing, if anyone ever bothered to ask. But nobody asks me much of anything, because I'm just ordinary Nurse Haskins with a bank account that's emptier than empty.

It's windy and dark without a single star on Christmas night and no help from the moonlight to find my way through the woods. Old-girl arthritis stabs at my knees every step as the snow crunches under my boots. I sneak up to the back door of the Wellfleet Health Clinic right around the time that nice holiday feeling goes sour from too much Christmas. Half the town is drunk or asleep by now, and when they wake up, my footprints better be slush.

Good Lord, I am so worn out from the prison-gray clouds of winter that I want to scream in somebody's ear. Anybody. Loud, like one of those lunatic mothers who lost her son on a ship at sea, but I have no son, and I never will. Too old. All that medical technology did squat for me.

HUSH LITTLE FIRE

Inside the clinic, I head for the meds closet but turn into the third examining room by mistake. *Don't you dare turn on a light.* I bump into the metal stirrups bolted to the table and stub my toe. For years, countless ladies have saddled up on this very table, parting their legs for a speculum instead of a bouncing lover. Mothers with too many kids already. Girls who got knocked up out of wedlock. Fifteen-year-old virgins who were in big trouble because of first-time careless sex and because one single sperm vigorously swam all the way to the egg, beating the mob of other sperm. Bull's-eye.

All kinds of women were ready to fix it with a big wad of ash. End it. Way back then, the word *abortion* was never used by Dr. Newcombe, as far as I can remember, and breaking the law was beside the point. My strategy with these patients was to nod and look concerned but never, ever look into their eyes, because if I did, they'd start crying, desperate to get it out and get the procedure over with. Fair enough. I did my best not to judge. It was not my sin. I was only helping other women.

Go get the pills.

Twenty-four steps from the bathroom to the pharmacy, turn left, and then five steps to a lifetime supply of drugs. I work my way down the hallway, tapping the walls with my fingertips just as the phone rings, cutting through the silence like a burglar alarm. Jimmy must be waiting nearby with that odd twitch in his eye, anxious for whatever pills I can grab. I peek between the window blinds into the Cape Cod night. He's out there, probably hiding behind a tree. *What a jackass. Good thing Dr. Newcombe didn't live long enough to see his nephew now.*

I snap the blinds closed and trip over a wastebasket, toppling out the contents. Forget about cleaning it up. On my tiptoes, I hurry past the hall mirror where I usually stop to fix my lipstick. Shiny pink lipstick and a sexed-up toss of my ponytail might have gotten me this job years ago, but lipstick won't help me now. In the beginning, I was required to dress in all white from head to toe, my dainty young feet so ugly in practical white nurse's shoes. There were many mornings I had to get rid of the blood splats that had speckled my clean white shoes after an especially messy procedure. I built a tiny trapdoor in my mind that slammed shut when I started to worry about the hatchet jobs when Dr. Newcombe messed up. I taught myself to focus on shaky thighs and sterilized tools and never, ever think about life or death or little beating hearts. Hearts way smaller than an eraser head.

Teeny tiny thumbs half the size of my eyelash.

Dr. Newcombe would smile at the teenage girl, pat her shoulder, and say as he hovered too close to her face, "This is your decision."

He always made sure I carefully counted the cash before he began his speech in his smooth radio broadcaster voice that made me feel like puking. When the speech was over, he filled the room with a stuffy silence as he examined the girls methodically. He scraped. He suctioned. He blotted the errant blood. And after that, he counted the money again.

Don't get distracted. I remind myself that tonight I'm here at the clinic for one reason: to grab Oxy and Xannies as fast as I can. I try to do the math on how much money I'll get for the pills, but the ghosts of teenage girls keep interrupting my count as they scurry through the hallway.

Is that Gina over there with her painted pink toenails, writhing around in the stirrups? Thirteen-year-old Gina Doanne, who'd hardly made the connection between menstrual blood and sex. Sweet Gina, who had enormous breasts that made men whistle, and she barely knew why they did that. Dr. Newcombe had worked quickly on Gina and the young ones, spewing out reassuring sentences.

Relax, breathe deeply, we'll be done in a jiffy was the main part of his dumb speech. When he said that after suctioning sessions, my heart cracked open for the girls who came alone, whimpering from start to finish. I wanted to hold every girl's hand and give a much better radio broadcast speech. *Yes, your life will be full of female predicaments, big and small, but don't let anyone tell you what's best for you.*

The married women were the easiest. They didn't cry when Dr. Newcombe finished up with a few easy snips and clips and a stitch or two like with a Thanksgiving turkey. All done. The women paid him to end it, but it wasn't so much of an ending but the beginning of how to get on with their lives. He was dirty and holy at the same time when he scraped away their troubles in less than an hour. Ladies of all ages loved him, the pregnant, the barren, the menopausal, the flirty widows, and so they kept coming.

"You can't wipe a baby's ass with a Bible," Mrs. Crocker once said, laughing before a procedure. She begged Dr. Newcombe to cut her fallopian tubes.

"No more babies, please, oh please."

Dr. Newcombe finally relented after he made a bundle off Mrs. Crocker, the wife of the chief of police. Chief Calvin Crocker was a Catholic most of the time, a man who simply loved sex and wouldn't wear a rubber. Too tight. One time she confided in me how easy it was to slip a rubber on a practice cucumber but not the chief. No. He was a hefty man and a father of six who looked the other way when Mrs. Crocker visited with Dr. Newcombe.

"Afterward, she gave me British tea in a real china teacup, so lovely of Nurse Barbara," I heard Mrs. Crocker whisper into the office telephone, looking a bit green after her fourth procedure.

It seemed like every girl on the Cape, every mother, every auntie knew about Dr. Newcombe, and at the same time pretended they knew nothing about it. Keep it quiet over the Bourne Bridge, an unspoken pact between Dr. Newcombe and Mrs. Crocker, sealed with a wink.

The secret procedures were going great for a while, and the cash rolled in until *Roe v. Wade* ruined everything for us. I had warned him that his cash cow side business was about to dry up. And sure enough, in the middle of another miserable Cape Cod winter, January 22, 1973, *Roe v. Wade* became the law of the land, and Dr. Newcombe was screwed. No more cash business. Kaput. For a couple of weeks, he mulled over his next move, talking to me in dreamy sentences he couldn't complete. In the middle of February, deep into a sleet storm, Dr. Newcombe called me into his office for advice.

"I've been thinking about how to retool my medical practice in light of the fact that family medicine won't financially . . ." And then he fell forward flat on his face with a massive heart attack. I tried pouring cold coffee all over his face to wake him up, but Dr. Newcombe died anyway, inches from my clean white nursing shoes.

Put that man out of your mind and get back to business. I close my eyes and shake my head castanet quick. So many years have gone by, so really, what does all that stuff matter? My fingers tremble as I unlock the pharmacy door and punch in the combination to the meds closet. An old grammar school panic pops in my chest as the red light on the keyboard glows green. Jimmy and his sidekick Patrick will have to pay more for this

HUSH LITTLE FIRE

9

haul of pills. I pull the office step stool out of the closet, and the sound of it scraping across the floor shoots a shiver straight up my knees. Just as I steady my feet on the top step, someone calls my name.

Bar-bar-a.

I whip around and bonk my head on the cabinet door, losing my balance, spinning to the floor. Someone is standing in the shadows, wheezing. I hear a loud crack from the other room, but in an instant, I realize it's a hard whack to my skull. A cherry-bomb light flash goes off in my head. Everything goes black.

★   ★   ★

I wake up hot and sweaty, my cheek pressed against the linoleum floor, and I can't lift my head. A sharp pain spears through the middle of my face. I smell smoke. In the distance, I hear sirens louder and closer. The room is sauna hot. The building is on fire.

Oh Lord, who will think to look for me inside on Christmas night? I recite faint jumbled-up verses of what I can remember of the twenty-third psalm, because I heard that's what people do when they're scared shitless.

"'The Lord is my shepherd, I shall not want . . .'"

Sweat drips into my eyes. I can't see. I've forgotten most of the prayer, so I switch to a simple Christmas carol.

"'Joy to the world, the Lord is come.'"

Sing. I must keep singing. No passing out.

The walls dissolve into a blur of smoke. More sirens chirp in the distance, or is it a barking dog? I squint at my thumb, which lies inches from my cheek on the sticky linoleum floor. The room fills up with smoke, and my thumbnail is so close to my eyes that it looks like the face of a long-lost friend. I stare at my thumb until I have an overwhelming urge to pop it in my mouth and suck it. Suck my thumb, I do, and it tastes salty and good. It soothes me as the world begins to fade away, until all I can think about is my thumb.

♦ 3 ♦

MISS MARY NEWCOMBE
BACK ON THE
CROOKED PENINSULA

Mary

THREE DAYS BEFORE CHRISTMAS, I put up a sign on my studio door in Brooklyn: *Mary Newcombe Pottery School— Closed Until Jan. 2.*

But I took it down because it was just an invitation to bad-boy burglars. This week is my annual obligatory Christmas vacation in Wellfleet—do jail time with my mother, be nice, and then zip back to Brooklyn. Now that Danny is twelve, he's stopped complaining that I didn't give him brothers and sisters to play with. Good thing Santa brought him brand-new earbuds to keep him company. For better or worse.

Since we arrived in Wellfleet, I laze around in my childhood bed every morning under the old wilting canopy that shelters me from bad dreams. Today is December 28, the limbo after Christmas that dawdles toward New Year's Eve. I had hoped to catch up on sleep during this holiday visit, but my mother won't let me.

"Wake up, rise and shine, Miss Mary Newcombe. Time's a-wasting," she cheerfully warbles in my face and then pulls the pillow out from under my head. I open the window for fresh air, but she closes it quickly, grouching that a smoke smell from that terrible fire snuck into the house and is making her cough.

Beatrice Birdie Newcombe—everyone likes to call my mother Birdie—has been downing cups of tea, one after another, because Cousin Jimmy won't answer his phone. First thing this morning, she got fast-breaking news from the elderly ladies about how the town fire started. When I press Birdie for what she knows, her phony soprano voice gets higher and higher as she hurries downstairs to the kitchen, moving around too fast like a bumblebee that can't find an open window. I make my way to the kitchen and carefully stand behind her to ask, "What's wrong?"

"Nothing much . . . Have you or Danny talked to Jimmy since last summer?" She vigorously rustles the ties on a garbage bag without looking up.

"No. Why?"

"Everything seemed fine with Jimmy until I suggested that Danny help him clean up *Angel Baby* during school vacation. It's been a filthy mess inside that boat for months. Don't forget, the boat is mine now, but the mess is one hundred percent theirs."

I'm guessing Jimmy's idea of tidy translates to Danny's idea of neat, which translates to Birdie's idea of filthy.

"You know, I asked him nicely, but he blew up at me and started spewing out awful things about Danny."

"Like what?"

"I just can't repeat it. He was nasty."

"Tell me!"

She sighs. "He said Danny can never set foot on *Angel Baby* again. He called your son an *effing pussy*."

"Danny's not a sissy. My God, that *word* is so retro. And it's mean."

HUSH LITTLE FIRE 13

"I said *pussy*, not sissy. Oh, never mind all that. Just find him before the police bring him in for questioning."

"You think *Jimmy* has something to do with the fire in Daddy's old clinic?"

Birdie doesn't answer as she stands over the kitchen sink squeezing water out of a sponge too many times.

You can bet the town of Wellfleet is buzzing with theories about arson and hell fires much faster than the gossips can sort them out. Count on the Old Ladies Gossip Militia of Wellfleet to sand and polish their opinions about how the fire started. I'm not a gossip and certainly not a white-haired busybody, not yet, but my mother reminds me too often I'm one of those "older mothers" who's well on her way.

"After chores, would you please drive around and find that cousin of yours."

This is an order. Not a question. I'm fifty-two years old, but my mother still likes to boss me around. What I really need is a hug, but when I raise my arms to find her, she darts to her purse, looking for something more important. I put on a cheerful face over my try-not-to-be-upset face. But what do sissies and pussies have to do with my son? Birdie gives me the Birdie frown, which is code for *Do what I say,* so I scoot out the door, not properly caffeinated.

Danny decides to come along for the ride, but he's a silent lump in the back seat. I peek in the rearview mirror, but he slumps down sideways with that white earbud thing poking out of his ear. He is far away in another land, the land of his phone that never includes me. I miss my little boy.

This mission to look for Jimmy is probably a waste of time, so first we cruise by Newcomb Hollow Beach to say hello to the sea, and it calms me down like it always does. A fine spray of sand blows up from the dunes and peppers my windshield between splashes of winter rain. Today the sea is munitions gray, wild waves rolling and pounding the shore. Danny is lying down in the back seat, feet up on the window, and the boy doesn't even notice where we are. So off to the Wellfleet Market we go to find Jimmy, and maybe there's some news about how the clinic burned down.

I dread running into anyone I know; still, I force myself to go inside before it gets busy at the market's coffee bar. That's where fishermen hang out in the winter when they have nothing to do. Within earshot, I mingle with my hood up and grab cream and napkins, gliding and feinting with my face turned away.

Dave, the harbor master, insists he heard from somebody, who heard from somebody else that over fifty gawkers came out in the frigid weather on Christmas night to watch the giant orange flames go berserk in the sky. Mike, the shellfish constable, complains the firefighters were much too late as they scrambled to extinguish the monster. Kevin, who owns the liquor store, reports the fire started with a sudden crackle and then exploded into giant sheets of flames expanding and shrinking, strange and liquid like mercury. Suddenly he pivots to me and whispers in a preacher voice, "Sorry you had to witness your dad's old clinic burn down."

"But I wasn't there."

He squints. "Didn't I see you in the crowd?"

"It must have been someone else."

"But you *waved* to me. I'm pretty sure it was—"

"Not me. I was home all night."

Or was I?

It creeps me out that they're all looking over and staring at me like I'm a liar.

Kevin turns back to his audience of fishermen coffee drinkers and sheepishly declares it was the most outstanding inferno he ever witnessed. He laughs out loud and says it looked pretty funny the way a dog, a German shepherd, was frantically running in circles next to the burning building. Until he heard a woman scream out, "Maybe the dog is trying to tell us that someone is trapped in the building!"

Kevin tells anyone who'll listen that Nurse Haskins's body on the gurney was twitching like crazy. When they hoisted her up into the ambulance, a bystander let loose a groan that passed through the crowd in a whisper. "Nurse Haskins didn't have any hair, more of a charred and bloody mess on her head," he says, chewing a toothpick.

It all happened so fast, he admits he isn't sure if she even had a face, but he could see she was still alive. Buy a bottle of wine and get the entire story at his liquor store.

Jimmy never shows up at the coffee bar, so back to the house we go to corner Birdie for any bit of information she might be hoarding. She's an expert hoarder of all things important that she locks away, and she's the only one with the key. I find her in the kitchen, sitting at the table with a cup of tea, silently stewing about something. A pinprick of panic zaps my eyes because I don't remember much about Christmas night. I fiddle with my silver lighter, rolling it between my fingers, which usually helps me sort things out. Birdie flits out of the kitchen without a word. I open the freezer door and look for answers in the cookie dough.

All I can remember about Christmas is that Birdie's best friend, Mrs. Cream Sherry, arrived early for our holiday brunch.

16 JUDITH NEWCOMB STILES

In my head is a hazy picture of Birdie balancing a teacup full of Mrs. Sherry in one hand while flipping pancakes for Danny with the other. Happiness comes in a teacup filled with her sherry, which is how a Wellfleet grandmother gets her drinkie before noon.

I admit that I, too, had a few nips of her holiday breakfast drink, and after that, I guzzled my fair share of Mr. Sparkling Burgundy with the roast beef. By the time Mr. Cognac arrived for plum pudding, I was sailing through another jolly Christmas, wondering if Jimmy would ever stop by for his presents. The Christmas tree made me sneeze a lot, so I raided my mother's cabinet for an allergy pill but swallowed a few Valium instead, which is probably why my memory of the terrible fire is one big blank. I woke up the day after Christmas, shivering on Birdie's old stuffed chair. But I wouldn't say I had an alcoholic blackout either. That's just a touchy phrase invented by guilty AA people. Nouveau Puritans, Birdie calls them.

But I must say, there is something about being back in Wellfleet that makes me want to drink my brains out. And it's not just me. The seasons change, the tides go in and out, and for everyone, time can stop here like a broken clock.

Birdie insists that before the fire, she *went out and about* with Danny, and she knows nothing. I don't believe her, because when I ask her if she thinks Nurse Haskins will recover, a teeny tiny smile creeps into the corner of her mouth before she turns away. Danny's no help either when he says, "I dunno," his pat answer to just about everything. *I dunno. I dunno. I dunno.*

It worries Birdie no end, and it scares me too—why are the cops running around town, asking if anyone saw Jimmy Newcombe on Christmas night?

♦ 4 ♦

THE BIG TIPSY
ANNOUNCEMENT

Mary

I HEARD FROM BIRDIE that Jimmy got a gig at the Wellfleet Market doing food demonstrations for the tourists when he ran out of money. She said he showed up in his waders to demonstrate shucking oysters while he bragged to pretty ladies from New York that he's the *fastest motherfuckershucker* on Cape Cod.

It's high tide around now, and all the oyster beds are under-water, so there's a chance we'll find Jimmy with a bunch of oyster farmers who flock to the coffee bar at high tide to recharge and shoot the shit. I lure Danny back into the car with a bribe of candy and new sneakers if he'll come with me to check it out one more time. We park behind a cop car, and I shake Danny's shoulder to get his attention. He rubs his face and gives me his best manly-man scowl.

"Go see if Jimmy's at the coffee bar. Hurry up."

"Do I have to?"

I blow him a *pretty please* kiss, but he swats it away and bolts out of the car. He trots through the cold rain and disappears into the market, and I wish I could read his mind, because every time I mention Jimmy's name, he goes poker face on me and shuts down.

Me, myself, and I don't have the energy to follow him into the market, because it's depressing when the regulars snub me as an out-of-towner. Even Nancy, that busybody cashier, is wary to say more than hello. We're the same age, we went to school together, but she treats me like an outlier. Thanks to the elderly ladies who dole out tidbits of facts when they feel like it, everyone knows I'm a Newcombe but not quite a Newcombe. Nancy gives me the *not quite* look whenever I see her. She has several jawboning aunties, and I used to pray to God on my knees that one of them would finally come forward and straighten out the stork story of what really happened when I was born. No use asking Birdie to explain it. I tried many times. *Other mother—real mother— other mother* is a loop that plays over and over in my head ever since Birdie broke the news to me on one of her rainy tipsy days. I was only nine years old when she handed me a bag of Hershey's Kisses and made the big announcement as a spiked orange juice dribbled down the sleeve of her terry-cloth bathrobe.

"A very nice stork brought you to us, Mary."

"A what?"

"Mary Newcombe, you're adopted, and don't think for a second that Mommy doesn't love you a million times over."

"A million times over what?"

Birdie tossed back the rest of her orange juice drinkie, lay down on the couch, and passed out in front of the TV. She was facedown on the cushion, so this was my big chance. I flattened my hand like a little fish and slithered inside her bathrobe pocket for the silver monogrammed cigarette lighter,

HUSH LITTLE FIRE

19

engraved with curlicue letters: *Dr. Newcombe*. She took it from him, so I took it from her.

I don't remember much else about Birdie's orange juice nap that afternoon, except that my so-called father was out of town, which left me without a second parent to fact-check and tell me the truth. I brooded over her announcement with some leftover sips from her glass—that I was born from a different woman. No information about my biological father, except one thing: Birdie had said the nuns claimed he was a *no-good foreigner*. After her nap, when I got up the courage to ask a few questions, she poured me a glass of milk and told me not to worry, but she herself looked worried with her scary Birdie frown. She picked up her knitting needles and seemed offended as she clickity-clacked away on a sweater she said was for me.

That day of her tipsy announcement—it felt like she punctured a hole in my heart with her knitting needle, the way she made me feel ungrateful and guilty for asking a few lonely questions. She never talked about my adoption after that, so I took to picking my scabs and making them bleed, freaked out by the bright-red blood and her silence. I kept wondering if a trace of my birth mother was hidden somewhere in my blood, but I was afraid to ask.

It was a big help when I learned in school how the human heart grows—that my nine-year-old left ventricle pumped oxygen-rich blood to every part of my body, to the far recesses of my toes, to my cheeks to rosy them up, and to my little girl's womb to prepare for a period and my own baby someday. I still worry about the comings and goings of blood in my body, which always leads to obsessing about my bloodlines. *Who is my birth mother? Is she happy or sad? Is she even alive?*

Danny is taking too long in the market. Either my boy's inside talking to Jimmy, or he's making his way through the

JUDITH NEWCOMB STILES

candy aisle. By now, my windshield is covered in winter rain or sleet or is it snow? Cape Codders, especially Birdie, love to fret about the persnickety Cape Cod sky that can't seem to make up its mind. Analyzing the weather is a favorite pastime, especially in the dead of winter. If she ever doesn't want to answer a question, Birdie goes on and on about rain, snow, sleet, hail, nor'easters, hurricanes, storm surges, blizzards, and any kind of New England weather disaster.

I crack the window open and catch a faint fire smell, acrid like a burning hair dryer. This waiting, waiting, waiting is something I was never good at. I flick my silver lighter for a quick smoke, just one, and practically suck the filter off, trying to remember if I drove this car on Christmas night.

A baby-faced police officer knocks on my window and signals he wants to talk to me. His peach-fuzzy moustache looks comical on his tough-guy grimace.

"License and registration, ma'am."

"But, sir, I'm just parked." I use my most refined kiss-ass voice because he's police.

"Are you Birdie Newcombe's daughter?"

"Yes, sir, I am. Officer, do you think we're heading for a nor'easter? Maybe a storm surge?"

Officer Babyface looks up at that sky and mutters, "Didn't see any such thing on the weather channel." He wiggles his belt buckle. "We're trying to locate your cousin Jimmy Newcombe. Do you know his whereabouts?"

"No, sir, I haven't seen him since last summer." I want to spank this ten-year-old in a police uniform and make him go away.

"Mr. Newcombe's truck has been parked for a week at the Mobil station, but he's been spotted down near the oyster beds in Katie Snow's Honda."

HUSH LITTLE FIRE

21

"That's surprising. He doesn't usually work there in the winter."

He points to my New York State inspection sticker that expired last month. "Better take care of that, Miss Newcombe, when you're back in the big city. Happy New Year. But if you see your cousin, call me immediately. Agreed?"

"Yes, sir."

Officer Babyface tries to look important as he salutes me with an awkward bow. But now I recognize the little salute, a weird gesture some of the local guys used to do in high school. I wonder if he's making fun of me in a Cape Codder sexist pig kind of way. Jimmy did the salute and bow when he teased me or when Birdie insisted he apologize after his naughty shenanigans.

It never occurred to me to look out for a Honda when I drove by the flats where Jimmy's oyster bed used to be. I only saw one lone woman in the distance working fast, trying to beat the incoming tide. *Mr. Late* was Birdie's other name for Jimmy, needling him for never getting the hang of the fast-moving tides. I never called him Mr. Late, but many times I watched the incoming tide threaten to swallow his tires—cold murky water licking his ankles, ready to flood his knees.

I heard from the Old Ladies Gossip Militia that his trouble with oysters began with an argument he'd had with another oyster farmer—a woman. It was Katie Snow, as a matter of fact, a mother who tends her beds with her baby strapped up in a backpack. Birdie said Katie Snow was ready for a good fight with anyone, seeing how every day her baby clawed at her hair and drooled down her neck as she raked.

"It's too cold. You shouldn't be out here with a baby," Jimmy had shouted at her, knee deep in water—at least that's what Birdie told me the elderly ladies told her that Katie had told them.

"Fuck you. You wanna fuss with babysitting at five in the morning?" is supposedly what Katie said to Jimmy, which Nancy, the market's cashier, reported as solid fact, angling for me to add something to the tip jar by the register.

Birdie said that the very next day, Jimmy filed a complaint in front of the Board of Selectmen that Katie was stealing his oysters, but she showed up at town meeting to defend herself, carrying her cute baby for sympathy, and it worked. In Wellfleet, if you lose at town meeting, the humiliation stings and spreads through every cup of coffee, every beer at the Bomb Shelter Bar, and all over Cape Cod thanks to the Old Ladies Gossip Militia. It makes me laugh, but it's true that Birdie and her posse in the Gossip Militia seem to know what's going to happen before it happens. They predicted the town would let poor single mother Katie Snow take over Jimmy's oyster grant if he went bankrupt. Birdie warned Katie that his oysters were tainted from neglect and that too many men were like Jimmy because too many babies were dropped on their heads.

Officer Babyface is gone, the town is deserted, my car radio is broken, the battery died on my phone, and I have nothing much to do, so I sit in this damn car and zone out. Other women daydream about their love life or lack of it, or their children, or winning the lottery, or what it's like in heaven or hell, but I smoke another cigarette and daydream about tinkering with a different temperature in my next firing. And just as I picture the roar of the kiln burners and how I turn them up to the limit because I absolutely love listening to the squall of fire, Danny comes running out of the market. He opens the car door and just stands there, and I can tell he's cranky. The sleet

HUSH LITTLE FIRE

flattens his blond curls that I love so much, and I want to grab him, pull him inside and dry him off.

"What's that smell?" Danny grumbles and jumps in the front seat.

"Smoke, left over from the terrible fire, I guess." When he looks away, I roll down the window a crack and drop the cigarette butt out. Time to quit. It makes my allergies worse, and I don't want to turn into another raspy old Cape Codder with cigarette breath. In Wellfleet, the wind from the sea sends the smoke smell across the shore, reminding us of things we should never forget. Hold my nose. Plug my ears. I can't remember.

"I'm gonna walk home."

"But you'll get soaked."

"He's not in the market, and I don't want to see him. Not now, not tomorrow, not ever."

"Why? What's wrong?"

Danny tips his head back and swallows a handful of candy in one gulp. His crabby vibes bounce off the dashboard as he puts his hood up and steps out of the car.

"Where are you going? We're supposed to find Jimmy."

"Stop yelling at me."

"I'm not yelling."

"Go find him yourself. I can't stand him." Danny spits out a spray of candy near the side of the car and kicks the door closed. My son—my only child—sprints away in the sleet that is turning to rain as I call after him with some motherly nonsense.

♦ 5 ♦

LISA'S CRYSTAL BALL SINK DRAIN

Lisa

I WEAR MY *LISA DOANNE—CLEAN MACHINE INC.* T-shirt to the Clean Machine office when I clock in, then immediately remove it as soon as I'm out the door. My name is plastered on the shirt just over my right breast in a golden circle. It looks like target practice for an arrow. The T-shirt has been washed so many times the letters have faded and practically disappeared. But Clean Machine charges us employees twenty-five dollars for a shirt *they* make us wear, so I'll wear this one until my boss hassles me to buy a new one.

Everyone says I'm lucky to have a job cleaning the Woodwards' McMansion once a week, since Patrick doesn't have a job. Lucky me. My boss thinks I'm a reliable cleaning lady, but this morning I take my time and am sloppy because the Woodwards live in New York and rarely come to Wellfleet. When my mom was alive, she taught me how to clean with a *lick and a promise* for those homeowners who rarely come up from New York. I clean a lot of houses that people don't really live in. Too bad Birdie Newcombe's snobby daughter and her kid

HUSH LITTLE FIRE

25

are back for Christmas, because that means no money cleaning the Newcombe house. Mrs. Newcombe doesn't want to see my face while they're here, so I get laid off for a few weeks, just like that. It's so unfair.

By lunchtime, I've collected enough coins scattered around the house in drawers and in the clothes dryer to go out and buy some food. I think of it as a tip. Dunkin' Donuts is deserted, so I get my food fast. With tasty jelly doughnuts and two espressos, I make my way back to the Woodwards' for an important coffee break. I sprawl out on the comfy white couch and marvel at what a good job I do keeping it white. Never mind the crumbs left under the cushions. The Woodwards' fancy sound system blasts holiday music throughout the house, and even though Christmas Day has come and gone, the sound of some jerk crooning "Auld Lang Syne" brings out my sentimental streak every time. I can't stop thinking about Mom and how she died from working too hard after a lifetime of cleaning houses. Don Carlson, the dingbat at Carlson's Funeral Parlor, whispered a joke about what to carve on her tombstone when he thought I couldn't hear him. *Saint Gina Doanne: Our Lady of Cleaning.* I hate him.

I gulp my espresso and choke on the doughnut, because it occurs to me that maybe God decided to punish my mother. An elderly know-it-all aunt told me that *Sweet Gina found herself in a girlie predicament more than once, with several secret visits to Dr. Newcombe.*

"And you know . . . your mother . . . well . . . she needed an emergency procedure when she was barely thirteen and two more before she was old enough to vote."

Aunt Elrie was fake friendly with that old nurse, what's her first name, the one who got whacked in the fire by the Lord. My mother used to gripe that Nurse Haskins was haughty, and my aunt never liked her either. I should have asked Aunt Elrie how come the Lord let Mom die so young, just like that, *bam*, a blood clot in the middle of scrubbing some tourist's jammed-up sink. Nobody knows when God will be cruel, and it spooks me how on Cape Cod, the wet wind likes to punish us mortals. God's wind. When the big ones swoop in off the ocean in late August, vacations are ruined, and worse, my crackers wilt. Sponges never dry. Envelopes seal themselves when I'm not looking. I'm so glad the tourists don't bother to visit the Cape after autumn. In the winter, clouds park over the rooftops for months, so forget about those starry summer nights. The sea slaps the twisted peninsula from three sides with a blanket of gray sky and defeat. *Don't get too happy, you lowly mortals. It's winter. Slap. Slap.*

When the music is over, I clean the downstairs bathroom like I always do, but this time my work feels different. I lean over to clean the toilet, and charged with two espressos, I'm ready for anything. Even though today is another wretched winter day in Wellfleet, I'm convinced my luck is changing. I hope and pray this is a special kind of nausea rolling around in my belly, because it would mean I am *finally* pregnant. Scrubbing toilets gives me time to think about exactly how a baby spurts forth in the universe. From nothingness to something. A new life.

I slide off my rubber gloves and flick my braids back over my shoulder so they don't land in the toilet bowl again. I have the urge to stop cleaning the Woodwards' bathroom and cut the braids right off, but Patrick likes my hair long. A large silver cross hangs down my chest, something that Patrick bought me at the flea market. I tuck it into the gully between my breasts, so it won't bang into my teeth when I bend down. Up and down, clean, clean, clean, the never-ending residue of the Woodward family.

HUSH LITTLE FIRE

When Patrick gave me the silver cross, he spoke to me so sweet and tender, which made me feel loved and appreciated. I secretly hoped this was a preview gift to an engagement ring. But then he got that sneaky look on his face when he told me I must wear it all the time.

"Whaaat? Every single day?"

"Be sure to wear it at the Lighthouse when you're waitressing." He glowered at the shiny cross resting crooked on my breasts. As he poked it into place, he said, "Wow. The cross makes you look super trustworthy!"

"It does?"

"Your boss won't keep his eye on you all the time at the register. You look really honest now."

At first, I thought wearing a cross was just another harebrained idea of Patrick's, but after a week, I began folding my hands in prayer at odd random moments. I know this praying thing is more like cutting deals with God, but maybe it could actually work. So far today at the Woodwards', I've said a prayer in each room. Why not.

Vacuuming the living room: *I pray, dear Lord, I promise to be a nicer person if you just let me win the Mega Millions this Friday.*

Mopping the kitchen floor: *I pray, dear Lord, if I win lots of money, I'll even donate to the do-gooder fundraiser to build a new clinic after the fire.*

In the bathroom: I stay on my knees near the base of the toilet and toss the sponge aside: *I pray, dear Lord, this is Lisa, sorry to bother you again, but I won't pocket bills from the register anymore if you just let me be pregnant this time.*

Every month for God knows how long, I've been buying pregnancy test kits and failing them. Pink means pregnant. Blue means failed. I ache for a baby of my own that I can hug and kiss whenever I want. I'm so sick of babysitting other people's brats, but waitressing at the Lighthouse and cleaning don't bring in enough money.

I check out my body again in front of their fancy hall mirror. Will Patrick still call me a *looker* when my belly gets big? I pucker my lips and pinch my cheeks to liven up the god-awful paleness. Winter drains the color right out of me. Patrick squints a lot and probably needs glasses, so I hope he hasn't noticed the new frown lines on my face now that I'm thirty-five. Never mind that.

A polka dot of a person is growing inside me.

When I vacuum my way into the living room, I spot spider webs threaded in the corner between a chair and a bookcase where I haven't bothered to vacuum for months. Spiders are such tattletales. I lug the Electrolux over to the bookcase to attack the spiders because when Mrs. Woodward phoned me, she announced in her squeaky-bitch voice (supposedly her cheerful voice), "We love Wellfleet so much we're coming back to see what it's like in the winter!"

"Assholes," I muttered. But only after they hung up. The Woodwards are supposed to arrive in three days, giving me hardly any wiggle room to take shortcuts. I snatch up a silver-framed wedding picture of Mr. and Mrs. Woodward smiling like goons into the camera. I spit on it and polish it with the bottom of my shirt.

In some ways, I love cleaning houses, because it's a job with a beginning, middle, and end. Big mess, clean-clean-clean, and then it's all done with results you can actually see. Round and round scrubbing sink drains is my favorite, because sometimes it's like a crystal ball when a solution to the latest problem all of a sudden pops into my head. The sink drain has answers. I know it sounds weird, but I rely on the drain oracle.

HUSH LITTLE FIRE

I tiptoe back to the bathroom for a final scrub and ask the crystal ball sink drain one more question.

When the hell will things get better?

My mom always said, "If at first you don't succeed, try, try again." But by now, I'm pretty sure that's bullshit. I miss my mother and often visit the cemetery, bending on my knees to kiss the small marker for Gina Ann Doanne. The plastic flowers are still going strong, although the colors have faded, and sometimes they blow over in the wind. The Woodwards are too hotsy-totsy to have plastic flowers in the house, but they can't fool me—their philodendron plant never dies because it's made of silk and paper. I found that out when I tried to water it.

Unfortunately, I'm short, so I have to stand on a chair to vacuum the spiderweb crud off the ceiling. I wave the vacuum cleaner wand at a daddy longlegs creeping up the wall, and it gets sucked up before I can blink. A pang of guilt hits me that the innocent little spider will die a slow, miserable death lost inside the dirty vacuum cleaner bag. I feel cold all over, and guess what . . . the cheapskate Woodwards locked the thermostat way down. Why oh why did I give away my nice wool sweater to Trudy Bale just because she's Patrick's mom? Well, I gave it to her partly because it was itchy, and mostly because I've felt sorry for my soon-to-be mother-in-law ever since she lost her upper dentures when she was drunk at the Bomby. I hope she'll find a way to get new dentures, because lately Trudy's been shoving her tongue under her upper lip, which makes her look like a wacko homeless person. I love Trudy, kind of like a replacement mother, and because she has the same friendly blue eyes and tired old skin as my own mother used to have. But thinking of this and the dead spider, I panic

30 JUDITH NEWCOMB STILES

and hurry to vacuum up every last crumb in the couch because I worry it's bad luck to do a lousy job cleaning.

Wait a minute . . . I drop the vacuum cleaner wand.

Maybe Mom and little polka dot are passing each other in the universe.

The space in this house—on this road—on this planet—in this universe—feels too big, so I drop to the floor for one more quick prayer. Someone is knocking at the back door, and it might be Lester, the cook at the Lighthouse, who knows exactly where to find me when he needs to borrow money.

"Hey, Lisa!" Lester says in his best silky deep voice, standing in the doorway with a big grin. He definitely needs money. "What are you doing on the floor like that?"

"Cleaning the carpet. What do you think I'm doing?" I jump up and face Lester as his musky cologne floats through the air. The unusual scent must be packed with pheromones, because every time I smell it, I have the urge to grab him and slow dance. I tried to get some for Patrick this Christmas, but Lester only had one bottle of the sexy brew that his mother sent from Jamaica.

"Is there any way you can spot me twenty?" he asks, shifting from foot to foot, shivering.

"Sure, when I get my paycheck Friday, but you gotta pay me back."

Lester is wiry and lean from doing a lot of grunt work for white people—washing dishes, hauling garbage, and scrubbing other people's boats. He hustles a smile a lot when he speaks so the old ladies of Wellfleet won't be scared of him. I'm surprised how he clicks into a different rhythm and a serious face when he carries on with his friends in Patois.

"I forgot to tell you two detectives stopped by the restaurant yesterday looking for a Mr. Lester Fielding." I wave a dust

HUSH LITTLE FIRE

31

mop near his face to catch his attention. "They wanted to know where you were Christmas night and if you're related to Bon Bon, that kingpin guy in Provincetown."

"The cops think everyone from Jamaica is related to each other. What else?"

"A big cop I didn't recognize asked me if I knew where you were when the clinic burned down. I was tempted to say you were sitting on Santa's lap, asking why you didn't get a new car for Christmas."

"Thanks, Lisa, but my car works fine."

"They wanted Bon Bon's address. So, *are* you related to Bon Bon?"

"Lisa, you should tell Patrick to stay away from Bon Bon." Lester has small black eyes that carefully camouflage whatever feelings are hiding behind his small talk. He leans in and speaks quietly, as if someone might overhear. "Before Christmas, I saw Jimmy and Patrick at Dunkin' Donuts in Wellfleet with that old nurse, and they were just sitting there, and nobody was eating or drinking."

"What nurse? You mean Barbara Haskins who got burned in the fire? My mother never liked that bitch."

"Yep, her. And what's worse, I heard Jimmy and Patrick were in Provincetown looking for Bon Bon. Word is out they had some kind of meeting about deliveries of a certain kind. Not lobsters. Did *you* do their deliveries? Forget it. Don't tell me. You know, the cops are watching Bon Bon, and if they're watching Bon Bon, then they're watching Patrick, and that means they're watching you. You better be careful, Lisa."

♦ 6 ♦

THE SMELL OF A ROSE
IS A TEASE

Mary

I T'S LIKE THE WIND'S only job is to remind me, *Mary Newcombe, winter weather is fickle on the crooked peninsula of Massachusetts, and if you start your day full of hope, look out.* When I wake up after a long nap in Birdie's house, the rain and sleet have stopped, leaving behind a blue sky with just a few snowflakes blowing sideways outside my window. I lie on my back and stare at the faded wallpaper with loops of bad weather stains dripping down. Some stains look like creepy eyeballs that stare back at me through a thicket of paper roses, nagging me to stop being such a coward and confront Birdie about my other mother.

Last year, I spent ninety dollars on a 23andMe genetic test but chickened out and let it expire. Finally, I got up my courage and ordered a new 23andMe test for another ninety dollars, took the test, and the results are now being tracked through cyberspace. My milky spit was sent to a faraway lab to reveal the essence of who I am, and that scares the shit out of me. But this is my last hope unless my adoption papers are hidden somewhere in this house. I stare at the wallpaper eyeballs, and the

HUSH LITTLE FIRE

roses look like faces. The wallpaper is older than I am, but the roses aren't talking either.

Although the mansard roof leaks and the wallpaper is rotten, Birdie is so proud of living in one of Wellfleet's historic houses. At the Historical Society where she volunteers, she explains to visitors in her serious low voice that the Newcombe house was the first to have indoor plumbing, but I think she made that up. Sometimes it cuts me in two that she never, ever tells anyone the history of how I came to live under this roof. Here in the attic space turned bedroom for Birdie's only child, me, it feels like the slanted roof might cave in on me any second, so I better wash my face and get out of the house.

My new plan is to cruise by the harbor to look for Jimmy, but instead I drive past the burned-down clinic, then to the ocean, and I can't help myself, I circle right back to the clinic. Did I drive here on Christmas night? The smell of a rose is a tease, gone the second you step away, but smoke from a fire invites itself into your clothes, charcoal bitter, and it stays. I sniff my sleeve like a dog as I drive, but all I get is wet wool.

It's easy to slip under the yellow police tape, because nobody is guarding the site. Once a simple white clapboard building, now a pile of black rubble and ruin that makes me gag as I lean against a tree. A tree branch snaps back at my cheek, perhaps a slap for daring to come here. And oh, how I still hate this spot, and the way Birdie used to force me to walk here to deliver my father's lunch on Saturdays. He had no time left over for me after he tended to sprained ankles, severe sunburns, vomiting from shellfish allergies, things Nurse Haskins could have handled alone.

Your father is a busy doctor and can't possibly run home for lunch on a Saturday. Birdie said this a zillion times.

One time when I dutifully arrived with his lunch, I suddenly felt woozy, so I locked myself in the ladies' room and dropped the lunch bag on the floor. I looked in the bathroom mirror and gently asked the girl staring back at me, "Why does he come home for lunch on weekdays when I'm in school and not Saturdays when I'm home?"

"Figure it out, stupid," the mirror girl answered. I kicked his bag of lunch.

My father was an orderly man ruled by habits, and every Saturday he would embrace me with a tepid thank-you that poked his stethoscope into my face.

"Thank you, my little chickadee, for bringing my lunch," he would say. It was bad enough that he called Mom Birdie, so embarrassing, and I never felt like his chickadee either. It was hard to breathe when I had to look at the receptionist's face, and I worried my throat would close up, so I stared at the floor and shriveled up with shame, wondering how many people in the waiting room knew I was adopted. Every time I brought his lunch, that mean mirror girl liked to woodpecker me with questions like:

Was it his idea or her idea to adopt?

Get a baby.

Buy a baby.

Arrange for an adoption.

It was all the same gobbledygook way of saying it businesslike—procure a person.

And the procured person was me.

I used to long for my father to put away his stethoscope and stop fixing all those strange people. I wanted him to come home at lunchtime and fix my broken bike. Fix my heart. But it was Jimmy who fixed my bike.

At first, I don't pay attention to the crunching of footsteps behind me, twigs breaking and boots scuffing the shells on

HUSH LITTLE FIRE

what's left of the parking lot. Before I can turn around, somebody taps my shoulder—I flinch—and I find myself eye to eye with Officer Babyface again.

"Ma'am, you're not allowed on this side of the yellow tape."

"Sorry, I was just looking. My dad used to work here."

"He sure did. Are you looking for something in particular?"

"No, sir."

"Ma'am, you're trespassing."

"I'm so sorry, sir."

I glance up above his head at the empty sky, no more clouds, and there it is, the great fireball—the sun—listing down west after one more day of warming the earth, which is another useful fire activity. The sun pokes out of the clouds, a beautiful disk of orange fire about to drop out of sight behind Officer Babyface's head. And if his fat face would please go away, I might stand here for a while and warm my face in the sunlight from my favorite fire that burns in the universe twenty-seven million degrees hotter than my kiln ever gets. Birdie warned me never to stare at the sun or it will burn my retinas and I'll go blind, so instead I look at Officer Babyface's chubby cheeks and say I'm sorry a few more times. I'm tempted to ask him if he heard news of Nurse Haskins and how's she doing in the hospital, but I don't. Besides, I never really knew her. I have almost no memories of Nurse Haskins except a few years ago on Easter when she almost ran over my mother's foot with her shopping cart at Stop & Shop. Neither of them said hello to the other, but after Nurse Haskins rolled away, I got a litany of complaints from Birdie.

She looks like an aging ingenue with that ponytail.

The librarian says she's a communist.

She still dyes her hair blond. It looks so trashy.

She dented my car and wouldn't pay the deductible.

She sent her Labrador to poop in my garden.

She was what they call an enabler *with all those girls back then.*

But now, I imagine, Nurse Haskins no longer has much hair of any color. Maybe a few sprouts, like Officer Babyface's wannabe moustache. He stands up straight, both hands on his belt buckle, revving up to boss me around, but before he opens his mouth, I apologize ten times and walk back to my car.

In the distance, I notice another police officer sitting in the squad car, yapping away on his cell phone. It looks like Walter Stone, my old friend from high school who makes pottery as a hobby now, or so Birdie told me. Cop by day. Potter by night. Walter was my honey in high school—not as in boyfriend-type honey but as in art friend honey, who could draw an exact likeness of John Lennon and Paul McCartney. Walter's mother had put a lid on art and practically forced him to join the police force, and Walter gave in like a good son. But Birdie told me he has an art studio bigger than a barn with three different kilns and all the materials that have been hard for me to get. And I wish this weren't such an awkward time to ask if he happens to have any of that rare copper for my red glazes.

I slink around toward the police car and make sure it's really Walter glued to his phone, because this means I can call him later and insinuate myself into borrowing some glazes. Now is not a good time to ask him for anything, but as I leave, I catch how his big potter's hand waves through the air, doing karate chops, just like how he waved his hand when he finished a drawing.

In a few days, maybe I'll cozy up to Walter for some glaze materials and sneak in a few questions about the clinic fire. I'll use my laid-back *nothing important* voice.

On the other hand, maybe I *don't* want to talk to Walter the cop. Could be risky.

♦ 7 ♦

NO CAKE AND NO STEAK FOR LISA

Lisa

I'LL SKIP CLEANING THE Woodwards' gigantic hall mirror because I got rid of the smears last week, even though it was me who'd smeared it up. Smear, clean, smear, clean it up in an empty vacation house that wishes somebody would stay here more than two weeks. There must be a better way to earn a living. I worry I'm morphing into my mother and I'll grow old and die cleaning houses. *Clean, clean, clean, Gina Doanne—now die.* Is that what God told my mother to do with her life?

I study my body in the sparkling hall mirror and want to hug myself, because someday soon my Clean Machine T-shirt will stick way out with a beach ball of a baby who is one-half me and one-half Patrick Bale. I love miracles.

Those do-good churchgoers do good all the time because they think God will toss them a miracle or two if they're good. I tried that. No miracles for me so far.

So I have a new motto:

It's easier to be bad than good.

On the ride home from the Woodwards' McMansion, the back-and-forth scraping of the windshield wipers gives me a depressing feeling that praying and this do-gooder stuff isn't helping. Even though I've been experimenting with the hidden powers of the silver cross, the effort, the smiling, the pleasantries of doing good deeds leaves me exhausted with very little payoff.

"This sucks," I say out loud to the steering wheel.

"Your refrigerator is empty. Get groceries before you go home. Peanut butter has its limits," the steering wheel yells back.

I carefully pick out twenty-five dollars' worth of groceries at Stop & Shop, and while waiting in the checkout line, I overhear two expert gossips reviewing the latest on Barbara Haskins's burns. They stick out their chins with righteous concern and quickly move on to chitchat about what a shame it is that the High Tide Motel was sold and turned into the run-down High Tide Apartments.

"Since it's no longer a motel, there's no upkeep. Such an eyesore. Those tenants are a bunch of hoboes," one of them cackles to her friend way too loud in my direction.

Back at the High Tide Apartments, I park Patrick's dilapidated truck and carry my bag of groceries to our apartment. Plodding through the snow in my sneakers, I blink the falling snowflakes out of my eyes. I feel like crying because the Stop & Shop ladies were right. Everyone in town knows a lot of wheeling and dealing goes on here among the bottom-feeder tenants. Like lobsters on food stamps, we're always scavenging beneath the big fish in the sea. My home is really a hodgepodge apartment, two motel rooms merged together with a rickety refrigerator crammed into the corner. An old motel bed with two dents in the shape of bodies sags in the corner.

HUSH LITTLE FIRE

The High Tide Apartments still has the ghost of a swimming pool left over from High Tide Motel days. My fingers are cold and raw, so I stop near the pool pit, filled with leaves and snow, and blow some warm breath on my palms before I switch hands with the bag. I look down into the hole, and the empty pool stares back at me with a big wide-open mouth, shouting out, "Ha-ha, Lisa, you still live in this awful dump with awful neighbors!"

By now, the white paint outside the building has all peeled off and landed on the windowsill with a pretty dusting of snow. From a distance, it reminds me of shredded-coconut cake icing. I wish I'd bought a coconut cake at Stop & Shop. Steak and cake for Patrick and me. Could be very cozy.

I hurry to my front door and hope I don't bump into any neighbors. Too bad Jimmy Newcombe decided to move in next door so he could be closer to Patrick, which is a big problem for me. All they talk about now is how they'll make tons of money with their new business ideas. Start-up this. Start-up that. Jimmy and Patrick went bankrupt with their oyster grants, so they turned to lobster trapping last summer, but that didn't go so well either. A stoner lobsterman buddy recommended cans of cat food for bait because it's cheaper, but what kind of knucklehead fishing partners buy a case of cat food for bait just when the season is winding down? Jimmy and Patrick, that's who.

I wiggle open the makeshift padlock on my front door and nudge the bag inside with my wet sneakers. I had told Mrs. Woodward in my most sincere voice that all the meat in their McMansion freezer was turning gray with freezer burn, so Mrs. Woodward promptly ordered me to throw it all out. The frosty meat is a slight exaggeration, but I tell myself I earned the pricey steaks like another tip. I depend on tips.

Patrick is passed out on the couch with his feet dangling over the armrest. He looks like such a ninny with his mouth hanging open like that. His favorite glass bong, a slutty red mermaid, sits next to him, and lately she just lies there on the coffee table, the center of his attention, with little left over for me. Patrick doesn't even know I've been trying to get pregnant. A baby will shape him up quick. I open the wobbly refrigerator door and stuff the steaks inside.

In the off-season, Patrick rarely shaves because of the cold, so he says, but being stoned all the time makes him lazy. He and Jimmy would look so handsome if they'd shave more and get haircuts. If they did that, maybe the old biddies in town would stop pointing a finger at them like they're the scruffy lowlifes who might have burned down the clinic. Patrick is snoring underneath a dirty brown skullcap pulled over his eyes with his black hair peeking out like a bad Halloween wig. *Oh, where is the Patrick I used to know?* Blame Jimmy Newcombe and his never-ending plastic-lobsters scheme. If only the two of them would stick to live lobsters.

I lean over Patrick to give him a wake-up kiss, but never mind, he has an ugly cold sore on his upper lip. His cheeks have patches of stubble where he missed with the razor like he was mowing the lawn in a hurry. This shaving job makes him look deranged.

On Christmas morning, he had shaved properly—he looked handsome, and for one beautiful morning, I thought my old Patrick had come back. The high school senior of yesteryear, the great kisser with a sultry mouth and lips that made him look like a guy in the movies. Kisses that rang up my lust with a gong.

By ten AM Christmas morning, everything was going so well. Bolstered by that old holiday ting-a-ling feeling, I kissed him full throttle as I handed him a present.

HUSH LITTLE FIRE 41

"Merry Christmas, Patrick!" A big thick book called *Cape Cod Fishing Tips*.

"You're out of your mind. This book can't be for me," he groaned, and proceeded to roll a joint.

"You and Jimmy are always talking about making more money, and it's way better than your stupid plastic-lobsters scheme."

Our Christmas had ended by noon.

I could cry all over again, but I hum to myself and wash his dirty dishes in piles of billowing soapsuds that keep me company. He finally wakes up and mumbles, "Oh, hi," through his stoner fog as he hobbles off to the bathroom in mismatched socks, one white, one black. He leaves the door wide open behind him, and I'm suddenly overwhelmed with a crushing sadness. A warm oozing wet rushes through my jeans between my legs. I'm getting my period. No baby.

I look at Patrick through the door of the bathroom as he fumbles with his zipper and leaves the toilet seat up again. Like the snow outside, ice crystals begin forming all around me, outside me, inside me, closing in, and slowing my hopes for a baby to a complete halt. I had left one steak out to defrost, but instead I dump it into the garbage. No cake. No steak.

The one great thing about the High Tide Apartments is the lime-colored bathtub, suited for vacationers with strong water pressure and perfect hot and cold calibration like in a high-class hotel. Exactly the way I like it. I probably shouldn't take a bath with this bleeding, but I need one. Patrick steps into his boots, and without tying the laces, he shuffles out the front door, muttering, "I'm gonna get the keys to Jimmy's storage unit tonight if I have to choke somebody."

I scream after him. I can't help myself—"Just who are you gonna choke, Patrick?" I slam the front door behind him and

42 JUDITH NEWCOMB STILES

click the slide bolt lock from inside and shout, "You and your stupid schemes. Sometimes I feel like choking *you*."

I lock myself in my perfectly clean bathroom, faucets shining—I shined them—so I can take a long hot bath with plenty of bubbles. With both hands under the water, I gently pat my belly. *Okay, not this month, but if at first I don't succeed, I will try, try, again.* I dump a fistful of lavender beads in the bath and turn the hot water up with my toes. If Jimmy and Patrick can come up with new ways to make money with that guy Bon Bon in Provincetown, well, so can I. And I can do better.

Perhaps Bon Bon needs a new business associate now that Nurse Haskins is toast. It's all about not letting good opportunities turn into lost opportunities, my mother used to say. I slip my body down into the bathwater right up to my ears so only my face sticks out. I gasp at how easy it could be to take charge of my future, and that includes having a baby no matter how long it takes—with or without Patrick. And now, with Nurse Haskins in the hospital, whatever they were scheming, this has become an opportunity, the kind my mother talked about. And it's most important the old nurse keeps her mouth shut and never ever mentions the arrangement with Patrick and Jimmy to sell pills. Time to pay a visit to Nurse Haskins in the hospital.

I'll think about the particulars later, but right now, I'm going to relax and pretend I'm a tourist taking a nice hot bath after a long, wonderful day at the beach.

♦ 8 ♦

WAI WONG AND THE DEBRIDEMENT OF NURSE HASKINS'

Barbara

I CLOSE MY EYES and count how many days I've been in the burn unit. A few days, a week? They can't even get my name right on the erasure board for the nurses. It says Barbara *Hawkins*— room 167. I am definitely not related to any of those bums in the Hawkins family. But I don't want to risk asking the nurse who monitors my vitals to change it because that would ruin my plan. When the morphine stupor wears off at the end of the day, I must be disciplined and not utter a word. So far, so good.

The doctors and nurses hover over my face, trying to cajole me into speaking, but I stay silent. I overhear a snatch of quiet chatter between two nurses about how *the patient must still be traumatized.* I know if I ever start speaking again, the nerdy psychiatrist and police detectives will bombard me with questions and all will be lost. If I even utter a simple yes or no, those few words could snowball down the long road that leads to prison. I vow to be mute. For now, I love the morphine drip and the way it makes the pain fade for long stretches of time. Is this what Jimmy Newcombe was talking about? Bliss from oxycodone.

44 JUDITH NEWCOMB STILES

Burn trauma, shock, damage from smoke inhalation, pulmonary edema, blistering of the oropharynx—I overhear the nurses whisper to each other.

"Barbara, when I ask you a question, simply blink once for yes and twice for no," the psychiatrist commands. "Can you hear me?" After a moment, I blink three times.

A few hours later, the doctors swoop through the door over to my bed, and they give the psychiatrist another shot at trying to get me to speak. He's short, like a tree stump, and he looks out of place with the other tall medical professionals who group together in a self-important scrum. I have no great love for doctors, and I don't like the short one with his pulpy forehead and madman eyes. Dr. Tree Stump suggests I move my left hand for yes and my right hand for no, which is just a variation on the blinking strategy. Only three of my fingertips jut out from the bandages that encase my torso like a banana peel. The psychiatrist flashes a phony smile and gets too close to my face when he asks me several questions in a talk-to-deaf-people-type voice, enunciating every word.

"Move your left hand. Please try, Barbara. If you can hear me, just move your hand and give us a little yes, won't you please."

Whatever they ask me to do, I'll do something else. No slipups. Then they will surely go back to their offices and puzzle over badly burned me. I have the sinking feeling that it's only a matter of time before another detective will come through the door and badger me into speaking about the Christmas fire. *And who is that cute volunteer firefighter who keeps coming back to quiz me about Jimmy?*

This particular dose of morphine is kicking in nicely, or is it Oxy? I don't blink or move my hands, so the shrink sighs and shuffles out the door.

When the morphine is full blast, I love the strange wild visions I have—dreams that must belong to other people, not

HUSH LITTLE FIRE

mine, that's for sure. In one dream, I'm a Chinese man on a quiz show, answering difficult questions in Mandarin, and the questions are projected on a big screen with colorful lights with yes-or-no answers. The audience stands up and applauds, and I give a thank-you bow to the people in my snappy three-piece suit. So weird, because the only Asian person I know on all of Cape Cod is Wai Wong, the server at the Lucky Dragon Restaurant. I used to eat there many times all alone, and we became friendly. He even taught me one word in Mandarin, *xièxiè*, for thank you. For a while, I really liked Wai and our civilized conversations, especially because I'm low on friends and have no family of my own. He gave me handfuls of extra fortune cookies, and we laughed and talked about the possible paths in life that were presented on a plateful of cookies. I enjoyed his company until Wai became overly friendly and hinted that I might become his bride so he could get his green card. After that, I never went back to the Lucky Dragon.

A male nurse with a choirboy face floats over to my bed, takes my blood pressure, and clicks his pen a few times before he speaks.

"You are fortunate the burns are isolated to the upper half of your body. Just think, Barbara, someday you'll be able to walk out of here."

Fortunate? I'm a mess after that skin graft. Oh yeah, I'm so fortunate to be able to walk out of here with a Freddie Krueger face.

When the nurse leaves the room, I hobble over to my chart, because the computer screen is still on my page. It says I had a procedure called *debridement. What's that? De-bride?* At least I still have a finger or two that work, so I look up the word on my phone. Debridement is the removal of dead or contaminated skin and foreign material from serious burn trauma. I can't help but wonder if this is bad karma for all I did with Dr. Newcombe decades ago.

Right now I want to shout out for more painkillers, because the cycle begins with feeling stoned, but as it wears off, the pain starts at skin level and then chisels down deep into my bones. When the IV drip bag is refilled and I'm stoned again, I become Barbara with wings as delightful energy rushes through my body like a summer breeze through lace curtains.

By noon, I am neither awake nor asleep, and I hallucinate that my bed is rolling down a long corridor with doors on both sides. I open the first black door, but there is the specter of Dr. Newcombe, standing alone about to kiss me, so I slam the door in his face. I drift along in the gurney to the second black door and open it to see a wide span of Cape Cod Bay with boats docked at the harbor. This is a pleasant sight for me, until I notice a ghostly white buoy bobbing up and down that looks like the face of young Cindy. Sad Cindy. Tangled seaweed morphs into Cindy's swampy brown hair, framing her scared, crying face. A long, long time ago, when fifteen-year-old Cindy visited Dr. Newcombe with her predicament, she bawled her eyes out the whole time in front of him until her face looked like a waterlogged blob from swimming all day. Many years later, I recognized Cindy as she tried on men's jeans at Watson's clothing store in Orleans. Her swampy brown hair had gone partially gray, and she had bad posture and downcast eyes. Cindy looked like she'd been carrying a giant rock on her back for years. Standing there in my bra and undies at Watson's, I suddenly remembered how Dr. Newcombe had stepped it up to a more complex procedure with her. He accidentally snipped Cindy's fallopian tubes. I looked on in horror when Cindy's bloody ovaries spilled out like snot balls with the fetus. How many years did it take for Cindy to figure out that she could never get pregnant again?

HUSH LITTLE FIRE

I've had enough of door two and slam it shut, hopefully forever. I am so stoned, neither awake nor asleep, when door three opens all by itself. Flames are everywhere, lapping at the walls, looking for my thumb. What's going on? Am I crazy? Where am I? Am I back at the clinic, or is this my hospital room? A nurse and a girl float through the door, speaking quietly to each other.

The nurse whispers, "We are limiting all visits to ten minutes. She doesn't have any visitors, so we're glad you came. Maybe you can cheer her up and get her to speak."

"My mother knew her very well, so I'm sure she'll be happy to see me. Hmmm, I guess she won't be able to eat this box of chocolates, but at least I brought her a Bible," says the strange young woman. This isn't a dream. *It's a real visitor. Who is it?*

When the nurse leaves the room, the girl looks back over her shoulder and closes the bedside curtains. She pulls a chair next to my IV and wraps her fingers around the pole.

"I brought you a Bible. I'll read some famous passages, the ones my mother, Gina, used to read. Do you remember my mother, Gina Doanne? A neighbor told me that behind my mom's back, you and Dr. Newcombe called her the *frequent flier* when she came to the clinic. That wasn't very nice. I'm Lisa, her daughter. Do you remember me?"

This strange Lisa visitor looks up at the security camera near the ceiling. She walks underneath, abruptly shoves a chair against the wall, and stands on the seat with her face below range of the camera. She pulls a wad of bubble gum out of her mouth and presses it smack on top of the lens. I don't move. I follow Lisa with my eyes and begin to panic.

Lisa sits down again and lays the Bible too close to my bandaged arm, pressing down hard on the mattress while reading a page. Halfway through the verses, she whispers into my bandaged ear, "My mother never liked you or that greedy Dr. Newcombe, but that's beside the point. Did you think for one minute I didn't know about your pill business with my boyfriend, Patrick? The three of you thought you were big-time dealers, but the way I see it, fishermen and nurses don't know the first thing about selling drugs. I guess you found out the hard way."

I pull the blanket up to my neck.

"My humble suggestion is, from here on in, when the cops ask you questions, well, you cannot remember anything about December twenty-fifth. If you say anything about Patrick to the police and he goes down, you will definitely go down harder. As my friend Lester always says, there are things way worse in life than jail time. I'm sure you catch my drift."

Lisa rests her hand on top of my exposed thumb and taps the peeling nail polish. "Nothing personal, Nurse Haskins, but now it's time to look out for myself. And you should look after yourself. Be careful in hospitals. They can be germ factories, you know. My mom always said, 'Pneumonia is an old person's friend.'"

Lisa plants a peck of a kiss on my forehead before she stands up. She slides a chair back under the security camera, jumps up, and removes the wad of bubble gum, popping it back in her mouth. She sashays back to me and pulls back the hospital curtain, standing exactly in range of the camera. I don't move. She clears her throat and says in a loud, cheerful voice so that cop Walter who guards the room in the hallway can hear, "Before my mother passed away, she said she'd never forget Nurse Barbara Haskins, and I won't forget you either. I'll be back." Lisa smiles at the cop, waves the peace sign, and prances down the hall.

♦ 9 ♦

MARY MAKES A POTTERY CREMATION URN FOR A DEAD CHIHUAHUA

Mary

IT FEELS LIKE A hundred years since I escaped Cape Cod to live in Brooklyn, and although Danny and I live 288 miles away from my mother, she camps out in my head most of the time with her dos and don'ts. Calling me on her phone is her lifeline, but it's funny how when I'm here for the holidays, we don't speak much. I see a note on the kitchen table, a note taped to the fridge, and various Post-its left in strategic places around the house in my mother's loopy handwriting. She's out and about with Danny buying him sneakers.

I haven't heard from Jimmy. Where is he?
Mrs. Reardon called the house phone. Call her back
immediately.
Danny didn't take out the garbage. Can you, please?
Mrs. Reardon called again.
If the police call, don't talk to them under any circumstances.
Mrs. Reardon called for the third time.

With all these annoying notes around the house, I'm tempted to leave a few for her.

Why don't you fucking look for Jimmy yourself?
Did you hide my original birth certificate in the house?
Do you ever wish you adopted a different baby?

But I don't leave any notes, and I don't call Mrs. Reardon back about her pottery order either. She can wait. She is first on my list of problem customers, which is why I haven't called her back. I made 110 coffee mugs for her—fine, not really; mugs are a pain in the ass—and now she wants to line up behind my mother to order one of my specialty cremation urns.

When I was back in Brooklyn before Christmas, out of the blue, my mother started bugging me to make a pottery cremation urn for her, and she's not dying, not even close. She called me up in the middle of the night, whispering in a scratchy voice that sounded way too near like she was on my pillow.

"Is this Miss Mary?" That's what she likes to call me, which is icky and sad and not at all motherly, because what mother calls her grown daughter *miss*?

"When are you going to make a pretty urn for my ashes? You can make me one out of Newcomb Hollow clay. I want an urn with an easel and paintbrushes on the lid and my name in gold letters."

"Really? You want one now?"

"Put ocean waves crashing on the base. That's what I want."

"Go back to sleep, Mother. I don't make cremation urns anymore." Then she hung up before I could say anything like *I love you*, which she skipped too.

Almost every potter I know squeaks through the winter on money from selling pots for holiday gifts. Before I came back

HUSH LITTLE FIRE

here, I completed an annoying order for the snooty Reardon & Farley law firm in Manhattan. Mr. Reardon had sent his wife slumming to buy crafty Christmas gifts in Brooklyn. She arrived in my studio to inspect my pots, wearing a fluffy brown mink coat that flopped open and closed on her body. She took awkward steps in her brown high heels that left marks on the clay-covered floor like animal tracks. She spent a lot of money. She was a shopper. Mrs. Reardon's cheeks were as gray as a crumpled wad of newspaper, and I couldn't tell if she was smiling or frowning. Her watery eyes seemed to recede into her skull, and I wondered how much time she had left on this planet. And just as I had that thought, *ping*, she started asking about urns for the deceased, because, I suppose, she found out from somebody uptown that I was the go-to girl for handmade cremation urns. She must have heard I used to make urns in all different shapes and sizes, mostly for rich people and many for people dying of AIDS.

"Actually, Mrs. Reardon, I don't really make them anymore."

"But I need one for my teacup Chihuahua. Happy passed away."

She told me she had several high-strung miniature Chihuahuas—really, upscale rats with big, perky ears—named after Snow White's seven dwarfs. No children in the Reardon household.

"And Doc and his brother Bashful aren't doing well either. They're almost fifteen, so that means more orders for you in the future; won't you please consider it?"

"Sorry, but I quit making cremation urns. Too depressing."

"I need you to make one with your pretty red glaze, just for Happy, and I'll pay you three hundred dollars, no matter how long it takes."

"I don't really have time."

"I'll pay a thousand. Money's no object."

JUDITH NEWCOMB STILES

"Oh. I would be happy to make Happy an urn, no problem."

And so it was—how I got roped back into the cremation urn business. I swore I'd never make another one after years of cranking them out like a mortician who makes money off other people's grief. I tried so hard to be Zen about the whole thing, especially when I had to transfer the ashes into one of my pots. With a soup ladle, I used to scoop a dead person's ashes into an urn, an entire life suddenly ash with little bone bits and pieces of teeth. Oh, if they could look in the mirror now—how much time they spent fussing over bad hair days, those hairdos gone forever, flamed away for eternity. Nobody likes to think about this, but urn makers like me and morticians think about these things when we go to work. Cremation urns are good money. Good profit. All things considered, a potter can only get so much money for an ordinary cookie jar with a lid, but call it a cremation urn, and funeral homes charge more than a thousand dollars for cheap ones banged out in Chinese factories.

I should get to work on Mrs. Reardon's dog urn this week. It should be small, less than a cup of ashes, and I know this because a pet crematorium in Brooklyn has a window where you can watch your pet on a purple velvet pillow get cremated. I went along with my friend Joyce to watch her cat Oscar go up in flames, and I held her hand when she cried. I didn't cry at all. The fire was spectacular. It was like a crescendo of hallelujahs and Hail Marys for me, but strange, because we couldn't hear the crackling flames behind the glass partition. It was like watching a silent movie. Everyone agrees cremations are the good kind of fire and the clinic burning down was bad fire, but when I stare at flames long enough, it's easy to forget if it's good or bad. It's not nice to say out loud,

HUSH LITTLE FIRE

but the truth is that Nurse Barbara Haskins was almost cremated in the clinic fire, and the whole town blames fire when the flames simply gobbled up oxygen and solid matter to sustain the burning.

I wonder if Mrs. Reardon attended Happy's cremation. I know I should have more compassion for her, but compassion is not an abundant New Englander trait. There's something utterly absurd—sad, really—about making a thousand-dollar cremation urn for a rich lady's dog, but I guess these dogs are her babies, so I rummage around for my better self and attempt to feel sorry for her.

I tried to warn her that even with high-tech factory kilns, there are no guarantees with copper red glazes.

"Please understand," I said. "When I cut down the oxygen flow with the kiln damper, the greedy flames become hungry for oxygen, so they pull it out of the copper glaze's $CuCO_3$, hopefully turning the green to red. But sometimes it comes out awful and spotty like a frog."

Mrs. Reardon looked completely confused but nodded as she brushed some clay dust off her minky sleeve.

I must say I love copper red glazes, with their formulas that go back almost a thousand years to the Ming dynasty, when they fired copper red on sacrificial cups for emperors who worshipped the sun. It's a different red from Christmas red, or fire-engine red, or Harvard crimson. The ancient potters described their beloved copper red glaze as the color of fresh blood. Even now, with all our technology and sophisticated digital kilns, potters still can't control the elusive red. It's like the fire has a mind of its own and all we can do is carefully adjust the oxygen flow and pray for a good red. That's why we make kiln gods out of clay and put them on top of the kiln for each firing. Pray for red.

Pray? That's a tricky one. Wellfleet used to be a town full of praying people, but now, not so much, other than the Old Ladies Gossip Militia, who are still in the habit of going to church. I wonder if they pray for Barbara Haskins to get better. According to Birdie, nobody liked her, but surely the minister at the Congregational Church will mention the fire in his sermon and will ask the people in the pews to pray for her recovery. The churchgoers most likely pray to a god with a beard on a throne up in heaven, but I pray to a shape made out of clay, the essence of our earth and a god of fire that rebonds molecules in a process we cannot control even though for thousands of years, we've tried. Both the churchgoers and I pray for good results. I pray for a good red glaze sometimes, but mostly I pray to find my birth mother.

♦ **10** ♦

GOOD NEWCOMBS VS. NAUGHTY NEWCOMBES IN THE CEMETERY

Mary

WITH BIRDIE AND DANNY out shopping, it might be a good time to snoop. I'll be extra careful to place everything back where I found it. Last time I came home, I combed through the top drawer of the desk in the TV room, and now in the bottom drawer, I find old newspaper clippings, but nothing about me except a report card for Mary Newcombe, all B's. There's a yellowed crumbly clipping that I carefully unfold about the Wellfleet Town Hall burning down in 1960 with all the paper records of this and that, deeds, and important town documents. The Gossip Militia and the newspaper pegged it as arson, probably a disgruntled landowner who didn't want to pay back taxes. Another old newspaper clipping falls apart in my hands, about my beloved Penney Patch Fudge Store when it mysteriously burned down in 1976. Most of Wellfleet's suspicious fires were before the time Jimmy started rubbing sticks for sparks to make fire. Or were they? I was his trusty assistant in several of his experiments.

56   JUDITH NEWCOMB STILES

Danny and Birdie are back. My son finds me by the desk, barely says hello, and dumps three boxes of sneakers on the rug at my feet.

"You two have been busy," I say, squatting down to admire his loot. My mother nudges the bottom drawer closed with her foot and then gives me the crinkled Birdie frown, like she knows I was snooping. She retreats to the kitchen, complaining about the high cost of shoes and exactly what she spent, which is a favorite topic in the Old Ladies Gossip Militia. Danny won't look at me as he tries on his new sneakers. He's been sullen and skittish since we've been here, but maybe it's just preadolescent hormones. It's not New Year's Eve yet, and he's already hounding me to go back to Brooklyn. I look out the window and the sirens of drinkie start calling me, but I don't take it personally because they call up everyone in the winter. Mrs. Sherry suggests I get out there and keep looking for Jimmy. He's not at his apartment and he doesn't answer his phone. But it's time to go to the ocean and find some good clay to start the urns.

It's a rare fifty degrees today, but I bundle up anyway in a parka and ride my old bike to Newcomb Hollow Beach. I hang an empty bucket off the handlebars to collect the best clay hidden in the sand dunes for Mrs. Reardon. Gray clay full of bentonite, a type of volcanic ash that has been aging in the folds of sea cliffs forever. Newcomb Hollow clay is stretchy and malleable and the best for throwing on the wheel. Ancient volcanic ash is also perfect for glazes, and a pinch is just enough to move some molecules around in the kiln firing to make way for the ashes of a dead Chihuahua.

"Come back! I made lunch—your favorite! Bologna and cheese. Mary, you can't go biking without a helmet at your age!" Birdie shouts after me as I head for Gross Hill Road with my bucket. I never told her I can't stand bologna and cheese.

HUSH LITTLE FIRE

At the top of Mill Hill, the light is red, but still I dart across Route 6, because this was Jimmy's favorite dare when we were kids. Rush across the highway without getting flattened by a car was his adrenaline game, not mine, but now I take the dare. Winter air blasts sharp into my lungs and wakes me up as I pump the pedals faster and faster. I'm a kid again now and squint at the road ahead to rewind my life to when Jimmy was leading the way on his bike. He was always considerate and didn't ride too fast, except when he lurched ahead to spit a big loogie so it wouldn't land on me.

The first stop on Gross Hill Road with Jimmy was to race the shell path in the Wellfleet Cemetery for a visit with the dead, so there's a slim chance I might find him here today. Here at the graveyard, the Newcombes are divided into two clans. I always wondered if there was a family fight hundreds of years ago when the upstanding Newcombs dropped the *e* at the end of their name to differentiate themselves from the naughty Newcombes. Good Newcombs. Naughty Newcombes. The grave site is cleaved down the middle, separated by a row of leafless lilac bushes. Most of the Old Ladies Gossip Militia favors the virtuous Newcombs (*e*-droppers) on one side of the bushes, while on this side, there are the Newcombes who set fires, got drunk a lot, and hoarded their bitterness like money. Even though I'm adopted and the stork story is flimsy, I think of myself as belonging to this hardscrabble tribe. I know my blood isn't the blood of these people, but my attachment runs deep. It's kind of a schizophrenic thing, with my love for Newcombes on one side of my brain and this impossible longing for my birth mother on the other.

Jimmy liked to stop at the cemetery to say a few words to his mother, Clara. Sometimes he'd dismount, throw his bike down, and kiss the grass where her ashes were buried in a metal canister that my mother said looked too much like a flask. Then he'd walk over to Benjamin Oliver Newcomb on the good-people side of the lilac bushes, and he'd kneel down in front of a bronze flag sticking out of a rock that says, *For bravery and perseverance in the rescue of the Brig Yillica, December 1, 1851.* My mother said Captain Newcomb saved every man from a sinking ship during a terrible December nor'easter when the *Brig Yillica* hit the shoals.

"Benjamin was indeed a brave man," my mother told us many times, raising the bar of goodness way too high for me and Jimmy. The state of Massachusetts named the site of the rescue after him—Newcomb Hollow Beach, the vast stretch of sand and sea that curves around the corner before bending out of sight into Truro. Birdie told me I'm named after his wife, a good Mary on the *e*-dropper side. I think the state of Massachusetts named a parking lot after us Newcombes who kept their *e*'s.

I know very little about the good Mary, but there's a small suitcase in the attic filled with keepsakes, tatting, and crocheted table runners from the time when she took in sewing as a widow. Birdie says that's how women made their own money back then. High up on a bookcase in Birdie's TV room, there's a mysterious blue vessel with painted blackbirds made out of earthenware pottery that is signed *Mary A. Newcomb, 1865* on the bottom. Birdie treasures the vase—who wouldn't? My eyes often wander away from the TV screen up to the birds fluttering across the blue curves of the pot. Birdie knows I covet this vase, and every time I ask her if I can take it back to Brooklyn, she says *not yet* and starts an argument about how Mary A. Newcomb's blackbirds look too much like crows.

I circle the Newcombe plot a few times, say my goodbyes, and continue on Gross Hill Road all the way to a secret dirt

HUSH LITTLE FIRE

path. It leads to an unmarked kettle pond, an ancient oasis—good for freshwater swimming in the middle of the woods. Jimmy and I would drop our bikes on the path, and I'd follow him all the way to the pond, running hard, grass slapping my legs. When we swam across the pond, Jimmy always stayed by my side with each stroke to make sure I didn't drown. On the other side, the glassy water was so clear I could stand up to my waist and see straight down to my feet on the sandy bottom. Sometimes we stood there, panting and dripping, and he would hug me for no reason, and I waited for those hugs. "Race you back!" Jimmy would say, but he never raced. He always swam close by.

I stand on the edge of Spectacle Pond and skim my hand across the water, messing up my reflection because this time it's only me and I wish he were here, just two kids on our bikes. One time, before we left Spectacle Pond, Jimmy traipsed deep into the woods to look for a particular clearing—a campfire spot where boys from school hung out with Jimmy and their crumpled beer cans. For days he had been bragging that he could start a fire without a match, but I didn't believe him. Rubbing a flint never worked, but then he pulled out of his pocket a strange-looking lens that some old guy had given him. He dried it off by sliding it up and down his arm in the sun as he chanted something low and wild. When he stopped chanting, he stomped around the edges of the clearing and collected dry pine needles into a pile. He dropped down on his knees and said to me, "Come closer, Sunshine."

By that pile of pine needles, Jimmy nicknamed me Sunshine when he kissed me for the first time—another Jimmy dare, which turned us into naughty kissing cousins. I had a sinking feeling this could lead to trouble, but I didn't care. From then on, he called me Sunshine, not Mary, and I loved being close to

JUDITH NEWCOMB STILES

him, especially when he put his hand on my hair and stroked it, although it was the exact same way he stroked a dog.

"Watch this, Sunshine," he said as he jiggled the lens back and forth until he found the perfect angle, and then poof, magic flames, and then a beautiful fire. He shouted, "Oh *yes!*" with the burst of flames, and he yelled it way too loud. The sparkling lens was enchanting to a girl like me, but also scary, like watching the devil from a distance. I knew from school that flames had burned Joan of Arc alive at the stake, and I knew it only took minutes. I had my silver lighter and Jimmy had his lens.

Up and down the steep hills, I ride toward Newcomb Hollow Beach, but I'm huffing and puffing so much I can't possibly make it all the way to the ocean. I turn around and walk my bike back down the hill, and just as I round the corner to Birdie's house, Gemma, the mail lady, jams on her brakes in front of our mailbox. Gemma is the daughter of Emma, the retired mail carrier who delivered mail door-to-door when I was a kid. Postal work runs in the family. I wheel my bike up to the mailbox, and Gemma drills me up and down with her eyes. I can tell by the look on her face that she's itchy for some good gossip, because she clutches our mail, not handing it over.

"How are ya doing, Mary? So nice you and your boy came back for the holidays."

I feel my throat close up. Gemma is warming up in the batter's box.

"Your cousin's mailbox is completely stuffed with magazines, and we'll have to stamp *return to sender* if he doesn't hurry up and fetch his mail. When you see Jimmy, don't forget to tell him."

"Sure thing, Gemma. I'll tell him."

She leans in close and squeezes my elbow, whispering right in my face without letting me get away. "You know Ruth on the west end mail route? She says she saw him down at Powers

HUSH LITTLE FIRE

Landing near his old oyster bed doing something he shouldn't be doing."

"What's that, Gemma?"

"I'm not one to gossip, but Ruth heard from somebody, I won't say who, that he's still mad at Katie Snow about the whole oyster thing."

"When'd you see him?"

Gemma shrugs and says she can't remember, and then the prime minister of gossip hands me the mail, which I dump in my empty bucket. I smile and say happy New Year with a few phony well wishes. Gemma nervously strokes the steering wheel like she wants to ask another question.

"I waved to you in the crowd when they saved Nurse Haskins, but maybe you didn't recognize me."

This again? "But I wasn't there that night."

She tilts her head. "Weren't you?"

I shake my head *nuh-uh*. "I fell asleep watching TV at home."

"That wasn't you?"

"Nope." I pleasantly say goodbye and walk away. Leave it be, Old Ladies Gossip Militia. Leave it be.

I go back inside the house with a bucketful of Birdie's mail and close my eyes to try and visualize Christmas fire. Did I see it, or did I stay home? It freaks me out that Kevin says Nurse Haskins might have started the fire from a careless smoke, but what freaks me out worse is that I can't stop imagining the clinic and hungry flames gobbling up oxygen and wood because maybe one dot of glowing ash dropped from a cigarette. Why didn't she get out of there and run for her life? Joan of Arc couldn't run, tied in place with rope, poor Joan, logs and kindling beneath her feet. What on earth was Joan thinking— what was Barbara thinking—in those last precious moments when her brain realized her body was on fire?

♦ 11 ♦

BON BON AND LISA DISPARAGE CHOPSTICKS

Lisa

EVEN THOUGH I WORKED the night shift at the Lighthouse, this morning I stop by there and find Lester making multiple breakfasts in the kitchen for people who leave lousy tips. He's flipping eggs over easy, buttering toast, turning bacon, and it looks like he has four arms. He moves on to pancakes as he sings his favorite Bob Marley tune, glomming the words together—whipping a wooden spoon round and round to the beat in a bowl full of gooey batter.

"Hi, Lisa. How'd I do on my homework?" Lester mouths the words on the breakfast order slips clipped to a clothesline near the grill, reading them like he's in second grade.

It took me quite a while to realize my friend Lester never learned how to read properly. He had covered this up for a long time by joking about my bad handwriting, so I had to shout the customer orders all the way back to the kitchen. One day when I confronted Lester about an order mix-up, his eyes glazed over when I crabbed at him about confusing *fries & choc shake* with *fries & choc cake*. I conceded to Lester that they sounded sort of

HUSH LITTLE FIRE

the same, but I had written the order in my best print after he had complained about my messy script.

"Lester! Read it! I wrote fries and choc shake, not fries and choc cake."

Lester's teeth growled down over his lower lip. "How can I read if I never went to school?"

"Oh . . . Lester . . . I didn't know you never went to school." I felt like a first-class shrew. "Well, no problem, maybe I can teach you to read. My mother always said I'd make a good teacher."

I picked up a phonics book for fifty cents at the flea market and went through it page by page with Lester. Now I give him homework assignments.

"You got a one hundred percent on last week's homework. You're on your way. In no time at all, you'll be writing a cookbook. Hey, Lester, can you do me a little favor?"

Lester does a spin on one foot and gives me a hug. "Anything you want. Anything at all."

"You can take me to Provincetown to meet Bon Bon."

Lester puts down his spatula and steps back. "No way. Not that."

"You promised anything at all. If you won't take me to him, at least tell me where he is."

"I know you. You're going to find him with or without me. So you have to do exactly what I say. Okay?"

"Okay."

"He eats his meals sometimes at the Chinese restaurant in Orleans, so make it like you're waiting for your takeout. And don't tell me why you want to see him, because if the police ever ask me, I'll say I don't know anything about it. Deal?"

"Okay, deal."

At lunchtime on Wednesday, I order takeout at the sole Chinese restaurant in Orleans. The Lucky Dragon. A skinny middle-aged Asian man writes down my takeout order as I dawdle, flirting with the same skinny fellow even after I pay. He tells me his name is Wai Wong. I pretend I'm interested in Wai as my eyes ping-pong from the tables to the door, wishing Bon Bon would arrive. I wait and wait. I'm wearing my tightest blue sweater to hopefully give me some kind of upper hand when I finally meet Bon Bon.

"I guess you like to eat your food cold?" Wai nods a few times with an eager but puzzled look on his face.

"I'll reheat it when I get home," I say, slowing down my exit even more by retreating to the ladies' room.

At dinnertime, I come back wearing a tight black sweater, and when I walk into the Lucky Dragon again, Wai Wong practically jumps for joy.

"Whoa, you really love Chinese food," says Wai, recommending the Peking duck.

In the far corner of the restaurant sits one customer with his back to the door in an alcove. It's the only table with candles and a linen tablecloth and linen napkins. I stick out my chest and bustle over to what could be Bon Bon to introduce myself.

"Hi, I'm a friend of Lester's. My name is Lisa. Are you Mr. Bon Bon, by any chance? I'm so pleased to finally meet you. I hope I'm not interrupting."

Bon Bon slowly puts down his fork and knife without speaking. He doesn't move his head to look at my face, but I can see his eyes are covering a lot of territory as they roam around, scanning me from top to bottom. His body is still as a sphinx. The alcove is dark and his expression is unreadable.

"Have a seat, young lady. My name is Hector Bonaparte. Only close friends call me Bon Bon. Why did Lester send you here?"

HUSH LITTLE FIRE

I slink into the other side of the booth, bat my eyelashes, and flash him my best smile. Bon Bon has on a white shirt, perfectly ironed and fresh like the best of Mr. Woodward's. He is muscular, with top-heavy arms, and his head looks like an oily bowling ball. A small glistening diamond twinkles on his earlobe, and I can't read his mood. I notice he uses fine silverware, the kind I polish for the Woodwards. This man cuts his meat with a bone-handle knife that shoots a little shiver up my neck.

"Oh no, Lester didn't send me here. I just need a few minutes of your time." I zero in on the rings on his stubby fingers. On his left hand are dazzling gold rings, on his right hand rings with cut stones that look a lot like the college ring from Yale Mr. Woodward brags about. Bon Bon slowly puts down the knife.

"So you like my rings." He laughs, lifting his fork with his pinkie up in the air like those British ladies on TV with their teacups. Bon Bon is sharp. He caught my sneaky glances. I better be on my toes, because this guy doesn't miss a thing.

"These rings are from famous American universities," he says, whisking his hand in front of my eyes, jutting out his jaw as he speaks. "Each one is a gift from my clients."

I wonder what dilemma would make a man give Bon Bon his sentimental college ring.

"Would you like to try some of this goat meat? Chef Chen makes this dish just for me."

"No thank you."

Bon Bon pulls out of his shirt pocket an expensive pen. A very thin blade suddenly pops out. "I like this knife better for cutting my food. One stroke across the meat, and the job's done. None of this cutting back and forth across the plate. I detest that noise, don't you?"

66 JUDITH NEWCOMB STILES

I nod and watch him slice through the thick lump of meat like butter with one nonchalant stroke of the blade.

"This year I bought ten goats and five sheep at a farm in Truro for a very good price. Cute goats. Good meat. The way it works, I simply call the farmer, and he readies one for Chef Chen. He slits the throat and hangs it upside down to let the blood run. The farm cats love the blood."

"Interesting," I say, trying to sound firm.

"I name each of my goats. You would like them. This week Chef Chen roasted Arthur. Delicious. But I'm upset because the pretty female, Bella, went missing. Such a shame. Perhaps somebody stole her. These days everything seems to go missing. You know what I mean?"

"I think so . . . sure." I swallow.

"No you don't, Miss Lisa. No you don't. My goat went missing. My hubcap went missing. My money's gone missing. Well, my hubcap fell off, but it feels like even my country's gone missing. I never felt quite right here on Cape Cod. Here they say even the codfish have gone missing. I hate the taste of fish. I never eat fish. We don't lose our fish in Jamaica."

Bon Bon picks up a pillbox on the table and takes out a pinch of powder. "You know what this is?"

I shake my head. "No."

"It's the best spices from my country, and I like to add them to my food." He sprinkles some over his meat. "A little crushed chili pepper, fresh coriander, other hometown ingredients—you should try some. If you were a spice, Lisa, I'd say you are ginger. Sweet, but prickly on the tongue. Should I call you Miss Ginger from now on?"

"You can if you want, but you don't have to."

Bon Bon puts down the pillbox and folds his hands together. His nostrils twitch while the rest of his face is still.

HUSH LITTLE FIRE

67

"Do you smell something?" Bon Bon closes his eyes. "Do you?"

"No, *sir*, I don't." Maybe calling him sir will calm him down. His lower jaw is pulsating, and I can see he's wound pretty tight.

"It's the odor a man gives off when he can't be trusted. A sour smell."

I nod.

"Miss Lisa, why would anyone, such as yourself, tell the police they saw me sitting in a car in Provincetown talking to a nurse and Jimmy Newcombe the night before that terrible fire in Wellfleet?"

I say nothing and keep my body still, because I know it would be bad if he traps me. It's time to stop acting like such a wuss or I'll never get anywhere with Bon Bon. I straighten my sweater, stick out my chest, and speak in my most confident voice.

"I didn't say anything to the police. You might think I did, but I didn't."

Bon Bon's eyes shrink into little slits. "Does Jimmy Newcombe owe you money?"

"Not exactly. Let's just say many things in my life have gone missing too."

"Never get in over your head. Be careful to only lend money to those who will pay you back. I'm well known in certain circles as a benevolent banker. I like to help people whenever I can."

"Oh yes, Lester tells me how kind you are."

"Whatever you do, be sure to get a good return on your investment. Your friend Mr. Newcombe is turning out to be—shall we say—a slow investment."

"I don't really know him, even though he fishes with my boyfriend."

Bon Bon is silent and stares at my chin while he chews.

"Lester tells me you have many investments and business enterprises, and I was just wondering, now that Nurse Haskins is in the hospital, maybe I can step in and take her place." I lean my boobs in. "Kind of like a substitute teacher. But that's not the only reason I came to see you."

"Well then, I'll get another plate for you, Miss Lisa, and you can stay for dinner."

Without turning around, Bon Bon lifts his college ring hand and clicks his fingers. In seconds Wai Wong is at his side.

"Another plate, please, for the lady." Wai scurries off. "Do you prefer chopsticks?"

"No thank you."

"Good girl. Chopsticks are for pretenders."

I smile, and Bon Bon flattens his lips with an upward turn that is not quite a smile but an affirmative, or so I'd like to believe. Bon Bon looks straight at me, not moving a muscle, and I recognize this as a power play. I imitate his look and say nothing, right back into his eyes. Suddenly, I blink first, because I have to suppress a thought that could possibly lead to a laugh, which might very well piss him off. I stare at Bon Bon's bowling-ball head and have a vision of Humpty Dumpty sitting down in our booth, and Humpty floats over and merges into the body of Bon Bon, just like in a TV cartoon.

Humpty Bon Bon sat on a wall.

Humpty Bon Bon had a great fall.

"Now, Miss Lisa, what else did you want to ask me?"

♦ 12 ♦

NURSE BARBARA
AND DR. NEWCOMBE'S
BILLY CLUB

Barbara

THIS MORNING—IS IT MORNING?—the nurse asks me in her most irritating crispy voice, "HOW ARE YOU, MISS HAWKINS, THIS LOVELY MORNING?" Of course I don't answer. My torso is in a nervous sweat, making the bandages extra soggy. I'm pretty sure it's still the holidays, because paper snowmen and reindeer line the green walls in the hospital. No Martin Luther King Jr. posters or Valentine's hearts yet.

Several cops march into my room not dressed at all like the local police. They wear white shirts and suit jackets, and I don't recognize any of them. I have the sinking feeling this isn't just about the Christmas fire. None of them are local cops, except that Officer Walter Stone who mostly sleeps in a chair outside my room. And then there's that handsome volunteer firefighter who keeps coming back asking questions. Did the orderly tell the nurse his name is Tom Murphy? An older cop with a Marines buzz cut lays several photos on a tray in front of me.

"Did you see any of these people on Christmas Day before or after you went to the clinic? All you have to do is point," orders the cop. On the tray are snapshots of nine people: Jimmy New-combe; his cousin Mary; that boy of hers, Danny; and Patrick Bale and his icky girlfriend, Lisa Doanne. And there are two strangers, plus one familiar face I recognize—that nice fellow Lester who shovels the walkway at the clinic. There is also a photo of Birdie Newcombe.

Marines Buzz Cut Cop leans in so close I can smell his aftershave, and he asks me three times if I saw any of them on Christmas outside the clinic. Driving in a car? Downtown? Near the clinic? Anywhere? I don't make a move. I'm annoyed they mention Mrs. Newcombe. *I* was supposed to be the real Mrs. Newcombe, the almost-wife of Dr. William Newcombe, my Bill, if it weren't for his sudden heart attack.

Decades ago when Bill died, I hid away an ache that I never got a chance to be married to him. When I was a young nurse, I truly believed I would someday become Mrs. William New-combe, his helpmeet, the real wife of the town doctor, just as soon as he divorced Birdie and dumped that kid of his, Mary.

"I promise we'll get married soon," he told me. Bill had bought me a diamond engagement ring that he asked me to keep in a box for safekeeping, but instead I flaunted the ring, wearing it on weekends at the mall. Bill used to laugh and talk about the fickle finger of fate, but the way I see it, fate farted in my face when Bill's chest suddenly exploded with a heart attack, spoiling absolutely everything for me.

Over the years, the feelings I had for Bill had wound down and practically disappeared from my memory until this horrid stay at the hospital. With all this time lying around in a hospital bed, I remember how much I loved him. In a black corner of my heart, I realize being a gullible young nurse was my downfall.

The cops finally leave, and I'm able to get out of bed and walk around slowly because the burn damage is mostly to my

HUSH LITTLE FIRE

71

upper body. I shuffle into the bathroom, wheeling my IV, and stare at my bandaged face in the small mirror over the sink. It isn't looking hopeful, and it's depressing how only a few bits of fuzzy hair are growing back in. I come down hard on myself for being so vain about my face before the fire. Why, it was just last Thanksgiving I was lamenting my new wrinkles and missing my young-girl life. When I was a young woman, Bill marveled at my youthful complexion and I turned heads in line at the bank and even Stop & Shop, where the competition with delicious food was fierce. By my forties, all that had faded, and I woke up to the truth that my smile and a sexed-up toss of my hair might have gotten me the job at the clinic years ago, but it no longer sparked much of anything in men. No more darting-eye-contact flirtation tango with strangers in the fresh-fruit section.

Then in my fifties, the wrinkles etched their way through my face, and I optimistically thought of them as a road map to all my experiences in life. But I know that the face of an old woman is misleading, perhaps deceitful in the way all those lines can hide terrible mistakes of the past. The grandmothers who come to the clinic for checkups, they find it so easy to live the part, baking cookies, charities, bingo on Friday nights, lots of harmless old-lady activities until their plump bodies are plopped into a coffin. I try to bring dignity to getting older, but where is the dignity in stealing pills? I failed to save any money for retirement, and they cut back my hours, so I had to move into so-called affordable housing with the scum of Wellfleet. It's true, things can always get worse. If I ever get out of the hospital, I dread how people will stare at me. Every set of eyes belonging to every person at Stop & Shop will surely land on my face. *Don't think about that now. Think about happier days.*

* * *

When I first started working at the clinic, I was happy and so proud of my new job. Everyone in town adored the wonderful Dr. Newcombe. He was tall, a bit skinny, nice looking, even in his clunky black eyeglasses. And although he wasn't as cute as his brother, Big James Newcombe, he was spry and had the stride of a young athlete, bouncing on his toes in the examining room. I would have considered him 100 percent dreamboat if only his ears didn't stick out quite so much. He wore his hair too long for a man his age, his hipster attempt to soften the big-ears look. They stuck out of his floppy Ringo Starr haircut like two white apple slices, which was kind of endearing. He was congenial even with the crankiest patients, especially those tourists from New York City who criticized the waiting room furniture and the dusty taste of the water cooler cups.

With the lure of extra cash, I had eagerly signed up to be his conscientious assistant on the night shift appointments penciled in on his secret calendar. That was the special time to help poor women out of their dilemmas, so he told me. Except they weren't all poor, and I was surprised at how much the procedures cost. All cash.

In the very beginning of the nighttime procedures, I noticed something peculiar about Dr. William Newcombe. The good doctor kept getting a bulge in his trousers when he divvied up the money at the end of the night. He seemed to be very excited—was it the money? Days later, I noticed him getting overly excited in the trousers area again when he held up a syringe to give a woman an injection. One night after an especially difficult procedure, he was counting the money, getting bulgy again, which led to a long, heartfelt speech about how bad things were with his wife, Birdie, and how much he was in love with me.

"But, Doctor, you hardly know me."

"But I love you, Barb."

HUSH LITTLE FIRE

"But you are married, Dr. Newcombe."

"But my wife and I don't sleep in the same room."

"But, but, but . . ." I sputtered as he took my hand and led me over to the examining table in a gentle, nonpushy way. He kept telling me how much he loved me, and I melted like butter in a frying pan. I lay back on the noisy paper, hiked up my nurse's skirt, and parted my young legs for the great Dr. Newcombe. I didn't even bother to kick off my white nursing shoes, I was so swept away by this man.

Pretty soon after that first night, we fell into a routine of sorts. I believed it was true love. Though I had to admit it was kind of odd that he would sometimes cry out, "Oh baby!" as we made love on the abortion examining table.

The routine with the patients went like this:

Lock all the doors to the clinic.
Talk to the patient.
Count the money.
Perform the abortion.
Unlock the doors.
Send the patient home.
Lock the doors again.
Recount the money.
Look for the bulge in his trousers as he counted.
Have sex on the examining table and ignore the crinkly paper.
Clean and mop up carefully with industrial detergent.

Afterward, Billy (when we made love, I called him Billy) would say a few words—only about himself, of course—and then I went home to my lonely apartment. I longed for our clandestine sex to be more of an event, something special, maybe in a hotel, or at least some kind of festive party to go along with the sex and money. Once when I pulled out a bottle of wine, he declined and refused to go to my apartment, which made me very upset. I had bought myself a big white canopy bed at the mall, just for the two of us to celebrate our love in a different context. Something more intimate, at least slightly more normal.

"For goodness' sake, Barb, we cannot be seen together until Birdie gives me a divorce."

"Did you ask her for one?"

"Not exactly."

I had dragged the pieces to the canopy bed all the way from the parking lot into my apartment and assembled it all by myself. All 167 parts, if I included the screws in the count. Part of me understood why he never wanted to leave the office with me and be seen, but part of me began to think that he enjoyed having sex on the same examining table where he had just put an end to another pregnancy. I often wondered about his odd attachment to that table. One night I suggested again, "Let's go to a hotel and have some more fun?"

"But we're having lots of fun right here, Barb."

"True, but I thought we could change things up. Try something different. How 'bout it?"

"Okay, if you want to change things. up, come on over here, and you may have the honor of sucking my billy club." He chortled.

I was aghast. "Respectable girls don't do that!"

"Okay, Barb, have it your way. But we're simply not going out in public together."

I accepted the arrangement and decided it would be better to focus on our love and our work together. Until a few months later when I observed how huggy-kissy Bill was with some of his lady patients, especially Dianne Crocker, the wife of the chief of

HUSH LITTLE FIRE 75

police. Mrs. Crocker was a pretty woman and a regular at the clinic for all kinds of ailments, including undesirable pregnancies. I almost fell on the floor in shock when Mrs. Crocker came to the clinic with her little boy, who had a bad case of poison ivy.

"Nice to see you again, Mrs. Crocker. Please tell me your son's name again?"

"Billy."

"Billy?"

"Billy Crocker. My son's name is such a popular name these days. Lots of boys named Billy." Dianne Crocker laughed too loud, her odd staccato ha-ha-ha ricocheting off the walls of the small examining room. I was shocked to see Billy Crocker's ears poking out of his hair like two freshly cut apple slices. My heart sank at the sight of his ears. I felt utterly bamboozled and just stared at this little Billy cub.

★ ★ ★

Lying here in the hospital bed, I might start crying, even though my tear ducts don't seem to be working with all the burns. I remind myself I must not make a peep. The week before Christmas, the drug business with Jimmy and Patrick was already collapsing, and Bon Bon was no help. I was in a panic every day because Jimmy and Patrick never admitted to me they were stepping it up without me. I realized they had bigger schemes for moving drugs when I overheard Jimmy discussing the pros and cons of importing the drugs by boat. All this effort I put into stealing drugs now seems so impossibly pointless as I lie here in this hospital bed. I hug the flat spongy pillow like it's my Billy of long ago. I wish I had a fluffier pillow to help me rest.

♦ 13 ♦

THE CAPE COD LOGIC
OF BURNING

Mary

TOMORROW IS NEW YEAR'S Eve, and after that Birdie will leave for her usual winter vacation in Florida and Danny and I will head back to Brooklyn. The three of us should be savoring the memory of a cheerful family get-together, but instead this whole week sits in my stomach under a pile of acid indigestion.

The great fireball in the sky is about twenty minutes away from sinking below the horizon, and I can never get used to how the astronomer Copernicus declared that the sun is not actually moving across the sky east to west; rather, I and everyone else, the continents, the sea, little ants, are spinning around the sun. The science teacher in middle school told us the earth at the equator moves at a speed of 460 meters per second, or roughly 1,000 miles per hour, but only my mind is spinning nonstop.

I'm trying to create at least one happy holiday memory as I drive down Chequessett Neck Road, but that's impossible when I arrive at Powers Landing and see a pathetic fire on the

HUSH LITTLE FIRE

77

beach. *Jimmy.* The winter sun cuts low and harsh on the water behind him, almost dark now, as if to tell him this is a race no man can win. His truck sits beside him like a faithful dog with the engine running, radio blasting with the driver's door wide open. I watch the incoming tide move close to Jimmy's fire on the shore, and soon the curling waves will stretch across the sand and snuff it out with a hiss. The nearby summer houses are boarded up for the winter—he's not bothering anybody—but he doesn't have an oyster grant here anymore, and I'm sure he doesn't have an open-burning permit from the fire department. Ever since we were kids, we agreed to skip the chatty stupid talk when we tend a fire, but this time I don't obey the no-talking rule.

"We missed you on Christmas. Your presents are still under the tree, and Birdie wants to speak with you. She's worried."

Jimmy tosses a bull rake and his waders into the fire.

"So sorry it didn't work out with your oyster grant, but I hear there's too much algae in the bay and tons of sharks and seals this year."

"Shoot the goddamn seals. And shoot the summah people while you're at it," Jimmy mumbles, tears dropping into his dirty beard. The flames are shrinking, so I stand by his side, jackets touching, and pass him a bunch of tangled nets to boost the fire. His eyes are red and wild, and his hair is all over the place like a crazy man who needs a shower. He takes a long swig from a fancy water bottle, which is probably a flask in disguise.

"Nice water bottle. Where'd you get it?"

"Someone left it behind at the Bomby."

"So you took it?"

"Finders keepers."

He flings a pair of rubber gloves to the greedy flames and hums as they melt and stink up the air.

"Don't you need those?"

Jimmy doesn't answer, and I recognize his zombie stare, a look I've seen over the years, like God or Gandhi will be released in the smoke and finally explain the purpose of misery.

It's cold at Powers Landing, so I toss off my mittens and hold out my hands to warm up. I find that exact line between scorching-hot fire and freezing-cold air when the sting on my face is electric, neither hot nor cold. Jimmy sways back and forth in front of the fire.

"Why are you burning up all this gear? You could sell it."

"Who'd pay money for this junk?"

"Lots of people."

He empties the bed of his truck. The nets are smoldering on top of twisted metal chunks and the water is inching up, ready to bury the fire in a few strokes. My hands are too close to the fire, and a pang of sadness runs through me, because I wish for those long-ago times with my cousin when he still had a chance with his life.

Our elders told us:

Burning old chairs and junk in the yard—is okay.

Burning pots in the inferno of a kiln—is okay.

Burning baby back ribs on the barbecue, little pigs—is okay.

Burning Joan of Arc—is not okay.

Burning up the neighbor's noisy drum set is okay or not okay, depending on if you are the burner or the burned. Cape Cod logic.

"So horrible that Dad's old clinic burned down on Christmas," I say, trying to ease into the big question. "The fire chief

HUSH LITTLE FIRE

79

doesn't know what caused it. Jimmy, I have to ask you, did you see it?"

"Nope."

"Me neither." I root around for something else to make conversation. "You still have presents under the tree, and Birdie wants to speak with you."

Jimmy won't look at me as he pokes at the fire.

"Danny couldn't come with me now, but he says hello." A lie.

Jimmy is quiet and crinkles up his mouth like Birdie does when she's mad. Danny's name hangs in the air.

"I can't thank you enough for taking him out on your boat last summer."

He says nothing and looks past me as he grabs the last few pieces of junk from the back of his truck. I follow him back and forth like a puppy dog. He pulls a bunch of photos out of an envelope and flips them into the fire one by one like playing cards.

"Wait, let me see those! Are any of those photos of the Newcombes?" I snatch one out of his hand, a snapshot of two men standing on a dune at Newcomb Hollow Beach, smiling into the camera like bozos. They're in their swim trunks, holding bottles of beer, and the short one has a cowlick sprouting out from a mop of dark hair like me. I spin onto my roller coaster obsession, looking for similarities, clues, anything. I have a cowlick just like the short guy, but so do half the men on the planet.

"They're photos of my dad before I was born, when he was on leave from the Navy," Jimmy says.

"Big James looks so young. Who's the other guy?"

"Beats me." He grabs the photo of the Navy boys and tosses it into the fire before I can stop him.

But *who* was the other guy? I slap myself for going there. I'll never know, and I should accept it, but a buzzing in my ear reminds me all over again that on one of her tipsy days, Birdie hissed out a story about how the nuns blamed my existence on some *foreigner.*

The last thing Jimmy pulls out of his truck is a can of lighter fluid, and he squirts it on the fire while he sings mixed-up screechy verses of "Auld Lang Syne." His balance seems off, so I grab his sleeve and gently pull him back from the bobbling flames. He's not drunk yet but well on his way. We sing the ballad together, but I mostly hum because I can't remember the words. A dog, a German shepherd, comes loping down the beach toward Jimmy and then to me with a slobbery mass of seaweed tangled around a crab carcass. The dog drops it at my feet smack onto my boots.

"Is this a present for me?" I ask the damn dog, trying to sound like a friendly dog lover because this must be Jimmy's dog. It wiggles over to Jimmy for a pat on the head and gallops back down the beach for more treasures.

The sky begins to darken with rain that usually turns to sleet that will tease of snow. We sing *should old acquaintance be forgot* together a few times, and then he climbs into his truck with the galloping dog and waves goodbye with a quick dismissal. He guns his engine, takes a drink from his water bottle, and drives off, which doesn't worry me too much, because men who live on the Cape have perfected the art of drunk driving. Watching his truck disappear into a dot down the road makes me crave a drink. Danny's right. It's time for us to leave Cape Cod. Very early tomorrow morning, I'll go to Newcomb Hollow Beach and dig some clay to take back to Brooklyn before the New Year's Eve traffic gets bad.

◆ **14** ◆

WALTER GETS A SPIFFY HAIRCUT FOR MARY NEWCOMBE

Walter

OTHER POLICE OFFICERS WOULD hate it, but the truth is, I don't mind being assigned to guard Nurse Haskins at all. Chief Crocker ordered me to stand outside her door for eight-hour shifts, and if Barbara begins to speak, I'm supposed to beep the chief so some detectives can rush over and question her. The paper-white snowmen and snowflakes on the green walls of the hospital like to torture me with their dumb cheerfulness. They look like ghouls with evil smiles and black button eyes, so I might take the decorations down when nobody's looking. Finally, I got permission to move a chair inside her room and sit down, but now my ass aches from sitting in this chair day after day. At least guarding Nurse Haskins gives me lots of time to think and take inventory of my life. What have I been doing all these years? What will I do after retirement? Nurse Haskins isn't speaking and she looks scared and squints her eyes a lot. She's really out of it, but sometimes I swear I can hear her thoughts drift over to my chair. This isn't the first time we've hung out together. Years ago, me and Barbara played darts at the Bomby, and although we weren't exactly friends, more than a few times we had a beer together and discussed various unmemorable things. She used to be nice looking, and even though she was ten years older, there definitely was a spark. There was an attraction that buzzed between us, but mostly we were loners, craving a bit of company over beer and darts and an occasional smoke outside under the stars. Barbara was kind to me.

"Walter Stone, you're a good-looking young man with your entire life ahead of you. Don't waste it. Stop fretting. Get married and start a family. Watch out, because your whole life will be behind you in a blink. And you don't get a do-over," she said more than once, bumming a cigarette off me.

Sitting here, I'm getting more and more agitated as I think about how women are full of advice that I never take. When I was a young man, beginning what I hoped would be an exciting life, my mother, Mildred, sat me down at the kitchen table and said, "Walt, don't go wanting too much out of life. It's the wanting that will do you in. It will eat you up."

"What do you mean by that?" I asked, fearing another one of my mother's endless rants against my father.

"Set your sights low. You must lower your expectations. I wanted too much at your age, and look where it got me."

"Where'd it get you, Mother?"

"Oh, Walt, you know what I mean. Don't go wanting too much, that's all. At your age, I wanted to be pretty, movie-star pretty, and all that wanting just made me older. Such a mistake. I wanted a bigger house. I wanted a daughter. I wanted more money. I wanted to move away from Cape Cod, and I wanted your father to remember my birthday, for pity's sake."

I often got an earful about wanting, and throughout her monologues, I would make like I agreed with her. At times like this it was best to escape, so I'd start an imaginary drawing

HUSH LITTLE FIRE 83

that I could see clearly in my mind when I closed my eyes. With a pretend black charcoal stick, I drew trees and horses and dogs, living creatures that would never rant like my mother. Her words turned into a peaceful drone, background noise to my elaborate drawings.

Oh good, it's break time. I'm outta here.

Why is it every time Chief Crocker allows me to drive his brand-new 2015 cruiser, he rides shotgun inside my head and yells, *Walter, slow down! You could kill somebody!* I should actually speed up and pull over the crappy old truck ahead of me because it has a taillight out. But I'm technically off duty and don't want to blast the siren and I don't want to do all the paperwork back at the station. All I want is a good cup of coffee from Cumberland Farms, and if I hurry, I'll be back guarding Nurse Haskins before my break is over. The broken-taillight driver must be Patrick Bale or his mother, Trudy, because who else would drive that clunker? Maybe Lisa Doanne, the girlfriend, who for some strange reason came to visit Nurse Haskins the other day.

Unfortunately, the coffee at Cumbies is lukewarm, and because I'm in uniform, I feel bold enough to ask the Cumbies girl at the register if she wouldn't mind making a fresh pot. She nervously agrees, kind of bowing to me with fearful eyes, the way most people do when I'm dressed as a cop. While she busies herself with the coffee, I go to the men's room to check out my new haircut, the one I got because Mary Newcombe's back in town. I try to channel my best Brad Pitt face, tousle what's left on the top, but what I see in the mirror makes me laugh. Movie-star hair looks ridiculous on me. I've been told I'm still handsome in my fifties, and not just by Mother. She says I have a friendly face and angular cheekbones, although I never understood why the ladies make such a big deal out of cheekbones. The haircut is weird—close-cut stubble above my ears that breaks into looser waves on top, like the barber suddenly got tired. The barber insisted this is a popular haircut, but maybe Mary Newcombe won't like it and she'll think I'm just a hick town boy turned middle-aged man with a wannabe haircut.

I take a leak and review in my mind all the possible ways I can ask her out, but why isn't this easier? This should be easy. We spent so much time together in high school, making art and hanging out in long beautiful silent streaks, which I loved, as opposed to what it was like with my mother, Mildred, who talks too much. Thank God she went into a nursing home, which somehow freed me up to refer to her as Mildred, like she's sort of not my mother anymore. Just about every woman I dated was nothing like Mildred, but each new dinner date didn't come close to those wonderful times back in high school with Mary Newcombe. Often, in various romantic moments like kissing, I pretended the girl was Mary.

I pour myself a large cup of coffee with milk and sugar and grab a prefab tuna sandwich before I leave Cumbies. I pause in front of the register to assess how guilty about this and that the cashier might be feeling, and sure enough, this feeling-guilty one blurts out, "It's on the house. My treat."

Jackpot. This is one of the perks of being a cop in Wellfleet.

When I step outside, the Bales' dilapidated truck pulls up, and out jumps Lisa Doanne and Trudy Bale. No way to avoid them.

"How's the investigation going? How's Barbara doing?" asks Trudy, who in my mind is a pathological liar.

I take a long, slow sip of coffee, because I know better than to discuss police business with the bigmouths of Wellfleet.

"It's going . . ."

HUSH LITTLE FIRE

85

Lisa is staring past me with that girl-at-the-register guilty look on her face, because I guess she knows—that I know— her boyfriend was selling drugs all over town. Ever since the fire, the gossip queens have spread rumors she was helping him. That's why she's drifting away from me as she rummages around in her coat pocket, pretending to look for something.

"Trude, I forgot my wallet," she says. "Did you bring money?"

Trudy nods her head yes one too many times and awkwardly grins at me instead of Lisa.

"Nice to bump into you two. You should tell your son to get his taillight fixed. He knows it's a violation. I already pulled him over once, but I gave him a pass."

"Thank you, thank you, thank you, Walt. You're so nice," says Lisa. "We appreciate your kindness more than you know. You're the sweetest guy on the force, isn't that right, Trude?" Trudy runs her tongue around in her toothless mouth.

Right now, I'm even more suspicious of Lisa—the way she sugared it up with *thank you* too many times. She's definitely hiding something. I can smell it. I won't tell them the truth that Chief Crocker has slowed the investigation ever since the FBI came to town, butting into Wellfleet's business like there's some kind of Cape Cod cartel in this dinky town.

"How's your mother doing at Rock Harbor?" Trudy asks in a high-pitched smarmy voice. "It must be a relief she's in such a good nursing home. Eldercare homes are so hard to get into these days with all those extra seniors moving to Cape Cod from New York. If I had more time, I'd go visit Mildred."

I'm grateful—in more ways than one—that Mildred is in a nursing home, but Trudy should cut the bullshit. I know Trudy doesn't really like Mildred and Mildred doesn't like Trudy.

"Oh yeah, Rock Harbor is great. Trudy, if you're thinking of it for yourself down the road, it's best to get on the waiting list now."

"I'm not thinking down the road, Walt."

But any Wellfleet woman who goes to church every Sunday and Bible study on Tuesdays and free church meals and one-on-one sessions with the minister is definitely thinking down the road. I'll never forget the Wellfleet ladies at the Methodist Church raffles, because for ten years I dutifully drove my mother to see her so-called friends for their gabfest. Once, in the car afterward, Mildred groused on and on that Trudy and the rest of them were backstabbers, except she herself was stabbing Trudy in the back when she called her a slut for having four daughters in a row with different men. And then she took a swipe at the fifth baby, that loser Patrick Bale. Every week they go on a tear about the old blonde, what's her name, Hillary Clinton who's running for president. You'd think they'd be happy a woman is running for president finally, but no, they spend twenty minutes making fun of her pantsuit that hides her cankles. What the hell are cankles? I looked it up on my phone and cankles are pudgy ankles, but so what. Does anybody ever think about President Obama's ankles? Not for a minute. It makes me sick the way they are so cozy and friendly on raffle nights and then gossip about each other behind their backs. I have learned such is the way with Wellfleet women.

Lisa opens the door to Cumbies but stops and asks, "Has Birdie Newcombe come to visit Nurse Haskins yet?"

"Not yet."

"Maybe you and Chief Crocker need to talk to Mrs. Newcombe."

"About what?"

HUSH LITTLE FIRE

"I dunno, except that I heard she had a quarrel with Nurse Haskins over a prescription she couldn't fill because it was Christmas Day—something about needing a different medication for her psoriasis. Of course, Trudy and I were home with Pat all day *and night* on Christmas, but I heard from somebody, I can't remember who, that Birdie Newcombe was annoyed, maybe more than annoyed about the prescription. I also heard from Nancy at the market that Mary Newcombe hung out at the coffee bar for over an hour, eavesdropping on private discussions. An hour is a long time to be stirring coffee, don't you think?"

I am disappointed, actually totally pissed, that I could have spent an hour with Mary Newcombe at the coffee bar.

I carefully raise the pitch of my voice to sound casual-nonchalant-ish, so I can ask Lisa, "Has Mary Newcombe been going to the coffee bar a lot since she's been back?"

"How would I know? I'm always working," snaps Lisa as she takes Trudy's arm and hustles through the door to Cumbies.

"One last thing, Walter," Lisa says. "I heard from somebody who heard from Kevin that Nurse Haskins ran up quite a tab at the liquor store for months. And somebody said that when Kevin nicely asked her to pay up, Nurse Haskins said to *charge it to Birdie Newcombe's account*. She insisted Birdie owes her money."

"Can you believe it?" Trudy mutters as she breezes past me, so fast but so close she could kiss my badge.

◆ 15 ◆

FINDING CLAY FOR DEAD CHIHUAHUA CREMATION URNS

Mary

MY 23ANDME TEST RESULTS are still out in the universe, so I chew my nails until there isn't much left to chew. I'm so uptight because last night I dreamed about my birth mother in full Technicolor. She was standing right next to me. Jimmy and I were in the woods playing Pilgrims, making a simple campfire. Innocent. My Technicolor mother suddenly shouted, "Be careful! The fire is spreading out of control!" And then she dissolved into nothing like dream people do.

In real life, Jimmy and I used to make baby fires for fun deep in the middle of the woods. We called them baby fires, like that somehow made us less naughty for lighting matches when grown-ups weren't around. He liked to hold two sticks over the fire and skewer marshmallows on the pointy tips. Maybe I ate too many marshmallows, but it always made me queasy the way he got so excited when the fire bounced too high and burned them black.

With pottery, there is no such thing as baby kiln firings— even a pit fire or a raku firing has flames that can easily spin

HUSH LITTLE FIRE

89

out of control. By now, I've watched a lot of pretend film footage in my mind of the clinic fire spreading, so fierce and wild—embellished with lots of sparks shooting out like a giant umbrella over the bystanders like the Fourth of July. Why did that bitchy mail carrier think she saw me there? It was dark. It was night. It was cold. And all I know is I had too much to drink.

I flip a switch in my brain and force myself to stop worrying, because I have a job to do this morning before I leave town. If I'm making a thousand-dollar cremation urn for Happy the dog, I should pick the right clay to take back to Brooklyn, and for that kind of money, it must be the very best clay. Out of respect for Happy, I go to Newcomb Hollow Beach to dig out the most luscious clay found inside the lower cliffs of the sand dunes. The outer layers of the cliffs are grains of ancient sand, and nobody is certain how old the sand is, but it's old, so when the sunbathers stretch out their towels to worship the sun and get tan, the warm sand gives them a nice churchy feeling without the church part.

I pick up a handful of sand at the bottom of the cliff, let it run through my fingers, and I wonder how long ago these tiny grains of sand washed up here. Each particle of sand is made up of molecules like me—we all know that, but I wish a scientist would explain more clearly how I went from nothing to a single cell that grew into twenty-six billion cells in the cave of my birth mother's womb. Yes, they explain what I'm made of, but that's not enough.

Jimmy was obsessed with molecules and atoms, but I usually zoned out when he got going with science talk. He told me some scientists believe that the mystery of life began in a blob of clay, and I believe that's possibly true. Potters' fingers get very close to these mysteries through the tips of our fingers, which is one of the reasons we work with clay. Most of all I want to know, where were my molecules before the nuns handed me over to the stork? And where were they before the single cell?

Okay, time to forget the molecules question and start digging in the clay cliff. There are ten steps to making a pottery cremation urn. I'd better get started. I need the money.

Step One: Finding the Right Clay

I burrow deep into the lower layers of the ocean sand cliffs for good clay, because Walter once tipped me off this is where the good clay hides. He said taste the clay and look for less-salty layers, because the deep clay is the oldest and most malleable. Good for throwing on the wheel. Turns out he's right. The top layer is acrid and so salty it makes me gag. The deeper I dig out the gray clay, the more pliable it is, with beautiful streaks of reddish-brown iron that look like marble cake. Bentonite, iron, kaolin, and silica have been marinating here for thousands of years, maybe more. This clay is squishy like cold bread dough, mixed in with an occasional pebble worn down and rolled smooth by the sea. I grab a fistful and slap the clay into balls like *pat-a-cake, baker's man, bake me a cake as fast as you can.* A tingling in my fingers shoots up my arms, and every second I dig clay, the rush brings me one step closer to the kiln firing. That's when I, Mary Newcombe, control the flames that destroy all the combustible stuff in the clay. Destroy the old and bring on the new—in the shape of a pot.

I load up my bucket in a hurry; I want to skip the next steps, be done with throwing on the wheel, and go straight to the kiln firing—the best part. In my mind, I'm already doing my favorite kiln dance, coaxing the mysterious flames to make

HUSH LITTLE FIRE 91

the perfect red for Mrs. Reardon and a dog I never met. As I walk along the shore close to the water, my boots gouge out holes in the wave-washed sand. I look back, and my footprints made a crooked line like a drunken sailor. Nobody is here but me, not even a seagull, although I know there are all kinds of creatures swimming right near me in the ocean. The sun goes behind a cloud—I turn and face the water, hoping to see a few brown seals. Jimmy and I rode our bikes to this exact spot when we got in trouble with Birdie, and when we came here, he put his arm around me and told me to cheer up.

"It's not as bad as you think. She'll cool off," he used to say when he was still an optimistic underage drinker.

"Mom is always mad."

"Don't think of her as your mom. Think of it this way: Your mom and everyone's mom are a lot like the first living creature that crawled out of the sea. The encyclopedia says you and I are descended from a long line of *Pneumodesmus.*"

"What's that?"

"If you think about it, we all come from the slimy *Pneumodesmus* that walked out of the sea four hundred million years ago."

"You just made that up to make me feel better."

"No, I didn't. It's true. I swear."

"Then you are trying to make me cry."

"It shouldn't make you sad that we all come from the sea."

Ever since Jimmy told me about *Pneumodesmus*, I like to stand here and watch the pounding breakers and think of the very first creature crawling out of ancient waves, like these waves, taking its first breath of air over four hundred million years ago.

Jimmy also told me this is the same spot where Howard Snow, also known as Pokey Snow the oysterman, froze to death, drunk, one winter—something the gossips reported all over town as fact. Everyone gets so sad when they speak of the frozen oysterman and his end, and the Old Ladies Gossip Militia of Wellfleet cluck to each other in pitying tones that Howard committed suicide under these clay cliffs. But as I scan the beauty of this magnificent beach, I think differently of him. Maybe Howard took charge of his death and decided to end it all in his own way, numbing his body with his favorite booze on his way out of the world at the most beautiful beach he could think of. Suddenly it seems like not such a bad way to go. Better than fading away in some hospital bed like Barbara Haskins. He ended his life dead drunk listening to the rhythm of the waves like the sounds of his start in the womb.

I whisper goodbye to Howard and carry my bucket full of clay back to the car. I am stealing. Birdie would disapprove of taking more than a thimbleful of clay from the beach, because in her mind, a bucketful of Newcomb Hollow clay is stealing from the US government. That's because the National Seashore of the US government long ago paid the Newcomb family (the good *e*-droppers) a paltry six thousand dollars for acres of oceanfront property that they seized under the John F. Kennedy eminent domain land grab. But in truth, who really owns the sand and the sea? God or Poseidon? Who knows. There is a bit of God deep inside these clay cliffs, an ancient exclamation of life that crawled out of the sea, and maybe that's why I linger here and try to picture Howard lying on the sand in the big sleep. Right here, hordes of people park their towels in the summer, and not because they love sunburn or sand in their sandwiches or freezing-cold water that makes their teeth chatter. They come here to listen to how the waves explain life. And maybe death. In my bucket is simple mud that I'm taking from its ancestral home to a new home in Brooklyn, and soon it will be a thousand-dollar urn for a dead dog. By the time we get back to Brooklyn, the clay will be bone dry and ready to purify and sift with extra-special ingredients that I'll add. And by the way, the balls of clay that I'll shape and fire with a red copper glaze will last over ten thousand years thanks to the power of a glorious kiln firing. Not much biodegrading there.

♦ **16** ♦

SMASHING DRY CLAY BALLS IS ACCEPTABLE BEHAVIOR

Mary

I'M EXHAUSTED. IT TOOK nine hours battling New Year's Eve traffic back to Brooklyn, and Danny and I hardly said a word because of his beloved earbuds. No partying last night on the streets of our Park Slope neighborhood, but I did have a ginger ale toast with poker-face Danny when the Times Square ball dropped on TV. Not much New Year's Eve fanfare, just the way I like it, and then I went to bed. Our funky apartment on the second floor is a convenient commute to my street-level pottery school—nineteen steps to arrive at work. The Fourth Avenue Pottery School isn't much of a school anymore since my business partner Jean, the other teacher, bailed on me. She fell in love with a wealthy person and moved to Manhattan, so she hardly ever comes here anymore. All the more space for me to work and make Chihuahua cremation urns without students hovering around with their endless questions.

I'm so glad to be back in Brooklyn, but every time the phone rings, I worry it's my mother calling with more bad news. Finding Jimmy drunk near his old oyster bed, burning

HUSH LITTLE FIRE 95

up his tools, just about did me in. My better self should have waited a day or two until he was sober. Talked to him. Listened to him, but lately I've been piggybacking on Danny's vibe that I just don't want to be around Jimmy. Birdie will let me know if things get worse. Her favorite thing is to call about a new crisis in town, which always gives me a whopper headache, but the Bourne Bridge, Rhode Island, and Connecticut gave me some long-distance breathing room from all that. Thank goodness.

The studio is cold and drafty this morning because my gas kiln named Aunt Rachel hasn't fired for a while. When I dig my fingers into the porcelain vat, the clay is cold and stiff. It's raining and the pottery studio still smells faintly of motor oil that seeped into the concrete floor. This garage building used to be a dive where a car could pull over and get a flat fixed in twenty minutes, or the customer could buy a stolen tire. When I drop my fettling knife, it rolls under the metal shelving, where I find old car lug nuts tucked away in the corner. On my knees, I fish around for my knife every which way. All the commotion upstairs is unnerving—Danny tromping back and forth from the TV to the refrigerator, so forget the fettling knife. Time to get started on the next step of making an urn.

Step Two: Prepare the Clay for Throwing

The melon-sized lumps of clay from Newcomb Hollow Beach are bone dry by now, so it's time to pulverize them. This is the fun part, where I pound the dry balls flat with a mallet, the one time in my life when it's all right to channel all my aggressive tendencies and basically beat the brains out of these balls of clay. Pounding down hard on crumbly chunks of clay with my whole upper body is one of the few times it's acceptable for a girl like me to attack and smash. *Whack. Whack. Whack.* In my mind, I'm not beating the brains out of anybody in particular, not Birdie anyway, but today I feel like pounding the nuns who were in charge of Baby Girl Number Two's life. And *whack-whack* to the stork, for sending me off into a world wrapped in secrets without a note pinned to my jumper with some basic facts about me.

I finish the pulverizing job with a mortar and pestle and run the clay dust through a wire mesh to catch any pebbles or detritus. I feel my body temperature rise—I'm excited—because this brings me one step closer to lighting the kiln and orchestrating a legal fire for ten hours straight. For the dog urns to survive the firing, I add a few other bagged materials to the mix, such as a handful of Goldart fireclay to give the clay body a spine. Plus gritty grog for tooth. Could the rest of my day be this easy? Run the detritus of my life through the mesh, toss away any problem stones and strange unrecognizable bits, and be left with a pure clay that will give me no trouble when I fire it?

Perhaps the finished clay urn will remain on Mrs. Reardon's mantelpiece and then make its way underground to a pet cemetery, and then who knows, perhaps a landfill, waiting for an archaeologist a thousand years from now.

There are enough bone-dry pots on the ware racks to do a bisque firing. I love the flame that shoots out of my monogrammed lighter, but I can't wait for the big fat flames to shoot out of the propane burners. I'll monitor the firing closely, because every potter knows that a loose piece of paper, a rustling skirt, or a burp in the gas line could easily set the building on fire. I roll a twisted wad of newspaper and touch it to the flame of my lighter before releasing a whoosh of gas out of the burner. Lighting burners is a holy moment for every potter

HUSH LITTLE FIRE

97

when we pray the firing will behave. I light the second burner and remind myself that fire can leap out of control in seconds. I must slow down. Pay close attention. I worry about the wood beams in this studio, wooden shelving and tables, so many combustibles everywhere, which gets me wondering how fast the fire gobbled up all the beams and clapboard in the clinic.

Pay attention, Mary Newcombe. Hungry fire has no mercy.

Why can't I remember if I was there?

As the bisque firing rolls along, I throw a few practice pots on the wheel to kill time before the intoxicating smell of burning bisque takes off. Just as I sit up straight to admire my handiwork, my cell phone ding-a-lings in my back pocket, and I can tell by the vibration on my ass that it's my mother. I don't answer. I slide the pot off the wheel and set it on a drying shelf before I wipe my hands and listen to her message.

"I'm so sorry to tell you this in voicemail, really I am." Birdie's sniffling into the phone. Her voice garbled. "But I'm about to board another plane in Miami, so I have to be quick. Jimmy passed away last night. He was killed in a car crash on Route 6. I'm so sorry. And I have a few problems that you must help me with, because I simply can't fly back now and deal with Chief Crocker. What a numbskull. They towed Jimmy's truck to the police station, and they'll charge us a hundred dollars a day if we don't pick it up, and well, you have to . . ."

I drop my phone on the concrete floor. The glass cracks and the message stops.

I don't understand. Why is Birdie talking about towing charges?

I stare at the cracked glass on my phone and carefully pick it up to listen again. The message continues and Birdie whines on and on about how Billy Crocker only made the police force because of his father, Chief Calvin Crocker. She sputters, "Billy is such a despicable . . ."

And listening to that part is okay, because this means I must have misheard the first part about a car crash—about Jimmy being dead.

But then the last thing she says to me is, "Listen to me carefully. Don't say anything about anyone to the police. Keep your mouth shut. And by the way, you should know, Jimmy was going ninety miles an hour when he hit a tree head-on. He was driving Katie Snow's Honda."

◆ 17 ◆

LISA LOSES THE GOLDFISH GAME

Lisa

I ACCIDENTALLY POKE MY boob with the pin back when I yank off my LISA name tag to take a bath. I must be some kind of reincarnated tropical fish, because I could stay in a bath 24/7. My knees, my back, my feet—everything hurts at the end of the day. Soaking in a super-hot bubble bath sometimes helps to sort out the bumps in my life, and tonight, the bumpy subject is Jimmy Newcombe. Just because he died in a car crash doesn't mean he's out of the way. I should feel sad Jimmy cracked up Katie Snow's car—I sincerely try to feel sad—but right now, all alone in this bathroom, I don't feel it.

When Jimmy moved into the apartment next door, he was just another bump in my life. Patrick glommed on to Jimmy, and they decided to become partners. They took *Angel Baby* out to sea and set out to make their fortune trapping lobsters. Although Jimmy was in his fifties and Patrick was in his thirties, the two of them carried on like ten-year-old boys most of the time. So annoying. Two heads were not better than one. Not with those two.

I relax my arms and legs in the hot water and think about other fishermen, the ones who are quiet men, out of sorts on land, and always restless to get back on a boat. Jimmy wasn't like that. He was talkative in spurts, he read tons of books, and when he was silent, I felt like he was watching my every move. Maybe I should slip a book into his coffin when they have the wake at Carlson's Funeral Parlor. His body will be rigid and cold, probably in a suit and shiny shoes, which he never wore. The whole outfit will miss the point of Jimmy. Behind those dark-brown eyes, Jimmy's wheels were always turning, but his eyes will be closed tight at the wake. Don Carlson will put a lot of makeup on him to try and make him look normal, but it will only make him look freaky. Jimmy used to be handsome underneath his craggy face, with skin and hair that blended into the color of sand. His body was strong, like a man who had wrestled the sea all his life, but Jimmy's struggle was definitely on land. If he'd never moved to the High Tide Apartments, we wouldn't be in this mess with the cops.

With my foot, I turn the hot water on full blast, but the hot water heater must be empty, because the water's cooling down. Everything in my life seems to start out hot and exciting before it goes cold. Same for the Jimmy-Patrick lobster business that went cold after a good run. Patrick started crabbing at me all the time like it was my fault, but I wasn't the one who crushed them with state regulations and Maine's low lobster prices. Patrick is always short on money to pay the bills, so I get stuck paying for everything. I wasted a lot of time praying for God to have mercy and send us some money, but I wasted much more time praying Jimmy would be a good influence on Patrick. Jimmy never turned mean when he smoked a lot of dope the way Patrick did. In fact, Jimmy wasn't all that bad when Patrick wasn't around, and it was so

HUSH LITTLE FIRE

lovely when Jimmy started calling me Sunshine. *Lisa, you're my Sunshine.* It felt like warm honey spreading over a piece of hot buttery toast. He was one of the few guys who talked to me without staring at my chest. He asked my opinion about things and listened to my answers. Even his odd ideas didn't bother me, like when he got worked up about sharks' rights and how we should make peace, not war with sharks. He said the ocean was their home long before people came along and decided to sunbathe and swim. Okay, so he was very stoned, but Jimmy didn't mock my idea that perhaps the shark population should be controlled better because tourists might stop coming to Cape Cod.

"Then we would lose customers, and then everyone, even the Board of Selectmen, would go broke," I told him.

"Broke? Money means nothing to me until I run out of it," Jimmy said between a long hard toke.

"But money is everything."

"Money is nothing to the fish that swim in the sea."

"Well, I'm on land, and I hate being broke. If I ever have a baby, I'll need a lot more money."

"You got that right. Your baby will suck up money from the cradle to the grave."

"That's a miserable way to look at it. Is that why Katie Snow's mad at you?"

Jimmy never answered my question, and after the babies-and-money conversation, he started loaning me books about world history and atoms and the universe. I never had time to read them, so he would summarize them for me. It blew my mind to hear the atoms in my body had been around 13.8 billion years, or so Jimmy told me, getting all worked up.

"Since the Big Bang? Is this really true? What *exactly* is a Big Bang theory?"

"That's the big story, but let me tell you the small story about quarks." Jimmy always talked too fast about science stuff, which only baffled me. "Miss Sunshine, are you listening? Do you wanna know the difference between a charmed quark and a strange quark?"

"What's a charmed quark? It sounds like a cocktail."

"A charmed quark is an elementary particle, a composite of subatomic particles. A piece of an atom. They got the name quark from a poem in James Joyce's *Finnegans Wake*."

"Who the hell is James Joyce?"

"He's a writer. *Finnegans Wake* is a long book with a longer story."

Holy moly! Philosophy and physics make me nervous, and I wonder, as I relax in the bath, why I bother to worry and plan all the time for such an insignificant little life on earth.

One night, Jimmy explained with a pint of vodka in hand that heaven and hell simply amount to the last seven seconds of what appears in your fading mind right before you die. He stood up and took a big swig from the bottle, declaring in his best imitation preacher voice, "You know, Sunshine . . . in those last seven seconds of your life . . . your very own mind will either drop you into the fiery pit of hell or send you through the pearly gates to hug your mother."

"That's nice."

"Don't get your hopes up. All that drivel in the Bible about heaven will be gone in an instant after the oxygen leaves your brain. Your dream of eternal life lasts no more than seven stinking seconds, and after that, there is nothing."

On my back, I dunk my hair in the water and think about the idea of nothing. By now, the skin on my fingertips looks like raisins. What Jimmy meant by *nothing* really stumps me. and I wonder about the *nothing* that lasts forever.

HUSH LITTLE FIRE 103

The bubbles have flattened, the water is cool, but I don't want to get out of this tub and get on with my life. Not yet. Out there in *the nothing*—in the universe—is my baby waiting to be born. Actually, that's not quite true, because her egg is right here inside me waiting for some sperm, any sperm. I gently rub my belly round and round and ask my eggs to be patient. It's a basic problem in the universe for humans that I can't make a baby without a sperm. Too bad Patrick has been such a dud lately. And too bad we have no money. Jimmy was right that a baby sucks up money from the cradle to the grave, so why can't Patrick come up with a better plan to earn a living?

The soothing soap bubbles help me drift back to the unusual events of Thanksgiving—the exact day when Jimmy went from a bump in my life to a mountain of trouble.

It began when Jimmy ordered boxes of plastic lobsters online with the idea that he and Patrick would mix them with live lobsters in vats as camouflage. Bon Bon had told them it was too risky to drive product over the bridge, because even white guys were getting stopped and searched. I knew they had a secret meeting with Bon Bon about bringing drugs in by boat.

When I went next door to tell Jimmy and Patrick that the delicious turkey I'd been roasting was ready, I found them at the card table with Jimmy huddled over a candle. He was concentrating and rotating the bottom of the plastic lobster as its tail burned and melted into a waxy puddle.

"What are you boys up to *now*?"

They were so stoned they didn't notice me.

"Don't forget to use real rubber bands on the plastic claws. That way, they'll blend right in," Patrick said to Jimmy, who was busy with his melting.

"Details. Details," barked Jimmy.

Right then and there, I told them smuggling drugs inside plastic lobsters was a very bad idea and they could easily wind up in prison. I said I wanted back the money I had loaned them. Fool that I was, I had agreed to invest in their phony snowplowing business, but the money went to plastic lobsters.

"Besides, the pills will surely get wet," I pleaded.

Patrick gave me a confused stoner look and then turned to Jimmy, who described his elaborate plan to put waterproof baggies of drugs inside the plastic lobsters, sealed with crazy glue.

"Jesus, you two are out of your minds."

"Hey, you won't say that when we get rich."

"Why on earth are you burning plastic lobsters?" I asked Jimmy, suddenly craving a drink.

"Trick and I are running an experiment to hide the cut after we stuff them."

"Jimmy, stop calling him Trick. His name is Pa-trick. Stop calling him that."

Spittle dribbled out of Patrick's mouth in the middle of his annoying stoner laugh.

"Thanksgiving dinner will be ready in fifteen minutes, you guys. And if I were you, I'd toss all those plastic lobsters in the garbage right now!"

The boys were high out of their minds, so I took a deep breath, sat down, and timidly proposed a better plan, something smarter, if they only would agree to take on another partner, such as me. Why not?

"You guys won't get caught if you stuff your product inside the jars of my homemade jam."

They knew my jam business was a moneymaker when I bought cheap jars of discount expired jam at Job Lot, steamed off the labels, tripled the price, and sold *Lisa's Finest. 100% Organic* to the sucker tourists at farmers' markets. But when I made my offer to help Jimmy and Patrick, they turned to each other and burst out laughing.

I figure my biggest mistake was pouring myself a drink at that moment. A tall Cape Codder without the cranberry juice. By then, the turkey was probably overcooked and ruined. On my second Cape Codder, Patrick stumbled over to the kitchen counter and grabbed a bag of Goldfish crackers.

"Come on, you guys, you'll spoil your appetite." But I knew what was coming next. The stoner Goldfish game. Arm wrestling. Fine. The Goldfish game. Not fine. They played this a lot, tossing the orange cracker up in the air to earn a point if they caught it in their mouths. As the game heated up, they made a face with their mouths puckered into fishy lips every time a point was earned. When Jimmy made fishy lips, he went cross-eyed, which made Patrick slide into one of his hysterical laughing fits. Jimmy was good at clowning it up and taking the boredom out of the off-season, but that day on Thanksgiving, everything changed at the end of the Goldfish game.

"How 'bout a kiss for the winner?" Jimmy turned to me. Without waiting for my answer, he sidled over to Patrick with that slinky walk of his and kissed him on the mouth with his goldfish lips. And it was not a peck. It was much more. The two of them made slurpy gurgling sounds over their tongues, and Patrick didn't seem the least bit surprised. I watched Patrick root around in Jimmy's mouth with his wild French kissing, just like he did with me.

At the end of my bath, I remove Patrick's silver cross from around my neck and chuck it across the room into the toilet. I rise up out of the water and flush the silver cross away. Gone.

It is easier to be bad than good.

Rosaries and crosses are a dime a dozen, so from now on, I'll wear my mother's mahogany cross so strangers will trust me.

I dry myself with an old worn-out towel and try not to picture dead Jimmy after his car crashed into a tree. If the cops come around the Lighthouse again, I'll tell them in a slow, clear voice that I remember seeing Jimmy on New Year's Eve before the car accident, arguing with his aunt Birdie. I will squeeze in a comment or two about how much Jimmy liked *open-burning* season, and I'll artfully slip in that I'm not sure he ever bothered to get a permit. I will emphasize how some of the nutcases in Wellfleet count the days until *open- burning*, when the fire department allows anyone to burn leaves, broken chairs, old junk, you name it—and how Jimmy loved to run a fire all day long. I'll describe how difficult it was to figure out what he was burning half the time. He was always burning something. I'll drop more hints about Jimmy and the clinic fire. I won't forget to mention how Jimmy had a matchbook collection hidden in an old suitcase and how he had an unnatural fascination with candles. Then the cops will surely think Jimmy Newcombe was a crazy fire-loving man.

I hang up the damp towel and tidy up the bathroom. With Jimmy gone, the only bump in my life now is Nurse Barbara Haskins. If Barbara gets better, she won't accept going to prison alone if she gets caught for stealing drugs. Barbara could rat out Patrick to the cops, which also could spell g-u-i-l-t-y for me just because I helped him with drug deliveries. That old nurse could easily go from a bump to a mountain of trouble. Maybe it's time to bring another box of chocolates to the hospital and help her eat them.

◆ 18 ◆

HURL THE PRECIOUS EARBUDS INTO THE SEA

Mary

FOR WEEKS, I AM zombie mom, going through my days in a stupor, because if I start that grieving thing they talk about in magazines, it will mean Jimmy is really gone. I add up on my fingers how many times I spoke with him in the past year; probably less than thirty words passed between us. I dropped Danny off at the beginning of the summer, picked him up at the end, and even then I had a feeling Jimmy was avoiding me.

Birdie keeps calling with assignments to hurry back to Wellfleet right away so I can make plans for a funeral. I want to scream at her to do it herself, but I don't. In her Newcombesque New England best, she won't talk about Jimmy's life or death—all she talks about is what to do with his truck. She leaves messages with long lists of arrangements to make that become the pathetic checklist of how he has left this earth forever. After many phone calls of her pleading, I cave.

Like obedient dogs, Danny and I drive all the way back to the Cape, but at least he has a long weekend for Martin Luther

King Jr.'s birthday. Once again, Danny is silent in the back seat. The deafening whir of cars won't drown out the fact that Jimmy is dead. I can't bear to think about what led up to his death, so instead I think about copper red glazes while sipping an imaginary Scotch on the rocks.

After we stop at the house, I propose a quick visit with dead relatives at the Wellfleet cemetery, keeping in mind order number five from my mother. *Mary, figure out where to fit Jimmy in the family plot. There should be some space between his mother and father.*

I stop at the entrance to the cemetery, freezing my face off in front of all this death covered in snow. My boots crunch across the crusty snow, a loud snare drum announcing my arrival. Danny follows behind, syncopating my steps. He's shivering, so I whip out a wool cap from my pocket and cover his red ears.

"Hey, stop!" he says, flinging the cap back. How could I forget there are particular dress codes with twelve-year-old boys? No cap.

"Can we go now?"

"We just got here."

"But I'm hungry."

I want to pluck those earbuds out of his ears and hurl all his contraptions far away into the sea. His head is bobbing to some music, and I wonder if he's already dreaming of sex, drugs, and rock 'n' roll.

"You can bury Jimmy anywhere here, right? So can we go now?"

I circle my son and wave a pack of Life Savers in his face. A peace offering. He grabs them and mumbles thanks.

"Jimmy died right away in the accident, that's true, right?" Danny asks.

"Yes, that's what the police said, so it must be true." I brush bits of snow off my father's headstone.

HUSH LITTLE FIRE 109

The whisperers reported that Jimmy hit a big tree straight on, like an arrow, without bouncing off any other trees. He was speeding down Route 6 in Katie Snow's new Honda right before midnight on New Year's Eve. It was her car but sort of his because he bought it, all cash, so Katie could drive the new baby to the doctor instead of walking. According to Birdie and her posse, Katie told the entire town Jimmy was her baby's father. Even Birdie and her posse can't figure out if he crashed into the tree on purpose or if he died because he was just another drunk-driving fool. An uneasy ticktock sputters up in my throat, and it's so cold I can barely form any words.

"You never really told me, did you see Jimmy on Christmas night?" I ask my son.

"I dunno."

"But were you with Gramma the night of the fire when I went to bed early?"

"Did you go to bed early?" Danny looks confused and goes back to his phone.

Suddenly I have the urge to hug my son, but instead I do like I usually do and start babbling about anything and everything.

"You know, when Jimmy was your age, he had a real job mowing lawns right here in this cemetery."

"So are you saying I should get a job mowing lawns?"

"Not exactly. Jimmy kept the mower in there." I walk over to an old green door to a shed that was built in the olden days for storing coffins when the ground was too frozen to dig a hole. I pry open the door to *The Room*, Jimmy's fun secret hangout place. He took me here to drink beer for the first time. The cold beer made my metal braces shiver when I suavely held the can to my lips. It tasted salty from the swim in the ocean that coated our skin.

Hello, beer.

Jimmy told me if I drank the can fast, it would feel as good as diving through the waves, even better. When I finished, he crumpled the empty can with one hand.

Beer. My new friend.

Danny opens the door and interrupts my daydream.

"When can I have Jimmy's lobster traps? He told me all the traps would be mine someday."

"None of this has been decided yet. We haven't even buried him. Be patient."

"I don't want all those stupid plastic lobsters of his, but I'll take the traps."

"What plastic lobsters?"

"I dunno. Never mind."

Danny walks to the car, eyes on his phone, and somehow he doesn't bump into a single headstone. I prop up a bouquet of grocery store carnations next to my father and say goodbye to the dead.

"What plastic lobsters are you talking about?" I shout after Danny. "The police are going around town investigating the fire, and they called me yesterday. They know you were on Jimmy's boat a lot last summer."

Danny steps away from me, so I can't see his face.

"If you talk to the police, you won't say anything that could complicate things." I grab his arm and turn him around to face me. "You won't, will you?"

He looks away, rolling something around in his hand that looks like Jimmy's old crystal lens.

"Where the fuck did you get that?"

"Jimmy gave it to me."

◆ 19 ◆

MARY HEARS ABOUT BONGO BUTT AT THE LIGHTHOUSE

Mary

Iɴ ᴛʜᴇ ᴇᴠᴇɴɪɴɢ, Dᴀɴɴʏ and I head to the Lighthouse in downtown Wellfleet, the only restaurant open in January, and thank God something is open. The waitress at the Lighthouse is glad to see us, because so far we're the only customers at dinnertime. Danny sits down at a table and taps his fingers to some rhythm I can't hear.

"Can I get you something to drink?" asks the waitress with a plastic name tag that reads ʟɪsᴀ. She shuffles her shoulders when she speaks, which makes her breasts jiggle precisely in line with Danny's nose. Strands of her blond braids are stuck in her name tag, and I hope they don't fall in our food. When this girl Lisa stops smiling, she nervously taps a wooden cross on her chest. She looks familiar and could easily be me, itchy to get off Cape Cod before she goes insane from the cold.

"I'll have a Coke and a cheeseburger with fries," Danny says as he hurries off to the men's room. His phone falls on the floor, and he almost steps on it. I pick it up and stuff it in his jacket pocket on top of Jimmy's lens and a puffy plastic bag that looks like weed. It *is* weed. Twelve years old. Red alert. Mother Mary isn't ready for this.

"I'll have the same, but make mine a Coke with a shot of rum—make that two shots," I tell waitress Lisa.

By the time Danny returns to the table, I'm so antsy, but I don't want to look upset and get in trouble for searching his pockets, because budding teenagers have a special talent for reversing blame.

Danny fidgets and keeps poking his finger toward the flame that shoots up from the decorative glass in the center of the table.

"Jimmy taught me that game, and I taught it to you. Do you remember?" I say.

"What?"

"Move your finger sideways, but quickly. Me and my friends used to play this game at slumber parties. Watch me. This is how you do it without getting burned."

Danny smiles, and we take turns gliding our fingers through the bouncing flame. There is no keeping score or winning or losing, and the longer we play, it becomes dangerously hypnotic.

Suddenly Danny stands up and jabs his finger into the center of the flame and holds it there.

"Stop!" I shout, and yank his hand away.

"Different game, Mom. Stick your finger in and see how long you can stand it." He lets loose a loud, hiccupping laugh I've never heard before. I take a look at his red hand before he snatches it back.

"I'm so thirsty." I gulp down my drink, and the rum settles my mind, unspooling me, like pouring warm milk over my dread. I can't figure out what's going on with him.

The waitress clicks her pen too close to my ear. "I hope you don't mind my asking, aren't you Jimmy Newcombe's

HUSH LITTLE FIRE   113

cousin? You don't know me, but I'm the person who cleans Mrs. Newcombe's house—she's your mother, right?"

"Yes, Mrs. Newcombe's my mom."

Danny removes an earbud and perks up as Lisa stands over him, her chest in full salute to his eyes.

"Please give my condolences to your gramma," she says to Danny as if I'm not here. "Such a shock about Jimmy. God rest his soul." Lisa caresses the oversized wooden cross around her neck. "And I guess you heard about the fundraiser to rebuild the clinic? The whole town is devastated, and so terrible about Barbara Haskins. She might not recover," she whispers to Danny. This Lisa girl grabs Danny's shoulder and squeezes a little too hard.

"It's so nice to finally see you," she says to Danny, her eyes wide like they might pop out of her head. "Do you have any extra photos of Jimmy? Maybe you could take me to his storage unit to sort through his photos. I so wish I had a nice photo of Jimmy to remember him by. I know he kept all kinds of stuff in there, and you have the keys, right?" Lisa's eyes narrow as her smile collapses.

I interrupt this chitty-chatty waitress and ask for another drink.

"I never had his keys. Hey, what happened to Jimmy's dog?" Danny asks as Lisa starts walking toward the bar.

"Don't worry. My boyfriend and I took Sunshine. That dog is a handful." She pivots and pinches Danny on the cheek.

"What did you say?" I don't like her. She's a cheek pincher.

"Sunshine was Jimmy's dog." Lisa beams and twirls her braid at me like a schoolgirl. "He named the dog after me. Jimmy always called me Sunshine."

A melting ice cube gets stuck in my throat like a bee sting. *No way is this snotty waitress his Sunshine. That nickname belongs to me.*

"Excuse me," I say. "A refill here when you get a chance."

Danny wolfs down his burger and returns to his music reverie as he nibbles on the last of the french fries. Since Danny won't talk to me, I'll go over my numbers. I down the rest of my drink and order another, because step two of drinking rum includes math. Let's see, I'll start with the number thirty-nine.

At thirty-nine, I got panicky about not being a mother when the fertility window was closing. I started hitting on just about everybody I could think of—men with good genes, old boyfriends, an ex-boyfriend of an old roommate. I started out with simple make-out sessions, but I always had a fertilized egg in the back of my mind. Jimmy and I were practiced at kissing, but all grown up, anything else made me uncomfortable. First base was all I could handle with him, even though he pressed for more. We never talked about what we meant to each other, but Jimmy thought make-out sessions were all right because, as he put it, "You're one of those adopted babies, so we're not really cousins, right?"

All these years, I've felt a weird kind of safety not knowing—and not wanting to know—whose sperm finally implanted my Danny egg. The Newcombe motto is *keep it simple*, so no contact with whoever contributed the sperm, which is probably the same way Birdie felt about me. *Seal Mary's adoption papers forever.*

"When you finish your Coke, can we go?" Danny clicks his teeth in the same way I do when I'm upset and need a good introduction to bad news. He blurts out, "I know what you're thinking."

"Oh, what am I thinking?"

"You're wondering why I asked you if I can have Jimmy's lobster traps."

HUSH LITTLE FIRE   115

"Look, you spent a lot of time with him, and I know keeping the traps is like saving a part of him."

"I want the traps so I can sell them. I need money."

"You need money for what?"

"A new phone."

"You already have one."

I bet he wants money for weed. He bangs both hands on the table like he did when we used to play crazy eights and he didn't get the cards he wanted.

I wait for my son to argue, and after a long silence, he looks up and hisses at me, "You've got it in your head that your *good ol' Jimmy* was such a great guy, but you have no idea what it was like out on his boat. He used to give me lots of beer. I mean *a lot*. And you know what? I took it. So what do you think about that, *Mother*?"

"Well, how much beer did he give you? My God, you're only twelve!"

"He started buying me beer when I was ten."

"Did Gramma Birdie know about this?"

"No, but she wouldn't care."

"Well, I care."

"You weren't there."

"Excuse me, I don't get the entire summer off. I have to work."

Danny pokes his finger through the flame again.

"At least you did a lot of fishing with Jimmy." I try to be upbeat. Arguing puts an unbearable distance between us.

"It's time to go." Danny gets up from the table.

By now, I am cruising past step three of rum drinking into step four.

"Let's stay. Let's talk a little longer." My feeble suggestion.

"Talk? You wanna *talk*?" Danny sits down again and reaches for my drink but pushes it back. "Fine. Jimmy and his stupid dog. I used to put my beer in Sunshine's dog dish because it was so funny to watch that dumb fucking dog get buzzed. Even his dog liked to drink."

I am buzzed. I say nothing.

"You have no idea what it was like. He said he'd pay me for helping him with the traps, but he never paid me. He tried to pay me in beer, but he drank most of it himself."

Danny takes a big gulp from my drink before I can say no.

"And you know what? Jimmy pushed me overboard last summer. Nice, huh?" Danny finishes my rum Coke fast before I can stop him. He is quiet for a minute and rubs his face. Twelve years old, and now he's got that boozy Newcombe look in his eyes.

"First, he showed me his collection of fishhooks and lures, all different sizes—they were awesome—the feathers." Danny turns red and gnaws a lemon wedge in half with his front teeth. "But then he went crazy—telling me how much fun I'll have getting laid and all the free blow jobs I'll get in high school. He wrestled me down. It really hurt."

Free blow jobs? Wrestling? "Are you kidding?"

"He wouldn't stop wrestling me. He pinned me down and tickled me with that club of his."

"What are you talking about? What club?"

"I dunno. It's the club he used to brain a sand shark before he threw it back in the water. He kept singing a dumb song about bongo butts. I stuck my fingers in my ears to make him shut up."

"*Bongo butts??? What's that?* Was he drunk?"

Danny gulps down what is left of the watery rum Coke. He tosses his phone from hand to hand with a bizarre grimace, curling up the corners of his mouth.

HUSH LITTLE FIRE 117

"You have no idea. He kept poking me in the back with his club. It was supposed to be fun, but he kept telling me I have an ass like a girl."

"What's that supposed to mean?"

"I dunno. He kept trying to spank me."

"He was *spanking* you?" It's time to order another drink.

"When I told him to stop, he turned psycho and called me a little shit." Danny grabs an idle spoon on the table. "He wouldn't stop singing, really weird, like barking, and then the dumb fucking dog started barking, and then he pushed me overboard before I could get my bathing suit back on."

"*What?*"

"And then he threw some beer bottles right near my head."

"I can't believe this. Why didn't you tell me or Gramma about this?"

"She's always napping."

"You should have said something to me."

Danny throws the spoon on the floor and claps his hands down flat on the table. I don't know what to do—or say—or think—about this, so I raise my glass to signal for another drink.

"And you know what?" Danny squeals. "When he pushed me overboard, he wouldn't let me back on the boat." Danny's hand drops down to his lap in a fist.

"I had to wait in the freezing-cold water until he passed out, and then I drove the boat back to the harbor. I'm not like you and Jimmy. I don't really like the taste of beer, and I'm a very good driver."

"What's that supposed to mean?"

"It means we should go now."

I spit on my fingers and pinch out the flame in the decorative glass, which has migrated to the edge of the table, so I slide it back to the center and leave enough money for the bill underneath. I want to grab Danny's hand and hold it like the old days, but he is all the way across the table.

"Give me the keys. Please, Mom. I'm saying please. I'll drive us home."

"You're twelve. You can't drive."

"Jimmy taught me how to drive. I'm a good driver."

"Okay, it's time to go, but you're absolutely *not* allowed to drive." I stand up. I must compose myself. My legs better do what they're told.

"And another thing. That's not what you think in my pocket. I saw you digging through my jacket when I went to the bathroom. It's a bag of peppermint tea." He pulls out the plastic bag and waves it too close to my face. The perky peppermint smell is nauseating. "Fran gave it to me. I hate the taste, but I like the way it smells. It smells like Fran's hair. Here, smell it." He shoves it in my face again.

"Who is Fran?"

I steady myself, and without any warning, a tiny Mary the size of a fly hops onto my shoulder and wanders across my clavicle. And then the tiny thing jumps into my ear and shouts, *You can't fool me, Miss Mary Newcombe. It's true you've become an expert at imitating the sober walk, but that's easy because you're not totally loaded and the news about Jimmy sure did zap your brain into focus. Awake now?*

I poke around inside my ear with my pinkie, attempting to clear out the fly.

According to my calculations, I dropped Danny off at the beginning of the summer and picked him up at the end. But plenty of mothers do that.

Outside on the sidewalk, I stand up straight in front of the Lighthouse with Danny. The streetlamp makes a halo over his face as he feverishly pecks at his phone, so I grab this chance to study my son's face—really *look* at him—because he is not a man yet, and not a little boy. He lingers in that place where the creases of sadness and disappointment have not yet invaded his features. His face is still free. But his freckles are fading, and soon enough, frown lines and crevices will form and catch the things that hurt him.

Tiny Mary gives up and hops off my shoulder, suggesting I go inside for one more nightcap, because a quick nightcap could make this all go away. I tell myself not to think about Danny on the boat until later, or tomorrow, or next week. Why didn't he ever mention this before? And who is this girl Fran anyway? What I really need is a cup of coffee. And a flyswatter.

◆ 20 ◆

MARY BUYS CABIN BOY DOUGHNUTS

Mary

I PULL THE COVERS over my head and curl up in a knot when I picture Danny's contorted face last night when he told me about wrestling with Jimmy on the boat. In my hangover fog, I construct a neat corral around everything he said to keep it in one place, and then maybe the horror show on the boat will shrink down to nothing more than a mishap. I want to believe that wrestling and going overboard was the worst of it. My son.

Time to get out of bed and find my way to coffee.

I shuffle downstairs toward the kitchen and stop to peek at Danny in the TV room. He's pulling at his hair, making a curtain over his eyes. He drops the TV remote on the floor and spreads his arms across his chest like he's hugging himself. I guess it's easier to follow the drone of a repeat sitcom than to face each other and talk. Not now.

Looking around Birdie's TV room of clutter—she calls it a sitting room—you'd never know she has a family. Old-lady china knickknacks smother every tabletop, as if she set booby traps for anyone who might dare to move her prized possessions.

HUSH LITTLE FIRE 121

Jammed on the bookshelves are framed photos of random scenes. No people. The Grand Canyon, Florida palm trees, the Empire State Building, and not a single picture of me. I try not to care, which clobbers my temples with a stubborn reminder that the pendulum always swings into the next day from being blotto to a nasty hangover. Thud. Lodged in the center of my headache is the news that the 23andMe test results are chugging along in the universe. I know this because the testers keep emailing me with progress reports. The essence of me is not yet decoded, but I'm getting closer. I should go online to check how many more days until the results come in, but I keep putting it off. Too scary and impossible to face with a hangover headache, and there's no caffeine in this house.

"I'm thinking of going to Dunkin' Donuts for coffee. Wanna come with me?"

Danny shakes his head no. I will sit him down with some tasty doughnuts so I can unload my guilt about how sorry I am for not being there for him last summer. *And who on earth is he texting?*

"How are you doing?" I ask. Perhaps he is pining for the mystery girl. "Who is this girl Fran anyway?" I try to be light, but my hangover voice is hoarse.

"A new student. From Canada."

"Is she twelve too?"

"Yeah, my age exactly. We were born a week apart. Both on Thursday. Fran and Dan. We're practically twins. She says we're spirit twins."

"You were born on a Wednesday."

"No I wasn't."

"Yes you were." I swallow a mouthful of air, wishing for a mouthful of rum Coke. "So, is this a casual friendship between you and Fran? Like a friend-friend kind of thing?"

122   JUDITH NEWCOMB STILES

Danny shoots me a fierce frown, a signal this is way too many questions for him.

I must listen to whatever my son has to say, even though he and his buddies in Brooklyn have pit bulls circling their private lives. Be a good listener, the psychology books tell me, except I never finished any of those books because they make me fall asleep. Suddenly I have the urge to drive back to the clinic even though the answers I need aren't there anymore, so off I go to the Temple of Sugar, Dunkin' Donuts.

The streets are empty. I pass two lone cars on the way and pull up next to a beat-up old truck with faded bumper stickers and fishing gear in the back. Wellfleet is a tough place to live year-round for anyone, especially fishermen. Feast to famine. Shopkeepers and restaurants endure a frenzy of business for two months, and then after October, the famine begins. Doughnuts for breakfast, lunch, and dinner.

The truck parked next to me is filled with plastic tubs and snarled nets. A large man in scruffy overalls and layers of padded clothing gets out of the truck, walking ahead of me toward the Temple of Sugar. Suddenly he turns around and blocks my way to the entrance. Before I can move, he puts his hand on his hip and asks, "Where's Cabin Boy?"

"Excuse me, are you talking to me?"

He rubs his forehead and claws his stringy hair that spills out of a ratty hat.

"You're a Newcombe, right? I need to talk to Cabin Boy."

He moves me out of the doorway, walking me backward into the parking lot as he pokes at my arm. I can smell his cigarette breath. I don't like it.

"I'm looking for Cabin Boy. Your son, duh. Jimmy owed me money. A lot. And Cabin Boy was the runner. Maybe he

HUSH LITTLE FIRE 123

knows where my money is. I never got my stuff, and it's not a good thing when the runner fucks up."

"Excuse me? I don't know what you're talking about." His sinkhole bloodshot eyes look me over as he waggles his finger inches from my face.

"Just tell your boy I'm looking for him. He knows me. I'm Patrick."

"Okay, Patrick, I don't know what you want with my son, but . . ."

He pushes me out of the way and hurries back to the truck. As I watch him drive away, I read one of his faded bumper stickers. *I'm Not on Your Vacation*.

And that is all I can figure out about this guy Patrick, except the tiny razor-burn bumps on his neck. I swear they looked like barnacles.

When I return with doughnuts and coffee, I stand directly in front of the TV and ask Danny about Jimmy and what money this man might be talking about. I am shaking.

"I dunno, Mom. Can you move?"

"Who is this guy Patrick, and what money is he talking about?" All my ideas about a heart-to-heart talk congeal into panic.

"Jimmy told me it was for lobsters. I was the runner. Like a delivery boy."

"Who is Cabin Boy?"

"That's me."

"What does this guy Patrick want with you?"

"Can you please move. I can't see my show. I dunno. You mean Trick, Jimmy's friend? Trick with the old truck?"

"Please turn the TV off and tell me what you were up to last summer. Tell me, right now."

"Jimmy got orders for lobsters. I picked up the money in a paper bag. Jimmy delivered the lobsters. That's all."

"How often were you doing this last summer?"

"Lots."

"What is *lots*?"

"I dunno. I never even looked in the bags. They were stapled shut."

"Please tell me again, why does he call you Cabin Boy?"

"Why are you asking me all these questions?" Danny tosses his cell phone on the rug so hard it bounces, and I can see he is rattled, because he just leaves it there and gazes at my feet.

◆ 21 ◆

BARBARA SWEARS IT WAS A PROPOSAL, NOT BLACKMAIL

Barbara

WALTER FELL ASLEEP IN the chair again. He only got up to wipe the name *Hawkins* off the nurse's erasure board, and then he neatly wrote *Miss Barbara Haskins*. Thank you, Walter Stone. It's not like he bothers me with a lot of questions either, but he moved his chair closer to my bed and keeps asking me, "Barb, are you awake?"

Why don't they have clocks or calendars in these rooms? I wish I had the password to the computer that would tell me the exact date and time. Instead, time swirls around in my head like a blob that moves forward and backward willy-nilly. *Maybe that's the way time is and the human race fools itself with clocks. The longer I stay here, the more I'm afraid I'll never leave.*

Somehow, someway, I have to concoct a reasonable excuse as to why I was in the clinic on Christmas night. I can't say unfinished work or that I forgot my keys. Nobody would believe that, although Walter might pretend he does because he's sort of a friend—at least, he's friendly with me at the Bomby when he's drunk. If someday I speak, it will only be to Walt, because he'd never want me to go to jail for pilfering drugs. He might even help me cover it up. All the evidence is burned to the ground, all the drugs gone, so the only weak link to getting caught is if asshole Patrick slips up. Before the IV bag gets filled again, I must be diligent and review every relevant detail that could get me in trouble with the cops. I wish I had Walter to talk to about this, except he *is* a cop.

The first relevant event that floats into my mind is something that happened back in November with Birdie Newcombe. It seems like so long ago. My old-woman future was beginning to look like a frightening wasteland, so I went to a new age herbal remedies shop that had just opened in Orleans. I bought myself an early Christmas present, because the only family member left in my world is a self-centered cousin in Seattle. Lying in the hospital bed, I can't help but think the pretty mystical crystal was really a bad omen, because when I dropped it down the stairs, it bounced down several steps and shattered into slivers. After I swept up the crystal slivers and worried some more about my life, I got the idea to go visit Birdie Newcombe. I remembered Dr. Newcombe, my Bill, once told me that he sent lots of cash to the Cayman Islands and bundles were hidden around his house and in a storage unit. An idea kept multiplying in my mind, a conviction that half of his money was rightfully mine. Okay, it's now decades later, but that money never belonged to Birdie Newcombe, who did nothing to help with the abortion business. It was *me* who mopped up every mess, disposed of gross remnants, and calmed all those hysterical girls. It was also *me* who was supposed to be the real Mrs. Newcombe, inheriting his wealth if he hadn't dropped dead from a heart attack.

HUSH LITTLE FIRE 127

And so it was, last November, I went to Birdie Newcombe and demanded cash. This is a very *relevant event*, which Birdie Newcombe better not mention to anyone. I strain my brain in my bandaged head to remember how the conversation went down. I kick the sheet off and sit up in bed. It was drizzling and cold out that day, with bouts of sleet blowing so hard they hit Birdie Newcombe's house from all different directions. Birdie never invited me inside—she just stood on the threshold of the Newcombe house with her arms folded, scowling past me into the stormy sky. Standing under the porch roof, Birdie held a big red umbrella, and instead of opening it, she waved it around as she spoke.

"You've got to be kidding. After all these years?" Birdie angrily tapped at the railing.

I didn't present my *proposal* in a tactless way. I wasn't so crude as to call it something such as blackmail. I simply threatened to tell every single person in town about how philandering Dr. Bill couldn't keep his fly zipped with Dianne Crocker. It would be mortifying if everyone found out the truth—that Dr. William Newcombe was the real father of Billy Crocker and Chief Calvin Crocker was not. Billy Crocker had grown up to be someone important in town, the chief of police, like his father before him. Chief Billy Crocker was well respected and had no idea about his twisted gene pool. That's because I expended a lot of energy over the years confusing the gossips by spreading outlandish rumors as decoys to cover up the truth about Dr. Newcombe's extracurricular activities. Every time I ran into old Chief Crocker, I deluged him with compliments about how little Billy had such an *outstanding, forthright, honest demeanor* just like his dad, which made him peacock with foolish pride every time. And I slathered similar decoy BS on every member of the Old Ladies Gossip Militia regarding Dr. Newcombe's appendage whenever I could. I even told the ladies that I took a sneak peek at his own medical records and was surprised to learn his testicles were undescended—*cryptorchidism* is the big word I used, which is a fancy way of saying *no balls*. I emphasized that's why he and Birdie had to adopt. *Low sperm count* and *please don't tell anyone he saw a psychiatrist because he couldn't get it up*. The ladies believed my every word and spread rumors as fast as they could. I went out of my way to protect him because I loved him. Stupid me.

But I'm not the stupid one anymore! I told Birdie straight up that day in November—that her husband had sired other children. And it would not look good for Mrs. Newcombe if everyone found out that the doctor had dropped his wild seed into the baskets of so many women. Even Birdie's church raffle friend, Trudy Bale, had four daughters and a son, sired by different men, so who knew if Dr. Newcombe was in the mix. Dr. Bill and his babies, plus Dr. Bill and his kinky hobbies, would fuel years of new town gossip. I had all the dirt and would dig it up and blow it into the ears of the Old Ladies Gossip Militia of Wellfleet, humiliating Birdie as best I could. Rumors take on a life of their own on Cape Cod as facts get lost in the muck of low tide. In a small town like Wellfleet, foraging for new gossip is a pastime, and the secrets I kept for years would be a bonanza for the ladies.

The highlight of that porch visit was that I made Birdie completely furious. Birdie waved around the big red umbrella and poked on the porch so hard the point of the umbrella got stuck between the floorboards. With a few jerky yanks, Birdie managed to unstick the umbrella tip. She hurled it into the yard, but then her mood suddenly flipped casual as she clucked out a few choice words.

HUSH LITTLE FIRE

"Never mind all that. I'll go to Florida and stay beyond the winter. I'll live there year-round. To hell with Wellfleet. You will never get your hands on my money."

And without another word, she turned into the house and slammed the front door in my face.

As I straighten up in my hospital bed, I pluck at the bandages across my nose and wonder if I might ever sneeze again. Such a simple thing in life might not be possible. What is left of my nose after the fire? I feel cold all over and wonder if Birdie Newcombe might have been furious enough to burn down the clinic knowing I was inside.

♦ 22 ♦

MARY MEETS
MR. FIXIT

Mary

I DON'T KNOW WHAT to say or do when Danny shuts down. Leave it be for now, except I catch myself twisting the edge of my bangs into a knot like that waitress Lisa. There's not much time to figure out this mess before Danny goes back to school, so I'll try to talk to him later, but first, I must throw his phone out the window.

Like my mother asked me to do, I call the police chief, Billy Crocker, and beg him in my special subservient-sweetness voice to have mercy and waive the fees for towing Jimmy's truck. He is brusque and says he'll consider it, but he wants to stop by the house to discuss something. Oh boy. When I ask him about Katie Snow's Honda, he mumbles, "Junkyard," and has no idea why Jimmy was driving her Honda.

All the energy drains out of my body when I write on my to-do list, *Pick up the box of ashes filled with Jimmy*. Don Carlson of Carlson's Funeral Parlor was kind enough to arrange the cremation, and someone from Simplicity Crematorium offered to help figure out the memorial service. When I went

HUSH LITTLE FIRE   131

there to pay them, I was shocked to see all that's left of Jimmy was stuffed into a white cardboard box with *J. Newcombe* scrawled in magic marker on top. I pretended I left my wallet at home and ran out the door so I wouldn't throw up. Birdie insists I should make an urn for his ashes before I make one for a dog. I just can't, because the thought that there's no more Jimmy is so surreal and awful. Mrs. Reardon keeps calling for a progress report on Happy's urn, and now another one of her Chihuahuas passed, so that's more money for me. Except I can't wrap my head around any of this, so I go home and sit in the chair next to Danny and watch buildings and cars explode in a video game. Tiny Mary hops in my ear and yells, *Play video games! They're perfect for erasing your sadness. If you play* Metal Gear Solid V: The Phantom Pain *game for ten hours straight, only breaking to pee, you will completely forget about Jimmy. I promise.*

The doorbell rings, I jump up, and on my way to the front door, I down two aspirins and take a swig of water straight from the kitchen tap.

"Hi, I'm Tom Murphy. I'm here to check the furnace and collect the mail for Mrs. Newcombe while she's in Florida. You must be Mary."

It's so cold the breath from his mouth billows out in big puffs. He keeps his hands in his pockets—no handshake for me, not in New England where men shake hands with men, not women.

"Yes, I'm Mary." I hold out my hand for a shake. He doesn't notice.

"Your mom mentioned you'd be coming up from Brooklyn. Don't worry. This'll only take a few minutes." He smiles at me big and wide. His friendly blue eyes scrunch down in his cheeks, and something about his energy—I think I could like this man.

"It's Sunday? Checking a furnace on a Sunday?" I pat my hair back and cautiously smile back at this man. He's a stranger, and I know nothing about him, but I need this so badly, because I know nothing about myself either, except Mary Newcombe is teetering on the edge of 23andMe test results. On the doorstep, he wipes his boots before stepping inside, and then he heads down the basement stairs, skipping steps.

"Is there something wrong with the furnace I should know about?" I follow him like a clueless duckling.

"I tried to fix it weeks ago. Problems with the pilot light." He pulls out a pair of wire-rimmed glasses and examines pipes and joints, poking around at valves and dials I know nothing about. I try to be attentive.

On his knees, he says, "Everything is A-okay. No more problem pipes in this house." He jumps up and rubs his hands together. This is a guy who fixes furnaces and things. I like that.

On my tiptoes, I'm in line with his collar, and my head would fit right under his chin. He has thinning brown curls with some respectable trustworthy gray hair peeking through. I want him to stay a little longer, so I ask him to check the circuit breakers.

"I'm not an electrician, but I'll take a look for Mrs. Newcombe." I stand next to him and look inside the circuit breaker box as I take in the lovely clean reliable smell of a man who just shaved. I inch up next to him and pretend to read the map on the breaker box door.

"It's right there, see? A hundred amps for a kiln and 220 volts." I want to impress him with my electrician-speak.

He moves in closer to me. "Hey, Mary, your mom told me it would be okay to ask you to take the dog for a night."

"What dog?"

HUSH LITTLE FIRE 133

"I'm so sorry to ask you."

"Whose dog?"

"The girl who works at the Lighthouse, Lisa—well, after your cousin passed away, she begged the guys at the firehouse to take his dog. She was his neighbor, but she couldn't handle the dog, so I've got him now. Temporarily."

"Whoa, whoa, whoa. Did you come here to check the furnace or drop off a dog?"

"The dog's in the car. Would it be okay? I brought dog food."

"So you want me to babysit Jimmy's dog?"

"Only for a night or two. Sunshine's a good dog. I promise. Excuse me for forgetting my manners. My condolences to you and your mother. I'm so sorry about Jimmy's passing."

"Did you even know Jimmy?" This Tom Murphy man darts out the door and doesn't answer. At least he left the pickup truck running so the damn dog wouldn't freeze to death. There's a red VOLUNTEER FIREMEN'S ASSOCIATION sticker on his window with a big dog pawing at the glass. Halfway to the truck, Tom Murphy spins around and points his finger at me.

"I did meet you before. Yes, I did. Now I remember. You were in the crowd Christmas night watching the fire at the clinic."

"No. I wasn't." *This is too weird. Kevin and the nosy mail lady asked me the same thing.*

"Weren't you there?"

"Are you a fireman?"

"No, I'm just a lowly citizen volunteer. But I got called up that night."

Tom Murphy, Mr. Volunteer Firefighter, Mr. Magnetic, Mr. Handsome, leads Sunshine, a well-behaved German shepherd, to the front porch along with a very large sack of dog food.

"Is Sunshine male or female?" I can't help myself from asking about *another* Sunshine.

"This dog's all girl." On the front porch, Mr. Murphy bends down and pats the dog on the head.

"Now, you be a good girl." He kisses the dog's ear. "Oh, wait a second. I probably should bring her inside to look around and get acclimatized before I leave."

They bound through the front door, and Sunshine leads Tom Murphy from room to room, sniffing the floor and the furniture. Strange how this dog is on a sniffing mission, a lot like those Brooklyn dogs trained to sniff out bedbugs.

"Mrs. Newcombe sure does get a lot of mail." Tom Murphy pulls out a yellow piece of paper from his pocket. "Here's a special delivery from the post office."

I hold out my hand to take it, but he won't let go. He puts his glasses on and reads the slip.

"The return address is in Shijiazhuang, China. If you sign here, I'll go pick it up for your mother. It's addressed to the Newcombe family. Probably junk mail."

"I don't think my mother orders things from China. It's from China?" I ask, trying to figure out if he's married. No ring.

"I can save you the trouble and pick it up. Just sign for it." He eagerly pulls out a pen from his pocket.

"No need. I'll stop by the post office before we leave."

Tom Murphy looks disappointed as he passes me the slip. He could be one of those guys who likes to help old widows, how very nice of him, or he's just plain meddlesome like the rest of Wellfleet. He doesn't have a Boston accent, and he doesn't look like a nerdy Good Samaritan who helps old ladies in his spare time.

"How do you even know my mother? Jimmy was the one who always collected her mail."

HUSH LITTLE FIRE

135

"I was assigned to Mrs. Newcombe because the Volunteer Firemen's Association helps out with the infirmed and elderly, so they assigned me to Widow Newcombe. Lucky me."

"Lucky you."

I pat the dog's head, which makes me want to cry and laugh all at once, because I wonder if Sunshine misses Jimmy.

"When your mother called me, she said you might stay longer, and we got to talking, and, well, we had the idea that I should invite you to dinner at Mahoney's on Saturday night."

"Are you asking me on a date? I don't go out on dates much—I mean, I'm not much of a dinner-dater." I wonder if this invitation is all Birdie's idea.

"I'd like to take you and Danny. That makes it not a date. I don't bite. Ask your mother." He winks.

"All right. Danny and me. That would be nice."

The good side of my motherly brain says, *How nice—he wants to include my son,* but the bad side of my motherly brain wants to go out to dinner with this nice-looking guy without Danny. No Danny. I want to be alone with this man who fixes furnaces and things.

With a wave goodbye, Tom Murphy leaves in a hurry, and I call after him, "Wait, what time?" But the red truck disappears down the road.

Danny emerges from the cave of the TV room. "What's that dog doing in the house? Who was that guy?" He pecks at his phone while Sunshine sits erect by the front door.

"It's Sunshine. Jimmy's dog."

Danny holds out his hand above Sunshine's front paw, but the dog just sits there and doesn't move.

"Mom, this isn't Sunshine." He rubs the dog's neck and frowns. "This is a German shepherd, but it isn't Jimmy's dog.

Sunshine has a white spot of fur on her neck, and she always gives me her paw. This is definitely not Sunshine."

"Yes it is."

This dog is unusually well behaved, sitting inches from the door like a dog statue. Danny scrolls through his phone and holds it up to my face.

"Look at this selfie of me and Sunshine. See the white spot? See it?"

"Maybe that's a reflection on your phone?"

"Sunshine would never sit still like this. *Who* was that guy anyway?"

"Sunshine is adjusting. She's fine. That man is a handyman fireman who fixed the furnace, and he's handy with lots of things that need fixing," I stutter.

The dog is still staring at me, so I pour a bowl of dry kibble and bring it over to Sunshine, who doesn't even sniff the bowl.

"Give the dog some beer. Sunshine loves beer," Danny says. "I'll go get some."

"You'll do no such thing." I raise my hand to pet Sunshine, who stands up on all fours and growls.

I go over a few facts about Mr. Fixit, and some things don't add up, so I call Birdie and quiz her about the dog and Tom Murphy. Birdie doesn't have anything to say about the dog, but she gushes with praise about this helpful, courteous, handsome man. Jeez, you'd think *Birdie* wants to date him. Birdie goes quiet, and this makes me wonder if perhaps a mating flicker lives on forever, even in the heart of a seventy-five-year-old woman. How gross. Suddenly my mother hangs up without a goodbye, as if she were listening in on my thoughts.

◆ 23 ◆

MARY AND THE IMPOSTOR DOG

Mary

THE GERMAN SHEPHERD SITTING by the front door is beginning to get on my nerves. I poke my head into the hallway and speak nicey-nice in a high voice, but he growls at me. Tom Murphy better pick him up soon. Like tomorrow.

I finally go online to track the progress of my 23andMe test, and in the glow of the computer, I float through cyberspace and wonder what the "connectors" to my genes are doing out there. On the website, I see an unfriendly graph that represents the search of my life with one bulbous blue dot halfway through a line that marks where I am. It says, "On to genotyping!"

What does that mean? The email of my life goes on to say, "We're able to read around 600,000 letters in your DNA, which power the 23andMe results." Okay, my five-foot-three body breaks down to six hundred thousand letters? "We use probes to turn your sample into knowledge." Suddenly my whole body is itchy. The sirens of drinkie start calling me—*calm down*—but today I am determined to quit alcohol, no more sherry, sparkling burgundy, cognac, or beer, because it's time to clean out my pipes. I must clear my mind and body before I throw on the wheel to make Happy's cremation urn, because even for a dog, it should be a spiritual act.

My potter friend Jean often recommended meditating instead of booze, perhaps a hippie kind of buzz. Breathe in. Breathe out. Jean thinks of herself as a meditation expert, a little bossy at times with her strict instructions about meditating—palms up, eyes closed, sit on the floor, and chant *om*. Nothing clicks right away, and when I open my eyes, my face is very close to my mother's dark TV, which is begging for me to turn it on.

Jean says I must sit cross-legged on the floor, but it feels ridiculous, like I'm attending a kindergarten story time. There are millions, maybe billions, of meditators in the world, so why doesn't this help me? I hum the mantra *om*, but it makes me tired, so I try my own medley, *Ola-tunji, Ola-tunji*, which sounds sort of spiritual, although it's really my old boyfriend Bruce's favorite jazz drummer. *Ola-tunji* helps me go back and reconstruct a picture in my mind of what I was doing the night of the Christmas fire. Bleached images of my mother and Danny cruise my horizon, but nothing specific shows up. *Olatunji, Olatunji.*

I sink deeper into a mini meditation trance, and a fuzzy round ball of light appears. I remember Birdie gave Danny a gift certificate to play ten games in the arcade in Provincetown. A Christmas gift *of blow 'em up and shoot 'em dead* video games that twelve-year-old boys love. Finally, Birdie confirmed they went to a P-town arcade late on Christmas Day so Danny could hang out in the Church of Electronics for game fiends and lost souls.

My heart begins to patter, and then it cranks up to the speed of a jogger, which is never supposed to happen with

HUSH LITTLE FIRE   139

meditating. The fuzzy orange ball in my mind's eye looks like a big fiery sun—my face is hot—but my hands are icy. I picture myself jogging faster and faster, my arms stretched out toward the blazing sun—me and the Mayans chasing the untouchable sun. I'm on a desperate run because, maybe, the sun holds answers to my questions and all that makes me afraid in the world. My arms and legs quiver—my eyes fly open to a panic attack hovering above my head. Why am I so worked up when meditating is supposed to relax me?

Danny walks into the room, munching on a jelly doughnut. "Mom? Are you watching TV on the floor? You should turn it on." And then he walks out just like that. From the kitchen he shouts, "Can't I go back to Brooklyn early?"

I babble about needing to spend a few more days to make arrangements for the memorial service, but the truth is, I want to stay. So I call Jean in New York, and since we've been friends forever and she's kind of Danny's auntie, she agrees to meet him at Port Authority when he steps off the bus. She's fine with him bunking at her place for a few days. Just as I hang up with Jean, my mother phones me from Florida, like she has a sixth sense I'm about to look through her drawers again.

"Hello there, Sunshine!"

"Ugh. You know what, please don't ever call me that again."

"I thought you like that nickname. You don't have to be disagreeable with me. Did that nice young man Tom pick up the mail yet?"

"It's piled in a box in the kitchen. Should I forward you the important stuff? You got a notice about a package from China."

"Mary, listen to me. Don't pick up any packages from China. Leave it at the post office. Ignore it. It is definitely not a package for me. Jimmy ordered things online and had them sent to Mrs. Newcombe, and I never knew what he was up to. He told me he was ordering fishing lures, and when I read my bills, I discovered he used my credit card. The police can't find out about this. We'll talk more when I see you. Don't touch any packages at the post office. Agreed?"

"Okay, okay." Before I can ask her anything more, she ends it with a curt goodbye, and then she's gone.

Danny walks into the TV room and flops down on a chair, holding a glass of milk and not his phone. I snatch up the remote and shove it under my chair when he's not looking, because this is my chance to talk.

If Danny were a daughter, I'd know what to say. I'd ask my daughter to help me bake a cake, and while creaming the butter and sugar, I would gently tease out the truth. *Do you know if Jimmy had anything to do with the fire? And tell me, how horrible was it for you when Jimmy went crazy mad last summer and pushed you off the boat?* Girls get talking to each other about feelings when they do things like baking and brushing hair. And boys? It's like touching the south end of a magnet to the south end of another magnet when I try to get my son to talk to me.

"I need to stay here a bit longer, so I was thinking you could take a bus back to New York and stay with Jean. How does that sound?"

"Great!" Danny's eyebrows shoot up, and he finally smiles.

Like with the itch I had to keep scratching during meditation, I ask him one more time.

"I need to know, because the police want to know. What did you and Gramma Birdie do on Christmas when I fell asleep?"

"Fell asleep? That's a good one, Mom," he snickers. "You got wasted."

"Did you and Gramma drive to the fire?"

HUSH LITTLE FIRE

"I dunno. There's nothing to do here. Can we go back home today?"

Danny's face folds into a pained expression for only a second, and then he lets loose a big grin. "I've got the bus schedule right here on my phone. There's one that leaves Hyannis in eight hours."

Sending Danny back on the bus solves my Danny-on-my-date problem, but if I stay, I better make the dog pottery here in Wellfleet. I need that money ASAP. There are some leftover balls of dried-up clay in the basement, and right now I want something to pummel. And now I must go find Walter and shower him with compliments so he'll let me use his studio. I have a big secret blooming in my chest about to pop out of my mouth. Half of the secret is—something mothers never admit—I desperately need a mini-vacation from motherhood. *Olatunji.* The other part is Walter. I'm so happy to see my old friend. He's not much of a talker and never an explainer, so when I stop by and ask him if I can make a few things in his studio, he says, "Sure thing," and goes back to throwing a gigantic pot on the wheel. His arms are covered in gooey stoneware slip as his hand dives down inside a wet cylinder of clay that spins on the wheel. Never disturb a handsome man throwing pots. He doesn't look up or ask me what I want to make. He mutters, "Take whatever you need." Potter short-hand communication.

Step Three: Wedging Clay for a Dead Chihuahua's Urn

I sift through Walter's bags of dry mix and add Georgia Kaolin to my bag of powdery Newcomb Hollow clay to create a porcelain-ish mixture, which will be a good canvas for copper red glazes. Next step: Mix my specialty clay formula in Walter's dough mixer, which is the same equipment bakers use to prepare dough. I add water slowly in the way Mildred, Walter's mean mom, dribbled water and ice cubes to make her perfect pie crust. Not too much and not too little. Birdie used to mock Mildred's picture-perfect pies at church raffles, and she said more than once, "Why put all that effort into baking a pie when it's gobbled up and gone in ten minutes?" And I agree. I'm happier making pots that will last ten thousand years.

Every potter knows you must wedge thoroughly, because if you don't, any air bubbles left in the clay will heat up and explode like popcorn. Bakers wedge air in and potters wedge air out, but we use the same energetic arm movements. Wedging is tedious so I wedge fast in fourth gear, because if I give it my all, my superstitious mind believes that the fates will have mercy and nothing will explode. And more important, if I wedge with all my might, my convoluted logic tells me, no explosions will foretell good news in my genetic test.

Fold and wedge hard. Fold and wedge harder. Suddenly my hands go limp, my tongue is dry, my fingers stop, and I drop the mound of clay. It never occurred to me until right now—are the police going to call *me* in for questioning too?

♦ 24 ♦

BARBARA DREAMS OF HER FINGERS

Barbara

I'M SO STONED ON the hospital's painkillers all the time, I'm beginning to think of myself as Barbara Hawkins. All the nurses still call me Hawkins like Barbara Haskins doesn't exist. And to make matters worse, I have a new roommate who snores. She wheezes noisily through her nose day and night. A candy striper pours golden apple juice in a cup for my roommate, but it just sits there on a tray. I'm thirsty, but not for the apple juice or the liquid protein they force on me—I'm thirsty for a whiskey sour. I dream of the olden days at the Bomby where the bartender Steve made the best cocktails just for me. As I imagine biting into a whiskey-soaked maraschino cherry, I think about sin.

I wonder if the doctors understand that the sins of a lifetime are now emblazoned on my face. I wiggle my right hand under the bandages and wish it would stay bandaged forever, so I won't have to look at the stubs of three fingers that were amputated at the knuckles.

This morning when the nurse changed my bandages, I wanted to scream holy hell, but all that came out of my mouth was a groan. From my last manicure, there is one spot left of pretty red nail polish on only my thumb, and I can't bear to think of what the surgeon did with the amputated parts of myself. I have nothing to do but lie here all day, so I rewind my life back to when I was a young nurse who had to clean up after the secret procedures, and how it was my responsibility to make all the blood and sloppy stuff disappear. When Dr. Newcombe spoke of the remnants of the late-term procedures, the ones after six months, he always spoke in code.

"Now Barb, wrap *Mousie* in a brown paper bag and dig a deep hole far into the woods. Barb, why the sad look on your face? Stop worrying. Think of this as compost for our beautiful trees. And please don't throw *Mousie* in the ocean, because you never know, it might wash up on shore."

I did as I was told that year in 1972, and ever since, I've been explaining to God why I did that. I tell God and myself that it was important to help other women, and besides, it was my duty as a nurse. But an old saying latches on like the IV in my arm—*what goes around, comes around*—and maybe that's why karma landed me here? On top of that, it makes me so sad there never was a chance to bury my fingers. I shudder, wondering what else burned up in the fire.

To pass the time, I think a lot about my fun times at the Bomby—what else can I do? I'm stuck here. The doctors have reduced my pain medication, and my mind is quite clear for stretches of time. I pretend I'm surrounded by loud thumping music from the jukebox, and that helps me drown out the snoring sounds from my roommate. I picture myself dressed up nice for Ladies Night at the Bomby, ready for a good game of pool. I concentrate hard on remembering the

HUSH LITTLE FIRE

inside of the bar, every detail, down to green felt on the pool table and the pretty bottles lined up behind the bar, and this brings me right back to the Bomby. Even though parts of my fingers are gone, I close my eyes and imagine rubbing the smooth wood on my favorite pool cue. I love to play pool even when men show up on Ladies Night and hog the pool table and darts. So many men flock to the Bomby on those nights, all of them on the prowl except Walter, who buys me drinks. I float my mind back to one significant night at the bar, back in 1984.

"Don't you dare touch my drink," I snapped at Trudy Bale, who looked guilty as hell, slinking away from my whiskey sour that sat on a nearby table. "I seen you over there, *Mizzus* Trudy Bale, waiting for me to fix my eyes on the cue ball so you can steal sips from my drink."

I was dressed in my tight black slacks and my best golden silky blouse that showed off my best feature, my boobs. I unbuttoned the top few buttons so that when I shook out my ponytail, it cascaded to my shoulders and blended perfectly with my golden blouse. I kept my eye on my drink and Trudy Bale, who pretended to be reading an abandoned newspaper. I knew Trudy didn't give a damn about the headline in giant black letters that said Ronald Reagan had won his second term by a landslide. Trudy could have been pretty if she tried, but after four children, all girl babies, her figure was shot to pieces. The real Trudy was hiding under layers of clothing, a flannel work shirt, and Farmer Grey overalls. Trudy's black hair was nicely poofed and styled for Ladies Night in a way that accented her fake pearl earrings. Other people at the bar might have wondered why the baggy-overalls outfit, but I had a hunch why Trudy was desperate to hide her belly. I felt sorry for the woman but at the same time annoyed with the drink stealer, so

I had the urge to tell Trudy to splurge for once and buy her own drink. But then *mean me* went away and *nice me* asked, "Trude, can I buy you a drink?"

"That would be cool, but you know the bartender is my cousin Elaine's brother-in-law, and he's under strict orders to make sure I don't drink."

"What business of his is that?"

"I'm pregnant."

"A few sips of beer won't hurt. Even nursing mothers drink beer. You must know that by now after four kids."

The new morphine drip is kicking in, and I try not to hallucinate, but it's so fun to travel back to the Bomby in my mind. I close my eyes, and my hands tingle as I watch a larger-than-life Mike Gooden go slobbering over to Trudy. I would pinch myself if I could, if my hands weren't such a wreck, because suddenly it's important to remember exactly what happened with Trudy Bale that night. I make a mental list of all the people who might have been angry with me over the years—enough to do me harm. Trudy Bale?

Back when Dr. Newcombe was giving those secret procedures at night before *Roe v. Wade* ruined everything for him, I remember he was so neat and clean with Trudy, even though he was whistling too much while he worked on her. Her having another procedure seemed reasonable to me, because when all was said and done, Trudy already had four daughters and no man to speak of. Trudy was grateful for that abortion, because babies 1, 2, 3, 4 had been born a year apart. She turned out to be a regular with Dr. Newcombe, because the pill made her sick and a diaphragm didn't work with her tilted uterus.

The nurse interrupts me and takes my blood pressure for the umpteenth time, and when she's finally done, I drift back one more time to the strange events that night at the Bomby

HUSH LITTLE FIRE

when everyone was partying, and not because Ronald Reagan had just been reelected. I'm not quite sure I remember correctly, but an image slides by of Mike Gooden tapping Trudy on the shoulder as he waved a five-dollar bill in her face. He told her to meet him in his car, and I remember their argument back and forth. Trudy kept pushing for ten dollars, but Mike laughed and made a crack about her being such an amateur at giving head. But now I remember clear as a bell on Ronald Reagan Ladies Night—when she was finished wanking off Mike Gooden and then some—when she came back from his car—I could see she was quite pregnant again, with a fifth in those baggy overalls.

As I lie in bed, my not-mad list keeps changing, and Trudy suddenly goes from the not-mad column to the mad-at-Barb column, because I clearly remember how she begged me to help her end another pregnancy and I refused.

"Don't be silly. I haven't done anything like that since they passed *Roe v. Wade*."

"But you seemed so in charge of everything back then. You know how to do it. I'm desperate. I really need your help."

"You don't need my help. Abortions have been completely legal and safe now for years. Why don't you just go to Boston Planned Parenthood? It's not even expensive there."

"I did. But they said I'm too far along, and they can't help me."

"How far?"

"Seven months. I just look fat, right?"

"The only thing I can tell you is I heard of some old remedies that might help, but I'm not sure what amount or in what combination. Don't quote me. Pennyroyal essential oil, and then there's weird stuff like crushed ants, the saliva of camels,

148 JUDITH NEWCOMB STILES

and the tail hairs of a black-tailed deer dissolved in the fat of bears. I'm not kidding. I read that. Maybe it's just an old wives' tale, so do some serious research first."

"Where am I supposed to get that stuff?"

"Please don't take this the wrong way, but why did you wait so long?"

"It's not that simple. The girls are finally in school. Listen, I go to Mass when I can. At least I think about going to church. And I believe in the Father, the Son, and the Holy Ghost, but the Holy Ghost isn't going to babysit for me."

"You should have dealt with this sooner."

"This one is a total surprise. You don't know what it's like. I'm on my own with the kids. I'll go insane if I have another one."

"Maybe you can get some help from the baby's father. Who's the father?"

"That's none of your business."

"I think you better stop thinking about pennyroyal and start thinking about what to name it."

"That's all you can say? I should think about a name?"

"How about Patricia? I always thought if I ever had a baby girl, I'd name her Patricia."

"I think it's a boy."

"How about Patrick? Patrick Bale. I like the sound of it. That's a stand-up name for a boy."

Thinking of that awful night at the Bomby, I frantically press the call button on my bed to ask the nurse for more pain medication. I must get Patrick Bale and his mother out of my mind. Funny how the last time Patrick showed up for a drug delivery, I was startled at how much he looks like his mother. I was mesmerized by his Trudy Bale–blue eyes, and I remember that conversation at the Bomby years ago, and how the pennyroyal essential oil, crushed ants, saliva of camels, and tail hairs of a black-tailed deer dissolved in bear fat must not have worked. Patrick Bale is alive and well, and the way he turned out to be such a loser, Trudy Bale could very well be mad at me after all these years.

Everything begins to blur quite nicely on the pleasant drug drip with only one image rising to the surface. It's a hazy image of the last time I saw Trudy Bale at the dentist and Trudy refused to acknowledge my presence in the waiting room. I overheard a discussion where the receptionist told Trudy about a liquid diet to follow as soon as the dentist pulled the rest of her teeth. Right before I sink into a morphine stupor, I click my own teeth together, relieved that I still have them.

♦ 25 ♦
WOMEN HAVE BABIES FOR ALL KINDS OF REASONS

Mary

I WATCH DANNY CAREFULLY comb and part his hair because he's so excited to be going back to the city alone. He walks down the porch steps more like an adult, and when he talks to me, he makes his voice sound lower. He throws his backpack in the car and calls me Mary instead of Mom. "Hurry up, Mary, or we'll miss the bus." It sounds so strange and makes me cough.

In the driveway, we snap on our seat belts at the same time, and instead of hiding in the back seat, he rides in front with me. We both reach for the knobs on the dashboard for the heater, and my hand lands on top of his and I hold it there for an extra second. I wait for Danny to say something as the silence roars through my head. Sometimes I think I love my son too much, the way I load him up with torrential one-way feelings. I can't stand the silence, so out of my mouth spills, "I'm so relieved you're getting off the Cape. I'll come back to Brooklyn as soon as this mess blows over."

"What mess?"

HUSH LITTLE FIRE 151

"The police are asking a lot of questions around town, and that guy Patrick gives me the creeps. You know what I'm saying?"

He flashes me a sideways frown, like he's worried I might change my mind about his traveling alone.

I reach over and rest my hand on his shoulder. "I've wanted to say something to you for the past few days—that I love you, and whatever happened last summer with Jimmy, I'm so sorry I wasn't there."

"I love you too. But you worry too much like Gramma."

"I'm not anything like her."

"Yes you are."

"But she's not my birth mother. You know that."

"So?"

Danny's mouth hangs open like he wants to say something more, but instead he plugs in his earbuds and peers out the window. For the rest of the way to Hyannis, we don't speak, and when we arrive, I blurt out in my most neutral motherly voice, "You be careful on the bus and watch your back. And call or text me the minute you get there."

My only son climbs the steps to the bus with his backpack slung over his shoulder like he's done this trip a million times. Every mother in the world would tell me to take a deep breath at moments like this, because milestone events, even the little ones, can give a mother whiplash.

Danny will probably forget my instructions, but Jean will surely call me. Tiny Mary shouts in my ear, *You have a job to do now besides making cremation urns. Check the progress of your 23andMe test. Do it. But I suggest you go back to Wellfleet and take a long nap first, because it tells you ways to find siblings if the siblings are registered. It just might blow your mind.*

I do not go home. Instead, I swing by Newcomb Hollow Beach to check in with the ocean, but really to be in a place that has zero Wi-Fi, where I can't possibly check anything. Today is an odd January thaw, warm enough to bring out the hardcore surfers in wetsuits who wear rubber slippers and gloves. The fog is dense, and it is one of those rare times when I look out toward Portugal and can't see the horizon line. The separation between the sea and the sky is gone, and I welcome the fog. The rolling mist floats over two young women carrying their boards as they plunge into the ocean. They bob up and down on the cresting waves like two seals with ponytails before they paddle a few strokes and disappear.

I know my birth mother is out there, close or far away from this ocean. The genetic test might give me clues to brothers and sisters, but right now, standing here at Newcomb Hollow, I only want to look for surfer girls. Funny how this gray looks a lot like smoke, like the time Birdie fell asleep and her mattress caught on fire and the house filled up with smoke and the fire truck came and squirted it all out. It was bad, and Birdie was frantic on the front lawn, apologizing to the firemen and cursing the water all over her floors. And I could see her guard was down, so I figured it would be a good time to ask her again. "Tell me, please, was I born on Cape Cod?" She popped a mint in her mouth and she shook her head no, but said nothing more.

Mrs. Reardon called me last night—another one of the seven dwarfs passed away, and she *put down* a third Chihuahua because it was blind. Three thousand dollars for me. Would I kill my dog, if I had a dog, if it went blind? Blind people, even dogs, see the world in foggy shadows. Time for foggy-me to go throw a few pots.

Step Four: Throwing on the Wheel for Dead Chihuahua Urns

Walter sits next to me, quietly throwing a very large vessel to the tune of a faintly whirring electric wheel. His studio has different equipment, so I throw on his brand-new Brent wheel instead of my Shimpo VL Whisper wheel, which feels like I'm wearing someone else's underwear. The fit is off and doesn't feel quite right, but this is the best I can do for now. Something is different with Walter this time, because he keeps looking up and grinning at me in the middle of throwing. He stops and turns his wheel off before finishing the lip on his bowl and offers me a cup of coffee. How gallant of Walter—what a friend—but did he just jolt his own pot into a sloppy stop just to offer me coffee?

Throwing on the wheel is the part where the potter must stop talking, stop thinking, stop obsessing. I left my phone in the car because it's time to give everything over to my hands, so they can be alert and sense what the clay is doing. Let the clay move. And move the clay. My fingers are stiff, and with goopy wet clay all over my hands, I can't possibly check a computer for genetic test news.

I sponge some water on the mound and let the whirling ball of silt take me away. Leaning over the spinning wet mound of clay, I make sure it's centered perfectly on the wheel, in the world, in the universe, because I am not. I cup my hands and rest them on top of the mound as it turns, neither pushing nor pulling, but with all the promise of a finished pot to come. Finally, I exhale everything I've got and plunge my thumbs into the center to open the pot. Begin.

◆ 26 ◆
FODDER FOR THE OLD LADIES GOSSIP MILITIA

Birdie

1963

I AM CERTAIN THE Old Ladies Gossip Militia was founded on the *Mayflower* in an informal, unorganized way when the women had time to talk while cooking, or sewing, or swabbing vomit off the deck into the sea. It's not in a history book or anything, but our women became the historians of all things Cape Cod for centuries without writing anything down. No membership fees or formal meetings, just information passed through the grapevine, was the best way to keep secrets from becoming too secret.

An anonymous member of the 1963 Old Ladies Gossip Militia was caught blabbing gossip about us Newcombe girls again. She said to anyone who'd listen that my sister-in-law, Clara Newcombe, and "Birdie Brains" (she called me that!) were spotted driving to Provincetown for art classes, and it was confirmed that neither of us housewives had a valid driver's license.

HUSH LITTLE FIRE

Clara was teaching me how to drive a stick shift without any help from a man. She drove her husband's truck with me shotgun while we argued about if it was tacky, maybe premature, to wear my new black beret to art class.

"Only artists in New York City wear berets," Clara said, turning down the radio, which was blasting President Johnson's speech at headache level.

"Turn it off! I can't think when he whines."

"Yes sirree!" I grabbed the knob on the radio so hard it popped off.

"The president is a nincompoop." Clara gunned the engine and checked her lipstick in the rearview mirror. She was pushing seventy miles an hour all the way to Provincetown so we wouldn't be late for our class with the cute painting teacher, who happened to be French.

The inspiring art teacher had changed everything for us, and we felt like real artists when we discovered how to observe and interpret the world in new ways. The seashore and sunsets were the subject of art classes in the summer, but the Cape Cod housewives of winter like us were introduced to the landscapes that were hiding in our minds. Besides, it was hard to get students to paint snow and flat gray skies, the dreary winter landscape of the Narrow Land. December was a rough time for everyone, and Antoine and the professional artists in Provincetown had bills to pay too, so they gave discount lessons to the local ladies, and I knew they only did that so they wouldn't starve.

In our first class, just before the water break, Antoine leaned over Clara's shoulder, his arm casually skimming her breast as he told her that the sky didn't have to be blue.

"You can paint the sky any color you want," he said as he added a dab of red to her sky, his elbow wiggling each breast.

That was probably the exact moment in time when he and Clara began their ravenous affair. And observing that red dab of paint land on Clara's flat blue sky catapulted me into my own ravenous spell of oil painting. It was also the moment when the sword fight of dos and don'ts broke out in the center of my mind. *Do this. Don't do that.* Something I heard all my life. But soon after the dab of red paint, I killed the bossy voice in my head and painted all kinds of Cape Cod scenes that were staked out in my memory. I liked to paint by the stove in my kitchen, and I often went to bed smelling of turpentine.

In Provincetown, Clara was so relieved to be away from her young son, Jimmy, who was a tornado of energy, driving poor Clara nuts. Every Saturday I kept an eye on Jimmy when Clara was off somewhere, screwing the painting teacher. Clara's extracurricular activities were fine with me because I knew Clara was lonely, living at home with a five-year-old and no adults to talk to. The affair with Antoine was not unusual for a woman who had to endure winter on the Narrow Land with a husband off at sea. People did lots of crazy things stuck under that gray sky day after day. Besides, Clara's marriage to Big James was like being married to a ghost.

At the time of the painting lessons, Mary was not yet a Mary. She was still a nothing, not born, not available for adoption yet, so I didn't know anything about parenting. Even though Big James had a son to raise, he was gone at sea, or so he said, although I knew he called from Las Vegas a few times. Big James was a man whose body seemed too big to live on land, bumping into my precious things whenever he came back to visit. Last time I saw him, he knocked over a lamp when his big restless fingers lunged under the shade, clumsily looking for the switch. The latest trip, he supposedly was on a tanker in the Red Sea, somewhere near India or Africa. Each

HUSH LITTLE FIRE   157

time Big James came back, he brought a cheap present for his son, like a plastic water pistol from Nova Scotia, and he made hollow promises that Jimmy could be the cabin boy on the next trip. I got in a loud argument with Big James, yelling at him that he must never promise that to Jimmy again.

"Every time you come back, you promise the poor boy he can come with you. Jimmy will be a cabin boy over my dead body," I said, trying to control the hissing in my voice.

"Why not?"

"I heard what cabin boys did in the olden days."

"You don't know what you're talking about. Cabin boys do chores and learn about life at sea."

"No way! A little boy out at sea for months with a bunch of horny old sailors. And what about school?" Big James just laughed, which made his eyelids quiver. But I knew, and all the elderly women on Cape Cod knew, that in the olden days, cabin boys did double duty sexually pleasuring the sailors who got too pent up at sea. Sailors and pirates who were much too far away from their wives and taverns, anxious to stick it in a hole somewhere. Big James adamantly denied any such thing ever happened on ships, but I couldn't help noticing how sheepish he looked as he stuffed the peanut butter sandwich into his mouth—the whole entire sandwich in one fibber's bite.

With the art classes, I started calling myself Beatrice again, and I whispered in the mirror, "Beatrice the artist." And although Emma the mail carrier and other ladies in town considered my paintings dilettantish, that didn't bother me one bit. What did they know. They weren't the bosses of art. My mind was becoming so open to light and color and shapes I'd never bothered to notice before. The world looked amazing. And Antoine emphasized the importance of light in every single class when he wasn't pinching Clara's rear. For the first time, I paid attention to the spectacular light on Cape Cod when the sun occasionally showed itself in the winter. Since the leaves had fallen from the trees, the light reflected off the ocean, then raced through the bare branches, a stunning light, bouncing off the sea from three sides, headed straight to my canvas.

For me, painting was a magical place of endless possibilities, even better than listening to Elvis. When I finished a painting, Clara and I talked about it for hours. What was the inspiration? Did it come from a deep place in my subconscious? Did it express a special longing? It was exciting to consider these things. Then I showed my first paintings to Bill when he came home.

"Very nice, but your trees sort of look like broccoli."

I took it as a compliment. My imagination had transformed ordinary trees into puffs of bluish-green broccoli heads with dabs of fiery red bursting across the canvas.

I was Beatrice again, not that ordinary housewife Birdie, so I bought myself a book on Henri Rousseau, and I donned the black beret, although I never wore it out of the house. One afternoon, it occurred to me I could have been a versatile artist, like a female Michelangelo, if only I had started making art earlier in life.

It bothered me a lot that random men—men like Big James—had a knack for invading my thoughts uninvited, especially in art class when the painting teacher droned on and on about famous men painters from France we should admire. I wished Antoine would shut up. I was dying to ask Clara what she thought of that lady from New York who went undercover and dressed up as a Playboy Bunny.

"You mean Gloria Steinem?" whispered Clara when Antoine left the room.

HUSH LITTLE FIRE

"Yeah, that one. I really like her hair. I love the extra streak of blond in the front."

I added a streak of yellow to my ocean waves. The coincidence was thrilling.

"I don't know; if she doesn't bleach that streak properly, she'll look like a skunk. Just one streak is enough," Clara whispered, frantically applying more lipstick. She blotted her lips on a tissue and muttered, "She's just another rich bitch from the city, telling us what we should and shouldn't do. Like, don't wear a bra. Oh please, that would make my boobies sag."

I liked to agree with Clara on most issues, because it was easier to agree than argue with my only friend. Since Clara was stuck as the wife of my husband's brother, and even though I hated Big James, I didn't want to ruin things with Clara. But what I really wanted to say to Clara, and all the other gossips in town, was *Gloria Steinem has gorgeous hair. She doesn't look like a skunk. And Gloria most definitely has a point. The way she talks—got me thinking that I have the right to paint in my kitchen whenever I want!*

During the year of exciting painting class, Clara became pregnant and tried to hide it even with me. I felt like Clara was ten steps ahead of me, ahead of the times, when she started talking about leaving Cape Cod and *liberating* herself from this place. At first, hiding the pregnancy worked okay, because everyone wore layers of clothing in the winter. Big James was still gone but coming back soon, and Clara was planning her escape from Cape Cod. She talked about Canada, because it was close but still another country. It was obvious that Clara was pregnant, and one night, without any warning, she packed her car to leave. But before she set out for Canada, she dropped Jimmy off at my house with a note pinned to his chest saying she would *be back soon to pick up Jimmy, but until then, please look after my boy. I know you understand. Love, Clara.*

Clara came back all right, but in an aluminum urn of ashes along with a small jar that held the ashes of a premature baby.

The painting classes ended for me, because when Clara died in childbirth, I felt like a big part of my soul drained out of my body and would never be refilled. The emptiness was back. I missed Clara terribly and hid the black beret from myself in a place where I'd never remember to find it. It became impossible to think about art with Clara gone. Sometimes I felt like blowing my brains out.

◆ 27 ◆

BIRDIE AND THE NOSY MAIL CARRIER

Birdie

1964

AT NIGHT I LAY in bed in the Cape Cod blackness, feeling depressed after the evening news. I'd been watching President Johnson on TV, and I was pretty sure he'd never changed a diaper in his life. Bill was too busy making money, so it was unthinkable he'd find the time to wipe the baby's bottom and help me. I'd wanted a baby, and he'd gotten me one, but he never asked why I felt so sad. I never said it out loud, but I missed Clara, and this new baby didn't fill up my love hole.

Lying alone in the dark, I wondered if he'd paid money to buy this baby. Sickening, if he did that, but Bill was into money. I knew some money was in our storage locker, but where was the money hidden in the house? Once, I helped Bill hide the money in the base of an antique lamp in the living room. I unscrewed the vase cap, and the porcelain was hollow inside, with plenty of room for bundles of cash that wouldn't burn if there ever was a fire, or so he told me. There were so many random fires in Wellfleet—everyone knew that those who went broke in the winter on Cape Cod—well, there was insurance money to be had.

I tried to fall asleep and dream about what the money could do for *me*, but the sheets on the bed kept me awake, wrapping me too tight as I rolled over. The sweaty linen was spoiling my chance to dream of how I would one day take the money and travel to an exotic place I'd read about in the encyclopedia, Sanibel Island in Florida. My favorite page. I wasn't sure when I would go, but I loved to whisper *Sanibel Island* to myself. I knew that place was never cold like Cape Cod, and the sun did not disappoint.

I felt like crying, but over what? It wasn't about being a barren woman anymore, because Bill had gotten us a baby. I slipped my hand inside the sheets like a pledge of allegiance over my belly that would never make a baby of its own, not a peep. All that *sexual intercoursing* turned out to be useless. That's what Bill called it, sexual intercourse-ing, his funny way of talking formal about screwing, balling, shagging, humping, dicking, and fucking. For years I put up with Bill pounding me up and down with about as much tenderness as a teenage boy on a diving board.

When a woman gets married, the husband expects it will be an easy deal to fill up her womb with life—with a baby. "Fill 'er up." Easy, like at the gas station. Progeny. That's what Bill just assumed. When you lift that big nozzle thing with a hose and then pump up the dark hole under that cute little metal door on the side of the car, gasoline pours out fast, no problem. But then the nights of intercoursing and the periods and the months and the years ticked by as I felt my womb grow harder with each intercoursing. All those years, instead of me getting pregnant, a strange emptiness moved through my body,

HUSH LITTLE FIRE 163

and Bill moved into his own bedroom. Up until then, I was certain that Bill truly believed my vagina was the portal to the unknown mysteries of existence. I was convinced that all men believed that, and yet at the same time feared it. Maybe resented it. They probably wondered, how come the split second of existence bursts into being inside a cunt and not a king? How come women have a direct line to all that forming and growing of the little fetus thing? No matter. At least all Bill's intercoursing stopped when he got the brainstorm to adopt. And it was fitting that Bill got a lump of a baby girl for an heir instead of a boy.

When Bill brought the new baby into our home from way up north, he declared, "Mary. That's her name. I know it." At the time, I thought perhaps the birth mother had already named this baby and Bill was going to honor that. But I remember feeling sick I didn't get a chance to even suggest a name for the infant. Oh no, instead I got to clean up explosions of poopy diapers and endure the endless crying. Bill was at the clinic all the time, of course, and I had no idea how to get Baby Mary to stop crying. Bottles of milk were good for ten minutes, and then the fussing would begin again. Rocking in a rocking chair didn't help, pacing the room, singing softly, or loudly, long car rides to the ocean—nothing soothed Baby Mary. Late one night, with stethoscope in hand, Bill brushed off all the crying as simple colic.

"She'll get over it." He padded back to his own bedroom in his plaid flannel pajamas and went back to sleep. A few days later, I thought I found the key to calming the baby when I was making a cup of tea for myself. The teakettle let out a long, loud whistle, which startled Baby Mary into silence. It worked once or twice, but not for long, and soon the red teakettle and Baby Mary screamed on and on together. I thought I would go out of my mind.

164 JUDITH NEWCOMB STILES

After the first five months, like the Dr. Spock book suggested, I began to feed Baby Mary cereal. Pale white sticky mush that didn't look much different from baby spit-up. However, the blessed baby cereal stopped the endless crying, and I started to feel better. One day Baby Mary randomly smiled, and then her face lit up into a bigger smile when I looked directly into her eyes. I felt tickles of happiness, like the happy hymns we sang in church. Was this what motherhood was supposed to feel like?

Motherhood-smotherhood, why was it so hard to fall asleep? When morning hit, the blinds and curtains were set just right so they wouldn't let in a smidgen of light. When a loud knocking at the front door began, I rolled over, dreaming about a boat in Sanibel Island that was knocking against a harbor wall. Knock. Knock. In the dream, I frantically tried to undo the rope so I could sail away, but the knocking was clipped and persistent. I woke up and yelled, "Just a minute. Who is it?"

I threw a raincoat on over my nightgown to answer the front door and was grateful Baby Mary was still asleep.

"Who's there?" When I opened the door, the sun was too bright as Emma, the mail lady, thrust a package at me. Emma noted the raincoat with a sneer, as if to say she'd caught me sleeping late. Fodder for town gossip.

"I didn't want to leave the package on the porch, and the mailbox is too small. Plus it has a strange scent. This package is so odoriferous."

"Odoriferous?" I was annoyed all over again with Emma, who had the habit of throwing around big words that didn't fit very well into any conversation.

The package smelled bad when I held it up to my nose and shook it.

HUSH LITTLE FIRE 165

"Need help opening it?" Emma was excited and whipped out a box cutter. Emma should have recognized that smell because she had that fussy daughter, Baby Gemma, to remind her ten times a day of that unexquisite-unmarvelous-undelightful baby smell.

"Here, I'll cut the string for you. Who's it from anyway?"

In my opinion, Emma was being nosy, but in a pleasant way, so without much thought, I let her linger and open the package. The brown paper fell off easily, and inside a shoebox there was something strange, a bunched-up baby's diaper that blasted an awful ammonia dirty-diaper stink straight up my nostrils. Just as Emma shrieked, out fell a postcard with no picture, just the words *BABY KILLER*.

◆ 28 ◆

WALTER AND BARBARA DISCUSS THE NEED FOR WIGS

Walter

2015

WHEN MARY REMEMBERED MY full name, Walter Jeremiah Stone, it felt so good, I wanted to shout, *I love you, Mary!* even though I think she was just buttering me up to borrow my glazes.

She whispered into the phone, "A little birdie told me Officer Walter Jeremiah Stone of the Wellfleet Police Department would be more than happy to lend me some precious glaze materials? Is that true?"

I gave Mary Newcombe my most expensive bentonite, my rare copper oxide, and I cleaned up my best Shimpo wheel just for her. And then I cleaned it again after she sent clay splats flying onto the wall when she threw on the wheel. I even served her coffee and homemade brownies, but still she seems oblivious to how I feel about her.

Keep trying, Barbara would surely tell me if we were drinking margaritas at the Bomby.

HUSH LITTLE FIRE   167

Today I have orders from the chief to spend the morning at the station before I go guard Nurse Haskins at the hospital. I find Chief Crocker sitting at his desk, waiting for somebody important from somewhere important to review the names of suspects involved in the Cape Cod drug ring. Since Jimmy Newcombe died, everyone at the station has stopped talking about the Christmas fire, and I want to know why.

When the chief gets nervous, he eats a lot, so he orders me to run out and buy him a meatball submarine sandwich for lunch. I don't want to make things worse by mentioning he already finished the ham-and-cheese sandwich Mrs. Crocker made him for lunch. When I drop off the submarine sandwich, the chief wants to eat it right away, which is why he immediately dismisses me to start hospital duty. It's obvious he's been biding his time, sucking on one of his red lollipops, because his tongue has a rosy-red glow that snitches on him about this bad habit. The chief keeps a big stash of lollipops in the top drawer of his desk, and he breaks the stick off when he sucks them to hide his clandestine relationship with lollipops.

At the hospital, when the nurses aren't looking, I read poetry to Barbara, but today I forgot my book. I play optimistic Pete Seeger songs on my phone to lift her spirits, yet Barbara seems to be wasting away, and she still hasn't uttered a word. Barbara has gotten so skinny that sometimes I can't make out the shape of her body under the sheets.

Chief Crocker gave me a list of questions I'm supposed to ask Nurse Haskins in order to stimulate conversation. Questions like *If you win a free dinner at Moby Dick's Restaurant, would you have their tasty salmon burger or the codfish sandwich?* The chief is always eating and chatting about food, so he thinks these questions will get her talking. But Barbara seems depressed under those bandages, and it might be cruel to mention good food.

JUDITH NEWCOMB STILES

To pass the time in the chair, I think about women. My luck with women has been lousy, but I know it's mostly my fault. Over the years, I dated different local girls, but then switched to women farther away from my mother's scrutinizing eye. The internet dates didn't work out either. Even when my mother never met my Boston girlfriends, she had a telepathic way of pinpointing their faults and the relationships fizzled out. Janice Dellapiazza was a beautiful girl with a long mane of straight black hair that flowed down her back like a blanket. She was nice, very intelligent, and was studying for a complicated degree in adolescent behavior. She liked to chew gum a lot and seemed to always have a minty gray wad in her mouth that flitted around when she talked. The relationship was chugging along, the sex was great—in fact, it was spectacular. I overlooked Janet's gum-chewing habit and I began to fantasize about our future together. Many times after jogging, after dinners, after coffee, after sex, Janice Dellapiazza offered me a stick of gum, and soon I became a frequent gum chewer.

"Walter, you look like a cow, chewing that nasty gum. Spit it out. It's a disgusting habit," my mother told me. Soon I broke up with Janice.

I settle into eating my own meatball submarine sandwich and have this wild idea that maybe Barbara will enjoy the smell and ask me for a bite. I wish I could have brought her a bottle of beer. You never know—just one beer might get her back on track. But when I study her sleeping face, she seems so much smaller in the hospital bed—her arms look like chicken bones with an IV that feeds her.

I crumple up my sandwich wrapper into a ball and toss it across the room into the wastebasket. It might perk her up if I tell her how much fun it is to make pottery. Maybe the exciting

HUSH LITTLE FIRE

169

details of how to fire a raku kiln will take her mind off her troubles. But no, it might upset her if I mention the word *fire*, so I'll talk about Mary Newcombe instead. It's easy to ask Barbara's advice when she's sound asleep.

"Listen, I really need your advice. Mary Newcombe is back in town, but I just can't seem to catch her attention. I do all these things for her, but she doesn't seem to get the idea that I really like her. Maybe I even love her after all these years? I don't know . . ."

Barbara parts her lips and says in a scratchy whisper, "*Keeeep trying.*"

"Oh my God, what did you say?"

Did Barbara just speak? I'm stunned and hurry to her bedside to hold her hand. I look into her eyes and am terrified to see life seeping out of her pupils. Death is beginning to take over. It is quiet fading-away type death. I can feel it.

Barbara lets out a hoarse moan.

"Waaal-ter, don't leave."

Barbara lifts her hand and touches the bandages on the flattish part where a nose should be, and I can see she is missing fingers.

"What do I look like?" Her voice is raspy and she's crying. "Tell me."

What's left of Barbara's other hand is very cold and I would rub it to warm her up, but that might hurt her, so I gently cup both my hands over her bandaged fingers like she's inside the middle of my prayer.

"Walter, I have no hair anymore."

"Don't worry, they make beautiful real-hair wigs now for cancer victims, and they can make one just for you."

Barbara raises her arm and taps the bandages in the same spot where a nose should be, her hand moving in slow motion.

"I can help you. I'll bring you a brochure about wigs."

"No thanks, but thanks anyway. What I need is a brochure about noses."

"Hey, it's not that bad." I smile and try to be upbeat, except I have the urge to cry, but a police officer is never supposed to cry.

"Walter, you look so gray. Why does everything look so gray?"

"You have to get better so we can have a good game of darts. We miss you at the Bomby. I promise I won't let you win."

"Look out the window. Gray skies every single day. Even these awful bandages are gray." Barbara holds her hand directly in front of my eyes.

"But the bandages are white." I gently pet her hand.

"No they're not! I feel like the inside of my body is turning gray."

"Don't think like that. Everything will be all right. I promise."

But I am not telling the truth. I have a horrible feeling that Barbara's insides are actually turning gray, rotting slowly toward death. It's as if the winter sky has been waiting, just waiting for Barbara to weaken, ready to snuff out her life once and for all.

I will never mention to Chief Crocker that Barbara finally spoke.

◆ 29 ◆

MARY'S BIG DINNER DATE

Mary

I ONLY HAVE AN hour to pull myself together before Tom Murphy and the big dinner date. To any other woman, it would be no big deal, but I haven't done the dating game for years. People usually gain weight over the holidays, but I lost five pounds because a thimbleful of spit left my mouth for the genetic test, and I'm scared. I finally moved the box of Jimmy's ashes into the pantry, then behind the TV, then under my bed, then to the basement. Pushing away everything I don't want to think about is more exhausting than lifting weights. Getting ready for a date is worse.

I'm sure all my hormonal juices have dried up, but perhaps this fix-it guy knows how to oil my hinges. When I met Tom Murphy, I instantly liked him, but certain things don't make sense, especially with that dog. First of all, Tom Murphy picks me up in an ordinary black sedan and not his red pickup truck, so is he a bachelor with two vehicles? When we park at Mahoney's Restaurant, he leaves his cell phone on the dashboard, but sitting inside, he pulls out a different phone from his pocket and answers with, "I'll call you back." A man with two cell phones? He taps in a quick text with a scowl and then looks across the table at me. Dormant romance vibes well up inside me, and I like this Tom Murphy a lot, but I hardly know why. He smiles so nicely at me. Just me.

The waitress has a dead look in her eyes. Pen and pad in hand, she doesn't look up when she asks if we want to start with a drink. Her uniform of a black button-down shirt and black slacks have been washed so many times that her clothes look weary. She doesn't try to muster up a smile or courteous small talk, and I guess she's grumpy because tips will be lean for many months to come. Tom Murphy orders a margarita, no ice, yes salt, and out of my mouth pops, "I'll have one too." The sirens of drinkie are calling, but I promise I'll only take one sip. Much to my surprise, Tom Murphy orders baby back ribs, my favorite, and parrot me orders the same.

Two sips of the lovely margarita, and it comes pouring out of my memory bank that this early stage with a new man is like an empty page in a teenage girl's diary. I can create in my mind a *charming, kind, honest, thoughtful, art-loving, wood-chopping, nice-to-children, politically independent volunteer firefighter Tom Murphy man* who likes to cook and fix things. But I put the brakes on this nonsense, *stop*, because as a new relationship progresses, there can be an ugly moment when what you imagined is not what you get. What am I about to get with this man sitting across from me? His hands are too smooth, with well-tended cuticles and not a single callus, when he picks up his drink. And it bothered me on the ride over that all he wanted to talk about was the clinic fire.

"So, do you like charbroiled ribs too?" He leans across the table.

HUSH LITTLE FIRE 173

"I *love* ribs. They're my favorite, quite nourishing in fact, and I especially love to barbecue ribs on the grill with my secret delicious recipe for sauce with a dash of beer, and . . . and . . . soaked overnight with overripe garden tomatoes and sometimes a splash of brandy." He nods enthusiastically.

"Do you prefer pork or beef?" he asks, carefully rotating his drink like this is some kind of profound question.

"Pork. But I try not to think about the actual pig, of course. Pork ribs are so delicious. I don't know why people are vegetarians, do you?"

"I never met anyone who stayed a true vegetarian for their entire life. You know, Mary, I have this theory about humans and eating meat. This may sound sort of heavy, and please don't take it the wrong way, but whenever I see a person eating meat, it's a reminder that every man at heart is a killer." Tom Murphy fondles his drink.

"What do you mean?"

"We certainly don't like to think of ourselves that way." He wipes his mouth slowly with a black cloth napkin. "It's kind of a philosophical theory, and it's *not* something I think about every day, but you know, we all have a disconnect about killing." He tilts his head and starts brushing imaginary crumbs off the table. "We don't like to admit that everyone who ever eats meat, even just once, is a killer once removed."

"Hmm. I never really thought of it that way," I say, lying once again. I've thought of this many times, but I wish he'd cut the philosophy talk and just kiss me.

"Chief Crocker thinks the Christmas fire was caused by a cigarette, but the fire inspector is looking at arson. I'm just a volunteer in the department, but it's an interesting question that the guys at the firehouse were batting around the other day. If a random fire was started with a careless cigarette, does that make the smoker a killer once removed?"

I snap a breadstick in two and brush my own pile of crumbs into a tiny hill on the table. Yikes. What kind of question is this for our very first date? And Nurse Haskins is still alive.

"These are really good breadsticks," I say as we sink into uncomfortable silence, so I order another margarita and pretend to study the candle on the table as I slowly turn it in circles. Moments like this are half the reason I stopped dating years ago, because each new possible guy was like peeling an onion. And dating became even more complicated when Danny was born. My last dinner date, was it over a year ago? The guy looked like an onion, round cheeks, a bulbous forehead, but I didn't mind. Paul seemed nice. I had grand designs that we had so much in common and could eventually become like a lovely scenic jigsaw puzzle where the pieces fit together. But dating is tricky, because I have a kid, a subject Paul, the nice onion, failed to mention once. I started out with this great idea of what we could become as a couple, but then fate handed me an onion and said, *Peel it*. So over several dinner dates and a visit to one god-awful-boring baseball game, I peeled back the layers of Paul and was pissed he'd never even thought of inviting Danny to see the game. Not to mention he never once continued a conversation when I casually brought up my son. So much for dinner dating, and now it is difficult for me to make polite conversation with Tom Murphy, because eating ribs requires a lot of concentration and I can't eat ribs with my fingers in this nice restaurant.

"These ribs look delicious," he says, eagerly picking up the bones with both hands. Great. Tom Murphy and I could be good.

HUSH LITTLE FIRE

"So tell me, what line of work did you retire from before you became a volunteer firefighter?"

"I was a builder. In the contracting business. It was a decent-size company, Murphy & Sons in Boston."

"Is it a family business?"

"I wish. The owner has a son Thomas Murphy, but unfortunately not me. But I was still able to retire early."

"Why Cape Cod?"

"You know the answer. The ocean, the beauty, the peacefulness."

"Funny, but you don't have hands like a construction worker. I'd have guessed you were a musician. I mean your hands are so nice."

"I worked in the office most of the time," he says, reaching over and touching my hand. "Tell me about Danny. I'm sorry he couldn't join us. When's he coming back to the Cape? I was going to ask him to help me on my boat. He likes boats, right?"

"I guess so."

"I can text him a picture of my boat. What's his text?"

"You want to text him?" Oh, where is Tiny Mary when I need her? Why all these questions? I certainly don't want a potential boyfriend texting my son.

"Who's he staying with while you're gone?"

"My friend Jean. She's from Wellfleet. We grew up together and then moved to New York many years ago." I hope this is enough of an answer and he won't ask me more.

"Is Jean a potter too?"

I put down my new margarita carefully. I could never explain the full story of Jean to this man I hardly know.

"The only thing I can tell you about Jean is that we started a small pottery school on Fourth Avenue and Ninth Street in Brooklyn in an old car-repair garage that we rented before Park Slope got ridiculously expensive. Danny and I live upstairs."

This is kind of a lie, a sort of half-truth, but how could I explain the Jean situation without sounding like a weirdo and sending Tom running in the other direction?

I don't have the nerve to tell him, not yet, that Jean and I drove over the Bourne Bridge after graduation from high school, and Jean has never been back to Wellfleet since. Birdie gave us an old station wagon and lots of money neatly folded in rubber bands. While Jean waited in the car, Birdie made me swear never to tell anyone where she hid the money around the house.

"When I'm dead and gone, in case you need money, I want *you* to know I have bills like this in every lamp in this house. Watch me. First, carefully unscrew the fixtures here under the vase cap, and see inside here? The money is safe. You should know too that I have many lamps like this in the Newcombe family storage unit."

That day, Birdie handed me wads of cash because she loved the idea of Jean and me escaping Cape Cod to become artists in New York. My mother had tears in her eyes when she waved goodbye, and for a second I wanted to bring her with us.

"Should I order you another margarita?"

"Oh no, I shouldn't."

"Tell me more about your potter friend Jean."

"On second thought, I'll take that drink."

What I can't tell this man without three more margaritas is that Jean and I planned to meet men in New York who were poets and painters, and we would marry them, and our children would grow up together and be best friends too. But Jean crapped out on me. When we went to Greenwich Village bars to meet guys, Jean had a habit of drifting off to meet someone

HUSH LITTLE FIRE

named Les, her *new friend*. Jean had fallen in love with Les, an accomplished personal injury lawyer who happened to have an enormous trust fund and drove a red Porsche. Jean was in love with Les and especially the red Porsche. She talked about the car incessantly, and Les was in love with young Jean, or so I was told many times back then.

It took me a while to get used to Les, real name Leslie, because, honestly, Leslie looked a little strange. Leslie's skin appeared to be stretched flat with a tight sheet of Saran Wrap, and it never seemed to change color, a summer tan under her helmet of spiky blond hair. A few months into the Jean-Leslie relationship, I learned why her skin looked like that. Leslie's trust fund came to her from her father, who had made a fortune in the sixties from inventing a spray-on preservative for fruit and vegetables called Forever Freshness. Grocers loved it because bananas and apples didn't go rotten for weeks. Forever Freshness was popular with all the supermarket chains, and Leslie's father got very rich until the FDA banned the spray. But he was a resourceful businessman, so he patented a similar solution as ladies' makeup. Soon millions of women were buying Forever Fresh Face. Leslie had so much money that for Jean's birthday one year, she bought the garage building that housed our pottery school, and she did this out of love for Jean when we were totally broke and close to bankrupt. Jean and I were about to crawl back to Wellfleet with our tails between our legs, but Leslie saved us with a casual stroke of a pen in her checkbook. Leslie was a thunderbolt of goodness in the history of our pottery school. And when I became pregnant with Danny, both Leslie and Jean were thrilled, and their stomachs puffed out a bit as if they were pregnant themselves. Or maybe in some roundabout way, they thought it best they assume the role of *other parent*, since Danny's father was unknown.

Not now, surely, but when is the right time to explain to Tom Murphy that Danny has no father and is being raised by me and two sort-of aunts who are in love with each other? They never had babies of their own but they go to Danny's school performances, they take him trick-or-treating, they went to parent-teacher conferences when I had the flu and went to parent-teacher conferences when I didn't have the flu, scolded Danny for not doing his math homework, got into arguments with his soccer coach, and the list goes on.

So I take a deep breath and say to Tom Murphy, "Danny's father has never been in the picture, and this week Danny is staying with Jean, who is in love with a woman named Leslie, and they take excellent care of him when I'm away."

"You are very lucky to have such good people as backup," he says, smiling.

Whoa. What an answer. I can finally think of him as just Tom.

Tom's cell phone ding-a-lings, and he immediately answers it, looking worried. He props the phone on his shoulder, pulls out three fifty-dollar bills and lays them on the table.

"I've been called up. There's a fire at the boatyard in Wellfleet. Let's go! You'll have to come with me."

As we hustle toward his car, Tom puts his arm around me and hurries me along. One-handed, he slaps onto the roof one of those suction-cup red-light bubbles that cops use, which announces that we're in a hurry to a fire. A cherry light, like on TV, is spinning on top of this car. So exciting for a girl like me.

◆ 30 ◆

WALTER WATCHES
ANGEL BABY BURN

Walter

B Y THE TIME I arrive at the boatyard with four of my police pals, the fire has spread, leaping from boat to boat, giving off the sickening smell of melting fiberglass. Chief Crocker is running around willy-nilly, monitoring the tow trucks as they move sailboats into the street away from the flames.

"*Walt!* You're in charge of crowd control!"

"Yes, sir," I shout back to the chief, wondering what crowd control really means in the middle of the night when hardly anybody's here. The motorboats are shrouded in white plastic covers stretched taut over the frames, and they look like mutant sea creatures being dragged against their will. The old clapboard office building is burning out of control near two large boats parked too close to the blazing building. No chance of saving them.

A town catastrophe and a decent fire will get Wellfleet people out of bed even after midnight, and in a blink, a handful of people arrive here to rubberneck at the fire. It's mildly annoying when that new volunteer firefighter rushes to the scene. Tom what's-his-name jumps out of his car and maneuvers the heavy firefighter gear over his clothes. He's such a washashore, showing off like Houdini when he jockeys the heavy helmet over his head and disappears into a pack of firefighters. My heart bounces up and down when Mary steps out of Houdini's car. Was she riding around with that chump? Were they on a *date*?

I spot Mary inching her way toward Lisa Doanne, who is standing in a small crowd, and why is Lisa hysterically crying? An older woman turns around to hug Lisa, and surprise, surprise, it's Trudy Bale. Good time to sneak over and schmooze with Mary.

"This is so terrible. What happened?" I overhear Mary say to Lisa.

"Oh, I could die! *Angel Baby* is completely ruined. What will we do now?" Lisa turns to Mary. "And I'm so sorry, I should introduce you two. This is Trudy Bale, Patrick's mom and the sweetest soon-to-be mother-in-law a girl could ever have."

Lisa is perky and smiling, with an odd disconnect from her histrionics a few seconds ago, and I wish I had a notepad to take notes. I squint at Trudy, who puts a cigarette between her caved-in lips. The shape of her forehead is a lot like Patrick's, with that fetal-alcohol flatness. Of course, I wouldn't take notes on the forehead—it's irrelevant—but both mother and son have meat-cleaver chins. In the glow of the fire, I can see life hasn't been good to Trudy Bale. She has a drinker's body, more like a blob on toothpick legs, and a splotchy red face not from sunburn. I wonder if it's hard to smoke without teeth.

"Patrick's on Nantucket. I just called him," Lisa shouts to Trudy. "He's devastated. He loved this boat like it was his baby." Her soon-to-be mother-in-law doesn't react, face

HUSH LITTLE FIRE 181

frozen, like nothing is wrong. I pull a grocery receipt out of my pocket and scribble a few notes on the back.

"*Angel Baby* was Jimmy and Patrick's boat." Lisa repeats this a few times, loud enough for everyone to hear.

"Actually, I don't think it was *their* boat." Mary sounds a tad grouchy. "As I understand it, the boat is in my mother's name now. She took over ownership of *Angel Baby* and paid all the bills. She'll be so upset, but I'll wait until morning to call her."

I hear Lisa whisper something in Trudy's ear that sounds vaguely like *fuck her.*

The firefighters are valiantly on the attack, with blasts of water rushing from several hoses. The flames are winning. I would never say this to anyone, but sometimes it seems unfair that people shake their heads and say things like *such a destructive fire* when the flames are simply looking for oxygen to uphold the burning. Nobody is inside the boatyard, nobody's hurt, so for a moment I allow myself to appreciate the awesome blaze.

"Stand back, everyone! You can't stand here. Move!" yells the chief. "*Stone*, you're supposed to be in charge of crowd control." I wave my arms and herd a group of people away, all of them walking backward like robots.

After a few minutes, I stand face-to-face with Mary. "I'm on duty now, but do you need me to give you a ride home?" Mary takes my hand and softens the way she did in high school when her casual touch teased me with hope of becoming her boyfriend.

"Thanks, but not yet, Walter. I'm not cold," she says through her chattering teeth. Is she planning to ride home with that chump?

I worry maybe Mary doesn't respect my work as a police officer. She must know I've been stagnating as a low-level cop in the Wellfleet Police Department all these years. The truth is I had a miserable time reading tests and failed the detective exams several times because, according to my mother, I was born with a *bad case of dyslexia*. Hard luck for me, I never got a significant promotion, but I never felt sorry for myself, so I hope Mary doesn't feel sorry for me either. I patrol the onlookers but don't stray far from Mary, and throughout, our eyes keep meeting. I won't forget to discuss my observations about Lisa's and Trudy's odd behavior with the chief. I won't mention a thing about Mary. Maybe I should offer Mary a ride home one more time?

♦ 31 ♦

CELIBATE MOTHER GETS TWO OFFERS IN ONE NIGHT

Mary

THE FIRE IS CHASTENED down to embers and puddles of water, so Tom and I are allowed to go home. I will never forget this fire. Dinner with Tom was nice, but wow, I got another chance to observe a fire *outside* a kiln, and it's like nothing else. I know fire. I've studied the fire of kilns for years, and I accept that the bricks serve a purpose, containing the miracle and keeping it from doing damage. But tonight I got to watch an inferno roam freely into the night—magnificent flames slapping at the sky, gobbling up oxygen, so much bigger than a beach fire—and now I have a colossal stiff neck from looking up so much. While Tom and the firefighters worked hard to snuff it out, I secretly wanted the fire to burn up the heavens a while longer, even though the firefighters were squelching it out. Tom's face and hands are smeared with black soot, like he's been working in a coal mine all day. Neither of us speaks as we get in his car. We've known each other less than a week, but this feels like we're easy friends who've known each other a long time. I wish.

On the ride home, Tom's left hand grips the steering wheel and his right wanders over and finds mine. He squeezes my hand and doesn't let go. His fingers curl nicely around mine all the way to Birdie's house, and I feel like singing a song, a quiet one.

Tom walks me to the front door and leans in to kiss my forehead. "Sorry for the interruption tonight. We must try dinner again."

"I'd love that."

I open the front door, and something feels off, like Miss Mary Newcombe is standing on a frozen pond about to crack under her feet. The drawers to a cabinet have been tossed on the floor, the door to the basement is wide open, and several lamps are shattered, with broken pieces littering the floor.

"You can't go inside. This is a crime scene."

"I want to see for myself. I live here."

"No, no, no, Mary. And you can't sleep here tonight. It's too dangerous. You can spend the night in my apartment. I'll sleep on the couch."

"Me? Sleep at your apartment? But you? On the couch?"

"Sure."

A police car pulls up, cherry lights flashing, and out jumps Walter and another cop. Walter hurries over to me and gives me a hug, pulling me in tight to his body.

"Are you all right?"

"For Chrissakes, I'm fine. It's the house that's been trashed, not me."

The other cop rushes inside with Tom, ordering Walter to stay with me. It's still really strange to see my art friend from long ago dressed up as a cop. I'm eye level with his badge.

"I hear you went out to dinner with Tom what's-his-name?"

"Tom Murphy."

HUSH LITTLE FIRE 185

"You know, he's not from around here. He's not like you and me. He's a washashore." Walter looks down into my eyes like a parent.

"Washashore? Don't be such a snob, Walt."

"I'm not being snobby."

"Yes you are. The Pilgrims were technically washashores, and anyway, you forget I'm adopted, so what does that make me?"

"Sorry, I don't mean to be rude. Hey, it's getting very late. If you need to, you can stay at my house for the rest of the night. I have a guest bedroom."

"Thanks, but I'm all set."

Who would have guessed that I, Miss Mary Newcombe, the zero-social-life celibate, would get two offers in one night.

"I'll be over bright and early in the morning to assess the situation so you can get back inside, hopefully by noon." Walter moves in so close I can feel his breath on my neck. "It's great you're staying in Wellfleet now. I want you to know, I've changed a lot since high school."

"So have we all."

It's past four in the morning, and no way do I want to think about high school. I want Walter to drink five cups of coffee, get on the case, and figure out who vandalized my mother's house. I look up at Walter's face, and maybe it's an animal thing, but he still gives off waves of kindness peppered with a sexy baseball energy. After all these years, his body's still solid, a pillar of goodness, and it's hard to describe, but here he is on my mother's front lawn, sending pheromones into the airwaves that land on me.

"Maybe you wanna come with me this Friday to free wine tasting at Kevin's."

It's the middle of the night and is Walter asking me out? Free wine tasting is not exactly a date.

186 JUDITH NEWCOMB STILES

"Free wine tasting would be nice. And of course, I'll pay you for the copper carbonate and the use of your studio as soon as I get paid."

"No need to pay me." Walter hugs me again. "You came back to Wellfleet at just the right time. Everything is changing so fast with my coming retirement. I'm excited. When I leave the force, I'm even gonna grow a beard."

"A beard? That's nice."

Nice, nice, nice—everything is *not* nice. I wonder where this middle-of-the-night conversation is going.

"Seriously, Mary. Sometimes I find myself wishing some things turned out differently. Hey, remember our senior year in high school, when you kissed me at graduation? I'll always remember that." Walter is rubbing my cold red hands between his cold red hands.

"Huh? I kissed you?"

"If I remember correctly, you were kind of drunk, and we were making out, and, well, then Jean and I were making out, and then you and I were making out again until you puked all over the refreshment table. But I was okay with it. Really, I was. Do you remember that?"

"Sort of," I lie.

Walter looks up at the stars and murmurs, "You hardly ever come back here. Well, I've only seen you a few times since high school, four times in fact, 1999, 2000, 2007, 2010, but now it's great hanging out with you in the studio."

"You always had a good memory."

"Stone! Put up the crime scene tape, pronto, so I can go home and get some sleep!" shouts the other officer.

"Yes, sir!"

Walter stomps away, but then he hurries back to give me a kiss on my mouth. Did Walter just kiss me? So much has happened to me since the graduation party in high school, and yet it seems like a lot of Walter's world has moved on too slowly. He unrolls yellow tape around the house, and I catch up with him to ask him about something that's been bugging me.

"Before you go, can I ask you, how well do you know Katie Snow? I don't really know Katie."

"If you're really asking me about her car and Jimmy, just say so. It's an open investigation, so I'm sorry, but I can't discuss it."

"Oh come on, we're old friends. It's public information that Jimmy was driving Katie's car when the accident happened."

"True."

"And it's public information that she took over his oyster beds when he went bankrupt, so how well do you know her?"

"Not very well, but I guess you heard from your mom that Jimmy was paying child support for the baby. Don't repeat this, but everyone knows she was just playing him to get money."

"What do you mean by that?"

"Everyone knows Katie Snow was fooling around with any guy that walked through the Bomby's front door. And between you and me, she talked Jimmy into believing the baby was his. He was paying for everything with that baby. Honorable guy. But my aunt told me—because her sister told her— that Jimmy took a test, and it turned out the baby wasn't his after all."

"What's the baby's name?"

"Everyone calls Katie's little one Sunshine."

♦ 32 ♦

TOM MURPHY'S SQUISHY DOUBLE BED

Mary

TOM'S PLACE IS IN the middle of the High Tide Apartments, but how in the world did he qualify for affordable housing? His apartment is tidy, like an empty stage set with no clutter, not even a small pile of mail. There is one cereal bowl in the dish drain and one towel on the towel rack. True to his word, I get to sleep in the bedroom on a squishy double bed while Tom sleeps on the couch.

In the morning, I sulk for a few minutes because Tom never tried to jump my bones last night. I slept lightly, hoping like a fool he'd slink through the dark and hop into bed with me. At least he's making a fine breakfast of eggs with three strips of bacon, and they're sunny-side up without a single nick to the yolks.

"Last night, I heard the police say that one of the boats damaged in the fire belonged to your cousin Jimmy. Is that where he kept his boat in the winter before he passed away?"

"I'm not sure. Jimmy and I lost touch."

"But I thought Danny went out on his boat with him every summer?"

HUSH LITTLE FIRE

"How do you know about that?"

"Your mother told me."

I twirl a circle in the egg yolks with my fork, my mind racing. How much has he been talking to my mother? Birdie bigmouth. Over too many margaritas at dinner, he kept asking me about Jimmy's fishing business. It should be obvious that my feelings about Jimmy are raw and I can't stand talking about him.

After breakfast, I borrow Tom's truck and drive over to Walter's studio to trim my half-finished pots. The studio is bigger than his house and looks more like an airplane hangar. His kiln shed is massive, and when I poke around, I lust after Walter's beautiful kilns, starting with a regular propane downdraft gas kiln, Connie, a raku kiln, and an electric Skutt kiln, Connie Junior, neatly arranged in a row. He could run a school with all this equipment.

Step Five: Trimming the Clay off the Chihuahuas' Urns

I don't know how other potters feel about trimming, but for me, it's akin to shaving my legs. My 23andMe is out in the universe, shaving me bald for the truth, but right now I must push away all the chaos in my life and focus only on making pots. This is why potters are potters, because when I sit at the wheel, all that other codswallop goes away and I'm free. I center the first leather-hard urn on the wheel head and hold it in place with clay waddies, which are little blobs of clay. I brace my arm on my thigh as I shave the foot of the urn with a sharp loop tool, and the excess clay spools off as the wheel turns. This is the part where it's easy to mess up, so go slowly and no daydreaming.

I trim the lid with the same loop tools, then check with calipers to measure if the lid has dried properly and will still fit on the flange of the urn. I take a damp sponge and smooth the surface. Other potters use natural sponges, but I like to cut up sponges from the car wash. At this leather-hard stage, other potters often carve their initials on the bottom, but I don't. I usually sign my pots later with a brush dipped in black stain, but I won't do that now, because it's not my place to have my name go with the deceased when they pass to the other side, wherever that is. However, I will carve an infinity sign on the bottom to encourage the dead Chihuahua on its way to the unknown.

I throw the shaved trimmings in a slurry bucket to slake down to goopy mud that can be recycled to make the next pot. Or should I throw this batch of trimmings back into the sea where the clay came from? No, I'll save it in case another one of the seven dwarfs croaks.

Walter is over at Birdie's house and calls me to say I can't go inside yet to clean up the mess, but he tells me he did some sweeping.

"Thanks for doing that. You didn't have to."

"Tell me, who goes in Birdie's house besides you and your son?"

"A girl named Lisa Doanne usually cleans the house once a week, but she was at the boatyard fire."

"Yep. She was there. We talked about the boats. Her boy-friend's boat, or rather your mother's boat now. I don't trust her."

"Me neither."

I cover my urns in plastic to dry and get ready for a bisque firing. I feel brave and decide to check my phone for any emails from 23andMe. And oh my God, they sent me a new one.

It tells me from cyberspace, "Are you getting excited to receive your results? We are! Here are two great tools you will be able to use to expand your family circle and deepen your personal connections. The result will be ready in one week."

The words in the email are cold and detached, but my head is on fire, because I'm one week away from answers.

"With DNA Relatives, you can find and connect with people that share DNA with you, compare your results with them and message them."

What message? Like *Dear Relative, please explain why she abandoned me?*

"With Share and Compare, you can view your genetic similarities and differences with close family and friends. Find out whether your mom or your dad gave you specific traits."

Like what? And siblings? It never occurred to me I could have brothers and sisters, let alone the possibility of meeting them. This has been such a black hole of sadness my whole life, and in one week, I'll get the results. They sign the email, "Uniquely Yours, The 23andMe Team."

♦ 33 ♦

MARY LOOKS FOR HER BIRTH MOTHER IN THE MIRROR

Mary

AGAINST WALTER'S ORDERS, I go back to my mother's house before the yellow tape is down. I pause in the hallway in front of the antique mirror and wonder if I look too old and ugly for dating. I spent a fair amount of time ogling myself in this mirror when I was a kid, and my favorite thing was to blink my eyes fast until I made myself dizzy, hoping that when I opened my eyes I'd see a ghost. Back then, I longed to see my real mother hiding inside the mirror, so I talked to the mirror and made puffs of steamy breath on the glass to help conjure her up. I played this game endlessly, the way children without brothers and sisters like to do. Now I exhale steamy breath on the mirror just for fun, but the girl in the mist looks like an exhausted raccoon, with deep circles under her eyes—no wonder Tom doesn't want to sleep with me. In the reflection, I see Walter behind me, ringing the doorbell. Uh-oh.

"Good morning. You shouldn't be inside here yet. That's why the tape's still up."

HUSH LITTLE FIRE

193

"Walter, my mother lives here. I live here."

"The chief says you have to come down to the station for fingerprints. I'm sorry. I'm sorry. I'm sorry." Walter says sorry some more as his cheeks swell up and turn red. "Last night, the nurse, Barbara Haskins . . . she was overcome."

"Overcome?"

"She died." His voice is shrill and shaky.

"Oh God, I hope she didn't suffer."

"Suffer? She did nothing but suffer. I know because I was assigned to stand outside her door and guard her. She suffered terribly, and then she got pneumonia, and then her heart gave out."

"May she rest in peace."

"*Rest in peace?* Where? I'd like to know where her soul is resting right now. She didn't go to church. She told me she stopped believing in God. This means she has no soul, as far as I know."

I can see Walter is taking this bad. I hardly knew Barbara Haskins, but I begin to sink down into Walter's despair.

"The chief sent me to find you. He wants to have a word with you."

"About what?"

"He also wants to speak with your son and Birdie."

"Danny's in school down in Brooklyn, and Birdie's in Florida."

"I told him that. Just come with me now. I'll be right there with you."

"You're making me nervous. Why does he want to talk to *me*?"

"Routine. Chief Crocker will explain everything. You remember Billy Crocker?"

JUDITH NEWCOMB STILES

"Sure. I saw him at the boatyard, but he didn't say hello. The last time I talked to Billy Crocker, he was about fifteen years old. Tell me, what's this all about?"

Walter stands up straight, arms at his side, feet together like he's about to march off in a marching band.

"Just come with me. I'm just following orders. You don't have to sit in the back of the squad car like you've been arrested or anything. Sit up front with me."

"Okay, but what should I expect when I get there?"

"You'll get fingerprinted. I'll do that. We have EZ Prints now, so no more dirty ink. It's revolutionary, and they can scan the prints for results in seconds."

"If he asks me about Nurse Haskins, I hardly remember her."

"Since Barbara passed, this is a murder investigation. And they're looking at arson. And when the chief asks you questions, just tell the truth."

I know the first question Chief Crocker will ask is, *Where were you on Christmas night at the time of the fire?*

I'm still not sure where I was. Olatunji.

I sit in the front seat of the squad car with Walter, grateful he stopped talking.

My cell phone rings, and big uh-oh, it's Jean and Leslie on speakerphone, which means double trouble if they're calling together.

"You have to come back. Danny is suspended from school."

"What happened?" *I'm not sure I really want to know.*

Jean starts out slowly, very controlled, but then bumps it up a few notches to her screaming-harpy voice. "He started a fire on school property!"

"Correction," interrupts Leslie. "It was outside on a nearby playground, which is technically Parks Department property."

HUSH LITTLE FIRE 195

"Nice to hear from you too . . . how's the weather down there in Brooklyn?" I go at it sweet and light for Walter's benefit.

"Mary, you sound strange. Have you been drinking?"

"I'm fine. I'm in the car with my old friend Walter Stone. Jeanie, you remember Walt from art class and the *police* force?"

"This is fucking serious. Let me spell it out for you. Danny set a trash can filled with paper on fire with a group of other students during school hours." I jam my phone to my ear so Walter can't hear.

"Jeanie, this is not a good time to talk," I sputter into the phone, and say goodbye. My stomach is squeezing up breakfast residue.

At the police station, I find the ladies' room and reassure Walter I'll be right back. Inside a stall, I whip out my cell phone. "I can't talk long, but what the hell happened?"

"We're on speakerphone, so Danny, go ahead. Tell your mother in your own words," orders Leslie.

"It's not fair. I wasn't trying to wreck anything. I was showing my friends Jimmy's cool lens. They didn't believe I could start a fire with that little fucker."

"*You started a fire* with Jimmy's old lens on Parks Department property?"

"It's not like you think. It was in a metal garbage can. It was only newspaper. Homeless guys burn shit in those cans all the time."

"This is bad, very bad. But I have to go. I'll call you tonight."

"One more thing, Mom. Please tell Aunt Jean I'm allowed to play video games since they won't let me go to school, right?"

"Wrong!"

196 JUDITH NEWCOMB STILES

★ ★ ★

Walter is pleasant during the EZ Prints process, patiently explaining what he is going to do next.

"They will question you in that room over there, but don't worry, I'll be with you the whole time, even though I won't actually be with you."

"You'll be with me, but you won't be with me?"

"What I mean is, I'll be watching on the surveillance cameras."

"Should I be worried about this? I'm totally freaked-out worried."

"Just tell the truth as best you can. If I think you need to stop and get a lawyer, I'll flash the overhead lights in the room."

"Maybe I should get a lawyer right now."

"The light switch is right by the vending machines, and I'll just happen to buy a candy bar and blink the lights off if I think you might get yourself in trouble without a lawyer."

"Walter, I think I'm going to faint."

Walter keeps repeating in a righteous whisper, "*Just tell the truth.*"

I wish I knew the truth. I want to grab him and shake the stars right out of his Boy Scout eyes.

◆ 34 ◆
EZ PRINTS AND OLATUNJI
Mary

I'M SITTING ACROSS AN EZ Prints spreadsheet on a computer printout with my name, *Mary Newcombe*, in bold letters above my address in Brooklyn, my birth date, and other personal information that's hard to read upside down. I know Walter warned me, but still I'm astonished at how much the interrogation room in Wellfleet looks like the set of a TV cop show. They tell me to sit at a cafeteria-type table in a cheap metal chair, surrounded by dirty walls and a bright overhead light that must be megawatts, because it shines right through my eyelids when I close them. *Olatunji. Olatunji.*

In walks Chief Billy Crocker, struggling to suck in his big belly. He looks like a kid playing dress-up cop, and his ears stick way out like two Wiffle balls glued to a balding buzz cut. I remember as kids, Jimmy and I made fun of his ears sticking out like that, which, of course, led Jimmy to make fun of my dad's ears. The funny stick-out ears must be one of those common recessive Cape Cod traits dating back to Myles Standish.

Billy Crocker's father, old Chief Crocker, was a stern-looking man, and he was good at scaring us kids. One look and Jimmy and I would scatter and run, but he had ordinary flat ears, which must have made his job much easier.

"Hello, Mary Newcombe. Long time no see. Well, not since the boatyard fire. How ya doing?"

"I'm fine, Chief Crocker. Nice to see you too." But what I really want to say is, *Hi, Billy, you look ridiculous in that costume, and by the way, it's too tight. Next size up would fit better.*

"Would you like some coffee, water, soda, anything I can get you?" the chief asks.

"No thank you."

There is a big clunky camera to record this meeting, not at all hidden, and as I stare into the eye of the camera, my hands begin to shake. I realign my rear on the metal chair just as two more people enter the interrogation room—a woman in an expensive mannish but womanized suit, and a cop who is wearing a white shirt and a sinister black tie. They both have ID tags hanging in front of their chests that I can't decipher, and both are clutching Styrofoam cups of coffee. Walter introduces them with a bogus lighthearted lilt to his voice.

"This is Sandra Cunningham and Carl Babinski, who stopped by to ask you a few questions. I'm going to take notes, and in addition, we will be recording this meeting. Are you okay with that?"

"I'm fine with that." It feels like Chief Crocker is winding an alarm clock tighter and tighter until it will ring and explode on me. *Olatunji. Olatunji.* Where did these two come from? State police?

"Good afternoon, I'm Special Agent Cunningham with the FBI, and we are here because we hope you can help us

HUSH LITTLE FIRE

199

reconstruct the events of December twenty-fifth that led to the death of Miss Barbara Haskins. Please state your name, address, and age."

"My name is Mary Newcombe. I'm fifty-two years old, and I live at 222 Fourth Avenue in Brooklyn, New York." Sandra is wearing a cashmere suit and silk blouse, and together with her shoes, her outfit must cost more than a truckload of clay and glazes. She has that Ivy League haircut, a straight blond pageboy, and her perky smile belies the predator in her green eyes. I can't stand hearing her Ivy League voice, a neutral tone with no accent—the way the Ivies beat out all traces of regional twangs in their students. What is she doing working for the FBI? Embedded in her speech is the simple reminder that Ivies are better and smarter than the little people. Special Agent Cunningham is getting ready to nail me for something, and the best thing that could happen would be that Miss Mary Newcombe falls on the floor and faints.

"Miss Newcombe, please tell us, where were you December twenty-fifth, the night of the fire at the Wellfleet Health Clinic?" She is smiling, but her eyes are attacking my face.

"I was home."

"We have a witness that places you at the scene of the fire."

"But I was home. I heard there were a lot of people there, so it must be a mistake."

"Did you know the deceased, Barbara Haskins?"

"I didn't know her well. She worked for my father before he died, but that was decades and decades ago." I've seen cop shows where Sandra's job is to get me to squirm my way into giving longer answers, but so far, so good, for Miss Mary Newcombe's short answers.

"How well did your mother know the deceased, Barbara Haskins?"

"Not well."

"Did your mother ever mention anything about an incident outside the Wellfleet Liquor Store when the police were summoned to break up a dispute between your mother and Miss Haskins?"

"No."

Sandra turns to her sidekick, Babinski, and asks him to read a page from a rather thick file.

"December 17, 2004, 6:45 PM. 309 Main Street sidewalk in front of Wellfleet Liquor Store.

"Summary: Observed altercation. Two women, Mrs. Newcombe and Miss Haskins, were pulling each other's hair. Mrs. Newcombe shouted something about an insurance deductible and dents in her car. Not exact words, but I heard something like 'Pay up, you slut. I could kill you.' More hair pulling.

"Bartender Roger McEleny witnessed the event and gave a written statement in attachment, signed 'Officer Walter Stone.'

"Roger McEleny's witness statement: 'I was serving drinks inside and heard shouting, so I went to the door to see what the ruckus was about. Awesome fight. Two old broads goin' at it. Couldn't tell who was winning, but one of them got a fistful of hair and—'"

"That's enough. Stop there." Cunningham looks annoyed.

I try to picture Birdie having a cat-fight brawl outside Kevin's liquor store.

It probably started after drinking a few glasses on Kevin's free-wine-tasting night. Birdie hated Barbara, and I imagine my mother fighting with her stiff brittle arms, swinging at

HUSH LITTLE FIRE   201

Barbara like a whirligig with decades of rage in her fist. At the time, my mother must have been in her sixties, which meant Haskins was about fifty. I picture a hair-pulling brawl like in TV cartoons where animals are people-ified, bonking each other to the tune of gongs and bops and ukulele music, and on some level, the fight seems really funny.

"No, I never heard about that," I answer.

"Your mother never mentioned this? Why are you laughing, Miss Newcombe?"

"Am I laughing? I'm not laughing."

"Did the deceased James Newcombe ever speak to you about Miss Haskins?"

"Jimmy or Big James? Big James was Jimmy's father, and no, neither of them said anything about her."

Chief Crocker wiggles his behind down into his chair. "Try and remember. You can relax. You and I, we've known each other a long, long time. It's like we're all one big family here in Wellfleet, so take a minute and try to remember."

"One big family?"

Sandra is drilling the table with her pen and shoots daggers at Billy Crocker, who is probably supposed to let her do all the talking.

"A witness, a UPS driver, sighted your mother and Miss Haskins last November, arguing on your mother's front porch. Are you aware of that argument?" Cunningham is twirling her pen.

"How do you know they were arguing?"

"The UPS driver was delivering a package, and I quote, 'The two women were shouting so much that I had to postpone the delivery because one of them was waving a red umbrella at the other woman, and then she threw it at me.'"

"I know nothing about that."

"Miss Newcombe, what was your son's relationship with Jimmy Newcombe?"

"Jimmy was my cousin. Danny helped him a few times on his lobster boat last summer."

"According to our records, your son went on a boat called *Angel Baby* twenty days in July and fourteen days in August, and not at all after that."

I am silent.

"What did your son do on *Angel Baby* in July and August?"

"He helped out."

"Do you know someone named Patrick Bale?"

"No."

"Patrick Bale was Jimmy Newcombe's fishing partner. Are you saying you don't know who he is?"

"I don't know who that is."

"You are not telling the truth, Miss Newcombe. But I'll get back to that in a minute."

Oh, she's good, snarky Sandra. Catches me in a lie, twiddles me with fear, and lets me sweat until she *gets back to that in a minute*. She must be good at catching fireflies. Punch holes in my jar for air so I can live a little longer.

"How often did you see your cousin Jimmy Newcombe between December twenty-fifth and New Year's Eve, when he died?"

"My mother and Jimmy had a falling-out, so he didn't come over for Christmas. I didn't see him at all."

"And your mother, did she see him?"

"You'll have to ask her."

"Miss Newcombe, the surveillance camera at Dunkin' Donuts shows you speaking with Patrick for four minutes and fifteen seconds. So, Miss Newcombe, why are you lying?"

At this exact moment, the alarm in my head explodes and the megawatt overhead light flashes on and off. *God bless you, Walter, my friend.*

"Chief Crocker, I think I need to get a lawyer."

♦ 35 ♦

MARY LOSES IT IN THE SQUAD CAR

Mary

CHIEF CROCKER SEEMS GLEEFUL that Agent Cunningham couldn't get me to say much. He doesn't like her because she's an out-of-towner, invading his sacred territory. Walter takes my arm and leads me down the hall, and I feel so light-headed, floating along on the conveyor belt of *what's next*. How in the world did I wind up in this building where cops are quizzing me about arson and murder? It's like snarky Sandra punched me in the stomach with a nasty game of *gotcha*.

As soon as I open the door to Walter's squad car, I sit down and barf all over the dashboard. Walter reaches under the seat for a pile of lunch napkins.

"Here, let me help you," he says, wiping the vomit off my chin like a mother with her toddler. "Move over a bit so I can clean up the dashboard and get you home."

"You're too good to me."

"That's my job. Be good to Mary Newcombe."

HUSH LITTLE FIRE   205

"Walter, see that red truck over there? Why is Tom Murphy's red truck parked at the police station? He's a volunteer firefighter, not police."

"I think you should ask him that yourself." Before Walter looks away, I watch his face close down on the dimmer switch of more trouble.

"Okay, never mind. Don't tell me. I should change my clothes and forget all this. I need to get on with my day. Is it all right if I come over and bisque my pots? You know, as soon as I finish them, I get paid. I really need the money."

"Sure thing. I'm doing a bisque firing tonight."

Walter drops me off at my mother's house; the yellow police tape is gone, but the house seems so empty and vulnerable. I go upstairs to Birdie's bedroom to look for something that might tell me more about her—or Jimmy—or me—or anything that could explain the missing pieces of our piddling little lives.

A stuffy whiff of flowery perfume bombards me when I open the door to Birdie's bedroom. The room is feminine, with flowery wallpaper and a fluffy beige quilt with matching pillows embroidered with doves. Looks like the vandals never made it upstairs, because Birdie's room looks untouched. I open every drawer in her desk and rummage through her chest of drawers. Nothing. No photos, no letters, and no important papers. But then, tucked underneath her socks behind a sachet in her underwear drawer, I find an old postcard, just one. It's a touristy thing that says *Welcome to Canada*, and it's signed *Love always, Clara*, postmarked 1963. It's over fifty years old—why did she save this?

Dear Beatrice,

Canada is beautiful! Hugs and kisses to my Jimmy! I miss my boy so much! I'll be back soon. In the meantime,

you should know, the gift is not from Antoine. I'm posi-
tive. We'll talk more when I see you. I hope we can still
be friends.

Love always,

Clara

What gift? Who is Antoine? What does she mean by *I hope we can still be friends*? This postcard is too discreet, but that's what women, even sisters-in-law, did back then. I'm a snooper, but now I'm a thief, because I slip this postcard into my pocket. I must bring it to Birdie when I see her. If Birdie caught me snooping in her room, she'd have a fit, but sneak-around me opens the antique curio cabinet anyway. It's filled with clay stat-uettes, teapots, crystal figurines, and terra-cotta busts tucked away on the lower shelves. On the bottom shelf there's a clay head—the spitting image of little-boy Jimmy. I remember when she made it in a makeshift art class she set up for kids in the kitchen. In Birdie's kitchen art classes, I tried to sculpt cats and dogs while she took all my discarded clay and transformed the wet clay into a likeness of Jimmy, her hands pinching out the features. She worked a mushy lump of clay like magic into something that seemed to document the inner battles of Jimmy's life—I can see that now. I understand why artists make clay busts, I do, but the face looks so real and strange without a body, like somebody cut off the head. In Birdie's kitchen art class, I remember her snapping at Jimmy a lot, annoyed with how he always had ants in his pants—and here it is, Jimmy's essence, radiating out of his crooked clay mouth. The clay eyes stare into space, the way Jimmy could see things out there that I couldn't.

"Aunt Birdie, where's the rest of my body?" Little Jimmy had joked about shrunken heads and decapitation in kitchen

HUSH LITTLE FIRE 207

art class. After so many years, the terra-cotta bust of Jimmy is chalky because it was never fired. I turn it around a few times, and then just for fun, I set it on the beige pillow with doves. For a moment, I feel so sad that little-boy Jimmy is dead and gone, but then I remember Danny describing that day on the boat last summer when grown-up Jimmy was spanking my son, plying him with beer, pushing him off the boat, having him carry money in paper bags, and for these things and for all that he might have done to my son, well, now I understand why the French chose decapitation as punishment. No need to explain to other mothers, because if I said I could kill someone if they ever harmed my son—before I finished the sentence, all the other mothers of the world would nod and agree. I snatch up the terra-cotta bust from the pillow and shove it back in the cabinet.

The postcard will stay with me in my pocket until I can show it to Birdie. It blows my mind that a living, breathing Clara held a pen once and wrote this in perfect handwriting over fifty years ago. What did it mean? I collapse on Birdie's bed, exhausted from all I can't figure out.

Oh, stop this fussing, right now! The voice is Tiny Mary's, although I don't see any flies in the room.

I get up and comb through the boxes in Birdie's closet—nothing much—and then I touch the small paintings on the wall. Six of them. They are signed *Beatrice 1963* in the lower right corner in a lovely ornate cursive that must have been hard to do with a brush. The paintings have a generosity to them, bright colors and vigorous, bold strokes, as if to say, *Look at this beautiful world; won't you join me?* I never knew much about Birdie's secret world of painting, but now I see.

Tiny Mary hops across my collarbone and into my ear. *Earth to Mary. Stop lollygagging around your mother's room! Get*

208 JUDITH NEWCOMB STILES

your mopey self over to Walter's studio and make those dog urns. The studio has that special copper glaze you want, and better yet, Walter has everything you need. Everything.

Step Six: Bisqueing the Dead Chihauhuas' Urns

Walter and I form two small kiln gods out of clay to sit by the kiln to bless the bisque firing and to keep the pots from exploding. I shape a mermaid kiln goddess, and his kiln god is an elephant with the trunk facing down instead of up, but according to Birdie, an elephant statue with the trunk facing down means all the good luck will pour out. I can't afford to have these urns explode, so I phone Walter at the station and we have a discussion, more like a semi-argument, about this. And since most potters are a superstitious lot, he tells me to toss the elephant and use my mermaid kiln goddess. She will guard against kiln disasters, and while she's at it, *please guard against any more trouble with Chief Crocker and snarky Sandra Cunningham.*

Walter's electric Skutt kilns are hexagonal chambers of firebrick encased in gleaming shiny metal, and they remind me of sci-fi spaceships. Like me, he names the kilns after favorite dead people to help the spirit of the firing. Walter named his favorite propane gas kiln Connie, after Connie Olinder, his beloved first customer, and so he named his electric kiln Connie Junior for good karma. If there's iron in the clay, Walter jokes about how bisque with iron comes out the same pink as a hairless baby rat. I thankfully have never seen a baby rat, but when our bisqued pots are unloaded from the firing, they are a strange pink and definitely not pottery you'd give to your favorite teacher.

I put on my to-do list *Tell Mrs. Reardon that it will take another week or so before I finish the urns.* I'll be subtle, but not too

HUSH LITTLE FIRE

209

subtle, and let her know that I have lots of extra-special clay from Newcomb Hollow, and that I made extra pots with lids in case another Chihuahua happens to climb the golden staircase, go the way of all flesh, meet one's maker, give up the ghost, kick the bucket. Most potters don't like the color and texture of bisqued pottery because it's unfinished, in limbo, and kind of ugly. I'm okay with pink-hairless-baby-rat pots that are chalky and unpleasant to the touch. But when I'm not looking, sadness grabs me from behind when I think of how my birth mother gave away her hairless pink baby rat.

♦ **36** ♦

LISA HAS IT OUT
WITH PATRICK

Lisa

THE ASSISTANT BARTENDER AT the Bomby told me Patrick called me "Queen Lisa the Cunt," but I think he just said that to make me hate Patrick because he secretly wants to date me. He's not that cute either, and anyway, Patrick hasn't been around the Bomby for a while, so he probably didn't call me that.

It's a couple of days after the boatyard fire and I'm feeling very good. Mission accomplished. Plenty of people saw me there, including Mary Newcombe, which was the whole point. I brought Trudy to witness the burning boats so that Mary could *witness* us *witnessing* the fire. Trudy reassured me many times that nobody knows Patrick didn't actually go to Nantucket. He never set foot on the ferry, but he has a ticket receipt to make like he was out of town. I reminded him ten times to wear rubber gloves when he broke into the Newcombe house. I pray he didn't forget.

At noon I go straight to the Woodwards' house for one more stinking day of cleaning up somebody else's mess. When

HUSH LITTLE FIRE 211

I step out of the car, my sneakers get soaked, and it feels like they've been wet all winter. I put my socks in the dryer and take a nap on the Woodwards' king-size bed.

After a leisurely lunch and an afternoon coffee break, it's already dark out by four, so it's time to head home in my dry socks. I trudge through the slush across the High Tide Apartments parking lot, and when I open the door, there's Patrick passed out on the couch again with his muddy boots, messing all over the cushions. Most likely he has gone from lying down to sitting to lying down all day, maybe a trip to the bathroom and the refrigerator. The mermaid bong is partially shoved under the couch with the red tail sticking out, rejected, because Patrick has graduated from weed to pills. I kick the tail of the slutty mermaid way under the couch.

In the bathroom, I rub my elbows, my knees, and my neck—my whole body is sore. I undress and unhook my bra, moving my arms too quickly, which jostles my tender breasts, which are almost as sore as my elbows. Time to get a new bra. My jeans are hard to zip up—they must have shrunk in the wash again. I give up on the zipper and count on my fingers— my period is late. *How can that be?* Patrick has been too stoned for sex all winter, and no matter how hard I try, nothing gets him aroused. He's been such a dud, and the mermaid bong would agree.

In the bedroom, I rifle through my underwear drawer to check my monthly menstrual cycle calendar. It has pathetic kiddie stickers in the margins, images of babies, ribbons, and presents I hope to receive someday at a baby shower. I believe it's important to know the exact date of conception if I ever get pregnant. There are no blue *S*'s for sex in December or January, thanks to Patrick, so the last time I had sex was

212   JUDITH NEWCOMB STILES

Thanksgiving, the day of the ruined turkey. Thanksgiving day has a big blue *S*. Oh God, it was the day of the stoner Goldfish game.

How can that be? I turn the page to that downer day of bleeding in late December, the day it felt like my whole entire world collapsed with a few trickles of blood. I drop the calendar on the floor when I suddenly remember my mother told me that some women have spotting, a little bleeding, even when they are pregnant. *Did I mistake the trickles of blood in December for a period?*

I hurry into the bathroom, unwrap a pregnancy kit, and pee on the wand. It turns pink. Pregnant. *Is this a mistake?* I lock the bathroom door and tear through my stash of pregnancy test kits—three more turn pink. Now the sore breasts and tight jeans make sense. I leave the wrappers on the bathroom floor and go stand next to the couch, wondering if this is a good time to tell him. Patrick is passed out, still as a corpse, and I can't imagine him helping me with feedings or diapers. His body stinks from not having showered in days, and ketchup is stuck to the stubble around his mouth. It looks like old blood and makes me think of Bon Bon's farm cats with furry faces, lapping up the spill from Arthur the goat. His arms begin to stir; he sits up and complains about something, lunging at the air like a drunk.

He looks at me crazy-angry and shouts, "You never told me what you said to the police about *Angel Baby*. You better not have fucked this up. What did you say?"

"The whole thing was your idea. And I never said anything to the police about the boat. Don't blame me for your stupid schemes. Even your mother thinks you'll get caught."

"I did nothing wrong. It was my boat too. For your information, I own half of Jimmy's half. We were business partners,

HUSH LITTLE FIRE

213

and I have a contract to prove it. That's at least fifteen thousand from insurance money. So there."

"The boat was worth a lot more than that, but your contract is worth shit because you should have known Jimmy didn't keep up with the payments, which means you didn't keep up with any payments, so he turned the boat over to his aunt. Birdie owns the boat. You can be so dense sometimes."

"If you knew that, you should have told me!"

"I didn't find out until Mary Newcombe told me at the boatyard fire. And *you* should have known that, not me."

"Shut the fuck up."

"So did you find any money at the Newcombe house? You better not have left any fingerprints on her lamps. Mrs. Newcombe can't find out I was spying on her when she stuffed a bunch of money inside those things."

"I'm not telling you anything ever again. You talk too much."

This is definitely not the right time to have a meaningful conversation about a baby.

His eyes and nose and cheeks are red and scrunched up into an angry knot that's about to burst. He lunges at my face—his grubby fisherman hands yank my throat and jerk me back. He shakes my head like I'm a bobble doll. "You bitch!" He punches my face.

I panic—and not because he could have broken my neck, but because his hands could hurt the baby that's growing inside me. I grab my purse by the door, no coat, and run out into the parking lot. My face is wet and sticky when I touch it in the dark, and I wish it were just ketchup. The skin on my cheek feels raw, like he slugged me with a cheese grater. This is my own blood that I share with a baby. *Keep going. Don't stop moving.*

I leave the High Tide Apartments, walking fast on the side of Route 6. With each quick step, I tell myself, *Let's go, baby. Let's go, baby.* The chant is soothing and gives me purpose, like it's moving me into the future with every single step. I'm never afraid of the dark, and it comforts me that the trees and buildings and colors are erased into a sea of black as I walk. I stop and feel around in my purse for my phone. *Call Lester.* My hands fumble over a comb and keys, and I pull out a pack of tissues to blot my bloody face. My fingers are shaking nonstop and I can barely press the numbers on my phone.

"Lester, can you come pick me up? I'm not that far from Wellfleet center. I'm walking."

"Ha. You're calling me for a ride? I'm about to go to bed. Is this a joke?"

"No, but can you come and get me? I'm walking on the ocean side of Route 6, and I'll cross over and walk toward Dunkin' Donuts. It's bad."

◆ 37 ◆

LISA GOES TO
THE TOOLSHED
WITH LESTER

Lisa

I STAND ON THE side of Route 6 in the dark, too embarrassed to go inside Dunkin' Donuts. Within minutes a white Lexus pulls over, screeching to a stop. Lester jumps out of the car with the engine running, door left open as he hurries over to me.

"Are you all right?" Lester pulls me toward him and spreads his arms around me. For the first time in a long time, I feel safe in a man's hug. A whiff of his cologne blocks out the entire world. He gently touches my face.

"Let's get you out of here. I'll take you back to my place. Try not to get mud on Bon Bon's leather seats." Lester helps me into Bon Bon's car. I carefully put the bloody tissues deep inside my purse.

"Thanks for coming." I press my winter scarf over my cheek to stop the bleeding. Everything is strange and out of order, and my world will never be the same. Patrick is out. Baby is in. And simplifying this in a decisive way makes me feel calm and a little bit better.

We don't speak a word on the ride to Lester's home, a cabin, which is really a toolshed in the woods. Lester lives on land owned by Peter Middleboro, a wealthy local who owns nine restaurants on the Cape. The Middleboros live in a McMansion on six acres up by Gull Pond. On his property are lots of toolsheds scattered among the trees, so-called housing for guest workers in the summer. Lester had agreed to be groundskeeper for Mr. Middleboro, so in exchange for maintaining the gardens and lawn, he was allowed to winterize one of the sheds and live here year-round. Most of the sheds except Lester's have three bunk beds crammed inside for the workers, like uncomfortable barracks in the Army. No toilet or running water, so the workers use a porta-potty on the premises. They all share a shower in a washroom that is nowhere near the McMansion. Toolshed housing is Wellfleet's dirty little secret, and it makes me grateful that my High Tide apartment has a flushing toilet and bathtub.

As we pull into the long dirt road to Lester's cabin, we pass the Middleboros' private beach on Gull Pond where the rich people swim, never Lester. He tells me not to worry, because he has no roommates, and his cabin is toasty warm with a new electric heater. Unlocking the door, Lester leads me inside with one arm hooked over my shoulder.

"I'm okay, really I am. I can walk just fine." I try not to cry.

"Sit down in this chair and let me clean up your wound, and then I'll heat a bowl of my stew. I make it with bone marrow broth—good for healing. Good for you."

He turns on a lamp and tips it toward me to get a better look at my face.

"Thanks. I appreciate it, but I hope it's not goat stew. I don't like the taste of goat. I tried some at the Lucky Dragon and it tastes so slimy." I want to make a joke about goat meat,

HUSH LITTLE FIRE

217

but it hurts to move my mouth. Lester dunks a clean white washcloth into the bucket of water and gently dabs my cheek. My left eye is swollen shut.

"Oh God, how am I going to wait tables looking like a monster?"

"Don't think about that. Not now . . . think about it in the morning. You can take the bottom bunk and I'll take the top. If you need to use a bathroom, I'll walk you up to a washroom past the barn, or you can use the porta-potty right out here."

"Thanks, you're so kind, but I can handle it myself." I totter out the door to the porta-potty, and the cold air feels good on my cheek. I blink a few times, but only my right eyelid moves. I look up at the stars, which look strange and not so far away, because seeing out of one eye distorts my vision. I feel like I could reach up and grab a little star, but I'm too tired and sore to bother.

The porta-potty is cold and stinks of chemicals, so I pretend I'm not really here. Peeing in the dark, in frigid weather, in a smelly porta-potty, in the middle of the woods—what has become of my life? Bare-assed, trying to pee without sitting, I remember the baby growing inside me.

I walk back to Lester's toolshed, and inside it's warm and cozy. I sink into his comfortable chair with a bowl of stew on my lap. It's hurts to chew. There's a two-burner hot plate next to a knee-high refrigerator and three clean buckets of water with lids. Now I know why Lester brings a tub of dishes to the Lighthouse to run through the dishwasher every few days.

Lester's place is so homey, with an old stuffed blue chair next to a card table, a nice sitting area wedged in tight next to a bunk bed. Top and bottom bunks have perfectly made sheets and blankets like in the military, and on the wall above the top bunk is a wooden cross and a faded picture of Jesus. Tucked next to the bottom bunk are two framed photos of a smiling boy and girl, and I know they're his kids in Jamaica, Lester Junior and Tanya. I guess Lester put the photos near his pillow so their smiling faces are the last thing he sees before falling asleep.

Lester turns out the light and says, "Good night, sweet dreams," to me, politely leaving me in the pitch-black toolshed to decide if I do or don't want to undress. I crawl into bed with my clothes on and bury myself beneath Lester's soft sheets. I listen to Lester rustle around above me. I am safe. It's so dark and quiet out in the woods, with hundreds and hundreds of trees separating me from Patrick.

Ever since I was a little girl, I liked to lie in bed like this and imagine I was out at sea, lying down in a dory. I pretended I was in a soft sleeping bag like a cocoon, stretched out on my back beneath the stars with miles of water separating me from my unbearable life on land. I visualize the dory when Lester suddenly whispers, "Everything will be all right."

It's as if he can hear my thoughts, riding in the dory too.

I roll over, and the pillow is painful next to my eye. I remember what happened with Patrick punching me. I remember walking to Dunkin' Donuts in the dark. I remember there's a baby to think about now. Bad and good all at once—so many mixed-up feelings at the same time as I start to fall asleep.

★   ★   ★

In the morning, I peek out the toolshed door, and there's a police car hobbling over the potholes on the dirt road that

HUSH LITTLE FIRE   219

leads to the shed. I shriek at Lester, "There's a police car coming up the road!" Lester jumps off the top bunk.

"Get away from the door. You better hide, so they don't know you're in my cabin."

I move away as Lester slips past me and goes outside. I peek through the crack in the door and recognize Officer Stone with a blond woman in plain clothes. Lester greets Officer Stone with one of his friendly full-moon smiles.

"Good morning, Officer Stone. How are you?"

"Hello, Lester. Chief Crocker would like you to come down to the station. He wants to ask you a few questions, that's all."

The blonde holds up a badge with a golden eagle and sneers at Walter, stepping in front of him.

"I'm Special Agent Cunningham, FBI, and we need you, Mr. Lester Fielding, to come down to the police station."

"What's this about?"

"This is regarding the Wellfleet Health Clinic fire on December twenty-fifth."

"But I only shovel the walkways. They don't have a snowplow."

Walter comes around and stands in front of Special Agent Cunningham, blocking her line of vision. "Just come with me. I promise it will be short. Come along."

"If you say so, Walt, I mean Officer Stone."

"You ride in the back of the squad car, but it's not like I'm arresting you or anything."

Lester walks to the police car in a T-shirt, no jacket. It's cold out, and I want to run out and give him something warmer to wear. I can't see his face, but his shoulders are slumped, and as his head drops down, he slides into the back seat like a common criminal. I have a hard time pulling out my phone from my purse, I'm shaking so hard. A baby is growing inside me, and everything is moving too fast. Maybe it's time to call an emergency meeting with Bon Bon.

✦ 38 ✦

LISA GETS A RIDE WITH CHANTRELLE TO THE CEMETERY

Lisa

BIG PHEW. THE COPS sent Lester home after questioning him, but he didn't say how it went. My face looks a tiny bit better, but even cover-up doesn't hide the black around my eye. My cheek's still swollen, but Lester promises my face will go back to normal.

There's a lot of time to do nothing in the cabin. If only I had wheels, I could go to the cemetery and visit my mother. I'm going insane wondering where Jimmy could possibly have hidden Bon Bon's money—or did he spend it? *Up his* for not telling anyone where it is.

Patrick bragged about all the loans Bon Bon gave Jimmy over the years, pretending he was in on the loan. Jimmy always paid them back on time, but the *problem* loan was when Jimmy borrowed forty thousand dollars cash in December. *Wow, so much money.* Jimmy and Patrick were planning something big, and I hope and pray it had nothing to do with those stupid plastic lobsters. The boys were holed up indoors, getting shit-faced every day between Christmas and New Year's Eve, so maybe they didn't have the brain cells to spend it. Where could the forty thousand be? Finding that much money would be like winning the Mega Millions in my miserable little world of always being broke. But I don't want to end up like one of the farm goats with my throat slit if Bon Bon doesn't get his money back. I review Jimmy's habits and try to visualize where he might have hidden so much money. Birdie's basement? Storage unit? His truck? Not the boat. Patrick had scoured *Angel Baby* and found nothing there, which was when he got the bright idea to set the boat on fire for insurance money. Major blockhead. I rub my temples and try to think the way Jimmy would think. Wherever the money is, Jimmy would want *me* to keep some of the stash, because he gave money to Katie Snow when she fooled him into thinking Sunshine was his baby. He was always nice to single mothers, and *he was nice to me*. Bottom line, I could really use some of that forty thousand.

If I get my hands on that money, I'll spritz myself with a lot of perfume before I return it to Bon Bon. I'll be sure to look meek and desperate until he asks me what's wrong. I will tell him I'm pregnant and out of work, and I'll remind him I'm good friends with Lester. I'll do my best to get him to take pity, because he just might slip some cash right back at me. Worth a try.

Lester's gone out again, so to pass the time, I clean every inch of his home. I'm careful to carry a lone spider outdoors, so it can live and I won't get bad luck. I open the door for a little fresh air, and there's a stranger driving up the long dirt road to the toolshed. I close the door and lock it. Through the crack in the door, I see a short woman with bug-eye sunglasses. She knocks on the door and waits, but I'm too nervous to answer. After a few minutes, the stranger climbs back into a Lexus. I've had nobody to talk to for hours and hours except

HUSH LITTLE FIRE

the spider, so I shriek after the woman, "Wait, please don't go. Are you looking for Lester?" It hurts to move my neck. I grab a coat and hurry over to the car. "Hi, I'm Lisa."

"I figured as much. I'm Chantrelle."

Chantrelle steps out of the white Lexus, a sturdy woman, thick in the torso with muscles like a body builder. She's wearing a dancer's black leotard with a billowy long white shirt down to her knees. Chantrelle is draped in gold, and the light catches her jewelry with a twinkle, like she knows important things. Her body is a smaller version of Bon Bon's, and she moves toward me like a tank.

"I'm Lester's friend and Bon Bon's sister. Come inside. It's cold out here." Chantrelle climbs back into the Lexus, summoning me with a long purple fingernail. The radio thunders and Chantrelle turns it down, carefully clicking her purple nails across the buttons. She has exquisite rings on every finger just like her brother, no college rings that I can see.

"You should put some ice on your eye. Maybe some arnica."

"What's arnica?"

"I can give you some. It's great for bruises. They say Swiss mountain climbers discovered the arnica flower and ate it because it promotes healing. I sell it in my shop. But since you're Lester's friend, I'll make you something special with dried arnica root and spices. You'll be better in no time at all."

"Thanks, but you don't have to do that. Have you heard from Lester? He's usually home by now."

"He told me to tell you not to worry. I told him to say nothing to the police until a lawyer is present. Never speak to the police without a lawyer, if you know what I mean. Bon Bon is sending his lawyer from Boston to help him."

"Do you have another phone number for Bon Bon? I tried his cell, but he doesn't answer. I need to talk to him."

"My brother doesn't like people to call him when it's personal. He will get in touch with you first. I'll ask him."

"Thanks. What's your name again? Channel?"

"Chan-trelle. Sometimes you can find him in my spice shop in Hyannis at the minimart. He has an office there. I have a fabulous little shop; have you been there?"

"No, I don't think so." *The last thing I want to talk about is shopping in any shop.*

"It's called Spice Up Your Life. You've never been there? Didn't my brother tell you? I own a spice shop. You should come by. I have something for everyone. Spice up your life, Lisa." Chantrelle laughs and clicks her nails together.

"I've never been to your shop. It sounds cool."

"I sell all kinds of rare spices and condiments and kitchen supplies—provisions, as they say on Cape Cod. My brother and I import them from all over the world."

"Chantrelle, would you mind giving me a lift to the cemetery? I need to pay a visit to my mother. Can you drop me off? I can walk back."

"No problem, but isn't it too cold out? You really want to go there? It's so windy."

"I visit my mother every week—well, maybe every other week in the winter."

On the ride to the cemetery, I don't say much as Chantrelle blathers away about spices and remedies. My mind keeps drifting to the money and where asshole Jimmy might have hidden it.

"I'm texting my brother and telling him where we are. He says hello and he'd like to meet with you again. He insists I wait and give you a ride back to Lester's."

I guess when Bon Bon gives orders, everyone jumps, including his sister.

HUSH LITTLE FIRE   225

"You don't have to, but if you don't mind, I'll be less than a half hour."

"That's fine. I'll run and get some coffee and then wait right here for you."

I hop out of the Lexus at the cemetery entrance, and Chantrelle drives away, leaving me alone and at peace for once, without a living person in sight. I turn around in a circle, looking up at the endless gray sky. The side of my face is painful, and I worry the pain can travel down to the baby through the placenta.

♦ **39** ♦

OLD MAN CHRISTOPHER KNOWS EVERYTHING ABOUT EVERYONE

Lisa

OLD MAN CHRISTOPHER, THE cemetery caretaker, shuffles toward me, pushing a rickety wheelbarrow full of branches. He moves slowly down a narrow path of white seashells, bending down here and there for twigs.

"Well, hello there, Lisa! How ya doing?"

Old Man Christopher has gotten so old that even up close, his white hair blends into his pale face like a ghost.

"You're walking the wrong way if you're looking for your mother." He snaps a twig and drops it in the wheelbarrow.

"Yes, I know. How are you doing, Christopher?"

"I'm all right, I suppose. Cleaning up the place. The wind keeps me busy in the winter. Sometimes the wind makes so much noise here, I think I'd rather be deaf."

"But it's so peaceful here today." I wish the old man would go away. "Can you please tell me where the Newcombe plot is, so I don't have to wander around looking?"

"It's up there next to the row of lilac bushes near the shed that's built in the hill with the green door. Which one of the

HUSH LITTLE FIRE   227

Newcombes are you visiting? They haven't buried Jimmy Newcombe yet."

"I'm really here to see my mother, but while I'm here, I also want to pay my respects to a few more people."

"The family should bury Jimmy next to his mother. Clara Newcombe's marker is the one with the fake slate and aluminum. You see it over there?" He points. "The cheap one. It scratches too easy with my mower."

"Thanks, Christopher. I'll be going now."

"Jimmy was a good man. Somebody ought to buy him and his parents a decent headstone."

"By any chance, do you have a hammer I could borrow?"

"What for?"

"I just want to straighten out my mom's plaque. It keeps shifting, and I want to fix it before it snows again."

"Ground's frozen."

"Says who? It doesn't look too frozen."

"I miss that Jimmy Newcombe. He used to come by here every week, sometimes twice a week." Old Man Christopher swings a hammer over the wheelbarrow before he hands it over.

"Wow, I think I saw him here too. Did you say he came here lots?"

"Yes sirree. He was a good man. He'd help me, and I never had to ask him. I'm getting too old for this kind of work."

"Oh, you don't look very old. There are tons of men older than you. There's a bunch of ninety-year-old fellas still driving cars around Wellfleet. That's what old is."

"I'll be eighty next July. Ten years till ninety feels like ten minutes when you're my age."

I do not want to get into a long discussion with Christopher, not now. I wish the old geezer would look for more twigs and leave me alone.

228 JUDITH NEWCOMB STILES

I stand in front of my mother's crooked plaque and realize this Gina Ann Doanne plaque is also made of a fake, plastic mixture, but it's a good imitation. Kind of like my mom. It has sunk and shifted and is cracked. I do a speed-reading of a prayer on a holy card I keep in my purse. I want to have a heart-to-heart conversation about finally getting pregnant, but I read and pray so fast even the Lord probably can't understand me.

"Sorry, Mom, I can't stay long. Chantrelle is waiting, so I have to talk fast, and I must see the Newcombes while I'm here. It's not what you think. I'm not going to scream at Dr. Newcombe like Aunt Elrie did that time she called him a greedy pig. As a matter of fact, I should thank him for *fixing it* for you a long time ago. You were too young to be a mother. Okay, I'll say it. It's a good thing he did *abortions* on you before I was born, because I might not be here if he didn't. If you had all those babies before me—you would have surely quit sex and I might never have been born. That's a longer discussion and I don't have time, but I know the Lord forgives you; at least I'm pretty sure he does. I think the Lord is angry, very angry, at the Flannery boys for tricking you into the woods for capture the flag when it was really capture Gina Doanne. The Lord punished their ugly hearts for ganging up on you like that. I know that for a fact. The Flannery brothers who died are in hell, and the youngest who's still alive is in prison for something else. The Lord forgives you, and anyway, you were barely thirteen the first time you got pregnant, just a baby yourself, so how were you supposed to take care of a baby?"

I whack the hammer again on the side of the plaque, but it still doesn't budge. Christopher was right; everything is frozen.

"Mom, I want you to know that I'm over-the-moon happy to finally be pregnant. You were a good mother to me, and I'll

HUSH LITTLE FIRE 229

be a good mother to this baby. I'm ready. I love you. Gotta go now and visit with the Newcombes."

It's easy to ditch Old Man Christopher when I zigzag my way around the headstones on the hills where his wheelbarrow would get stuck. I stop in front of the upstanding *e*-dropper Newcombs and notice they outnumber the naughty Newcombes. Three to one. I say a prayer to bless all of them, the naughty and the good, but I can't stop thinking about what a waste of land this is with all these dead people just lying here year after year. Somebody could build a house or two and move out of the High Tide Apartments.

"Jesus! You scared me, Christopher. Don't stand so close! Are you following me? What are you doing?"

"I'm cleaning up after the storm, pruning and such. What are you doin'? You checking on the Newcombes?"

"I'm here to pay my respects."

Three crummy plaques at my feet stare up at me, Jimmy's mother Clara, his father James, and then the sorry little plaque that says Baby Newcombe.

I kneel down and run my hand across the letters. "Tell me, Christopher, you might have heard, why didn't they give the baby a name? It's so sad. A baby should have a name."

"They buried the mother in a hurry for the sake of little Jimmy. It was years ago, but I remember like it was yesterday. You know everything is yesterday for a man like me. I remember Birdie Newcombe gave up on waiting for Big James to come home for his wife's burial, so they did it fast without him. Birdie said a boy needs a place, a marker, to go be with his mother. But Jimmy didn't know anything about what's down there. I never told him."

"What's down there?"

"Don't believe everything you hear in town about Jimmy Newcombe. I get so tired from riding the mower, and Jimmy would come by and finish the job. He'd swing my old Weedwacker, singing and whacking and dancing like it was a party. Oh, he made me laugh so hard sometimes, and he never broke my Weedwacker either."

"What are you talking about? What's down there? Don't you think it's wrong they didn't give the baby a name? I'd never do that."

"No need to name it. There aren't no baby ashes down there. I never had the heart to tell him."

"Tell who? Jimmy?"

"Birdie bought a cheap urn, and the lid didn't quite fit. I remember thinkin' it looked like a whiskey decanter."

"How old was Jimmy?"

"Not sure. Four or five, maybe. When the doctor laid Clara's urn in the ground, I remember Birdie collapsed, weeping and moaning so loud she had to leave and go sit in the car. Little Jimmy ran off howling right behind her. Dr. Newcombe was rattled when he laid Clara in her hole, shaking so hard he couldn't even finish the Lord's Prayer. There weren't no minister present to hold him up and keep going. Just me and my shovel."

"I'm glad you were there."

"The lid to the baby urn fell off, and all the ashes scattered, but the doctor didn't seem bothered at all. Me? I was worried sick. But he just tossed the empty urn and the lid into the hole and said something about fireplace ashes. No baby ashes down there, them's fireplace ashes down there, and he told me not to tell anyone, or else."

"Or else what? Are you sure they weren't people ashes?"

"As sure as I'm standing here today."

HUSH LITTLE FIRE 231

"I can't imagine anyone would do that."

"Hell, the crematoriums and funeral parlors do it all the time. They mix the ashes of cats and dogs and everybody. They burn up the dead together to save a few bucks and then scrape 'em into whatever cremation urns Carlson's Funeral Parlor can provide. Like I said, there ain't no baby ashes down there."

"That's so awful."

"Ashes and dirt, it's all the same, stuck in the ground. If you ask me, it'd be better to use the ashes for fertilizer. Ashes are the best for hydrangea and peonies. When I die, I don't want anyone to send me to the fires. Just throw me into the sea." Old Man Christopher throws something imaginary in the direction of the ocean.

I text Chantrelle and say I'll be at the cemetery entrance to meet her in a minute. As I start to leave, I suddenly remember something I saw on a TV show, how a murderer hid his gun underneath a dead person's headstone, and oh yes, on another mystery show, the killer hid the victim's body in a cemetery. No surveillance cameras, no people walking around to catch him. I remember sitting with Jimmy when he talked about *how babies suck up money from the cradle to the grave.* What a great place to hide money. I bet he watched the same TV shows as me. We might have watched them together. Old Man Christopher continues to wander around the headstones, so I yell over to him, "By any chance, do you have a crowbar I can borrow?"

◆ 40 ◆

MRS. O'MALLEY
THE THWARTER

Mary

MAKING POTTERY IS SUPPOSED to be fun, but not when I'm under pressure to get perfect red glazes for dead Chihuahuas. It is noon, and when I take a break from mixing glazes in Walter's studio, I start to worry about men, and I don't like worrying about men. Tom Murphy's cell phone is no longer in service. His landline is disconnected, and his apartment is empty. The fire department is taking messages, but Tom never calls me back. I dry my hands and float over to Walter's computer to look up Murphy & Sons in Boston, because maybe they know where he is. I find a Murphy & Sons Trucking Company, a tool company, piano movers, and there it is, a construction company. When I call to inquire about Tom Murphy, the receptionist singsongs her name, "Mrs. O'Malley speaking," like she's trying to cover up her piss-off mood today.

"Which Tom Murphy do you want, miss? There are three Tom Murphys who currently work here, including the owner's son."

HUSH LITTLE FIRE

I explain that my Tom Murphy retired and moved to Cape Cod, and she laughs and says since the company began in 1925, there must have been dozens of Tom Murphys who retired, mostly to Florida or Arizona. Receptionists in New England seem to fall into two categories, helpful or out to thwart you, and nothing in between. I can't tell by her voice how old Mrs. O'Malley is, but she's definitely a thwarter.

I ask Mrs. O'Malley if she ever knew the Tom Murphy who retired and loves dogs and drives a red truck. I lie for a worthy cause and tell her that the dog warden found his lost German shepherd, and in my most sincere voice, I say that I want to return his dog.

"I don't have time to keep track of all the former employees and their pets."

I wait through a long silence, hoping the thwarter might thaw.

"It's company policy to not give out contact information of current or former employees."

"Okay, thanks for all your help." *Not.*

When Mrs. O'Malley hangs up on me, the preamble to a panic attack starts messing with me. Where did Tom Murphy go, and where did he come from? All of a sudden, overnight, Tom disappeared into oblivion, a strange dark void. Kind of like when I was a kid and worried that maybe I wasn't born from a real person and maybe I came from the void. Because if I was born from a living, breathing woman, anybody knows a mother who has milk percolating in her breasts would never give away a wonderful baby such as me. A real mother wouldn't have put me up for adoption. I know it's silly, but as a kid, I worried that the void would pull me back and un-born me if I didn't behave. As an adult, I've had many conversations with myself about the void, especially when it comes to my father and his line of work. The void was also a place where doctors like my father sometimes had to ask a fetus to wait at the door while a woman with shaky legs suddenly went bonkers because she couldn't stick to her decision. No refunds in Dr. Newcombe's office, I bet. And now it scares me how Tom has disappeared. I know it's different, but really, it's all about the void.

Stop this right now. Be rational, Tiny Mary whispers, buzzing in circles and landing on my head. *Stick to the task at hand and finish mixing your copper red glaze.*

Just as Tiny Mary zips up to the ceiling out of sight, Walter comes through the door. "Hi, I'm home for lunch. Need any help mixing your glaze?"

"Maybe."

Walter gives me a surprise peck on the cheek and dons an apron over his police uniform. He unchains his gram scale and bags of dry ingredients, because it's a tradition, really a precaution, that potters bicycle chain their gram scales in place because they worry that drug dealers will sneak in and steal them. Potters all over the country do this, but who would steal a gram scale from a cop?

Step Seven: Mixing and Glazing the Old-Fashioned Way

My ten bisqued cremation urns are languishing on the ware rack like bald baby rats. I look over, and Walter is measuring the materials for a celadon glaze for his own pots. He is humming, but I can't tell what tune, maybe "God Bless America"?

He tells me the bags of copper carbonate are new but not yet tested, and they might be grade B materials, you never know.

HUSH LITTLE FIRE 235

Sometimes minuscule contaminants can screw things up. The gram scale is finicky, and I have to get this right. A pinch of this or that and Mrs. Reardon's copper red will turn frog green if I don't properly reduce the oxygen in the firing. I carefully stir the dry mix with my fingers before adding water. For the best results, I add just enough water to give it the consistency of heavy cream. Walter prefers half-and-half with two dunks.

"I don't know what I'll tell Mrs. Reardon if her expensive urns come out bad."

"If you want perfect colors, you should have become a house painter. Bor-ing. Don't worry so much. I often get surprises out of my kilns, but they're good accidents," Walter says, pointing his finger at me like a conductor and I'm his first violin.

"What on earth is a good accident?"

"Think like Japanese potters. They like accidents, and they even charge more for those pots."

"I think Japanese potters made up the idea of good accidents to put a positive spin on a fuckup."

"Not really. It's like when the scientist Fleming discovered penicillin from growing mold. He called it a happy accident."

Walter reminds me to take it easy and face the fact that once the flames are roaring, it's out of our hands and anything can happen. He shows me his new special technique of grabbing the pot with tongs and dipping it in a bucket of glaze, which is not really a new special technique, but it looks great because Walter dips and dunks and whistles with flair. So I imitate Walter's graceful arm movements and slosh my pots into the bucket of glaze until they're completely covered. Glazing done for now.

Tiny Mary buzzes down from the ceiling and hops on Walter's shoulder and then hops over to me, whispering that the results of 23andMe are sitting inside my computer with the truth of my existence. I don't want to log on when Walter's around, so I meticulously clean the tools and buckets and wait for Walter to go back to work.

My heart is thumpety-thumping like crazy, so the minute he leaves, I rush to his computer. There is an email with a picture of an envelope with digital confetti bursting out that says, "The 23andMe results for Mary Newcombe are in. A world of DNA discovery is waiting!"

I stare at the envelope, hold my breath, and think of five things to do before I read it, but instead of doing those five things, I open the pixilated envelope. So strange to see the essence, my life, broken down into numbers and percents. The results confuse me, and they must be wrong. It says, "99.5% European, which breaks down to 98.5% British with trace ancestry that's Southern European." That's it? Nothing exotic? Nothing complicated? The little girl in me had a ridiculous fantasy that everything about my birth mother would become clear and it would immediately lead me to a name, which would connect me to my people.

I read through the traits section, and it pretty much gets this part right about me—brown hair, brown eyes, 76 percent dimples, 93 percent earwax, and a longer big toe. A buzzing begins in my ears and migrates through my whole body when Tiny Mary reminds me that most of the old-time Cape Cod people are descended from the Brits. I get into an argument with Tiny Mary, who insists the numbers are correct and that English people share my DNA, and she reminds me that I shouldn't forget that the *Mayflower* people on Cape Cod are descended from tribes in England.

Tiny Mary warns me to take action and *don't even think of crying*, but I want to go home and crawl into Birdie's bed with the doves and cry. I want to know which British-DNA woman

HUSH LITTLE FIRE

is my birth mother before I grow old and die. I heard there are genealogists called search angels who will track down unknown relatives with the DNA information I just got. I may wind up calling a search angel, but right now it's time to get on an airplane and squeeze some answers out of Beatrice Birdie Newcombe, once and for all.

♦ **41** ♦

LISA DRIVES TO SPICE UP YOUR LIFE

Lisa

SITTING HERE ON LESTER'S comfortable chair, I couldn't be happier as I look at two big black plastic bags of money stuffed underneath the bottom bunk. I see a halo of hope surrounding them when the miraculous energy of money radiates throughout the cabin. Lester's still out, so I get up and move to his bunk bed to be closer to the bundles of bills. I should have figured it out sooner, no-brainer, that Jimmy hid the money in ordinary garbage bags under his mother's plaque in the cemetery.

Good news for me that Jimmy squirreled away another six thousand that I've already dipped into to get a new transmission for my car. I bought a vacuum cleaner for Lester's cabin and some secret baby blankets and yellow booties that I hid under the mattress. My whole body relaxes, knowing so much money is within arm's reach, and relaxing is good for the baby. Lester doesn't know about the pregnancy. Not yet. It might make him feel weird, and he might turn macho and side with the father, like when my uncle sided with my stepfather, even though Stepdad beat the crap out of my mother every other day. When it comes to fathers' rights, the men usually stick together, and then I wouldn't have a place to live.

I wonder if Bon Bon will really charge interest on the forty thousand? I better get organized and hurry over to Spice Up Your Life in Hyannis, because Chantrelle said Bon Bon has an office there. It's time to step out and make a move with the money. I'll have to walk to the Mobil station to pick up my car with its new transmission—or Old Man Christopher could drive me there if I butter him up with a ton of compliments. Forget that. I'll walk. He talks too much.

I'm so tired of hiding out at Lester's. Jimmy is dead, Barbara Haskins is dead, and Bon Bon will be happy to get his money back. That only leaves Patrick as the last big bump in my life. If the police bring him in for questioning, then Patrick will squeal, and he'll drag me down with him. I see the future as simple, like train tracks that suddenly fork. I can either live a long and happy life with my baby by taking the right fork, or I can go left and wind up in prison. And then they'll surely take my baby away, because I was stupid enough to help Jimmy and Patrick with deliveries. What do they call that on TV, an accessory to the crime?

Spice Up Your Life has a big splashy sign with palm trees and Jamaica's national flag painted on all four corners. I enter the shop and am hit with sweet and peppery smells that hang in the air wherever I turn. There are rows of canned food imported from Jamaica and bins of yams and plantains. In a trance, I stroll the aisles and fill my basket in no time. Lester cooked me tasty callaloo, a vegetable dish with spices and onion that looked like spinach, so I buy six cans for Lester. For the first time, I don't have to check any prices. I can fill my

240 JUDITH NEWCOMB STILES

grocery basket to the brim because I have a handful of hundred-dollar bills in my pocket. I grab ten packs of Ram-It-Up spices, a curry booster for goat. I hate goat meat, but maybe I'll get used to the taste because Lester likes it so much.

At the checkout counter, I ask the pretty girl with gold earrings in the shape of peace signs if Chantrelle or perhaps Mr. Bonaparte is in.

"Who should I say is calling?" In an instant, the girl loads the cans and plantains into a paper bag without damaging her long pink fingernails.

"I'm Lisa. Lisa Doanne."

The pretty girl picks up her cell phone in its pink rhinestone case and rattles off something in that secret Jamaican language that Lester uses with his friends.

"It's the door right past the ladies' room." A pink fingernail points to the back of the shop.

The door opens to a hallway with more doors, and the first, in golden letters, says *Chanty*. I knock, no answer, so I walk down the long hall, bouncing on the wall-to-wall carpet. The door at the end has a wooden sign framed in golden rosettes that says *Spice Up Your Life*, and I bet it's real gold. Before I knock, the door breezes open, and there is Bon Bon sitting at a large oval desk. I can tell it's mahogany, because I recognize fine furniture from cleaning the Woodwards' house. It's late morning, and Bon Bon is wearing workout clothes that look like they've never seen the inside of a gym. His office is pristine with almost nothing in it except four flat-screen TVs hung on the walls, all going at once with no sound. I look closer at rotating images of the Lucky Dragon Restaurant. Bon Bon has his feet up on the desk, leaning back, and doesn't look at me.

"Good morning, Miss Lisa. Have a seat. I was hoping you'd stop by. Do you recognize Chef Chen in the kitchen?"

HUSH LITTLE FIRE 241

He sits up straight and presses a button on the desk that closes the door behind me. I hear it lock.

The TV flashes a close-up of the neon sign at the Lucky Dragon. Bon Bon asks, eyes still on the TV, "Do you think I should order a larger sign for my restaurant? I like the signs to make a statement in my establishments. This one looks too small."

I sit down in the leather chair opposite Bon Bon and stick out my chest.

"The sign should definitely be larger, but not red letters. Red looks tacky. Try blue letters. Everyone likes blue. Script would look nice."

"Blue lettering. I like your suggestion. I might try that."

Now I know why Chef Chen makes those special meals of goat. Bon Bon owns the Lucky Dragon. Impressive.

After an unsettling silence, I sit up straight and fold my hands on my lap. "I brought you all the money that Jimmy and Patrick owe you."

"Thank you. Where is it? You understand I'm expecting forty thousand plus interest."

"I understand. But Lester was hoping you wouldn't charge interest because it's not really my loan."

"You say *Lester was hoping*?"

"Lester and I have been good friends for a very long time."

"I see."

I slide closer to the desk. "I have forty thousand right outside locked in my car. I'll go get it. But I was hoping you would waive the interest. And, more good news, I want to pay you for something else."

"What might that be? I assume you want help with your jam business. Organic sells well on the Cape and everywhere. You could use an investor. High profit margins with your

242   JUDITH NEWCOMB STILES

buy-sell jam from Job Lot. Their jam is just as good. Anyway, organic labels are overrated. Just a piece of paper with glue on the back. The labels are meaningless, you know why?"

"Why?"

"Because the water that grows the food in your country is bad. Full of pesticides and antidepressants. Think of millions of people urinating out drugs that find their way into the water table. Also, the drinking water here on Cape Cod is full of nitrates. It isn't safe for children. I have a daughter almost your age. Clever like you, but quiet. She studies marine biology at Yale and emails me interesting articles about all the chemicals in the water. I've been thinking of going into the bottled-water business. What do you think?"

"The water business could be good for you. But right now, I'm not thinking about water or my jam business much. It's still off-season. Besides, I'm going to have a baby. I'm pregnant."

"Well, what is it that I can help you with, Miss Lisa?"

"I can't possibly focus on improving my jam business with Patrick moping around the apartment all day. He's driving me nuts. I need to get Patrick out of my life."

"I assume Patrick is the father?"

"No. Not exactly."

"What do you mean, *not exactly*?" Bon Bon looks puzzled, and this is the first time he looks directly into my eyes. He shakes his head and clicks a remote a few times until all the screens are the same image of Chef Chen in the Lucky Dragon. Resting his arms on top of the mahogany desk, he taps the tips of his thumbs together. Tap, tap, tap. I wait.

"Did you ever try Chef Chen's octopus medley? He makes it with curry and roasted wild octopus, never farm raised. My daughter sent me a fascinating article about an octopus. In

HUSH LITTLE FIRE

243

captivity, an octopus will become very stressed and will eat its own limbs, which can lead to death from infection. It's an odd kind of self-cannibalism. Even an octopus has stress. Did you know that?"

"No, and that sounds awful. An octopus eating itself."

"I see your fingernails are bitten down. And your thumbs are very red. You seem out of sorts."

"A little bit. Well, sometimes."

"I like to help people, especially anyone who is friends with Lester. That's what business partners are for. If we can expand your jam business to Boston, that would relieve a lot of your financial stress. Are you stressed?"

"Well, I have a lot to think about with a baby coming." I hide my nails behind my back. "I need to get Patrick out of my life. Can you help me?"

♦ 42 ♦

LINCOLN ABRAHAM SMITH FILES HIS NAILS

Lisa

IN LESTER'S CABIN, I drop down on my knees and pray.

"Dear Lord, I thank you for this baby growing inside me. I hope it's a girl, but I will accept a boy. Maybe when you have a moment, you can send me a signal. Pink would be nice."

I stand up and straighten out my clothes. My boobs are enormous and very sore, but at least wearing Lester's big sweatshirt makes me feel better. Bon Bon didn't make me feel better, and I was glad to return the money and get out of his office.

I clean the window in the back of the cabin with ammonia and water, moving the rag in circles while I think about old boyfriends. The list of my old boyfriends is short, and I always liked them better when they were out of sight. Sometimes when Patrick was in the same room, irritation bubbled up out of nowhere, and when he slugged me, he destroyed any love we had. Forever.

With Lester, everything's so different. I'm happy just sitting by his side in the cabin. The subject of sleeping together has never come up, not even hinted at, even though Lester

HUSH LITTLE FIRE

245

puts his arm around me a lot. Anyway, there's no way I'd have sex with a man for a while, plugged up with a baby growing inside me. The thrusting of a man could loosen my baby. I haven't found the right moment to open my mouth and tell Lester I'm pregnant. I love the way he knows it's better to stick to small talk.

After cleaning the window so it sparkles, I've run out of chores in this cabin. My plan is to buy seeds and bags of soil to start a garden in the spring. I bought a small imitation Oriental rug at Job Lot and full-length canvas curtains with blue anchors that I installed myself. The curtain rods stick out too far and make the window look like a kid in an oversized hand-me-down outfit. Oh well, the cabin is definitely more homey.

I take a few steps toward the middle of the cabin, toss away my rag, and drop to the rug on my knees to pray for one more thing. As I kiss the middle of our Job Lot Oriental carpet, I think of Middle Eastern men in long robes, kissing prayer rugs. I wonder about all that praying they do every day. The only knowledge I have of Middle Eastern men comes from a cartoon about Ali Baba and the TV news about scary terrorists. But somehow I'm certain they go to a deep place of spiritual longing and prayer that connects them to a greater force in the universe, even though they don't share the same God with me. On my knees, I press my face into the rug and apologize to God for doing anything that might have led to the death of Barbara Haskins.

I pray, *Dear Lord, I know this might seem a little late, but I'm sorry Barbara Haskins died. I'm sorry for my evil thoughts when I visited her at the hospital, but I was afraid. As you might have noticed, I'm not usually a person who wishes harm on other people. It's just that I was trying to make my world safe. Really, who wants to go to jail? Sorry for rambling. I'm very sorry for everything. As you know,*

I'm going to have my first baby. I hope you noticed I gave up swearing. Oh Lord, can you forgive me?

My neck aches from being down on the prayer rug, and when I open the front door for fresh air, Patrick's brown pickup truck stumbles up the dirt road. I reach out with one hand to close the front door, but it won't close all the way. *Don't panic.* I scramble to the back window faster than a mouse, but I'll never make it if I try to climb out the little window. I hide behind the full-length canvas curtains and try to be still. Minutes feel like hours as Patrick slowly gets out of the truck. His anger is electric and zaps the ground in a tantrum as he stomps into the cabin. I've known him long enough to feel it in the air when he gets crazy in the head, and I feel it through the curtains. It occurs to me that this could be the last day of my life.

Oh dear God, please don't let him find me.

I hold my breath and peek through the curtains as Patrick opens drawers, the little refrigerator, his hands flying everywhere. He jerks the drawers onto the floor, rifling through Lester's clothes. He smashes Lester's nice glass bowl and sends the water bucket flying across the room when all of a sudden, a car screeches to a stop right in front of the cabin.

Lester jumps out of the car with another man. He stops at the door with his arms crossed and announces in a very loud voice, "My good friend here, Lincoln, was enjoying a smoke at the bottom of the road, watching the world go by, minding his own business. He was kind enough to text me when he saw your truck go up the driveway. *What the fuck* are you doing in my house?"

"I'm looking for my girlfriend. Where the fuck is she?"

Lincoln is the biggest man I've ever seen in my life, and the proof is that he has to bend down quite a bit to slide through the front door of the cabin. He politely stands behind Lester

HUSH LITTLE FIRE

with about as much emotion as the empty-eyed faces on Mount Rushmore. In one stroke, his enormous hands twist Patrick's arm, which sends Patrick lurching into a headlock. Lincoln yanks Patrick like a rubber band; one more inch and he could snap Patrick's head off. Patrick's eagle tattoo on his neck is all twisted, and his face is bulging red. Lester gets up close and looks into Patrick's face, eyeball to eyeball, without saying a word. Lester is about to explode.

"Patrick, let me introduce you to my friend here, Lincoln Abraham Smith. He is also Lisa's friend. He's a chef and an excellent fisherman. Do you see his hand?"

Patrick is grunting something I can't hear. His head is stuck in the vice of Lincoln's giant arm. Lincoln's other hand is smoothing the top of Patrick's head before he gives a cheeky tug to Patrick's ponytail.

"Lincoln, kindly tell Patrick what you do before you cook."

"Well, this hand here, you can see I polish my fingernails like the ladies do. I prefer clear epoxy to nail polish on my middle finger, and I paint the top side and the underside to make it very hard. Do you see that? Answer me."

Patrick gives Lincoln a wobbly nod.

"Then I file it to a nice point like the ladies *never* do, and I give it one more coat of epoxy. Fingernails are portable and perfect for gutting fish. Do you see how nice they are?"

Lincoln yanks Patrick's ponytail again and whispers into his ear, "I like to think of my middle finger as a kitchen knife. Perfect for filleting fish and such."

Lester moves in closer to Patrick and gets right in his face. "Lincoln might gut your eyeballs out if you ever disrespect him again. And if you ever go looking for Lisa again, Bon Bon will not be pleased. It takes Lincoln just a few seconds to gut a fish. Do you understand me?" And with that, Lester gives a flick of his finger on Patrick's forehead above each eye.

Patrick sputters, "I didn't really come here for Lisa. I came for my money. Some of that money is mine."

Lester paces the floor in a circle. "Go home now, Patrick. Go home. I'm going to give you some friendly advice, although you will never be my friend. You made life difficult for Hector Bonaparte, and that was a very bad idea."

Patrick wriggles his head, which makes Lincoln squeeze his neck tighter.

"Maybe you don't recognize the name Hector Bonaparte because you are ignorant. Hector goes by the name of Bon Bon, and he will get in touch with you in ten minutes about leaving Cape Cod for good. Until then, go to the bottom of the road and wait in your truck." With that, Lincoln Abraham Smith lifts Patrick in the air and hurls him out the front door. I take a few steps from behind the curtain and open my mouth to say something very important, but my lips let out a spray of squeaks before I fall facedown on the prayer rug and faint.

♦ 43 ♦

BIRDIE CRITICIZES
DR. NEWCOMBE'S USE
OF TWEEZERS

Mary

I AM MARY NEWCOMBE now, but who would I be if the nuns had given me to somebody else?

There's too much time while I wait at the airport, too much time to rip my history apart, so I sit here in a mish-mosh of dread. In the seating area, I wander over to the big glass window to look for the plane I'll take to Florida. I have such a childish wish Birdie will give me a big warm hello when I arrive—so glad to see me—and her arms will pull me to her and hold me close. But Birdie isn't a hugger.

I rehearse what I'll say to her over and over, so by the time I arrive at her apartment, I am beyond frazzled, poking her doorbell too many times.

"Come in. How was your flight?" Birdie is barefoot, wearing a long tie-dyed yellow dress. Her painted red toenails scuff the hem as she ushers me in without touching me. She won't look at me and fumbles through her purse for a pack of cigarettes and offers me one.

250 JUDITH NEWCOMB STILES

"No thanks, I'm trying to quit. I thought I was over allergies, but smoking makes me wheeze."

"You don't have allergies."

"If you say so."

"Allergies are for the weak people."

"Whatever."

Birdie seems on edge. I better be careful. Her different moods, the criticism, can slay me when I least expect it, and I never know which Birdie I'll get. I roll my suitcase into the living room and don't even try to guess.

"It's so unfair they have a no-smoking rule in this apartment complex." She snaps a match and lights up. "Sit down. Make yourself comfortable."

I pick a white lounge chair near the front door, not the big white whale of a couch that could swallow me up. The windows are shut and the air conditioner is roaring, but it feels like there's not enough air in the room for both of us to breathe.

"I'll make you some tea. But let's not beat around the bush. I think I know why you're here. You know, you could've done this over the phone, my dear."

"I needed to see you in person, Mother."

"I know it's serious when you call me Mother." Birdie exhales smoke out of the corner of her mouth and laughs. She abruptly stubs out her half-finished cigarette, which lands like a broken arm in the ashtray. She smooths her hair, plops down on the couch, and lights another cigarette—and oh, how I love her secondhand smoke. I inhale deeply when it wafts my way.

"I need to ask you, Mother, have you heard from the FBI or the police?"

HUSH LITTLE FIRE

251

"Don't be silly. You worry too much. I know how to handle them." She jumps up and putters around in her kitchenette, thrusting two mugs into the microwave. "I'll simply answer their questions in the vaguest, most confusing way, and then I'll drop little hints that I'm suffering from, you know, early-onset dementia. I'm seventy-five. I know how to act the part." She exhales a big ring of smoke with a flourish. "I'll move with a tremor, and I won't get my hair done all week."

"Are you kidding? You'd actually do that?"

"They already asked me about my relationship with Nurse Haskins on the phone, so I just played them some music on the radio and hung up. If they show up here, I'll do something like pour hand soap in my tea."

"Why not just tell them the truth?"

"What do you want me to say? That I'm sorry Barbara Haskins died? I'm too old to lie."

"Walter Stone said a UPS driver told the police he saw you having a heated argument with Nurse Haskins on your front porch last November. What was that about?"

Birdie is busy blotting some tea spilled on her saucer. "Oh, don't give me that patronizing look." She kneads the wet napkin into a ball. "The truth is I'm not sorry Barbara died. Some say she got what she deserved."

"Did she deserve to die like *that*?"

"Oh, that's not what I mean, and you know it. Honestly, I'm not qualified to say what she deserved, but I'm not sure God is qualified either. All I know is the tramp was trying to blackmail me."

"You shouldn't call her that."

"She said your father's money was really half hers, not mine, and *why*? I know she was broke, but so what. Did she think she had any right to the money just because the two of them gave out secret procedures like candy? Hell's bells, that was decades ago. She had the audacity to demand money after all this time."

"You should have told me."

"She said she kept an embarrassing note from Dianne Crocker all these years. Dianne begged Barbara to keep quiet about little Billy Crocker. She could have ruined me. Wellfleet's a small town. What would people think?"

"What did the note say about Billy Crocker?"

"Never mind all that. But then she told me about Cindy. I forget her married name. She said go ask Cindy if she could ever get pregnant again after your father botched the procedure and sterilized her by mistake."

"She said that?"

"It doesn't matter. If there were any medical records from back then, they're all gone now, thanks to the fire."

"*Thanks* to the fire???"

I want to take Birdie's hand and hold it to tease out the truth, but she has a teacup in one hand and a cigarette in the other.

"Mother, do you know who set the fire at the clinic? You can tell me."

"You shouldn't judge me." She looks out the window.

"I'm not judging you."

She stirs what's left of her tea, clickety-clicking her cup with a spoon.

"Sometimes I wonder how God will judge me, because I admit it, I often wished Nurse Barb would die. But you know what? After a while, I stopped wishing her dead, and I was grateful to Barb."

"Grateful?"

HUSH LITTLE FIRE 253

"Because she kept your father occupied. Him and his you-know-what. He decided to sleep in his own bedroom, and that was far enough away for me."

"Funny how I grew up thinking all mothers and fathers kept separate bedrooms."

"You have no idea what it was like with your father. He couldn't keep his fly zipped with that nurse. And there were others, and not just Dianne Crocker. It's bad enough he was unfaithful, but he never took responsibility for abortions that didn't go so well. Girls that got hurt. Tiny heartbeats snuffed out with a clip of tweezers."

"Tweezers?"

"Well, I know the surgical instruments aren't tweezers, but they certainly look like it. Imagine him ending a chance at life with a lousy pair of tweezers."

"So does this mean you're against . . ."

"Oh my goodness. Don't *you* start lecturing me with that catchy phrase. It's practically a cliché by now. *My body, my choice*? Oh please. Singsong baloney! Tell me, whose right is it to choose? What about a heartbeat's rights?"

"It's not that simple."

"My dear daughter, are you asking me if I'm against a woman's right to choose? Because my honest answer is *yes* and *no*. I admit that I waffle back and forth on the question, but most women have doubts at least once in their lives. Of course, you'd never admit it. In the end, you pro-choice girls are probably right about the whole thing, the concept anyway."

"It's not just a concept, Mother."

"If I were Trudy Bale with four daughters like that, I would have gotten the fifth one *fixed*, but her mistake was not taking care of it over the bridge soon enough."

"Over the bridge? What do you mean by that?"

"She drank too much and blabbed to everybody at the Bomby, including me, about how to get a late-term abortion. I knew she couldn't handle another kid on her own. She should have gone to Puerto Rico or Paris or someplace like that for help."

"Paris?"

"Rich people get late-term abortions, and it's completely hush-hush, rolled up and repackaged into a pretend miscarriage. But Trudy didn't have the money. It's a woman's decision, but still it's true, everyone has a little twinge at least once about the tiny heartbeat that ends with a lousy pair of tweezers."

"Please don't say tweezers. Tweezers are for plucking eyebrows. They use sterilized surgical instruments."

"Same difference. And if you must know, with your father, it was never about a woman's right to choose. It was about money. All cash."

"So what if Daddy made a lot of money? Back then what he did was so important. Women needed him."

"Don't be silly. Your father didn't give a damn about those girls."

"Well, a woman shouldn't be forced to have a baby if she doesn't want to. And what about all those women who died from coat hangers?"

"What about it?"

"Daddy saved lives."

"Very funny. Bill the lifesaver. That's a good one. Your father the lifesaver and your father the heart squasher."

"Good God, don't say that."

✦ 44 ✦

BIRDIE IS CERTAIN FAUX WOMBS ARE COMING

Mary

AN UGLY LITTLE FLY buzzes onto the sugar bowl and then lands on my shoulder and then zigzags in the air and bounces back to the sugar bowl. *Tiny Mary? How'd you get all the way down to Florida?* I wave my hand to shoo the fly away.

Tell your mother to throw out that flypaper over the sink right now. Can you think of anything worse than your feet getting stuck on something sticky until you shrivel up and die of starvation? Tell herzzzz!

I bat at the sugar bowl one handed and ask my mother, "Do you have a flyswatter?"

"No, and I'm out of flypaper. Now, where was I? Oh yes. Tweezers. I truly believe all this angsty nonsense and arguing about a woman's right to choose will be a moot point soon. Sooner than you think."

"How could our right to choose *ever* be a moot point?"

"They say in the Netherlands, someday soon it will be normal to grow babies in a petri dish, and it will be legal too. Scientists over there are supposedly close to inventing faux wombs for people. They already have them for lambs."

"Whaaat?"

"Picture this. Warm little containers with grow lights that will incubate babies in a plastic baggie full of amniotic fluid."

"No pregnant mothers anymore?"

"Nope. And it will be a fad for teenage girls to harvest their own eggs and save them for later. I bet you'll see this in your lifetime. Faux wombs."

"That sounds so bizarre."

"In the future, maybe in a decade or so, the reasoning behind *Roe v. Wade* will be obsolete. Young girls will think it's trendy to snip their fallopian tubes, and that way, no more pregnancy scares. You'll see. It will be fashionable to harvest eggs to fertilize and grow later in a fancy faux womb."

"No more human wombs? That's such a chilling thought."

Smack in the middle of my mother's rant, a faint buzzing sound gets louder as Tiny Mary zooms over and lands on Birdie's nose, then hops back to the sugar bowl, then back to Birdie's hair.

Ladiezzzzzz. Don't be so precious about hatching babies. I lay my eggs in your garbage, sometimes two thousand eggs a month. You have some nerve saying mean things about my maggot babies, who are kind enough to eat your leftovers and dead bodies. Mother Nature must have been asleep at the wheel when she invented nine months of pregnancy for humans. Ladiezzzz, your cumbersome long gestation period is very inefficient, so it's about time you switch to faux wombs.

Birdie is quiet as she taps the buttons on the air conditioner. She whispers, "I rather like the sound of faux wombs. It sounds so French."

"It sounds horrible to me. Too futuristic." I move from the chair and lie down on the white whale of a couch, exhausted, and it's not even noon yet. Birdie cranks up the air conditioner when I'm already freezing. "Do you have a blanket?"

HUSH LITTLE FIRE

257

"Are you cold? Should I turn down the air conditioner?"

"Please."

"Now that you're all grown up and a mother yourself, I can tell you this. Your father, he was different. Most doctors want to help others, and they have a guiding light that tells them to do good deeds in the world, but no, your father was guided by his pecker."

"This is way too much information. Stop talking about him like that."

"Pecker, pecker, pecker. That's what he was."

"I need to hear it from you first, Mother. So I'll ask you again: Did you burn down the clinic with Nurse Haskins inside?"

"I certainly did not. Nurse Haskins was very huffy with me that night when she showed up at the house last November. She had the nerve to tell me there's a statute of limitations on crimes but no statute of limitations on how she could destroy my reputation. But still, I didn't burn down the clinic."

"So what did you say when she threatened you?"

"I stood my ground. She had the gall to say she'd tell Billy Crocker that old Chief Crocker wasn't really his father."

"The police think you set the fire because you hated Barbara. The best thing you can do is tell the truth."

"Oh really? And where will the truth get me? Walter Stone hinted that the fire is linked to a bigger investigation about some drug ring on Cape Cod."

"The police don't think you were involved with the drugs, do they?"

"I hope not. But Jimmy used our mailing address to get drugs. Little yellow slips came in from the post office for *Beatrice Newcombe* for things I never ordered. Jimmy always picked up my mail. I think it was fentanyl from China that he was planning to sell, so where will it get me if I tell the truth? He used my credit card, and it wasn't for fishing lures."

"Oh God, that's bad."

"Bad for me and very bad for Danny. I found out Jimmy and Patrick made him deliver paper bags of drug money." Birdie is clutching the arms of the white whale couch.

"I have a lawyer friend in New York, and I'll talk to her about this. Sounds like you, I mean *we*, are in serious trouble."

"Are you in trouble, Miss Mary?"

"Don't call me that, please."

"Sorry, I forgot you don't like that."

"I hate it when you call me Miss Mary."

"Okay, *Mary* . . . And if you don't mind, there's something I've been wanting to ask you, and please don't get touchy with me. A witness, Lisa Doanne, told Chief Crocker you were hiding behind a van when the clinic burned down. Is that true?"

"She said she saw *me*? It was dark out. And I definitely didn't drive there. I don't drive drunk like half the people on Cape Cod, who shall remain nameless."

"You could have walked there."

"Oh right. In the cold. In the dark."

"But you walked there a hundred times to bring your father's lunch. Did you walk there that night?"

"I don't remember. I just don't. It's all a blur."

"Should I believe that?"

"Believe what you want . . . I can't *believe* you didn't see what was happening last summer. I counted on you to take good care of Danny when I was away."

"Cross my heart and hope to die, I didn't know what he was doing. I should have paid more attention, but I'm old, and besides, I have my own life."

HUSH LITTLE FIRE

"What life? What else were you doing that was more important?"

We stop talking and listen to the hum of the air conditioner. We both know she was busy watching important game shows on TV and stirring important cocktails.

"Why don't you stay a few days? I know you planned to fly back tonight, but we have so much catching up to do. I missed you."

"You missed me?"

"Please stay. Would you like a drinkie of some kind? I quit drinking, but can I make you a mimosa or something?" Birdie gets up from the couch and wanders over to the kitchenette.

"A glass of water is fine for now. I'm trying to quit smoking, and that's great you quit alcohol."

"I quit yesterday."

"I'm really proud of you. What made you finally quit?"

"Well . . . I ran out of sherry."

◆ 45 ◆

MARY CONFERS WITH WALTER ABOUT THE FEEL-GOOD SCALE

Mary

A SMALL PANG OF wanting to stay with my mother hunkers down inside me, so I agree to spend the night. When she said she missed me, I believed her. I want to believe her.

In the morning, I wake up earlier than Birdie, so I have a patch of time to review my 23andMe report and figure out how to talk to her about this. The chart of my DNA is screaming *British*, while Tiny Mary screams, *Calm down!*

Walter and I have been texting a lot about a pretty vase he made for Chief Crocker to give to his wife for her birthday, but at the last minute when he wrapped it, he noticed a hairline crack down the side. Walter was angsting-texting that it might leak on her table, and worse, she might get mad at the chief for a bad birthday present. This bad-firing-vase drama makes me want to call Walter and hear the sound of his voice.

"Hello there. I'm so glad you called. How's it going in Florida with your mother?"

HUSH LITTLE FIRE

261

"Fine."

"I know you. Fine means not so good, or less than so-so. On a scale of one to ten, ten is high, how are you feeling right now?"

"I have no idea. My scale of feelings is one big splatter of numbers, but thanks for asking."

"How's Birdie doing in Florida?"

"She looks so old. Actually, she's trying to look old on purpose for Agent Cunningham."

"Tell her not to worry about Cunningham. I've been quietly steering her north."

"Huh?"

"Cunningham pumps me for secrets about the comings and goings in Wellfleet, so I told her about some guys at the Bomby who insisted drugs are hidden down by the oyster beds. The guys at the Bomby thought this was hilarious, so they all got in the game. Charlie McAvoy pointed her in the direction of Maine and told her about fishermen in Portland who smuggle drugs in with codfish. Then his brother dropped hints about Nova Scotia, and if they keep it up, they'll send her all the way to the North Pole."

"Wouldn't that be nice." Walter and I have a good laugh about Agent Cunningham at the North Pole interrogating reindeer in her womanized man-suit. He suddenly goes serious on me and whispers, "Tell Birdie she should stay in Florida for now."

"Can you and the guys at the Bomby get in trouble for talking shit to the FBI?"

"Not me. I thought I told you, I'm taking early retirement, so I'm done in about sixty days. I'm already growing a beard."

"A beard? I love beards."

Walter's beard better be soft, not scratchy, if he ever decides to kiss me again.

"The chief is very unhappy with the way things are going, and he wants to believe the Christmas fire will go down in history as an accident."

"Let's hope so."

"He doesn't seem to care what really happened. But I do."

"Maybe we should all just let it go. You too."

Birdie's living room is blue and shaped like a fish tank, and as I listen to Walter, I feel like a lone goldfish swimming back and forth in her tank. By the time Walter finishes telling me about his latest kiln firing, Birdie wanders in with a hyper-cheerful look on her face.

"Sorry. Gotta go. I'll text you later. *She's up*," I say, surprising myself when I tack on a quiet "I miss you" before I say goodbye to Walter.

"Who were you talking to? I can always tell when you're talking to a boy. Was it Tom, by any chance?"

"Christ, I'm fifty-two years old. No, it's not a boy."

"How come you haven't mentioned Tom? I thought you went out on a date?"

"We did, sort of. But I haven't seen him since."

"You look deathly pale this morning. You must get some sun while you're here."

"My entire life, you've been telling me I look pale. I'm fine. Just fine."

"What? You don't believe me when I say you need to get out in the sun?" Birdie glowers at me. "Would you like me to make some tea with milk? I can go buy milk."

"I would love some tea, but no hand soap, please. And yes. I don't know what to believe anymore."

HUSH LITTLE FIRE 263

"Enough with all this small talk. I can tell you still have doubts." She bangs around in the cupboards, looking for something, and snarls, "Go ahead, ask me anything you want. Go ahead."

My mother turns around, looks right through me with her accusatory eyes on the offensive, like I have no right to ask her anything.

"Okay, Mother . . . Walter told me that Lisa Doanne told him that you went to see Jimmy on New Year's Eve a few hours before he died. She said you had a big fight. What about?"

"A fight? It takes two to fight. If you must know, I was doing all the shouting, and Jimmy, well, he just sat there like a . . . like a . . . potato. He was drunk. I wanted to slap him."

"A potato??? What did you say to him?" I touch her arm, but she pulls away.

"Look, I'm sorry . . . I could have done a better job looking after Danny, I know that, but I thought Jimmy was babysitting him." My mother crushes a soggy lump of sugar into little pieces on her teacup saucer. "I'm just Beatrice Birdie Newcombe, a foolish old lady. I was never any good at looking after children or taking care of babies."

"I wouldn't say that."

"I tried to be a good mother and a good aunt to Jimmy. I hope you will add that to my tombstone in big letters: *SHE TRIED*. All caps, please. That would be nice."

"Do you know what really happened on the boat that day when Jimmy pushed Danny overboard?"

"I should have never trusted him with Danny. I thought when Jimmy grew up and started fishing, he'd be better, but he was never any good at the fishing business."

"Did you know Danny drove the boat back to the harbor all by himself?"

264 JUDITH NEWCOMB STILES

"Jimmy swore that wasn't true. But if you must know, I had my suspicions about Jimmy. His attitude. And I always wondered if he was swinging both ways."

"What exactly do you mean by swinging?"

"Look. The world is changing fast right before our eyes. A middle-aged man, even someone like Jimmy, has the right to go for another man if that's what he wants. That's his own business."

"So what are you saying?"

"I'm saying Jimmy had a right to live his life however he pleased, but no man has a right to force his jiggety-jig on anyone. Not his wife, or his girlfriend, or a child. And especially not my grandson."

"Jiggety-jig? Is that some kind of sailor talk?" I am sick at the thought of Jimmy jiggety-jigging anywhere near my son.

"Big James used to joke with Clara when he came back from a long trip, and he'd ask her right in front of me if she missed his jiggety-jig."

"Gross."

"It's sailor talk, and yes, it's gross. Clara confided in me, he used to force himself on her. She told me he tried to make her play awful games in bed. And you can bet your bottom dollar, my grandson will never be anyone's *cabin boy*."

I clamp my hands over my ears. "I can't stand hearing any of this."

"I don't mean to upset you. I don't think it was all that bad with Jimmy and Danny. I gather, from a few things Danny said about that day in the boat, that Jimmy was drunk when he pushed him overboard, and nothing more. I can make you a nice Bellini with a touch of prosecco. It's still early, perhaps a Bloody Mary?"

HUSH LITTLE FIRE 265

"For God's sake, I thought you gave up drinking."

"I'll make one for you, not me. And anyway, what do my hobbies have to do with any of this?"

"Your hobbies?"

Birdie opens the refrigerator and sighs. The light glows yellow on her face as she whispers, "Once I asked Big James in my nicest voice, why on earth did he spank Jimmy so much? He just smiled and said, 'Because.'"

I don't remember much about Big James—he died years ago, and I'm not even sure when. But there was a photo in Jimmy's apartment of Big James with young Jimmy hugging his father's leg. Neither of them was smiling for the camera. It must have been right before Jimmy discovered the power of lighter fluid, which got him in lots of trouble with Big James. When we got caught making baby fires for fun too many times, Big James set up a wooden chair in the shed for the sole purpose of punishing his son. It was the spanking chair. That's what he called it. Little Jimmy knew there was a thin line between being good and bad, and he danced on that line too many times. We both knew roasting marshmallows was okay, but pouring too much lighter fluid on a hibachi of hot dogs near his father's toolshed was not okay. Jimmy laughed his ass off when the lighter fluid exploded the fire. Lucky for Jimmy, when the shed burned down, the fire department deemed it a careless accident. And lucky for me, Jimmy didn't tell the grown-ups that it was me who had squirted until the can was empty. We hated that shed. We were glad it burned down. For me, no more peeking through the door when Big James punished Jimmy—those times when I watched him spank Jimmy's bare bottom with a whack louder than a firecracker. It terrified me, and I held my breath so I wouldn't cough.

"Talk, talk, talk. It never makes much difference, does it," says Birdie as she ruffles her hair and walks over to the picture window. "Look at all those boats out there. You'll never catch me on a boat at high noon. Too much sun. You can get fried out there on the water. At least I always made sure Danny wore sun block."

"Well, I'm grateful for that."

"You know, Danny wouldn't talk about what happened on the boat, but Charlie McAvoy told me he saw Danny driving *Angel Baby* that day. I shouldn't have kept it a secret from you. You're Danny's mother."

"You and Dad kept a lot of secrets from me. *A lot.*"

Birdie is pushing random buttons on the air conditioner so hard she could blow a fuse in the apartment or in her head. "It was a terrible mistake I never told you about important things."

"*What* other important things?"

"I need to lie down for a minute. This heat is getting to me."

"But your apartment is totally air conditioned. *Mother*, you were about to tell me something important."

"I need to go lie down in the bedroom and collect myself, and then I'll run out and buy you some milk." Without looking back, Birdie retreats to the bedroom and slams the door on me.

♦ 46 ♦

MARY LEARNS THE TRUTH ON THE WHITE WHALE OF A COUCH

Mary

WHILE BIRDIE TAKES A nap, I watch junky soap operas on TV, and then I go out and buy some flypaper and wait for something to land on the sticky stuff. After her three-hour nap, Birdie bursts into the kitchen overly cheerful, looking rested and refreshed. "Shall we order some takeout for tonight?"

"Fine. Whatever you want to do. I've been waiting for you to wake up. Before your nap, we were having an important talk."

"Let's do Mexican tonight." Birdie shuffles through a stack of takeout menus.

"Don't change the subject."

Birdie looks surprised and puts down the menus.

"You were saying something about keeping secrets before your nap. What?"

Birdie spreads the takeout menus on the coffee table one by one. "Keeping secrets? Okay. Your father started it. And I guess you can call me a coward, because I couldn't stop."

"I asked you many times about my birth mother, and you never answered. Not once."

"If you must know, I didn't even find out the truth until I went looking through your father's personal papers after he died. It was like he handed me his dirty little secret, and I didn't know what to do, so I took it and kept it as my own for all these years."

I circle in close to my mother's face—so close she can't pop a cigarette in her mouth. "I want you to know that I took a 23andMe genetic test, and it came out ninety-nine percent of my genes are from England. *Who is my birth mother?*"

"That makes sense, but you're not from England. You're *Mayflower* English. Your birth records were in a locked box with old fishing lures that he never used. He thought I'd never look there, and I didn't until after he died. You were ten already, and there it was, the unadulterated truth in print, and I was horrified he never told me. I got so dizzy, I dropped the box and stepped on a hook—it went through my slipper."

"And? *And what?*"

I pull out the crumpled-up postcard I stole. It still has the perfumey smell of Birdie's underwear drawer. "I found this old postcard in your room. What does this mean?" I read it out loud to her without looking up.

Dear Beatrice,

Canada is beautiful! Hugs and kisses to my Jimmy! I'll be back soon. In the meantime, you should know, the gift is not from Antoine. I'm positive. We'll talk more when I see you. I hope we can still be friends.

Love always,

Clara

HUSH LITTLE FIRE

My mother snatches the card away. "You always were a little snoop."

"Why did you save this? What does this mean?"

"All right, all right, let me catch my breath. Give me a minute." She lights a cigarette in slow motion. "Before we adopted you, your father came back from Canada with the ashes of Clara and Baby Newcombe. I thought it was over. I thought we buried them. The end."

"The end?" I want to rip up the smelly postcard and throw the pieces at her.

"But three months later, on a second trip to Canada, he brought back a screaming baby. *You.* He lied to me and said the mother was fifteen years old and we had to respect the privacy of the family, so he said he couldn't tell me the mother's name."

"So I'm Canadian?"

"I was so overwhelmed, home alone with a newborn, I dropped the subject and stopped asking about the parents. I thought I'd go insane with all the fussing and crying. I didn't have the energy to question anything. I should have asked, but I didn't want him to think that Beatrice Newcombe couldn't manage, so I slogged through your first few months, trying not to go out of my mind."

"*Who* is my birth mother?"

"She passed away a long time ago."

"I may never be able to forgive you for keeping it a secret. Who was she?"

"I'm an old woman now, but it doesn't make this any easier. Clara's baby didn't die. You were born premature while Clara was hemorrhaging to death in Canada. Your father went to pick you up after you grew strong enough to travel a few months later. *Clara* was your birth mother."

"I don't believe you."

"It's true. I'm sorry."

I'm going to jump out the window or lock myself in the bathroom and vomit. "So Jimmy is my half brother?"

"Not exactly . . ."

Birdie's scary frown is bigger than I've ever seen it. I can barely hear her choking out the words. "At first, I prayed for God to forgive Clara, but something felt wrong. The father of the baby couldn't have been Big James. He was working on a tanker that year. Since Clara had been fooling around with the painting teacher, I went to Provincetown and hunted down Antoine, but he swore on a stack of Bibles that he couldn't be the father because he'd had a vasectomy."

"What do you mean, Jimmy is *not exactly* my half brother?" The question crumbles out of my mouth and falls away. I'm not sure I'm ready for the answer. My legs start moving toward the bathroom, although I'm not sure it's me who is moving them. I can't breathe. I'm furious there's a window in this bathroom, because I don't want anyone to look in and see me, Mary Newcombe, the *sort of* half sister of Jimmy, who was not my cousin after all. I move over to the sink and grab the faucets with both hands and look up. The girl in the mirror woodpeckers me with questions. She shouts, *Adoption is a game for adults, and the winner gets a baby.*

"Shut up!" I scream at the girl in the mirror and sit down on the floor, but that doesn't help, so I lie down flat on my back and stare at Birdie's ugly bathroom ceiling. The ceiling is supposed to be blue like the sky, but it's a hideous blue, like glossy magazine advertisements for the tropics where everything is fake. It's all been a lie. I had make-out sessions with a man who turned out to be a blood relative. We almost slept

HUSH LITTLE FIRE

together. Jeez. I could have had a secret-twisted-gene-pool baby with three heads if Jimmy and I had gone any further.

"*Please* come out of the bathroom and talk to me. I'm so sorry I never told you. But I could never figure out the right way, and the longer it went on, the further it drifted into the past. I was afraid you would love Clara, the golden mother, and you would hate me for all my shortcomings. I was afraid I wouldn't stand a chance with you."

I focus my eyes on the ceiling light fixture in the center of the fake blue ceiling, but it's expanding and shrinking all at once. Birdie stands in the doorway, looking down at me with her arms folded. Her face looks so strange upside down with its crinkled Birdie frown.

"I didn't know anything about Clara being your birth mother until you were ten, when I saw your original birth certificate for the first time. When I found it, I didn't tell you because I wasn't a big enough person to let you love another mother, your birth mother."

"Did Jimmy ever know any of this?"

"If he did, he didn't say so to me. The last time I saw him before the terrible car crash, he bitterly complained about women who lie, but I think he was really talking about Katie Snow. Please come out of the bathroom. There's something else important I must tell you."

I don't know if I can take anymore . . . What else?"

"First I need to run to the store and buy more milk."

♦ 47 ♦

UNWANTED BABIES PASSED OFF TO FARAWAY RELATIVES

Mary

I WAIT A LONG time for Birdie, who finally returns with two gallons of milk for our two cups of tea.

"Oh dear, should I have gotten cream instead of milk for your tea?"

"Milk is fine. Now, what else do you want to tell me? I've been waiting fifty-two years."

"Okay . . . okay . . . the truth is, your original birth certificate listed Clara Newcombe as the mother and William Newcombe as the father. He didn't want me to find out. He never told me about his fling with Clara, and I never paid attention to how flirty they were."

"This can't be true. *Daddy?*"

"Your daddy and Clara. She bragged all the time about free love, blah, blah, blah, and how women's liberation was so important for her freedom and the freedom of all women. What a joke. She was like a cat in heat without any concern for anyone's feelings—for *my* feelings. Look where it got her. And me?"

"I don't believe what you're telling me."

HUSH LITTLE FIRE

273

Birdie is at the kitchen table with both hands covering her face, and I can tell she's trying not to cry. She drops her hands from her face. "One thing I want to know—how come the birth mother gets to sit on a throne like a saint when I did all the work? How come?"

"That's not true."

"I'm the one who kept you from climbing out windows, from eating ant traps, from falling down the stairs. Miss Mary Newcombe, you put everything in your mouth . . . I'm not crying. I'm not." She wipes her nose with a dish towel.

"Are you saying that Dad knew he was my biological father?"

"He kept it to himself. He had a phony adoption birth certificate made up in Canada, and I didn't know anything until I found the original with a letter after he died."

"What letter?"

"It was on disgusting stationery that smelled like roses, written in her perfect script. He hid it inside the tackle box with the original birth certificate. I threw it out after I read it. Clara wrote to him that the baby was his and soon they would be together. No mention of me. What about *me*?"

"Please tell me more about Clara." *I've waited all my life for something—anything—about her.*

Birdie is quiet for a while, kneading the dish towel. "What can I tell you? She's not British, if that's what you're asking. She came from a long line of Cape Cod stock like your father. Her family has been on the Cape going all the way back to the original men who signed the Mayflower Compact. The Newcombes with an *e* go way back to England, and your father and Clara always kidded around that we're all blood relatives somewhere back on the family tree."

"Do you have any pictures of her?"

274 JUDITH NEWCOMB STILES

"I gave them to Jimmy. She was beautiful. Dark hair like yours, and beautiful pale skin like a pearl."

"But you always criticize me for being pale."

"You have the same complexion and the same eyes. You do."

"I wish you still had a picture."

"She was a restless woman, always hungry for more, and I just knew she would leave someday. I didn't know about the fling with your father. And worse, I never knew that Big James couldn't make a baby, so she turned to good old Dr. Newcombe to get pregnant with her first child. Jimmy. Big James never even knew. The Newcombe brothers looked enough alike for her to get away with it. Same obnoxious gene pool. You have to understand, Clara was my only friend. She knew how to make me laugh when everything was falling apart, and I loved being around her."

I sink down on the white whale of a couch and wish it would swallow me whole and take me out to sea. A sudden sharp pain attacks my potter's knee, and I'm not even lifting heavy bags of clay. Tiny Mary insists that a big heavy bag of sadness parks itself in my knee when things get to be too much and news has nowhere else to go.

"Can you tell me, why is it for ten years of my life, Daddy didn't tell me or you?"

"He was New England to the bone. Back then, unwanted babies were passed off to older sisters, cousins, aunties, faraway relatives, more than you think. And it was all done in secret, because that's the way women did things back then. He must have known it would break me to find out about him and Clara. Your father was an expert at secrets. Think of those girls who went in and out of his clinic. I'm so glad I never have to look at that horrible building again."

"Okay, okay. This is way too much for one day."

HUSH LITTLE FIRE 275

Birdie pats my leg and sits at my feet on the other end of the couch as she looks at takeout menus again. I stretch out my legs toward her, and she lifts my feet and rests them on her lap. Her strong bony fingers massage my heel, my instep, and then my toes. Without saying a word, she wiggles my toes one by one. I peak out of the corner of my eye—she is crying. Her fingers move to my other set of toes, and she whispers a ditty. "*This little piggy went to market. This little piggy stayed home.*"

I put my hand to my chest and feel for my heartbeat. It's still pumping away, old faithful, doing the job it was meant to do. Now I know that the blood running through my body, whooshing through my heart, is the blood of the Newcombe family. Now I know. And at this moment, my father, my birth mother, and my brother are a pile of dust unto dust, and all the while this woman, Beatrice Birdie Newcombe, cradles my feet.

"Miss Mary—oh, sorry, I didn't mean to call you that . . . just so you know, I won't be going back to the Cape in the spring. This is my home now. I've always wanted to live in Sanibel Island, and I'm staying. I'm signed up to take a painting class here. It starts next week."

"Walter thinks you should stay here too, until everything blows over."

"I know. He called me. And Tom called me. Those two boys should be calling my daughter."

"When did Tom call?"

"Two days ago. He said he's worried about you, but then he asked me, very pushy-like, if I saw you at the fire on Christmas night. I told him I was in my car when I watched the fire. There were lots of people there, and I said you stayed home. I think Lisa and all those buttinskies thought they saw you at the fire because Danny is about your height by now and he was wearing your orange hat with the sparkly pom pom. I made him wear it! His frozen red ears were about to fall off!"

"At least he listens to you. I can never get him to wear a hat."

Suddenly, I need to get away from this air-conditioner air and breathe some real air. I have a tremendous urge to go swimming. I'll do the breaststroke, the crawl, the backstroke, and the butterfly in the salty waters of Florida until I wear myself out. I'll swim all the way back to Cape Cod and sort things out with each stroke.

"Can people swim down near the boats? I want to go swimming before I leave."

"Oh yes, we can pack some takeout in my picnic basket and bring my new beach towels and—"

"No, Mom. I need to go swimming alone."

◆ 48 ◆

LISA SERVES BLACKOUT CAKE WITH DIRTY FORKS

Lisa

I'M GLAD TO BE back waiting tables at the Lighthouse, even though my eye still looks puffy. I flick my braid over my shoulder so it hangs straight down my back, because somehow this helps with my dignity. I need a straight back to serve the Woodwards, who are here, plowing through their dinner, ready for a dessert menu. Mrs. Woodward can be so condescending even when she just glances at me.

"Would you like some dessert? We have some delicious key lime pie and blackout cake tonight." I look down at Mr. Woodward's bald spot.

Mrs. Woodward wrinkles her nose. "I won't be having any dessert tonight. And you, Charles?" Mrs. Woodward's eyes are assessing my belly that's gotten bigger, but I figure she's too WASP-y polite to dare ask if I'm pregnant.

"Do you recommend the blackout cake? Is it locally made?" asks Mr. Woodward.

I want to say, *It's made with stale glue and old recycled candy bars, and I highly recommend it for you.* But before I can say anything, Mrs. Woodward butts in.

"Charles won't be having any chocolate cake. He's watching his cholesterol." She pats her lips with her napkin and winks at Charles.

"Charles *will* be having the blackout cake. Thank you, Lisa, and I'd also like two scoops of vanilla ice cream on the side," Mr. Woodward announces as his wife pats her lips again, frowning so hard she goes cross-eyed.

"Would you like two forks?" I waltz away before they can answer.

In the kitchen, Lester is joking around with Lincoln Abraham Smith, who was hired as a dishwasher even though he's a fine chef. The two of them are speaking in funny British accents, pretending they're having a duel with forks. I grab the two forks and wipe them on my apron.

"Those are dirty," says Lincoln as he rubs the sweat off his forehead.

"No problem. And please cut me a slice of blackout cake for the Woodwards. A big slice with two scoop of vanilla ice cream."

I return to the Woodwards' table and place the plate of dessert exactly in the middle of the table. Mrs. Woodward's eyes widen with lust for the cake as she pushes it over to Mr. Woodward.

"Would you like some coffee? Tea, perhaps?" I place a fork in front of each of them.

"Charles will have tea, and just water for me." Mrs. Woodward reaches across the table and stabs a piece of cake with her fork. They gobble up the cake together.

Lincoln bends down to pass through the kitchen doorway to bus the tables. He wipes his sweaty face on a rag and carefully stacks plates and utensils on his arm from a nearby empty table.

HUSH LITTLE FIRE

279

"I'd like to introduce you to my friend Lincoln. He's going to help me with my cleaning jobs when I have to move heavy furniture. He offered to help me this week at your house, so I can vacuum way under your couch."

Lincoln holds out his hand toward Mr. Woodward for a handshake. Mr. Woodward looks puzzled as he awkwardly reaches up, probably wondering why he has to shake hands with a busboy. His fingers disappear into Lincoln's giant palm, and I think I see Lincoln give a quick tickle to Mr. Woodward's wrist with his pointy fish-gutting fingernail. Lincoln smiles with his friendly best at Mrs. Woodward, but she doesn't shake hands. She bobs her head sideways and looks up at Lincoln.

"Nice to meet you. Where do you come from? Kingston? They make such gorgeous black mahogany furniture there. I just *love* Jamaica."

"I'm from here. I come from here. My home is Massachusetts." Lincoln is frowning now, looking like he's considering taking a jab at Mrs. Woodward, but he quietly gathers more dishes and returns to the kitchen.

Just as I look toward the exit, wishing I could run away, in walks Mary Newcombe, marching straight over to me, and she's steamed about something.

"Hi. I need to speak with you alone. It's very important," Mary says, like she wants to punch me.

"I thought you finally left town," I say with a perfectly straight back. "Would you like to see a menu?"

"No thanks. Is there some place we can talk privately?" Mary moves directly in front of me, too near. The Woodwards are watching closely.

"I'm off in an hour. Let's meet at the pier. What's this about?"

"I have a message for you and your boyfriend from my mother."

◆ 49 ◆

MARY AND LISA SPAR OVER THE REAL SUNSHINE

Mary

I T IS FOGGY AND cold at the harbor, so I keep the heat running in my car and look for Lisa. The moon and stars are hidden behind clouds, and the water looks black, with a few bobbling rowboats that are patiently waiting for warmer weather. Spring will come late like it always does, with a few more months of righteous suffering for all those on Cape Cod who thrive on suffering.

Lisa pulls up in a dented old car, so I circle around with my car next to her window, like two stagecoaches meeting in a field.

"Can I join you inside to talk?" I ask. The red tip of her cigarette glows in the night.

"Sure, hop in."

"You shouldn't be smoking. But I think you already know that."

"For your information, I'm not inhaling. I'm a little tense, and this relaxes me."

"It sure looks like you're smoking. Anyway, let's get down to business. First, my mother says hello. She's worried you won't be able to clean her house anymore. You're pregnant, right?"

"How did you know?"

"Everyone knows. This is Wellfleet."

Lisa picks something out from her teeth and examines it. "What else do you want to talk about?"

"She'll be glad to hear you can still clean houses. She says you do a really a good job and she'll recommend your work to a new neighbor. Word of mouth is everything, especially if you want more work. What I'm trying to say is, she'll help you if you help her. She has a favor to ask you."

"What's that?"

"That you and your boyfriend keep Danny out of any discussions you have with the police. Say he never had anything to do with your boyfriend's work."

"Don't worry about Patrick. He had to leave town. He's not coming back."

"Where'd he go?"

"That's none of your business."

"My son's just a little boy. You have to tell the police Danny had nothing to do with their side hustle."

"Don't be ridiculous. Jimmy is dead. Barbara Haskins is dead. Patrick disappeared. They were small-time dealers anyway. Besides, Chief Crocker claims the fire was an accident, so there's nothing to worry about. The state cops and FBI chick moved on to nab bigger dealers in Maine. And I heard that cute boyfriend of yours is up north in some fishing village where the smugglers live."

"My boyfriend?"

"Tom Murphy. That really cute narc."

"Huh?"

Lisa snorts and giggles too loud in my face. "Oh wow, you didn't know he was undercover, did you? State narcotics unit. Part of the Cape Cod Drug Task Force. Tom Murphy isn't even his real name."

"*A fucking narc?* How do you know he was a narc?"

"The guys at the Bomby told me. He wasn't exactly nosing around your house with that dog because he likes you. That dog was a sniffer from the K9 unit. And I heard your boyfriend brought that German shepherd to your house to look for dope."

I flash on Tom's apartment with nothing in it. That strange dog that looked like Sunshine, sniffing its way through Birdie's kitchen. Danny noticed right away it didn't have Sunshine's white spot on the neck. And the two cell phones. How could I have been such a sucker?

"So why did Tom leave town so suddenly?"

"Reassigned, I guess."

"Did you know all along about the dogs?"

"The police dog left town with the narcs, and Patrick had Sunshine put to sleep when she bit him. She was kind of cute. If only dogs didn't bark. And to think, Jimmy named the dog after me."

"No he didn't."

"Yes he did."

"You're not Sunshine. I am."

"No you're not. Don't get all New York City technical on me. Just because he was your cousin doesn't mean you really knew him. Jimmy named his dog Sunshine after me, and for your information, he called Katie's Snow's baby Sunshine when he thought it was his kid. I know your type. You think

HUSH LITTLE FIRE

283

I'm trash. Well, if I'm trash, then you're the dump, or do you like to call it the transfer station?"

"Take it easy. I need you to keep quiet about Danny's involvement."

"That goes for you too. If I were you, I'd think twice about saying anything to the police about *me*. That is, if your son is important to you."

"Are you threatening me?"

"Look, it's very simple. I don't want to go to jail. They'll take my baby away. And if they take my baby away, guess what? They'll put *your baby* in juvie because Danny was the runner."

"Danny didn't know what he was doing."

"And it could take years for you to prove it in court. In the meantime, they'll throw him in foster care. You get what I'm saying, city girl?"

I want to scream at Lisa or slap her, slap somebody, but it's me who deserves a slap. Tiny Mary is nowhere to be found when I need her. She would probably tell me, *Be direct. Just ask her.*

"What do you know about the fire?" I try to sound casual.

"If I knew who started the fire and I happened to make a decision not to tell, that would make me an accessory to the crime, wouldn't it? You must think I'm dense." Lisa leans over and whispers with one hand on her belly. "*But* we're alone right now. Nobody can hear what I'm saying. No witnesses. Just you and me and my baby. Do you understand?"

"Sort of."

"What if I told you that Jimmy was too drunk to meet Barbara for the pickup on Christmas night, so Patrick and I went instead? I had nothing to do with any of it, so I waited in the car."

"That's an interesting way of looking at it."

"I'm warning you. Don't cause trouble. I'll do anything to protect my baby."

"I get that. Take it easy."

"Patrick was stoned out of his mind, and the last thing he said to me before he went into the clinic was something about *Who needs a middleman? Who needs Barbara?* Mind you, I stayed in the truck the whole time." Suddenly Lisa slaps her hand on the window. "How the hell did a fly get in my car?"

"A fly? I don't see any fly."

"Over there."

Lisa swats at the dashboard, the windshield, the horn, and opens the window and lets a fly out.

"Please tell me what happened after that? I promise I won't tell a soul."

"Patrick said it was too dark inside the clinic that night and he couldn't find Barbara. He told me when he called her name, she jumped out of her skin and fell off a ladder. She hit her head. He swears it wasn't his fault. But between you and me, I know Patrick, and I'd bet the farm he knocked her out to shut her up. Because he did admit that he *tapped her* to get her attention. Next thing you know, the greedy fuck comes running out with big bags of pills and asks me what *we* should do about Barbara. I freaked out on him, so he calls his mommy, blubbering away like a baby. Thirty-six years old and the jerk still calls Trudy every time he's in trouble. I heard him tell her that Barbara was out cold and he couldn't tell if she was breathing. We had a big fight, he threw his phone at me, so I left and walked home. That's all I know."

"So you think Patrick started the fire?"

"I swear before God, it wasn't me who started any fire. Chief Crocker says it was electrical and I'm gonna stick with that."

"What about Patrick?"

HUSH LITTLE FIRE 285

"As far as the cops know, Patrick and I were at his mom's all Christmas night, the three of us exchanging presents. Trudy will swear to it. She's the kind of mother who'll do anything for her kids. She knows if Patrick goes down, I go down with him, and the bottom line is, you and Danny will go down too. You don't want this kind of trouble, especially when I let you in on a little surprise."

Lisa is texting, holding the phone under the steering wheel so I can't possibly read it. Her fingers fly across the phone as she mutters, "It's just Trudy. You know Trudy. God, I love that woman so much. She's like a mother to me. Too bad her son is such a fool."

I want to shake Lisa. "What in the world is your surprise?"

◆ 50 ◆

PREGNANT WOMEN TAKE A LONG TIME TO DO ANYTHING

Mary

PREGNANT WOMEN WHO DO things in a quick manner are rare on this planet, so I sit here in the dark with pregnant Lisa, scratching my arms, waiting for her to get off the phone and tell me the big surprise. The engine is running, the dashboard glows green, and it's like I'm looking at the world through those flimsy wraparound glasses that eye doctors give out for free. But nothing is free, and my head hurts, my eyes ache, and I wonder what Lisa's surprise is going to cost me.

"Like I said, it all comes down to the fact that us mothers are in this together all the way, deeper than you think. What I'm about to tell you, can you keep it a secret?"

"Of course," I lie.

"I'd been trying to get pregnant for years with Patrick, but nothing worked with him because I think his sperm is defective. But all of a sudden, I got pregnant last Thanksgiving—I keep a journal—so I know the exact date when I had sex. It was the same day I made a turkey for the boys on Thanksgiving."

HUSH LITTLE FIRE 287

"The boys? You call them boys?"

She is biting her nails like I do, but what nails does she have left? She switches to chewing the tip of her braid.

"Jimmy was getting super stoned, and the boys were playing the Goldfish game when Jimmy proposed we have a threesome. Patrick was so drunk he rolled off the couch, and it was like a hot dog rolling out of a bun, and—oh my God—Jimmy and I couldn't stop laughing at him. It felt so good to laugh."

"I don't get what you're saying."

"Patrick was on the floor for the rest of the night, and, well, Jimmy and I went at it. We did. We were both pretty wasted, and I got pregnant, and now I'm having Jimmy's baby. You know, I'm thinking if it's a boy, I should name him James, after his father. What do you think?"

"Good God, we don't need another James Newcombe in this world."

"Yeah, I'm glad you said that. But since we're going to be family, I thought it'd be the decent thing to ask you. If it's a girl, should I name her Thankful? It's such a nice old Cape Cod name. Baby Thankful. Conceived on Thanksgiving. What do you think?"

"It's kind of old-fashioned. Uhhh . . . so are we really relatives now?"

"As soon as the baby's born, we will be. So, if you're the cousin of my baby's father, do you know what that makes you? My Aunt Elrie told me about a relative being *once removed*, so I think it makes you what they call an aunt once removed."

I stare at Lisa, wishing to be once removed, and then completely removed from this news. Lisa is quiet as she picks the fuzz off her sweater. This aunt once removed must wake up from a very bad dream right now, because if this isn't a very bad dream, Aunt Once Removed is about to implode from this very bad news. Or is it good news?

"So this means I'm going to be an aunt of sorts?"

"Yep."

I decide right now I will absolutely never tell Lisa that Jimmy was actually my brother, but then, all of sudden like lightning, or God trying to smite me, I realize this is how a family secret gets hatched. This is how a gnarly painful family secret begins.

"Are you *sure* Jimmy's the father?" I ask her.

"Don't be so insulting. I would never say he's the father just to get money. I'm not like Katie Snow. There were no other guys, and this isn't an immaculate conception. It's not like I'm gonna ask you to babysit or anything. But you can if you want."

"I might consider babysitting your baby . . . Would you mind if I put my hand on your belly, now that I'm about to become an aunt once removed?"

"Sure." Lisa gently takes my hand and rests it on her baby bump. "They say someday soon, I'll feel a little flutter kick from my baby if I'm lucky."

Lisa's baby bump is warm, no flutter kicks, but it blows my mind to pieces that a little Jimmy is percolating inside there. At moments like this, I usually excuse myself, politely leave, and then go somewhere and get hammered. Shots would be good. But so far in my life, I've never had a single moment like this with so many new facts pummeling my brain.

Fact one: I wasn't a randomly adopted child, not like from an orphanage. Clara was my birth mother, and my adoptive father was bullshit, not really an adoptive father—he was my

HUSH LITTLE FIRE

289

biological father, who lied to his wife and me and the nuns and everyone on Cape Cod.

Fact two: I was unwittingly having make-out sessions with my brother—who wasn't really my cousin—although we thought it was okay to kiss because we thought we weren't blood relatives—except it turned out we were—and then he fucked my least favorite waitress, Lisa, the Junior Sunshine—who is considering naming my secret nephew James if it's a boy—or perhaps that hideous pilgrim name, Thankful, if it's a girl. *Oh help.* The umbilical cords in the Newcombe family have turned out to be impossible Gordian knots, and Lisa wants me to be okay with this? My family tree is a pricker bush, and I, Mary Newcombe, am stuck in the middle.

"Are you all right with being an aunt once removed? You look kind of pale."

"I'm okay, but I have to go now, and so do you. This is way too much information for one night."

"Suit yourself. But don't be sad. Be happy for my new baby. A new life in the world. I'm so happy. Lester has been such a big help. I think we're going to get a real place to live. He has two kids in Jamaica, so he knows a lot about feeding babies. And you know what?"

"*What now?*"

"Lester and I are going to get married, so I can qualify faster for affordable housing. Then I get to live in a regular house. It's not like we're in love or anything, but when we get married, Lester will get his green card, which will make him supremely happy, and then like after a few years, we can get divorced if we want to."

"That sounds good on paper, but how will it really work out?"

"Oh, there you go again with your holier-than-thou crap. It's not like Danny has a father."

I'm not about to get into the historical facts about who might be Danny's biological father. Instead, I drop my head between my knees to settle my stomach so I don't barf my brains out.

"Are you okay?" Lisa rolls down the window for air and pats my shoulder.

All my life, I've had this bad habit of making a silly joke at the wrong time, like when something isn't funny at all. As a kid, I made jokes to cope with all the scary things in my world, but now, not a single joke pops into my head.

"Are you crying?" Lisa leans over and holds my hand. And maybe because neither of us can stand all my sobbing, Lisa wraps her arms around me tight. This helps a little, it feels nice, but it is time to make my exit and go get hammered. Or is it time to call my friend Walter? Lisa turns the radio on to some loud grunge music.

"You know what I realized, now that I'm finally about to become a mother? I think you and me and everyone else— we're all a bunch of animals screwing each other and making babies. For thousands of years, we've tried to be civilized and make families, but nobody cares about that anymore. So it doesn't matter so much if my baby's father is a fuckup who's dead, does it?"

I sit up and search my purse for a tissue. Maybe Lisa is right and we are drifting back to being animals that roam the earth and get pregnant now and then. Do mother cats and mother dogs ever worry about who knocked them up? I'm getting so confused—it's time to call Walter.

51

THE MERMAID KILN
GODDESS GETS READY

Mary

M Y BODY HAS BEEN on a long trip to outer space, like an astronaut who changed her mind halfway to the moon. I wanted to know, then I didn't want to know, and now I know who was on the other end of my umbilical cord. Clara. I'm back on earth, hanging out in Walter's studio, because it's time to finish the cremation urns.

"It's been ages since I took the order from Mrs. Reardon," I whisper to Walter. "I think she's running out of patience with me."

Walter can't wait any longer to start the firing, so he carefully carries a tray of his teapots over to the car kiln. While I was in Florida, he was kind enough to dip the last two of my urns into the milky glaze with tongs so they would be dry and ready for firing. That step is a sacred baptism of pots, but I wasn't there for glazing the last of my urns. A potter should always glaze their own work, and I thank Walter for doing the holy deed.

Step Eight: Loading the Kiln with Cremation Urns

We arrange the mermaid kiln goddess on the top of the brick chamber for good luck. Walter's kiln is gorgeous, a fine car kiln where the bed is loaded with wares and then rolls on short railroad tracks into the chamber. I stand on one side of the car kiln bed, with Walter on the other side, as we position the remaining pots on the proper shelves. We stack slowly and vertically until all the wares are loaded on silicon carbide shelves held up with firebrick posts. Some of Walter's pots are huge, so he takes the bottom row, which tends to be cooler. He is gracious to let my Chihuahua urns take the middle, where the heat is even in most firings. We roll the bed carefully into the chamber, which looks like a house of cards. I hold my breath until the bed is snugly inside. We pack the leaky seams to the door with Kaowool, which is a prickly flame-resistant fiber that looks like Santa's beard.

Walter twists newspaper into a wand, and I click my silver monogrammed lighter to ignite the wand so we can light the pilots. It is a wise custom for potters to leave the kiln on low overnight, kind of like preheating the oven when baking a loaf of bread. Walter bustles around the burners in the back of the kiln, checking to make sure his Kiln Connie is functioning properly. Just as he ducks out of view to check the damper, I catch him making a quick sign of the cross like a priest. I whisper my own prayer for a good firing, for great reds, and to find peace and understanding of all that went down. In spite of all the science-based knowledge, I accept that mysterious forces will move molecules inside the kiln in unpredictable ways. Likewise, I must learn to accept and find peace with all the mysterious knots in the Newcombe family, lies piled on lies over the years, and for what?

HUSH LITTLE FIRE

Walter scoots out from behind the kiln and sits near me on a stool. He spins the wheel head on his favorite potter's wheel with his knuckles, like we are on a merry-go-round, passing the time. This is the preheat recess in the firing where we will let the kiln idle on low overnight.

"You can go home now if you want," says Walter as he strokes his handsome salt-and-pepper stubble that is working its way to a full-blown beard. In his potter's apron and budding beard, he looks handsome. Right now, he is the artist he always wanted to be.

"Okay, I'll check in tomorrow when the temperature is climbing." Before I leave, Walter looks in the peepholes with a flashlight to make sure the temperature cones are lined up properly. He grumbles, "I guess there will always be gaps that we can't do much about."

♦ 52 ♦

DR. WOLFE-SOMETHING MAKES A SUGGESTION TO DANNY

Mary

THE NEWCOMBE HOUSE HAS a dusty unused smell, so I open the windows in the kitchen and let fresh air inside to shake things up. I have Walter on speakerphone as I toss old food from the refrigerator out the back door to leave treats for the crows.

"I get the feeling you'd rather do the firing without me, since it's your special kiln."

"It's not that I don't want you here, Mary, but Kiln Connie is moody. She has a lot of idiosyncrasies that only I understand. If two people control the turn-ups, it's too many cooks in the kitchen. You know what I mean?"

"Sort of. But the firing is a critical step. If it's not done correctly, all my cremation urns could be ruined."

"Don't worry. I built Kiln Connie myself. I know everything about her and everything that could possibly go wrong."

Step Nine: A Bad Firing will be Entirely Walter's Fault

Missing step nine—the holy firing—is like I'm missing labor and delivery of a baby. But Walter is finicky about doing the

HUSH LITTLE FIRE

temperature turn-ups his way, and there's not much room for a second opinion. Still, I phone him a few more times, probably too many times.

"Promise after the firing is cool, you won't unload the wares without me."

"Of course, but I have to go. I'm right in the middle of heat reduction."

"The flames better be scouring the atmosphere for oxygen and sucking it out of my copper red glaze. Cross your fingers. I wish I were there with you to tinker with the damper. How far are you closing it?"

"Trust me. The flames are shooting out of the spy hole a perfect yellow white. Kiln Connie's been going eight hours and twenty-three minutes since body reduction, and we're getting near the finish line. How's your karma?"

"Could be better."

"We're in the final stage, so it's out of our control right now, like everything else in the universe." Walter laughs.

"When the temperature hits twenty-four hundred degrees and cone nine is flat, please remember to shut it down quickly before cone ten goes flat. Please, oh please, cool the kiln slowly and wait until I'm back to open it."

"Will do."

Walter goes quiet, and I can hear him breathing. "There's something I want to tell you about the chief, but it's confidential. Can you keep a secret?"

Oh boy. I'm too exhausted to handle one more secret. "Sure."

"I snuck into the chief's office and read a report on his computer from the fire investigators that I wasn't supposed to read. But when I went back to read it again, he had deleted everything."

"What did it say?"

"The report from the inspectors said the sniffer dog detected an ILR pour pattern in the clinic fire on the concrete where the basement floor used to be. But the chief conveniently left that piece of information out in his press release."

"What's ILR?"

"Ignitable liquid residue. They detected gasoline in a pour pattern, which proves there were accelerant liquids in the basement, and that means somebody poured something flammable on the floor. Crocker didn't mention the pour pattern to anyone."

"Does Chief Crocker know you read the file?"

"No, but I needled him about why he told the public it wasn't arson. The chief looked rattled and pulled at his ears, a sure sign he was upset."

"So you're saying Chief Crocker is stretching the truth?"

"When I tried to bring it up, he said the FBI is closing in on a drug ring and I should drop it. He told me to forget about it. But before I retire, I'm going to find out who burned the clinic down. I owe that much to Barbara."

I say goodbye to Walter and beg him one more time to let it go before I hang up. The old broom in the closet springs to life in my hands, so I frantically sweep the kitchen floor, even though I already swept it. But I forgot that sweeping old Cape Cod floorboards sends dirt and dust into the cracks to fester, so I vacuum up every single crack in the floorboards to remove the dirt in every single room.

I call Danny to see how he's doing after his therapy session.

"I'm good. Leslie bought me some new sneakers. Two pairs."

"Nice, but how many pairs do you really need? Anyway, how was the therapy session?"

HUSH LITTLE FIRE

"The therapist says I have what she calls—just a second—I'll read it to you—'deep-rooted unresolved issues that need to be addressed.' But she complimented my Air Jordans. And then she told me it means—well, her summary says—'Patient has an unconscious desire to play basketball.' I *really* don't, but I didn't tell her that."

"Is this the therapist the school recommended to Jean and Leslie?"

"Yep. She's hard to talk to. She smiles at me no matter what I say, and she has really bad BO. But she says I can take a genetic test to find out who my father is."

"*What* did she say?"

"She said I need parental permission first. We can do it all online. She says 23andMe is a good place to start."

I choke on the glass of water I'm sipping. "Oh . . . I didn't know you were curious about those types of things."

"Mom, I asked you a hundred times who my father is, but you always change the subject."

"Do I?"

"The therapist says I shouldn't make you feel bad, like, this doesn't mean you're a bad parent or anything. Also, she said I don't have to go to Jimmy's memorial service on Easter if I don't want to."

"Wow, I'd like to meet this therapist. She's full of ideas. What's her name again?"

"Dr. Wolfe-Something. She's one of those people with two last names. Please think about the test and then say yes. Gotta go. Leslie is giving me Ping-Pong lessons. Talk to you later."

At least he's talking to me and didn't say the word *like* every five seconds. Now it's time to swim the butterfly, the crawl, and the breaststroke all the way through the stratosphere to New York City—to Danny—if it takes everything out of me, because

I want to shorten the gap between us. I want to take him on a long walk to get him talking until he's ready to fly off and live a good life in this world. I want to be a branch on a tree that he can fly back to when he needs to, when he needs his mother. *Easier said than done,* I say to the therapists of the world.

Danny and I are doing just fine as a family, thank you very much, I would remind Dr. Wolfe-Something. I hate her. I would tell her I do all the mother/father parenting things that need to be done, and all rolled up into one parent makes life easier.

Even without a 23andMe test for Danny, I have an idea who might have contributed the sperm to Danny's existence. I do. I narrowed it down to one of two men, both of them in a respectable medical profession, so at least the fellow is smart. In some crazy cracked-up puritanical punishing twist of fate, I've been afraid I might bump into Danny's biological father if I ever go to a new dentist. Because Danny's biological father is one of two good-looking exchange students from the NYU School of Dentistry, the ones I met years ago.

I met Sklar and Otto, no last names exchanged, in a downtown bar long gone on a street I can never remember in Greenwich Village. My fortieth birthday had been looming like the guillotine of fertility, and I remember a murderous full moon, urging me to be wild. My body was in heat worse than a dog. I got drunk but kept my manners and politely accepted the offer to join them for a visit to their studio apartment on Ninth Street, one of those studio apartments with a bathtub in the kitchen. I'm pretty sure Sklar or Otto is Danny's father, because the timing is right. Danny is blond like Sklar but has curls like Otto, so who knows which one was the donor. I never knew their last names, but if Danny hires a search angel and follows the shrink's advice to take a genetic test, this might lead him to a last name, which leads me to a very high state of anxiety.

Earth to Mary? Stop all this angsting. Tiny Mary is back on my shoulder. *Get over it. Families are a messy business. Life is messy. Take it easy. Besides, Walter is taking good care of the firing. Get some rest.*

◆ 53 ◆
MARY'S JACK-IN-THE-BOX
OF LOVE—AND HATE

Mary

REST? I WAKE UP in the middle of the night sweating and sit up in bed to clear a dream out of my head. In the dream, Jimmy and I were young and kissing each other in the dark, and it was a tender make-out session. Two magnets that couldn't be pulled apart. In the dream, I felt his warm breath on my cheek when he exhaled rat-a-tat puffs of laughing and pleasure. But dear God have mercy, I never knew he was my brother, and what could have happened if we didn't stop? Not one old biddy in the Gossip Militia ever told me the truth about us, but maybe they didn't know. And if I were a Catholic, I would go to confession and confess right now that it almost went too far with my not-really cousin.

I'm marooned between feelings of pleasure and horror, and the more I wake up, the more the pleasure drifts away and the Puritan in my blood fills me with shame. Dreams can be so confusing. I convinced myself I hated Jimmy after he tried to spank my son on the boat, but this dream popped open a little jack-in-the-box, and in the box was all the goodness I once

HUSH LITTLE FIRE

knew in Jimmy. Now I lie in bed in the dark and feel itchy hives on my arms turning into welts. Love can do that. So can hate.

All morning I slather calamine lotion on the itchy welts. In the afternoon when it's time to unload the kiln, I rinse off, and the hives have flattened into pink islands on my face. Jean told me once that hives are the dis-ease of the body, *no ease*. She said disease is about inner turmoil roiling around in the body. My head is spinning with Walter's news that somebody set fire to the clinic and it wasn't an accident. I think Lisa knows exactly what happened, which is why she chewed off all her fingernails. I look down and check my fingernails.

"What's that on your face, poison ivy?" Walter asks me as I stand close to him while we monitor the temperature on the cooling kiln.

"Yeah, poison ivy, I think." I tap the blotches on my arm.

"Try not to scratch. I have some calamine lotion in the bathroom I can give you."

"Thanks, but let's unload the kiln first."

Step Ten: Unloading the Kiln with the Dead Chihuahuas' Urns

I have to trust the firing was in good hands with Walter and the mermaid kiln goddess. I love the thrill of unloading a big kiln, even though the results can be Christmas or Halloween. The heat at peak temperature is almost six times hotter than my oven on broil, and strange things can happen if the kiln overfires. Kiln Connie can melt the wares into pancakes, or dependable glazes can drip into puddles, and then there's crazing, cracking, pitting, white-spotting, and crawling problems that occur randomly. It's so brilliant of Japanese potters to

302 JUDITH NEWCOMB STILES

incorporate fuckups into their philosophy of pricing their pots. A big crack on a porcelain vase? No problem, just emphasize the crack with gold foil and call it special. But it will be a tough sell with Mrs. Reardon if the red glaze flops after she's waited so long.

The kiln is stone cold, so we don't need gloves to unpack the Kaowool. The cremation urns are eye level with me, and as I peak at the lids on the urns, I'm speechless and over-the-moon happy because the glaze is a deep copper red. Exhale. I unload ten dog-sized cremation urns, and the last one has a beautiful tan, almost golden, circle around the red on the lid like a halo. I am flummoxed by this strange marking on only one lid, because I used the same glaze on the same clay body and they were fired in the same heat zone. I can't figure out the variable.

"Everything looks good so far," Walter says as he tiptoes by me and pinches my ass.

We celebrate the wonderful firing with a shot of Jack Daniel's in his grandfather's shot glasses. I carefully examine the red urns again for glaze flaws, and they're all perfect, except the one with the stunning halo.

It takes me an hour to clean the kiln shelves, and I'm extra careful to sweep the floor and tidy things up, which is a potters' custom for giving thanks to a fellow potter for sharing a kiln. Walter seems amused by my flurry of studio domesticity, and with his feet up on the wheel head, he sits back and watches me work. He is starting to get loopy on Jack Daniel's, the Cape Cod way, but he can still talk and hold a pen. He makes scribbly notes in his kiln log.

"The best I can guess about the odd halo is that the bag of copper oxide from China had residue from the smelter, possibly zinc or titanium dioxide that sometimes creates a golden color," Walter says, scribbling the numbers to the glaze formula.

"It's so beautiful. So unusual."

"In China, the smelters aren't always cleaned properly." He crosses out the fractions on the page and starts again. "It's all so unpredictable, like the rest of life."

What it all comes down to is this: The smelter on the other side of the earth created this happy accident in the tiny town of Wellfleet on Cape Cod under the supervision of the mermaid kiln goddess. I want to say this out loud to Walter, but I don't.

I carefully pack my wares in newspaper so they can safely travel back to Brooklyn, but the newsprint keeps distracting me. Before I roll the pots in the paper, I scan the pages to see if there are any new headlines about Chief Crocker and the Christmas fire. There are none.

Walter sucks up the last drops from his glass and polishes off what's left in my glass as his face flickers with worry. "Are you going back to Brooklyn today?"

"I'm leaving in about an hour, but I'll be back for Easter when we have the memorial service for Jimmy." I sidle over to Walter and pinch his ass back. "I've been meaning to tell you, your beard looks great." I look up at him, and a red childish blush creeps up to his forehead as he smiles through his elegant beard.

"Call me when you get there." He gives me a kiss on the forehead and rubs my shoulders with his big hands.

"Mary, you should keep the happy-accident urn for yourself and give Mrs. Reardon a different one. The glaze is so rare."

"Maybe I will. Maybe I'll give it to you if you promise not to stir up trouble with the chief. It'll be your happy-accident sugar bowl."

"I can't promise that."

"If you keep nosing around, somebody will get hurt. I'm only gone for a while, until April, and for God's sake, you'll be fully retired, so what's the point?"

"The point is I spent all those weeks with Barbara in the hospital, and I got to know her better. I don't want to end my career in the force with this up in the air. I want to know the truth."

54

IT BEGINS WITH A SIMPLE CANDLE

Mary

I'VE BEEN HOODWINKED INTO hosting a memorial service for Jimmy when it's really my mother's job. March dragged on and on and I'm very good at procrastinating, blaming the crappy weather for not organizing any of it. Today is Good Friday, not much good about it. Easter is in two days, and Birdie insists it's a good time for a ceremony. She promised to come back on Easter and asked would I please make all the arrangements—book a wake at Carlson's Funeral Home, find a minister to emcee, pick out a prayer and a poem to read at the burial, make refreshments for guests—all of which I did not do, because my mother is not coming back. Dr. Wolfe-Something gave Danny permission to skip it too, so in the end, I'm hosting a one-woman service. I didn't make Jimmy an urn; instead, I will scatter his ashes in his favorite places, because that's what he'd want me to do. I ordered a nice plaque for the cemetery, real marble, to sit between his parents and next to Baby Newcombe. And it's fitting that there won't be any trace of his real person underneath the ground along with Baby Newcombe, who isn't there either. I am here.

The real Baby Newcombe is hosting the one-woman funeral service.

I try calling Danny and my mother, but they don't answer, which leaves me all alone on the front porch, feeling bad. I sip coffee and stare at a broken porch rail and tuck my knees together under my chin. On Walter's feel-good scale of one to ten—if ten is feeling great and one is feeling awful—I am definitely a one. And if there's a number lower than one, that would be me.

Jean would tell me to meditate at a stressful time like this, but there are so many important things about transcendental meditation, half of which I can't remember. She told me when she closes her eyes and focuses, she can hear the stones, the roots of the trees, the light from the sun, and she can hear the Holy Spirit. That sounded a little kooky to me, but come to think of it, I've been talking to the Holy Spirit for years, so it would be nice to hear something back. I close my eyes to listen, but I don't hear any stones, or roots, or light beams, or the Holy Spirit—perhaps I'm trying too hard, or maybe I'm not trying hard enough?

I give up on meditating and look down at the brown dead grass that is beginning to turn green. And when I look up, tiny green buds are beginning to pop out of the branches on trees. The sun is warm on my face, and on a scale of one to ten, I think my needle is beginning to move off of one. No matter how awful this winter was, the green is coming, and it's coming no matter what.

I look around the yard, and a breeze rustles a bunch of little flowers—white snowdrops that are jiggling and laughing at something, maybe me. I notice green poking through the dirt across the road, and a bunch of crocuses are bursting purple. I think my needle is moving closer to ten. Spring will do that.

HUSH LITTLE FIRE

307

I finish my coffee, which is cold by now, and shuffle to the kitchen for a refill. I look through all the kitchen drawers for a candle, because it begins with a simple candle—this need to purge my life of all the hush-hush family lies that I lived with all these years.

I have a small pile of photos from Birdie's storage unit that I stuffed in my purse to marinate, hoping they'd explain my childhood to me. I dig out the envelope of photos and sit down at the kitchen table to study them for the millionth time. I light the candle, and the flame bounces and wiggles, cheering me on.

The first photo I hold up is from my first day of kindergarten, the three of us standing together, me looking goofy, my mother looking out of sorts, and my father with his photo face ripped out, a hole where his head used to be. I bet Birdie did that. With the touch of a flame, I burn what is left of little-girl me, and in an instant my father's body and his meandering pecker flare up, and at the same time Beatrice Birdie Newcombe's face melts away with a quick yellow burst. This is a good kind of voodoo. The remnants are now sticky ash bits resting on the Formica table. Goodbye, secrets of the past.

"I smell something burning!" says Walter as he rushes through the doorway to the kitchen, his hands behind his back. "Sorry I didn't ring the doorbell. What's burning?"

"It's okay, it's just a candle and paper and me burning a few things."

Walter steps closer to me—his hand whirls around from behind his back, holding up a tiny bouquet of snowdrops and crocuses. He grins and doesn't say a word.

"Are these for me? Thanks. How nice of you." I blow out the candle, and the flowers warm me all over, like they are smiling at this young-love gesture from a middle-aged police officer with his reliable and elegant beard. And I'm not feeling too old either to receive an itsy-bitsy bouquet from Officer Walter Stone. I look up at this man with the beard that I wish would part at the mouth someday with a French kiss just for me.

"I picked them because they made me think of you."

"How lovely of you. Where are they from?"

"The side yard of the police station."

"Hmmm, I hope Chief Crocker didn't see you."

"Every day since you've been gone, I look out the side window and think of you. I can't concentrate, and I keep dropping my paperwork on the floor."

"I've been thinking about you too, Walter."

"I have one more week on the force, that's all. I cleared out a space in the studio for you to work this summer if you come back. Maybe you want to teach classes up here this summer."

"That sounds great."

I put down the flowers on the table, look up at Walter, and wrap my arms around his waist. Walter cups the back of my head with his big hand as tenderly as he'd hold a baby.

"I hear there won't be a funeral after all," says Walter.

"That's right. Birdie canceled, so I'm going it alone. I'll scatter Jimmy's ashes at Power's Landing, Spectacle Pond, and better yet, in the bay off of the jetty before the boats come back. I've already left a sprinkle of his ashes on the clay cliff at Newcomb Hollow."

"He would like that."

"How's it going over at the station?"

"It's going. No new leads on the clinic fire, if that's what you're afraid to ask me."

"We need to talk about this. Want to join me for a picnic lunch at Mayo Beach?"

HUSH LITTLE FIRE 309

"Sorry, gotta get back to work."

Walter won't look at me as he turns to go, so I put the Miss Mary Newcombe passive-aggressive squeeze on him.

"You agreed not to do anything that would put Danny in a difficult situation with the police, right?"

Walter frowns, rubs his beard, and I can't tell if that's a yes or a no. He leaves, closing the door behind him, too carefully.

◆ 55 ◆

TRUDY SPITS IN THE SAND AND WALKS AWAY

Mary

A T MAYO BEACH, IT'S too cold to swim, but the sun is warm, so I stand near the water and plan a phone call to my mother. So many things I want to tell her, and all of it points to one big *thank you*. I want to thank her for telling me the truth about my birth mother. I want to thank her for being a friend to Clara. I want to thank her for trying to mother Jimmy and me, and tell her I will never put on her tombstone the epithet *SHE TRIED* like she asked me to. Never. Warts and all, she deserves better than that.

Mayo Beach is deserted, except in the distance I see a woman in a white apron, no jacket, like she just walked out of the Bomby from across the street. She must be on a kitchen break. Her face looks familiar, and she keeps turning around, giving the world an angry look. It's Trudy Bale. On another day, I might be tempted to bum a smoke from her, but I don't crave one for once, with the salty fresh air blowing across the water. She waves to me, and I wave back as she traipses across the sand to join me. I'm trapped.

HUSH LITTLE FIRE

311

"You wouldn't happen to have a light, by any chance?"

"Hello, Trudy, long time no see." I pull out my silver monogrammed lighter. Trudy cups her hands around the flame and rotates her neck, as if her head has been stuck in a vise for twenty years. She puffs hard, like it's the last smoke of her life.

"What brings you back to town? I hear your mother canceled Jimmy's memorial service."

"Where'd you hear that?"

"This is Wellfleet." Trudy laughs and scuffs the sand with her sneaker. She squints and her eyes dart sideways, like she's worried somebody might sneak up on us. "Things are looking up since I saw you last. Lisa's moving in with me this weekend. I'm going to help her when my grandbaby comes, since Patrick's away. He's about to get a good job."

"Where?"

"I don't know yet. I'm waiting for him to call and send money. I keep telling Lisa babies are expensive; even so, she was kind enough to buy me new dentures." Trudy slings a big mouthy grin my way with dentures that don't quite fit her face. "Such a sweet girl. I'll quit my dishwashing job at the Bomby as soon as the baby comes. My grandbaby is on the way. Isn't it exciting?"

Trudy pokes her finger in the back of her mouth and gives a little upward twist to her dentures. It turns my stomach to think Lisa may never tell her that Patrick is not the baby's father.

"Just so you know, Patrick left town. Without his boat *Angel Baby*, he had to look for work elsewhere. The boatyard fire ruined everything for him. Hard for my son to fish if he doesn't have a boat."

"At least nobody got hurt in that fire."

312 JUDITH NEWCOMB STILES

Trudy drops the rest of her cigarette in the sand and covers it with her sneaker. She rolls her tongue across her lips.

"Do me a favor and tell your friend Walter to stop hassling Lisa about *Angel Baby*. Stress is bad for the pregnancy."

"I didn't know he was bothering her. I hardly ever speak to Officer Stone," I lie.

Trudy turns bright red, coughing and sputtering something that sounds rehearsed, but I can't understand any of it until she speaks up, practically shouting. "I told Walter, and it's on the official police report, the three of us were at my place every minute of Christmas Eve, Christmas Day, and Christmas night. We were reading important passages from the Bible and singing Christmas carols on the piano, so like I told him, none of us even heard the explosion."

"What explosion?"

"From the gas."

"What gas?"

"That big explosion when the furnace at the clinic blew up. That's what it said in the paper."

"That wasn't in the newspaper."

"Yes it was." Trudy's voice is calm, but she's blushing.

"The clinic didn't have a gas furnace. It had electric heat."

"Well, it must have been gas from an old lawn mower or something. There's always flammable stuff in basements."

"Walter said there was a pour pattern of gasoline."

"Listen, Walter thinks he's such a genius. Don't start that crap with me. I know you've been talking to him. This might rub you the wrong way, but you and I better keep our stories straight for the sake of your son."

"What do you know about my son?"

"More than you know."

"How much did Lisa tell you?"

HUSH LITTLE FIRE 313

"Your boy was the runner. I warned Pat that this whole thing was a bad idea. He never listens. And wouldn't you know, he called me up, wondering what to do."

"About what?"

"Pat has nothing to worry about. In the paper it said Barbara fell and hit her head."

"I didn't read that. Where'd you read that?"

"Well, maybe it wasn't in the paper, but everyone knows she fell. You know it. I know it. The chief knows it. End of story."

"Really?"

"Really. I know Lisa had a talk with you about all this. She tells me everything. She guaranteed you'll keep quiet. Right?"

"Absolutely," I lie.

"Between you and me, I'll tell you this much, mother to mother. Pat called me crying like a baby that night. And from what he was saying—I know my son—he *might* have clocked her by accident. He gets upset so easily, but it's not his fault. He was born that way."

"Why didn't anyone call an ambulance or the police?"

"Look, he's my son. I do what I can to help him."

"You should have called an ambulance."

"If Pat bopped her, he wasn't thinking. He didn't mean to hurt her. He had nothing against her. You and me have to protect our own."

"That depends."

"You must know by now your life will be ruined if you open your mouth about any of this. I'll explain in a sec why this could be very bad for the runner."

"Keep Danny out of it!"

Listen up, Miss Righteous Newcombe. Here's how it went down. When I got there, Pat had pissed in his pants and Barbara was lying in a big puddle of blood. I didn't think she was breathing. I felt her neck for a pulse, but her neck's kinda fat. So I said a prayer anyway over her body for last rites, like a priest would have done. I asked the Lord to have mercy, all in front of Pat, so he could pray too. I told him not to worry, but he kept walking around in circles, cursing the Lord."

Trudy makes the sign of the cross, looking out over the water. "When he wasn't looking, I took the can of gas out of Pat's truck, and then I told him to go home. I waited until he was gone, and then I poured in the shape of a cross in the basement, so God wouldn't misinterpret my intentions. I got a sign from above that it was what I was meant to do. I saved some gas to make a stream to the door, so it wouldn't blow up in my face, and then I left the building fast."

"*You?*"

"Before I went home, I texted Danny that we had a last-minute delivery and he should come right over and meet me for an extra forty bucks. He texted back he'd be happy to help, but the brat said he wouldn't help me for less than sixty bucks. It's in writing. I saved the text."

"He had nothing to do with this!"

"Says who?"

"He was with his grandmother all day!"

"And people saw him at the fire with Birdie. Hard to wiggle his way out of those texts. Look, what's done is done. I only tell you all this because I know you'll keep quiet for your boy's sake. We're stuck in the same boat. If I sink, you sink. Stop nosing around. Then everything will be fine. Agreed?"

"Okay. Okay . . ." But a corner of my brain knows it's not okay to keep my mouth shut. Except Tiny Mary would tell me

I better keep quiet about this so things don't get a lot worse for Danny.

Trudy gives me a wild-woman smile and says, "Us mothers do what we have to do. I think you get it. If I were a man, I'd shake your hand on that, but never mind. Now run along and be a good mother." Trudy spits in the sand and walks away.

✦ 56 ✦

MARY'S WHITE PLASTIC SWAN HOSTS THE FUNERAL

Mary

I HAD ELABORATE PLANS for my one-woman memorial service, but it's all falling apart. I sit in my car in a bummer bad mood. The box of Jimmy's ashes is on my lap, and I pet the lid to calm me down. And then I call my mother.

"Did you ever find a good clergyman to officiate at the service?" Birdie has no idea how bizarre this sounds.

"It was too last minute. I'm going to keep it simple and read a poem or something."

"Just a poem? Sorry I couldn't be there, but you know I'm having so much trouble with my tooth."

Birdie sounds grumpy, so I want to cheer her up, and maybe that will cheer me up. I look out the window and describe the beautiful parade of seagulls that soar and dive into the waves at Mayo Beach. One seagull breaks with the group, circles above the parking lot, and drops an oyster from above. It cracks open on the pavement, and the gull swoops down to grab the meat. I start to tell Birdie about the

HUSH LITTLE FIRE 317

industrious seagull and the crocuses in her yard, but she cuts me off.

"You won't believe what periodontists do these days. After Dr. Scott pulled my tooth, he put powdered bone with adhesive in the hole. The bone powder was from a cadaver, so I asked Dr. Scott *from whom* might I be getting this bone? He laughed and said it could be anyone. Imagine that—cadaver in my mouth. Now I really have one foot in the grave."

I indulge her and listen as she babbles on, and I make a mental note to never again babble like that with Danny. Maybe not on this call, but maybe the next one, I will tell her I decided to make the cremation urn she wants. But only if she puts the lid away for safekeeping and uses the vessel for flowers throughout the rest of her long and wonderful life. I hope she'll say she likes my copper red, and we will joke about how it is no big deal to prepare for death by making a vessel out of mud.

"My tooth hurts. I need aspirin. Call me after the service. Call me when you're safely back to Brooklyn." And once again, without saying goodbye, Birdie hangs up.

I drive to the edge of the jetty and walk across the rocks, carrying five things.

1. Box of Jimmy
2. My silver monogrammed lighter
3. Lighter fluid
4. Wicker basket
5. Plastic swan inner tube

And no Bible. I carry the box of Jimmy in one hand with lighter fluid resting on top and a wicker basket tucked inside the circle of my old white swan inner tube. I found the swan in the basement and blew it up. Perfect for a funeral. The swan was my best friend at Mayo Beach—she taught me not to be afraid of the water.

I step across the jetty stones, careful not to slip on the slimy rocks, and walk all the way to the end. The water laps the lower stones, like an audience clapping for me to get started with my one-woman service. At this very moment, somebody, somewhere, is casting some other dead soul's ashes into this water—water that twists and turns around continents throughout the world. I read that somewhere in Varanasi, India, there is an entire industry devoted to building funeral pyres to cremate the dead out on the Ganges River, which is what gave me the idea for this one-woman funeral. Jimmy would love this. I rest the wicker basket on top of my swan, high enough so it won't get wet. I squirt the entire can of lighter fluid all over the wicker and place the box of Jimmy inside the basket. I gently slide my homemade funeral pyre off the jetty. Nobody is watching, no boats nearby, so I flick my silver monogrammed lighter and toss it goodbye right into the basket with Jimmy. The flames burst on the water, and the swan's neck collapses in an instant. I recite from the twenty-third psalm, *Yea though I walk through the valley of the shadow of death, I will fear no evil, for thou art with me.* This I say for Jimmy Newcombe with my pounding heart, and before I can finish, the water snuffs out the flames and swallows the swan.

In the car, I call Danny, but of course I get voicemail, so I call Jean and ask her to pass the phone to Danny, and sure enough, he's right there playing video games.

"Didn't you hear your phone when I tried to call you?"

"Yes."

"Did Jean tell you I'm coming back tonight?"

"No."

HUSH LITTLE FIRE

My son and his dreaded one-word answers.

"Mom, I gotta go. I'm not supposed to talk on the phone. Aunt Leslie is paying me fifty dollars a day *not* to use my phone, and so far, we're on day two."

"It's a good idea to lay off your phone, but Danny, this sounds like a bribe."

"Don't worry. I'm fine. Gotta go."

Danny will be all right in the long run, and somehow I know this. Walter says this summer he'll put Danny to work handling techie stuff for his online pottery sales, plus he wants to teach him how to build a rowboat. And maybe they'll plant heirloom tomatoes for Walter's specialty spaghetti sauce. All the things I never made time to do with my son. And I'm sure once I explain to Walter the complete unadulterated truth of Danny's involvement, he'll see that it's best to protect him. Maybe I'll have to sleep with him a lot and have wild and wonderful sex to persuade him to let go of the investigation, and that would be great.

I make one last stop at the Mobil station before I leave, and there are two other women pumping their own gas. Birdie always made me fill up her car, because she has a fear of spilling gasoline on her hands. On one of her rainy tipsy days, I remember her jabbering about how pumping gas makes her think of a *man's privates.* The gas pours out, and I clutch the nozzle as my mind squeamishly wanders off to the NYU dental students. How amazing it is that Sklar and Otto each had over forty million sperm that swam upstream in one shot toward my fallopian tubes on their mission to fertilize an egg. This means that over eighty million sperm were occupying my territory when I was partying with the dentists. What a party. And when the race to the egg was over, bingo, Danny, the happy accident. It all makes me dizzy, but maybe I'm smelling too much gas.

I have frittered away a good part of this day on the one-woman funeral, but I am happy that some part of Jimmy is back in the water, going in the opposite direction of the *Pneumodesmus*, back into the sea, mother to all of us. In a way, we spend our lives looking for the mothers we wish we could have instead of the ones we got. I found my birth mother and father after all these years, and it brings me peace, but the real peace comes from knowing family is not just about bloodlines. In searching for my birth mother, I learned that I must try to be a better mother to Danny, and I must learn to mother myself.

The sun is in my eyes, so I pull down the visor over the yellow ball in the sky that shows up for work every day, often unnoticed by us mortals who are too busy. By this time of year, the Pilgrims had moved on to Plymouth, and out of a hundred and two people, only fifty-one made it through to see spring. Since then, so many Cape Cod babies have been born, babies have died, and now I know that the baby down in the cemetery is fireplace ash and not a baby.

When I drive my car past the Wellfleet police station, I have a guilty conscience, just a little one, because Miss Mary Newcombe the petty thief pocketed the mermaid kiln angel from Walter's studio without asking, which is a no-no in the world of potters. The lovely mermaid kiln angel is riding back to Brooklyn with me, dangling from the rearview mirror, leading the way. She's a professional amongst kiln gods, and I need her on my road trip.

As I look across the street to the Wellfleet fire department, the sun is going down, and I see Captain Kinshaw took down the *open-burning* sign, which must mean it's officially spring. I barrel over a pothole, which makes the mermaid kiln angel spin and bounce like a dervish. Here we go. Say goodbye to

Wellfleet and hello to the Bourne Bridge that will take me off this crooked peninsula back to the rest of the world. I squint and aim my car straight at the magnificent fireball in the sky as it turns from orange to fiery red, floating on the horizon, about to drop.

THE END

ACKNOWLEDGMENTS

I EARN MY LIVING turning mud into money in the guise of colorful utilitarian pots that last ten thousand years. Throwing on the wheel gave me plenty of head space to write this story over the past eight years, and I am forever grateful to these people who helped me bring this book to life.

Big thank-you to Adriana Stimola of Stimola Literary Studio, who lives by the sea and immediately plugged in to this Cape Cod tale and found it a home. Triple thanks to Jess Verdi at Alcove Press, who took a chance on me and this wild story because she sees the world with her prescient third eye. Thank you, Elissa Altman, for giving me *Permission* (her wonderful book) *to give myself permission* to find the humor in many dark and difficult years for women before *Roe v. Wade.*

Although he is dust unto dust by now, thank you, John Ciardi, for telling me that I am a writer during a time in my life when I was only thinking about teenage boys.

A girl needs a team—and this book would never have been born without the hard work of amazing creatives at Alcove Press: Rebecca Nelson, Thai Fantauzzi Perez, Dulce Botello,

ACKNOWLEDGMENTS

Mikaela Bender, Stephanie Manova, Megan Matti, Doug White, Matt Martz, Monica Manzo, Cassidy Graham, Rachel Keith, and cover designer Lila Selle.

Thank you, Saint Cindy Sirko and the Dragonmoms, who taught me how a flabby middle-aged woman can reinvent herself on the soccer pitch while writing a book. Manny D'Almeida, the guru of goodness. My friend. My compass. Debra McKay and Dian Hamilton, for jump-starting our better selves in the Raw Vulgarians Club—writers of all things raw. Rosalind Pace and the Truro Memoirs gang, who were the midwives of this story. My early readers, John Snow (wonderful insights) and his sidekick Leaky Bucket (great cocktails). Always and forever, I thank Guido Moltedo, the brilliant editor-in-chief of YtaliGLOBAL, who dared to publish my article "Who Is the Boss of Her Body?" in Italian and English, which planted a seed in this book about the complicated future of abortion. Many thanks to Darcey Gohring, Daphne Gregory Thomas, and Jenni Dawn Muro for their laser-sharp insights into writing. Joyce Wlodarczyk, who opened the door and pushed me through (gently). Monica McLean, my third arm, and her creative genius. Kazuko Takizawa, who is still here in my heart, reminding me to stop wasting time—go outside and look for the sun. Thank you, Maria Rodale, the embodiment of *Love Nature Magic* (her book), for pointing me in the right direction with this story. Carol Bergen, the High Priestess of softball and all things writing. Michelle Axelson, the backbone of feminist and LGBTQ rants and ruminations for Porch Readings at Womencrafts in Provincetown. Nan Cinnater, Amy Raff, and the Rose Dorothea schooner in the magical land of books at the Provincetown Library, where much of my work was fertilized.

Lynne Hugo and Adam Chromy who tapped my shoulder at the Provincetown Book Festival. And of course, Caroline

ACKNOWLEDGMENTS 325

Leavitt who was my very first reader – I'm so grateful for her creative mind and spot-on comments.

Big thanks to Julia, Jane, Johnny (my children), and Mr. O'Hara for putting up with a mother who burned too many dinners because she was busy writing and firing kilns in the studio. Debbie, Josh, and Jed, my siblings (upstanding Newcomb *e*-droppers). Together we soaked up the wondrous beauty of Newcomb Hollow—a beach that became a character in this book. Cecil Newcomb, the beloved leader of our tribe, who taught me about lobsters, fishing, Vietnam, and to never forget that our tides go in and out. Aunt Rachel Theodora Stiles, for mailing me a book every month even though she lived nearby. The grandboys, for inviting me to play in The Deep Wild, a place where imagination runs amok with pirates and Moby Dick.

Now I live in the Cape Cod house of my great-grandmother, Mary Newcomb (*e*-dropper), and I thank her for marrying the fellow whose quote I taped to my front door, so I will read it every day before I go out into the world:

"There is an open way for love. Ages and ages of human experience have shown that love works well. The universe, by and large, is on the side of love."
—*Reverend William Curtis Stiles*